Awakened

A Curse of Rose and Snow

Savannah J. Foley

INALTA PRESS

AWAKENED

Inalta Press
www.inaltapress.com

ISBN: 979-8-9955856-1-9 (paperback)
ISBN: 979-8-9955856-0-2 (ebook)
ISBN: 979-8-9955856-2-6 (hardcover)
eISBN: 9798995585602

First Edition: June 2026

Cover Art by Muhammad Kaleem
Cover Layout by Stephen Mesker
Divider flourishes by Randli
Title font is Cinzel, by Google Fonts

for Ciera

Before

Once upon a time, far away and very long ago, I perched in the boughs of a tree and waited to steal from thieves. It was the dawn of my seventeenth summer. Homespun wool dyed green and brown disguised me among the canopy. The forest floor was damp and spicy with last winter's debris, but up in the branches a perfumed wind swished through the leaves, and I breathed it in with rising excitement.

This would be a good haul. Tall Tom's boy, Wulf, had sprinted from his spyhole to let us know of the incoming carriage, richly adorned and minimally guarded. Foolish of them. My thighs gripped a thick branch as I waited with an arrow nocked, alert for sounds of the approaching carriage and my father's whistled signal.

Times were hard. The Usurper's iron-fisted lords and tax collectors plagued us worse than summer ticks. We were mountain folk, proud and independent, but living off the land and trading our crafts was no longer enough to bring prosperity. Thus, with little moral compunction, some in my village turned to banditry, and my father was our cheerful captain.

Everyone had their place. My team waited in the trees, our arrows intended to bewilder and threaten instead of kill. Others crouched behind bushes or nets of woven grass, a more hands-on force ready to take possession of our prize.

As the carriage came into view, I understood why so few guards attended it. This prize had already been stolen, and now we would snatch it from those who thought to keep it.

The two men on the driver's bench did not wear uniforms, as one might expect for a gilded carriage of this quality. Their clothing, as humble as our own, was more stained and grimy than a single scuffle might cause, and their beards were unkempt. These were highwaymen, little better than mercenaries.

My father's troupe caused no harm to man or animal when possible. These men had likely killed the original guards—the driver's bench was stained with blood. Arrow marks splintered the painted wood of the sides and doors. A third man clung to the back like a footman, but matched the others in shoddy appearance.

No doubt there had been more of them, to overpower whatever guard force originally accompanied the carriage. The prize it contained must be too large to carry by horseback, and precious enough to risk escorting in its original flamboyant container.

Before the carriage could pass under my perch it was forced to stop and remove the log we'd placed over the road. Wisely suspecting a trap, the three bandits drew their weapons and looked around as they tried to roll the log off the road as fast as possible. Before they made much progress, my father's birdcall twittered through the air. Heart leaping, I lifted my bow and sighted an arrow.

Thunk!

A merry chorus of arrows hitting home drummed through the trees. The men shouted in alarm, but our treed force was forgotten as the ground team leaped from their hiding places onto the road. One bandit stepped toward my father, shortsword raised. He was impossibly outnumbered, but some men don't know when to quit.

My arrow might have just grazed his nose as it passed by him to stick into the wood of the carriage. The message was clear. To my relief, he stood down.

"Off you go then, boys," Father said cheerfully, and I scrambled down from my tree as our troupe intimidated the three bandits into retreating down the road.

They simmered with rage and shouted insults, long past the point when the words were lost to distance. I shook my head in disgust—we'd let them keep their weapons and meager supplies. What more could they ask for, really?

I joined the team on the road. Father calmed the wild-eyed horses with his deep, soothing voice, while others yanked open the carriage door. I craned to see over their shoulders, eager to discover if our prize was coin, weapons, or even fine trading goods like fabrics or barreled brandies.

But it was none of those.

"It's a nobleman!" Joph exclaimed.

Anya and Tall Tom pulled the man from the carriage. He wore clean finery, but his hands were tied, and a grain bag covered his head. Judging by the choked sounds emerging from the bag, he'd been gagged as well.

Joph poked his head into the carriage. "There's nothing else! Just him."

"Hostages," Finn grumbled, and everyone made a face.

I supposed we'd have to send him down the road after the outlaws, but Father disagreed. "Not a hostage," he said, a playful gleam entering his dark eyes. "Ransom. A handsome ransom, no doubt."

I smiled at the joke. Let's see how handsome this ransom would be. In the shuffling I'd drawn close to where Anya and

Tall Tom held our noble between them. I reached out to pull the bag off his head, and revealed—

One

Sleep is a world all its own. I wandered in those dark lands, unaware of myself or the passing of time. Dreams did not find me, only an emptiness that might have lasted a moment or an eternity.

And then it happened.

In that second before waking, I knew surprise and dismay. Had I truly forgotten the way out of this timeless mire? But it was so simple! I could have left at any time if only I'd remembered—

The knowledge flew from me, like trying to grasp a handful of moonlight.

My eyes opened. Disoriented, all I knew at first was terrible cold. It was freezing in here! Had the hearth fire gone out and an unseasonal frost crept into my family's hut? Alair would hate that—my beloved little brother was a frail and sickly child, and Mother swore the cold made his coughing worse. I should get up and stoke the fire, maybe lay another blanket across my brother's bed.

I went to throw back my own blankets and froze as a strange rustling met my movements. Slowly, I sat up, trying to make sense of my surroundings.

I was not in my own bed in my family's home. The bed I lay on was gigantic, fit for a king, and centered in a stone room. One wall had fallen away, revealing gray clouds swirling with snow. The view and the moaning wind implied height, like I was in a tower somewhere.

Had I fallen ill and been taken to Lorensile? It was the closest city, but the stronghold there boasted no towers, and why would a sick person be left in this decrepit, freezing room? Strangely, I was not wearing the simple linens of a bedbound patient, but the finest gown I'd ever seen, with thick skirts and a bejeweled bodice.

Strangest of all, the bed was covered in roses.

Not fresh-plucked blooms. These were dried and desiccated, thorns mummified and petals sinking into ash. I brushed them from me, panic rising as they caught in the foreign gown, and my fingers trembled with cold or fear.

Rose.

A whisper, full of longing, filled the room with my name.

Then I saw him.

He stood against the far wall, black cape flickering around his boots. He seemed like a boy my age, but his face... I blinked again and again, but the scars didn't fade. They covered his skin in a net fine as spider webs. Even his hands, bare against the wind, bore the marks of violence.

"You're awake," he said, breathless. "Rose."

The boy stepped towards me, and I flinched, roses rustling. "Who are you?" I demanded, though my voice was no more than a whisper.

"I—" He took another step closer, awe turning to devastation. "You don't remember me?"

"Stay away from me," I warned, voice shaking. Horror blurred my thoughts. Was I captive to a madman? He wore a sheath at his side, but I had no weapon to threaten this stranger or defend myself if he attacked. I tried to swing my legs over the bed to run, but they ached and I cried out.

The boy stayed frozen in place, so I gritted my teeth and guided each knee up beneath the rosy skirts. Someone must have put me in this dress, and I didn't appreciate the thought. How long had I been captive here? A sound caught my attention. The stranger had fallen to the floor. No, not fallen.

He was kneeling.

"Your Highness," he said, voice different now. Empty.

I stilled. "What did you say?"

"Your Highness," he repeated, and rose to his feet. His eyes had been so hopeful, but now they were bitter. "Please, princess, let me help you."

"Stay back," I warned again, and he complied.

I glared at him while my mind raced. Was it to my advantage that he mistook me for royalty? Because nothing could be further from the truth.

I had come to my family by way of a dying stranger at the midsummer festival handing her newborn to my startled mother. In those days even isolated villages like mine trickled down the old mountain paths to the city of Lorensile twice a year for fellowship and trade. My mother had thought herself barren, so my surprise adoption was the answer to a long-held wish.

She named me Rose, for the color of my baby hair. I did not look like a northerner, growing up to be pale and strawberry-blonde instead of swarthy and dark-haired, but even after my brother Alair was born years later, my parents always treated me like their trueborn child.

Where were they? How on the gods' green Earth did I come to be here, mistaken for a princess? It made no sense—what kind of princess slept on a bed covered in dead roses, in a room open to winter's fury?

"I'm not a princess," I said slowly, examining his reaction.

"You are." He displayed only gentle tolerance. "Look behind you."

I glanced over my shoulder, seeing nothing but the headboard carved with roses, and beyond it to the stone wall. A glitter drew my attention downward.

Resting on the pillow, as if it had fallen from my head while I slept, lay a tiara.

I turned back, eyes wide.

"Princess," the boy said soothingly, though the word made me anything but calm. "What's the last thing you remember?"

I took deep breaths to steady myself, not taking my eyes off him while I silently tried to answer his question.

The carriage. The bandits, and my father's joke about a handsome ransom. I remember the nobleman, hands bound and face hidden by a grain bag.

And after that... nothing. I didn't remember what the nobleman looked like, or what we did with him. My memories stopped with that moment.

I re-focused on the stranger before me and cleared my throat. "I remember hunting with my family. We rescued someone, a nobleman, I think."

The stranger smiled as if he saw through my lie. "That nobleman was Prince Halen."

My heart skipped a beat. Surely we didn't attempt to hold the heir to the throne hostage for ransom? That might explain imprisonment in this frigid room, but not my dress, or the lavish bed. Not my memory loss. Not a stranger calling me 'Your Highness,' or the piles of dead roses.

"Prince Halen?" I repeated. "Son of the Usurper?"

"The very one." The boy continued his wild story. "You and the prince fell in love while he waited for rescue, and you came here as his intended bride."

A bubble of laughter escaped my throat. Me, in love with some soft nobleman and engaged to the crown prince of Valeria?

"That's crazy, that's..." My laughter died as I met the stranger's solemn, golden eyes. Wind swirled through the room again, biting me to seriousness. It was crazy, and yet there we were: a fanciful dress, a tiara, and a stranger who called me a princess. The stone walls around us meant we must be in the castle, in our nation's capital city, hundreds of miles from my home.

"Why can't I remember any of this?" I demanded.

"I don't know," he admitted. "It must be a side effect of the curse that kept you asleep all this time."

"Curse?" The idea was so bizarre I couldn't make sense of it. Curses were the stuff of legends, when Fae walked the earth and magic was common.

"Much has happened, princess," the stranger was saying. "There's a fireplace in the other room, let's get you warmed up and I'll explain—"

"How long have I been asleep?" I interrupted.

He thought for a moment. "It should be spring now."

It had been early summer the day we took the carriage from the bandits. Almost an entire year had passed, and I remembered none of it. "What about my family?"

He paused.

In that pause I saw a thousand terrible fates for my family. My father, who gave bear hugs and told epic tales at night by the fire. My hardworking mother, with rough hands that turned soft when touching my cheek or ministering to Alair. He was only ten years old, and he'd been ill again. Had something happened to him, to any of them?

“Tell me,” I demanded, and the boy gave me a reassuring smile.

“I’m sure your family is fine.”

“But you don’t know?” I pressed.

“Princess—”

“Stop calling me that.”

He pressed his lips together. “Rose, then,” he said gently. “Let me help you, and I’ll explain everything.”

I shivered and wrapped my arms around myself. “And who exactly are you?”

“My name is Soren,” he said. “You knew me before. I’m here to serve.”

“Aren’t there any women who could help me?”

“Unfortunately, no.” He spoke softly, as if to a spooked horse. “There’s only us.”

Another impossible fact: only the two of us, in the entire castle? Where had everyone gone? I shook my head, biting off my questions. They would only beget more questions, and the answers would likely be just as unbelievable. Best to start at the beginning.

Finally, I nodded my consent, and the stranger approached. What choice did I have? If he wanted to attack me I couldn’t be more helpless. And besides, he wasn’t what I needed to remember. There was something more important, something familiar and simple. Something, I felt sure, that would unlock my confusion about this situation.

It eluded me, as dreams often do upon waking.

The boy who called himself Soren touched my legs with gentle fingers, swinging me around so I sat on the edge of the bed. He wrapped a woolen cloak around my shoulders. Brittle thorns of the long-dead roses caught on it, and around me petals collapsed into ash, staining the white bedspread.

Soren helped me stand, but my legs gave out. He caught me, supporting my weight as I clung to his shoulders and my feet scrabbled along the stone floor in thin slippers. "Sorry," I breathed into his neck, blushing at our closeness. He smelled hot, with a sharpness like the sting in my nose after lighting a match. The scent was familiar, and thus comforting, but it also reminded me of a danger I couldn't yet name.

"That's all right," he said, voice rumbling in his chest. "Take your time."

I was as weak as a newborn colt struggling to walk. Soren guided me toward a doorway while the wind licked us with an icy tongue. I shivered violently by the time he set me down on a blanket before an empty fireplace. Soren busied himself before it, and when he pulled back giant flames appeared to warm me. The heat was wonderful, but something was wrong.

There was no wood. The fire burned bright and tall, springing from the stone itself.

I studied Soren as he sat on the blanket beside me. The scars covering him were wispy and white, not pink and thick like the various ones I'd acquired on my legs and arms. His cape of midnight pooled around him, passing through his boots like a shadow. I remembered why his scent was familiar—I'd smelled it every time the erdwitch, Maeve, had come down from her cave to visit. The spice, the strangeness, at once comforting and exciting:

Magic.

Over the centuries magic had died out in humans, until only the old royal family claimed to possess powers. But they were all gone, murdered by the Usurper. So how was this possible? Magic, curses, winter in springtime, lost memories… The hair on the back of my neck prickled, and this time not with cold.

“Explain,” I said, voice sharp even as my insides quivered.

Soren cleared his throat softly. His index finger tapped on his knee three times, and after a quiet intake of breath he announced, “The Fae are back.”

The prickle on my neck spread through my whole body.

The Fae were a mythical species, beautiful and powerful, yet cruel and capricious. Our oldest tales said they grew tired of human expansion, and in a rare partnership both Fae and humans worked together to create two new worlds. One was named Avalon, to be the home and utopia of the Fae. The other was called Shadelorn, a prison for the magical beasts that tormented humanity with their violence. This left Earth to the humans alone, and seemed a peaceful solution for everyone.

The doorways to these new worlds were sealed with the blood of a Fae king, and a human hero called Valiant. It was after this pivotal event that Valiant took the name Aerendel, meaning Dawnbringer, and became king of the lands named Valeria in his honor.

And the Aerendel line continued for a thousand years… until the Usurper murdered them.

“All is not well in Avalon,” Soren continued. “The Queen’s sister, Silaine, tried to kill the Fae King Oberon and take the throne. She failed, and was exiled to Earth, but the portal was broken on the Fae side. They no longer need the king’s blood to open it. More and more Fae have come to Earth, joining Silaine’s rebellion. She’s been here for years, since the days of the last true king. She helped the Usurper take the crown, and in return he didn’t interfere with her growing forces in the north.”

I was horrified to realize this actually made sense. My village was located in the mountains to the north, but there were many people living more north than us. Sinister stories had trickled down in recent years of strange creatures, and whole villages disappearing without a trace. And it explained how the Usurper held his tenuous power, though dislike of him seemed to be universal.

"How do you even know this?" I asked, mind whirling.

Soren shrugged one shoulder. "It's common knowledge now. You've missed… quite a lot. The Usurper had made a blood deal with Silaine to take the throne, but he was a fool. Silaine broke their agreement. She came to the castle and…" His words failed, eyes fastened on a sorrowful past.

He didn't have to say it. If we were really the only two left, that meant a whole castle full of people was just… gone. Courtiers and servants, soldiers and scullery maids. The Usurper, yes, but his son, too. The boy I had supposedly fallen in love with.

I slumped, slowly accepting the gravity of what had happened here. Was it possible to mourn someone you'd never met? Or at least the idea of them? If Soren were right, I'd been in love. Now I would never know him.

"Silaine used their blood to bring the snow," Soren said, eyes refocusing on me. "She cursed you to sleep without waking, and I… I've been waiting for you to wake, hoping…"

"And my family?" I breathed.

He looked away from me. "It's winter where they are, too."

I closed my eyes in relief.

"I'm sure they're fine. Many people evacuated to Shalimar. That's where I'm taking you. I don't know why Silaine didn't kill you, too," he said, answering my next question, "but it doesn't matter. Now that you're awake I'm getting you as far away from here as possible." He rose, and I stiffened, but he only walked to a cloth pack by the fireplace and rummaged through it.

I wanted to call him a liar and spit in his face. I wanted to leap from the thin blanket and run from this room with its magic and the boy with the spiderwebs of scars. I wanted to deny everything he said.

The problem was I believed him.

Soren's hand emerged from the pack with a pot. He set this over the impossible fire, and when I could see the pot again it brimmed with hot porridge.

"You can do magic," I said, daring him to deny it.

He paused, before reaching into the limp sack on the floor and pulling out a silver spoon and bowl. Something else flashed within, but I didn't trust my eyes. What I saw would be far too long and bulky for that thin sack.

"Only since the… tragedy," he said, and served me up a bowl of porridge. "Many old stories have come to life."

He handed me the spoon with a grim smile. Had magic given him all those scars? I shoved a spoonful of the hot grain into my mouth, before remembering I was supposedly a princess, and should probably affect better manners. But to the shades with it. If they had given me any princess training I'd forgotten it now, and anyway there was only Soren to see. *I'm here to serve*, he'd said. Had he been a servant to Prince Halen? To me?

"Something woke me, though," I said when I'd polished off the bowl. "Something happened to wake me up. What was it? And why now?"

I hoped he would reveal the elusive anchor that brought me back to consciousness, still hovering there like a word I couldn't quite name. But his eyes left mine for a moment before returning, as if determined to meet my gaze. "I don't know."

I picked at the edge of my cloak. It was thick, and brown, and seemed perfectly normal. "I think you're lying."

A smile spread across Soren's face, slow and sincere. It pinched the scars on his cheeks but for a moment I didn't even see them. "Why am I not surprised?" he said. "Come on, princess. Let's get you safely into Shalimar before you freeze to death. We can find your family, and figure out how to break this curse of winter." He stood, and held out his hand.

I eyed it, considering. Why were the two of us chosen to survive the massacre at the castle? And why couldn't I remember it? Could I trust this boy whom a Fae had spared?

He waited, observing me without impatience. Light from the fire glinted off his tawny, curly hair. His eyes were unnaturally gold, a color I'd never seen on anyone else before. A result of the magic? His small, high cheekbones and deep-set eyes would read as handsome among southerners, if one ignored the threads of scars on his skin. Among my people his slim frame would be a weakness. We preferred stoutness and strength. Soren didn't look like he could win a fistfight, brace a spear against a charging boar, or carry home the body of a deer on his back.

But he was here, and all I had. What could make a stranger wait for me to wake, in the aftermath of so much violence and destruction?

After a moment I took his hand.

Soren gave me layers of clean linen and wool, pulled yet again from the seemingly-endless depths of his mysterious pack. He waited in the frigid wind of the other room while I changed, grateful he'd supplied me with pants and a tunic instead of a winter dress. I pulled on leather boots and wrapped the cloak around me, and these layers combined with a belly of hot porridge finally allowed my shivering to cease. Next, I arranged my hair into one long, thick braid down my back, and tied it off with a string Soren procured for me. I felt like myself again.

"Is there a knife I could have? Or maybe a bow?" I asked hopefully.

His mouth quirked in a wry smile, and he found me a fine little belt knife, small but sharp. I missed the one my father made for me with the deer horn handle, wondering where in the world it might be now. I'd used it for everything, from paring my nails to cleaning fish from the river. A pang of homesickness—would I ever see my little village again? How would I find my family among countless refugees in Shalimar?

Soren strapped a thin, plain sword to his back, lit a torch, then extinguished the magical fire and packed our supplies into the suspicious bag. Its brown, woven sides lay flat, even when lifted from the ground, and nothing clanked within it. As I followed him down a dizzying spiral staircase I tried to catch hold of his cloak, but it passed through my fingers like a cool breeze.

My lingering suspicion of the fantastical things he told me faded. The halls were strangers to me, but there could be no doubt we fled through a castle. We passed rooms with tapestries frozen to the walls, weapons from long-dead guards scattered at the doorways, and furniture covered in icicles.

But no bodies. For that I was grateful.

Soren led me into the white outdoors, and fresh cold caught in my lungs. The air was thick with the taste of snow. Everything around us stood still and peaceful. We approached what used to be a courtyard, large and square-shaped, but covered unevenly with white drifts. Soren turned and beckoned me onward. My boots made their first crunches on the snow, and then I looked up into the sky.

I couldn't tell what time of day it was, for the clouds were dark and pregnant with flurries. A few snowflakes floated towards me, as if welcoming me back to the world, and one caught on my lips. I brushed it away, and then the memory fell upon me just as gently, the truth behind what had woken me:

A kiss.

TWO

I touched a gloved hand to my lips. It wasn't just the feel of something on my lips that had been there when I woke. The familiar thing was a kiss, with all the tenderness that went with it.

I looked at Soren's retreating back, his magical cloak billowing behind him, and once again caution prickled my scalp.

Had Soren kissed me?

"Princess, we need to hurry," he called. "Please!"

I plunged after him, sinking halfway to my knees. I caught up to Soren, pacing my breaths with my steps and finding the rhythm to our travel. I'd done this a thousand times before, trekking about the forest in the dead of winter, checking traps and always ready with my bow for any game that crossed my path.

We approached the border of the castle walls where something had torn through the iron gates, leaving space for Soren and I to slip out. Magic? No—claw marks scored the iron.

Soren turned back to find me touching the gouges in the bars. Nothing could do this, not bears or wolves, or anything I'd ever encountered in the forest. I shot him a questioning glance.

He swallowed. "Silaine has set many monsters loose upon the land. We need to hurry."

My eyebrows lifted. I was about to ask what else this murderous Fae had changed in the world since I'd been asleep, but as we passed through the gate my concern was replaced with another.

Just beyond the castle walls stood a wall of thorns.

Black vines surged from the snow to distant heights. Some trunks were as thick as my waist, gleaming with a sheen of ice covering foot-long thorns whose very tips seemed dipped in blood.

Soren touched me, and I jumped. "Stay close," he said, and I stepped towards him. "No, closer." He wrapped an arm around me and our breath mingled in the freezing air. "Don't worry about them. Just look forward, and stay with me."

I nodded. As we drew near the thorns creaked, groaned, and *moved*, pulling back to make an archway that held as we passed through. I almost froze in panic, but Soren moved me bodily forward, and we stumbled awkwardly together under the hideous vines.

That journey of moments felt like a thousand years. I sighed in relief after we crossed safely, and reluctantly left the warmth of Soren's grasp. We turned to begin the true journey but a cracking sound shot across the snow.

The thorn wall shuddered and wobbled, as if shaken by a private earthquake. Soren grabbed my hand and we ran for our lives as the thorns toppled behind us. From a safe distance we stopped and looked back at the wreckage. My stomach twisted in horror as the vines vanished beneath the snow like a sinking ship, leaving not a trace behind.

"What the hell was that?" I panted.

"We should go," Soren said. "Hurry."

The speed of our travel left no breath for questions. I managed to examine the snow around us as we fled: no animal tracks, not even from bird feet, but judging by how the snowflakes fell and the look of the clouds, any tracks made more than four hours ago would have been filled completely. This light snowfall was a break in the storm. It did not surprise me when the winds picked up and the snow fell in flurries, clinging to my eyelashes and making it hard to see.

Soren's black cape was the only thing helping me see him in the storm. The castle was built at the top of a hill, and as we went on the grade of the land sank sharply. We descended on a winding road, but when we came to a crossroads Soren paused.

"Do you know the way?" I asked. I knew the trails in the forest around my village intimately, but I'd never been to the capital, and these roads were all strangers.

Soren hesitated, a moment too long. "Yes," he said, and led us to the left.

Not long after I called out to him, "Soren! I can't feel my face." We stopped while he pulled a scarf from his strange bag, blushing with apologies. "It's all right," I said. "I need to rest anyway."

The confession embarrassed me, but the energy from the porridge had worn off. I knew I should have been able to go much longer without taking a break, but my muscles were weak. We paused, two statues in the wilderness while I caught my breath. The wind whistled around us, delivering snow in great clumps.

Then, a change in the noise, like a tuning of the wind.

I whirled on instinct, but Soren was already shoving me to the ground. "Watch out!"

Something screamed above us. As I fell I glimpsed a hulking shape with wings—and claws—graze the air where I'd stood. Heart racing, I lay still in the snow, though it chilled me to the bone.

I reached across my shoulder for my bow before

remembering I didn't have one.

Metal rasped as Soren ripped his sword from its sheath. I sat up to find him bent in a defensive position, blade in both hands. I struggled to my feet.

"Stay down," he called, voice clogged through the scarf.

"What is it?"

"Gargrayles. Monsters from Silaine."

A shape loomed out of the thick flurries, its growing silhouette revealing black wings and eyes that caught the light in a flash of red. It swooped low and Soren swung. I flinched as the monster screamed while dark blood fell to the snow with a hiss of steam.

Rolling onto my knees, I crawled to the side of the road and dove into the ditch. I scrambled to a crouch in time to see Soren spinning in a circle as wings swished overhead. Two sets. Two beasts bigger than the mammoth bed I'd woken in.

I shrieked for him before it happened—one attacked from the front and the other from behind while he was distracted, slicing through his shadow cloak and the shirt beneath, spilling Soren's blood to the white road.

His back arched at the cut. He missed the swing into the attacker from the front, and its eyes focused on me next. Its talons flexed as it finished the swoop and I rolled. They struck snow not a foot from where I lay, before the great beast heaved itself back into the sky.

This was not going to work.

I could barely see in the falling snow, yet felt the wings of the gargrayles riding the air and knew they were rising up to fall down on us again. Just like hawks in a field, and we were the mice. Now was my chance.

I hurled myself onto the road, crawling to where Soren's bag lay deserted. He cursed at me to get back but I'd seen flashes of what he was carrying in that mysterious pack.

The gold of the hilt glinted, beckoning. I had rarely handled swords, but what choice did I have? My frozen fingers tore at the ties as the beast screeched above me. I yanked the blade from its sheath and thrust the heavy sword above my head, its hilt providing a strange warmth even through my mittened hands. The beast swooped, claws opened wide. I twisted left at the last possible second and sliced through the air—

I connected with flesh.

The creature's rot-scented blood fell like a sheet of rain, and it cried so loud the noise reverberated down the blade to my hands. The blade sang.

"Damn it, get down," Soren kept yelling but I ignored him, stepping towards the blood-flecked circle he had stomped out with frantic twirling.

"Shut up," I hissed, and turned my back to him. "Be ready!"

The snow pelted my eyes and I narrowed them to slits, seeking the body of a beast within the gusts of wind and shadows of falling snow.

"They're coming!" I tensed, sword pointed above my right shoulder. It hummed with awareness, a friend who whispered support and confidence. It would take care of me, tell me what to do.

I crouched down, pretending I was small as a sparrow, and the beast fell towards me. I looked up and my world narrowed to jaws filled with fat needles, ears pointed like a wolf, and a furry body framed by leathery wings. There was nowhere to hide, no time to change my mind.

Those terrible talons opened.

I screamed a hoarse cry, leaping up and reaching as high as

I could. Though its talons closed around my chest I swung hard, slicing through the neck of the beast.

I had hoped for another gash—a complete beheading should have been impossible, but my shock didn't have time to register. Headless, the body couldn't break its fall, and it slammed me to the ground, claws biting into my skin. Its breastbone thumped into my ribs and a blanket of musky fur pressed against my nose and mouth. Dimly I heard shouts of the battle Soren still fought with the other gargrayle.

Something hot and wet touched my head and trickled down my face. Blood. It gushed into the snow above me.

I squirmed, but the weight was immense. I pushed my head back into the snow to catch a breath, barely finding space between the creature's body and the air. Pushing and pulling despite complaining muscles, I eventually wriggled out from under the beast.

Red snow invaded the top of my tunic and scraped at my neck as I freed my head and arms. Then Soren was there, pushing his whole body against the dead gargrayle and rolling it off me. Its claws tore my cloak. "Are you all right?"

I gasped for air, blood chilling on my head and one cheek numb against the snow. I nodded. He helped me up onto shaking legs.

"Rose, next time you have to listen to me. The world is a lot more dangerous than it used to be. Those things could have killed you."

"You're injured, and you can't fight two at once," I said, teeth chattering. "They would have killed us anyway."

He dabbed at the blood on my face with his sleeve. "I heal fast," he said grimly. "Next time, let me fight alone."

I didn't dignify that with a response. The sense of danger had fled, but when I looked around—"Where's the other one?"

"It got away. And we need to leave, too. There could be more."

I kicked at the decapitated head of the gargrayle, its red eyes still glaring. I knelt to the ground to clean off my sword in the snow, then wiped it on the inside of my cloak. It was a fine blade, expertly crafted and apparently sharper than my instincts told me should be possible. The hilt had gold and silver finishes, adorned with a large sapphire. If I could pry the gemstone off—but no, now wasn't the time to worry about scavenging.

Soren pulled a cloth from his pack, and wiped more gargrayle blood from my head and neck.

"Thank you," I said.

"Of course." He reached out to take the sword from me, but I jerked it away. His eyebrows raised in surprise. In truth I surprised myself. But I felt oddly protective of the sword, and didn't want to give it up.

"You shouldn't be handling that," he said.

My eyes narrowed. "I guess I know how to use it well enough. I killed the gargrayle, didn't I?"

Soren dropped his hand and I clutched the sword closer to me. "It'll slow you down," he said.

"You were carrying two, apparently. I can be suffered enough to carry one."

Wind whistled through the tops of skeletal trees on either side of the road. What would I do if he insisted—raise a weapon against this boy who had watched over me while I slept? To my relief it didn't come to that.

Soren sighed. "Fine. Let me get you a belt for it."

Stand-off dissolved, Soren cinched the leather around my waist, his body a warm blockade against the wind. I closed my eyes for a moment and caught the unexpected scent of him again.

Fire. The sweet sting of magic.

He finished and pulled back, watching as I slid the sword into the scabbard at my left side. The weight clung to me, heavier than the daggers I used to carry, but I still caught my breath in pleasure. It felt so right.

Soren observed me with his golden eyes.

"What?" I asked, defensive. We were still so close I didn't have to shout over the wind.

He shook his head and smiled at me. "Nothing. It's just that you are a very remarkable princess."

Something moved within me. Maybe it was the look in his eyes or the way he smelled, or the way my lips tingled when he drew near, but there was definitely something he wasn't telling me.

About us.

We stared at each other in the whipping snow, but between us was only the silent crackle of magic. I recalled how my name had filled the room in the tower, tender and full of longing.

Finally I asked the question pressing on my heart. "Are you Prince Halen?" What I meant was, *Are you the boy I fell in love with*?

His eyes were filled with honey and sadness. "No," he said softly. "But I wish I was."

"Who were you, then?" I pressed. "...To me?"

Now his eyes flinched away. "We can discuss this later," he said gruffly, walking past me to his bag. "We have to get moving. Night will be here soon."

"I want you to tell me now."

"Rose—Your Highness—" He picked up the strange bag and strapped it to his back once more. "I don't think you understand how dangerous it is for us here. I'll explain everything once we're in Shalimar. I promise."

I wanted to push the issue, but the sudden fear in his eyes made me relent. I'd get the truth out of him later. I wrapped the scarf around my head and followed him, but then I tore it off again.

"Wait, we're going the wrong way."

We were hiking back up the hill, not down it.

"No. I made a mistake... This was the wrong path."

What could I do? Even if he was confused, he knew more than me, so I followed him back up to the crossroads, where we took the road to the right. We hiked through a frozen, empty town at the base of the hill, and then further on, until the sky grew so dark I could barely see the snow falling in front of my face. The mystery of Soren and I was pushed to the back of my mind by the difficulty of the journey.

We did not see the gargrayles again, but I felt movement around us occasionally. Soren paused now and then as well, sometimes lighting up the road with a burst of red emanating from his hand, and then the feeling of being watched diminished.

Traveling in this way, we encountered no disturbances… until nightfall.

THREE

Soren wished we were further in our journey. I could see it in his darting eyes, and in the way he kept pausing to listen to the darkness around us while setting up camp. His small pack yielded a complete set of tent poles and coverings from magical depths, and he held hands over them, whispering words I couldn't hear. They flew together in the blink of an eye and formed a well-structured tent. Soren crouched over the ground and held his hand across the snow. Fire burst forth.

I watched with fascination. By this point I was sure he was misleading me, but I couldn't put my finger on how, or why. The abandoned castle, the tiara, the winter, and the beasts—these were all points in his favor. But his other claims didn't make any sense. Why would a Fae kill everyone but he and I? Why would I lose my memories, conveniently forgetting everything up until the point Soren claimed my life changed?

And then there was the last piece of confusion: the kiss.

I believed with all my heart the curse of sleep had been broken by his kiss, and that lingering memory of tenderness made me trust him. The way he held me when I was weak, how he carefully wiped blood off my brow, his panic when facing down creatures intent on hurting me—all these actions were evidence Soren cared about me. Was he simply a servant, like he said, secretly in love with his master's intended bride? Or had we both been in love, and had to hide it? But then why was he hiding it from me now, especially if Prince Halen was dead?

With the camp assembled, Soren fussed over me, drawing me closer to the fire and conjuring food to warm my belly. As I ate he walked about, establishing a perimeter and picking out defensive positions.

"I want to take a shift," I said as he circled back around.

"What?"

"You're planning on guarding the camp. I know you're as tired as I am, so let me take a shift."

"Princess, I'm honestly surprised you made it this far today. You haven't had to use your muscles in a long time, and you need rest far more than I do. Don't worry about me. I can magic myself awake. You can barely keep your eyes open."

It was true. Belly full, my body focused on its next need: sleep.

"I'm going to get answers in the morning," I warned him, and one side of his mouth quirked up, but he still ordered me into the tent. I fell asleep before I could take my boots off.

My dreams came fast and frantic: the eyes of the beast, the bed with a thousand dead roses, and a sword found in the snow. Someone familiar rushed with me through a forest alive with green and song, a bow slung across my back, deerskin slippers pounding over a ground covered in pine needles. Then the terrible dread of entering the cave, a knife in the witch's hand, red blood sizzling in a tiny vial, shouting, a flash, an army—

I woke dazed and suffocating in the blankets, slowly coming to the realization that the shouting didn't end with my return to consciousness. Something ripped behind me. A knife dug through the back of the tent.

My frantic fingers struggled with my sword, but before I could unsheathe it large, strong arms guided by a red-bearded face reached in to pull me out into the frigid cold.

I screamed and thrashed but he held me tight, dragging me backwards through the woods while I could only witness the chaos around us.

The tiny campfire had swelled to ten times its original size, and Soren yelled with fury to match outside its circle of light, blasting our attackers with magic and dark shadows, sparkling shields defending against flocks of arrows. Dark shapes crouched behind trees, blades glinting in the firelight. One figure, tall and dark, stood out in the open, battling Soren, matching each magical blow with one of his own.

I shouted his name and it seemed everyone paused in their attacks for a breathless moment before renewing with twice the ferocity. I still held my sword in my left hand, though it was sheathed, and I smacked it against the legs of my kidnapper.

"Oof! Stop that, now." Redbeard had a strange accent, and a kind—if mildly annoyed—voice, but though I hit him repeatedly he didn't try to shake the sword from my hand. We reached a group of four other men waiting on horses, their swords and bows drawn.

I screamed again. "Let me go!"

"Shh, it's all right, Rose, we got you," Redbeard said as he set my swinging legs on the ground.

Rose?

Not princess. Not Your Highness. Just Rose.

"Who are you?" I demanded.

"We're here to save you," Redbeard said as he lifted me onto the horse, then hauled himself up after.

The group spurred their horses on, my would-be kidnapper

in the lead. We charged through the dark forest, barely able to see the trees in front of us.

They'd still made no attempt to take my sword, and I remembered the belt knife Soren gave me. I could gut Redbeard, slip through his arms, roll to the ground, and have my sword drawn by the time the others doubled back. If I could get a hold of one of those bows, I was sure I could easily be a match for them. Then I could return and somehow help Soren beat whoever was left behind. We could escape and he could tell me why they were fighting, why these men had come in the night to steal me, and why the way Redbeard spoke to me made me not want to kill these men at all, but find out what they were after.

Because this didn't feel like a kidnapping.

"Hold on, Rose, just a few more miles." Redbeard shouted to make himself heard over the wind and the galloping. "You're safe now."

No, it felt like a rescue.

We burst through the tree line and raced across a field shaded blue by moonlight. The grade of the land had lessened. As we approached the other side the men slowed their horses and retreated carefully into the woods, waiting for the rest of the party.

Everyone panted, the horses sending up white streams of breath to dissolve in the cool air. A shiver coursed through my body, and my teeth chattered. Redbeard switched the reins to one hand, gathered his cloak, and then threw both arms around me. He smelled like horse and sweat, but he was warm. We waited for a few tense minutes, snow falling around us peacefully as if a battle had not taken place miles from where we stood.

"Who are you?" I demanded again.

"Hush now," he said, terse but not unkind. "Answers come.

Look there."

The rest of the party appeared across the field, and the men around us expressed relief. At the head of the attackers rode a man in a dark cloak—the one who had wielded magic against Soren.

They came to a thundering stop and the leader's large, black horse drew alongside the one I shared with Redbeard. His face was half-covered by a scarf, but his dark eyes looked at me with eagerness and joy. Absent was the cloud of reserved secrecy I had seen in Soren.

The newcomer unhitched the scarf from his face and I blinked in surprise. He was my age! Or perhaps a bit older. He had a dark look: bronzed skin, black eyes, black hair. The same coloring as the people of the north. My people. Was he really leading these men? He gave me an enthusiastic grin as if we shared some secret, and reached out a hand.

"Up you go, girl," Redbeard said, making to lift me onto the newcomer's mount.

My right foot clumsily reached for the space between the leader and his horse's neck, and I was thrown rather unceremoniously forward. Before I could recover my seat the leader whirled his horse around, one arm encircling my waist protectively, and we were off again.

"Are you all right?" he spoke urgently into my ear, without Redbeard's accent. He said his words like Soren. Like me.

"Yes," I answered as best I could between the bumpy ride and the frigid air whipping in my face. "But who are you?"

"Alair sent us. Give us a few miles to outdistance that traitor and I'll explain," he shouted back.

My stomach leaped to hear of my brother Alair, before the strangeness of his words sobered me. My brother was ten years old—how had he sent a team of men to find me? Why hadn't my father done so? Why wasn't my father with these men?

Why did he call Soren a traitor?

The snow grew lighter the further we traveled, and the leader kept his arm firmly about my waist, his hand like a hot stone on my stomach. He smelled like Soren, covered in hard work and the tang of magic.

Finally the snowfall ceased, and the landscape glowed in pale blue. Above us the wind had pushed the clouds away, and we traveled under a starry night, sometimes passing clusters of huts covered in sheets of ice. The leader signaled his men to slow, and the horses walked through the frozen wasteland.

He let go of my waist and reached up to undo the scarf covering his nose and mouth. "My name is Rowan. I'm sorry we had to take you like this, but please believe me, he's not what you think."

I frowned, trying to untangle everything in my mind. "Who's not?" I asked first, the chilly air hurting my throat. "Soren?"

"Sor—What?"

"Soren. The boy with me." My words were met with silence. I tensed, full of panic. "Did you kill him?"

"No, we can't—Rose, don't you know who he is?"

"No," I confessed, deciding to share the truth with this stranger who seemed to know me. "I woke up today in the tower, and Soren was there, and that's all I know. The last thing I remember is hunting with my village."

Rowan whistled low in disbelief, and the horse flicked its ears back. "You don't remember... anything after that? He didn't—Are you sure?"

I shook my head.

"So what did he—Soren—tell you?"

It sounded strange inside my head, and would be ridiculous said aloud. "He said the Fae have returned to Earth. He said I'd agreed to marry the son of the Usurper, but a Fae named Silaine killed everyone in the castle, and brought the early winter, and cursed me to sleep. Is any of that true?"

"Unfortunately yes," he said and my heart sank. "It's more complicated than that, but yes."

"Oh." I'd held on to a tiny hope that Soren had been lying. "So who is Soren, really?"

"We call him the Betrayer," Rowan said, voice taking on a touch of iron. "He is the *damnsoír* of Silaine. I'm going to kill her one day."

Damnsoír. I mouthed the word silently, tasting each syllable. Damn-so-ere. The word tasted foreign but familiar, and I remembered it from a story my father used to tell. *Damnsoír* meant a slave.

To the Fae.

I shivered, with fear and confusion. Was it possible the boy who had treated me so tenderly was working for the Fae? I couldn't resist any longer. I exploded with questions. "So Soren's still alive? Why did Silaine curse me? Where are we going? Where is my family?"

"Listen, we didn't know you wouldn't have all your memories," Rowan said instead of answering my questions. "Alair can explain everything."

"So my family's all right? I don't understand why Alair would be this far south. Are my parents with him?"

Rowan faltered. "Rose…"

Another terrifying pause. I tensed, relief and curiosity evaporating. Suddenly I didn't want to hear any more explanations.

"You've been asleep for a long time," Rowan said gently. "Your family…"

"How long?" I demanded.

"I don't know how to tell you, I shouldn't be the one—"

"*How long?*"

Another pause. "Over a hundred years."

His answer didn't make sense. I could accept falling in love with a prince—barely. I could accept Fae in the world again, and even the true nature of Soren's identity. Hadn't I witnessed his alien magic? With the Fae involved, sleeping curses and long winters and terrible beasts were possible... But not this.

Not this.

Everything I had known was… gone. I could see the ravages of time now in the trees around us. Mummified trunks, canopies dead yet frozen together. Decades and decades of snow and ice, melting and refreezing again. The castle, with its unattended walls crumbling away. The roads that bore no tracks except for mine and Soren's—Soren, who had lied about my family to get me to go with him. So I wouldn't be paralyzed like I was now, with the overwhelming loss of everything and everyone I ever knew and loved.

Except Alair.

My little brother, ten years old when I last remembered seeing him. How had he lived for another century?

"We waited for you a long time," Rowan said, holding me closer. "I'm so sorry, Rose. Everything will be all right. Alair will explain."

I closed my eyes and felt hot tears trace down my cheeks, turning cold long before they reached my chin.

Some time passed before Rowan gently announced that we'd arrived, and I finally opened my eyes to see our destination.

It was a small village, centered in a field like an island in an ocean of snow. A high wooden wall surrounded the village, defensive spikes circling the wall to impale anything that drew too near.

"The last village of Valeria," Rowan said proudly. "We call it Briar. In honor of… well, you."

His words were like a shard of glass to the heart. Briar Rose. It's what my family sometimes called me. My father used to say that daggers and arrows were my thorns.

He would never call me Briar Rose again.

We descended the last slope toward Briar and a flare shot up from one of the towers along the wall. Rowan's posture straightened as we returned, his chest brushing my back. After a few minutes, a frenzied noise worked its way out of the barricades, and part of the wall lowered to let us inside.

The horses marched forward, Rowan and I at their lead, straight into a waiting crowd who cheered and whistled when they saw my face. They were mostly men, and of all ages, some dressed in rags while others wore fine armor. Some faces were dirty, and many beards unkempt, but excitement shone from every eye. I could only stare at them, thinking that none of these people were even born when I was last awake.

The camp was filled with mud instead of snow. We passed work tables and fire pits, then rows of long wooden buildings. My eyes widened. Briar had every appearance of a military encampment.

The ragtag crowd of soldiers escorted us in good cheer until we reached a structure in the center of the village. It was different from the featureless barracks. It had a chimney and a porch, like a house.

A hunched man wrapped in a fur cloak stood waiting for us there, leaning on a cane for support. He had a face so old the depth of his wrinkles startled me, and the top of his head sported more liver spots than white hairs. His beard was long, but scraggly, and he grinned a toothless smile of joy.

Rowan pulled the horse to a stop. The crowd surged, but didn't come between us and the house with its elderly occupant. Rowan dismounted and helped me down, holding my hands for a moment as I recovered my balance. He winked at me.

We approached the porch. I didn't know how to greet the old man, and a stone of dread sat in my stomach. The entire camp held their breath for his words.

"Welcome," he said, voice strong despite his appearance. "My sister, welcome home at last!"

FOUR

The old man wrapped his frail arms around me and hugged me tightly. I returned the gesture automatically, stunned into silence.

Rowan put a hand on the old man's shoulder. "She doesn't remember what happened," he said softly. "The curse must have..."

My elderly brother finally pulled back and looked at me with glistening brown eyes. "Never mind that." He squeezed my arms. "I will remember for you. Now come in, come in."

Rowan met my gaze in shared surprise at the old man's equanimity before he ushered us away from the now-cheering crowd into the house.

We entered a single large room divided into sections by its furniture. Tallow candles held back the shadows, except at the far end, where a glowing hearth burned merrily. It was here we sat, at a small table before the fireplace.

Rowan served a starchy soup bubbling over the flames while the old man held my hand and grinned at me like someone blind seeing the world for the first time.

"Oh, my sister, when I last saw you I was your younger brother. Now I am older by almost a century."

I looked down at our hands, my skin smooth and unblemished, his translucent and spotted with age. I peered into his face, trying to find some hint of my little brother. When I found it my stomach clenched anew—so it was true.

A hundred years had passed.

"Alair?" I whispered, his face transforming before me as I reconciled memory with reality.

I was nearly seven years old when he was born, and helped my mother care for him, as proud of him as if he was my own child. I showed him how to fish on the river, gave him monthly haircuts, and when he fell sick I was the one who sought out herbs for his medicine. I found that little boy in the curve of the old man's cheeks, in the color of his eyes and the way he smiled. This was my brother.

"I'm sorry," I said, realizing the silence had gone on too long. My voice was rough. "It's just that I didn't know it had been so long. Soren told me it had been less than a year…"

At the mention of Soren's name the smile fell from Alair's face. "Soren is a liar," he said, hands shaking in mine. He pulled them back, and gripped his spoon like a knife. "Filth. The scum of all men."

"Grandfather—" Rowan said, but Alair held up a hand.

Grandfather? That would make me Rowan's… great aunt. Suddenly the implication of a century of absence hit me in a different way: the world had not paused, life had gone on. Even my nieces and nephews, if I had any, would be old enough to be my parents. It wasn't just my immediate family I'd lost—it was generations of them.

"She should know the truth," Alair said. "Soren is her enemy, too."

"Please, tell me what happened," I said. "Everything. The last thing I remember is capturing a carriage with a nobleman inside. Was that Prince Halen?"

"It was. But our story begins earlier." Alair sighed and asked Rowan to bring him his pipe.

I explained to Alair everything Soren told me while Rowan returned with a pipe and a tiny packet of tobacco. As the flap opened the scent brought forth a thousand memories of nights just like this, sitting with my family in the glow of the fire while Father told us stories or whittled toys for Alair. He'd had a whole family of painted wooden ducks, and they could float on the river.

I bit my lower lip and held my breath to stop the tears. Now wasn't the time for crying. I had to listen, to find out what turned my world upside down. Alair passed his fingers over the stuffed end of the pipe and smoke curled into the air. I blinked, realizing I witnessed yet more magic. How had my little brother acquired magical powers? How had Rowan, for that matter? Could everyone do magic in this strange new future?

"The Fae Silaine uses the blood of humans to create monsters," Alair began. "When she started growing her powers in the north, word of her wickedness reached the old king, Stefan Aerendel. Silaine sent word that she would let him live and leave his kingdom in peace if he would give her the northlands to do with as she wished. But Stefan was a good man, and refused. All might have been well, and that foul Fae wiped from this earth under the strength of Valeria's army, but a traitor struck from within."

"The Usurper," I guessed, and Alair nodded.

"Correct. He sought out Silaine and proposed a deal. Lord Cynric, as he was known then, would dispose of King Stefan and his rightful heirs, if Silaine would grant Cynric the power to hold the kingship. They made a blood oath, to hold each other to their promise."

I nodded. This was all in line with what Soren had told me, and blood oaths were common in the legends of the past.

“Cynric slew King Stefan, Queen Briallen, and their children. All except one. A newborn babe, smuggled from her cradle.” Alair smiled at me.

I raised an eyebrow. This was the first I’d heard of one of the royal children surviving. But as Alair’s smile stretched on and on I paled. It was impossible. It couldn’t be… “*Me?*”

My brother inclined his head. “You, my dear. You are the lost Princess Talia Aerendel.”

I sat back in my chair, unbelieving. I’d grown up hearing the story of how a woman in Lorensile had stumbled out of an alley and given her baby to my mother during the summer festival. My adoption had never been a secret in our village. It hardly could have been—I was pale and tall, with hair that couldn’t quite decide if it was yellow or orange, and my family were true people of the mountains, dark of hair and tan of skin. But several families in our village had taken in orphans or distant relatives, so I was hardly special in that regard.

Alair continued his impossible tale. “Our dear Maeve happened to be visiting the castle while Lord Cynric committed his murders. She stole you away, and gave you to our parents to raise as their own.”

I held up a hand, needing a moment to take this in.

Maeve was an erdwitch—a being sprung from the earth fully formed, to balance the elements and do the will of the gods on earth. She lived in a cave nearby and was a healer to the villages in the area. She helped with Alair’s illnesses more than once, and though I knew she had a fondness for me I never suspected it was because she saved my life.

I shook my head to clear away my shock. “*I’m* a member of the royal family? Why didn’t anyone ever tell me?” A sense of betrayal cut through the hurt. “Why would our parents lie about where I came from?"

"They didn't," Alair reassured me. "Witches can change shape, you know. Maeve appeared as a desperate young mother when she gave you away. Our parents never knew a thing about you being a princess. Maeve didn't even tell you until you went with Prince Halen to ask her blessing for your marriage. She was very concerned. His father had tried to kill you, after all."

I winced. "All right," I said, willing to suspend my disbelief. "So I was born an Aerendel. But tell me about Halen. Did we really… fall in love?"

Alair puffed on his pipe, and Rowan watched him intently. Alair shrugged. "I don't remember much. I was very young, you know, and jealous that someone was taking my sister away from me. I'm sorry."

I hadn't realized I'd harbored a tiny hope until it perished. Unless I recovered my memories I'd never learn about this boy I had loved.

"He was our captive, at first, but refused to tell us his name, and there was no chance he'd survive if he escaped through the woods, so he lived with us as a sort of prisoner-guest. You taught him to shoot a bow if I recall correctly. It was around this time I grew deathly ill. You and Halen went to Maeve to plead for my life, and she agreed to save me with the magic in her blood, with the understanding that it would… change me. Maeve shared her essence with me, imparting some of her erdwitch powers. I learned the craft from her, and passed down the ability to my son, and his son." He smiled at Rowan. "When you returned to our village, a troupe of royal guards was waiting for you. Halen went back to the capital and you were heartbroken. But weeks later he returned with the news that his father had given him permission to marry you, if you would accept. Much of the village was to go with you to the palace in celebration."

In front of me I caught Rowan's frown. He opened his mouth, but Alair held up a hand and Rowan fell silent. "I was left behind with Maeve," Alair continued. "Still too sick to travel. What happened next has been a source of speculation for a hundred years."

My heartbeat quickened. Here was the truth about my family at last.

"On the day you should have reached the palace, a terrible wind blew through the mountains. Temperatures dropped, and snow fell in the middle of summer. It never left. When I was fully healed, Maeve let me travel to the palace to discover what happened to my family. The snow was endless, and the closer I got to the capital the stranger the rumors became. Many had already fled, and the city outside the palace was completely deserted.

"Inside the palace I found only death. In the throne room were the bodies of our villagers and the royal family." Alair's eyes left mine for a moment to flick towards his grandson. "Including Halen. Slaughtered. Only you were missing. I searched every room in the palace, and finally found you in the tallest tower, asleep on a bed of roses. Sleeping so peacefully, like nothing at all was amiss."

Here our memories could intersect. I remembered the ashy petals, now mere husks of the flowers they'd been a hundred years ago. I wondered for the first time what they had looked like when fresh, colors vibrant and strong, cradling me with their softness and fragrance. Who put the roses on the bed, if not Alair?

"I tried to wake you, but you would not stir. It was the curse. I was still yelling for you when Soren arrived. He was a noble who somehow convinced Silaine to spare his life. He'd become the first *damnsoír* since the Fae last walked the Earth. Powerful. Immortal. He is a monster, a villain, and an enemy to us all. *You must never trust him.*"

My brother growled the last sentence, and my heart seized. So this was why Rowan called him the Betrayer. It explained why he'd stayed so young though a hundred years had passed, and why he could do magic.

But not the kiss.

"Now wait a moment," I interrupted. "Soren could have hurt me—killed me—a thousand times over. But he didn't. He was… kind to me."

Another glance between Alair and his grandson. "That doesn't mean he wasn't going to harm you. Let me finish, I am coming to it."

I frowned, but kept listening.

"I expected to die in that room with you, but Soren let me live. He said it was so I might spread word that the winter would be everlasting, and that Valeria now belonged to Silaine. And you... Soren explained you were cursed with sleep, that only Silaine could order you to wake. When I returned to Maeve, she told me what had been hidden all those years. My lovely, fair-haired sister was not a random orphan, but Princess Talia Aerendel. You are the last member of the ancient royal line, the one that helped to seal the portals between worlds those ages ago."

I swallowed. The old royal family was supposed to have magic powers. Did *I* have magic, by ignorance never revealed?

Alair continued. "For my country I did as Soren ordered, spreading word that the land was cursed and the Fae Silaine now ruled over it. Our remaining people fled, even Maeve and I. But when I became a man and learned how to control my powers, I returned and founded this village, waiting for the day when you would wake again."

He stopped and waited for my reaction. I swallowed, and tears rose to my eyes. He waited a hundred years for me. Alair beamed, and I felt a rush of love and gratitude for my little brother.

Rowan cleared his throat when it became apparent Alair would not continue. "There's more to our story," he said. "From what my father and grandfather have learned over the years, Silaine is different from the other Fae. They have strict rules and customs. She practically broke the laws of nature when she tried to usurp their King. The snow she made acts as a blockade, and for the past hundred years no one's bothered her. Save us, of course. No one wants to march through a hundred miles of ice storms to pester a dangerous Fae. Despite how we've tried to convince them that waiting will only make it worse. Silaine has waited this past century, growing her forces, preying on villages near the border, and anyone who wanders too close to her lands. She's using Earth as the staging ground for her final battle against Avalon. And it doesn't really matter if she wins or loses. We'll all die in the process."

"But…" I pursed my lips in frustration. "But what does all this have to do with me? Why did she make me sleep instead of just killing me like everyone else? And why did I wake up *now*, after a hundred years?"

Alair pulled his hands back from mine and fiddled with his tobacco pouch again. Rowan opened his mouth to speak, then shut it.

"What?" I asked. "You're not telling me something. What is it?" My voice rose until I was almost shouting. I *needed* to know everything.

It was Alair who finally spoke. "We don't know why Silaine cursed you with sleep. No one else survived the massacre at the castle, and since you don't remember it, we may never know. It may have something to do with your heritage as an Aerendel, but Silaine couldn't have known that about you, then... Although I believe your blood is the reason for your awakening now."

I sat back in my chair, disappointed. My brother could tell me so much, but some mysteries would persist unless my lost memories returned. "Why did you leave me there? Why didn't you take me somewhere safe, where Silaine and her... *damnsoír*... could never get to me?"

Alair nodded. "A fair question. You may not have noticed, but the room where you slept was heavily laden with enchantments, both mine and of the Fae. A stalemate, of sorts. You couldn't be moved unless you woke, and when you did, I was alerted. To be honest, it benefitted us to leave you there. The wall of thorns would only part at magical direction. You were safe from thieves and other trouble-makers." Alair ventured a smile at me. "To keep Briar going, and to make sure no one forgot you, I spread the legend that a princess slept in the tower." His smile turned mischievous. "It was true, but only Maeve and I knew that. Every now and then I brought important people to see you. In that bed, with your beautiful dress and tiara... no one could doubt you were a princess. The mysterious sleeping princess of Valeria."

It disturbed me to think of Alair bringing strangers to watch me sleep. But at least he had his reasons. Soren had also said he'd waited for me to wake, but that must have been a lie.

Alair's voice grew grave. "Unfortunately, we suffered a

tragedy recently. My son, Ferras—Rowan's father—led a group of our men on a scouting journey to monitor Silaine's activities. They have not returned."

Rowan held his face carefully blank, but his eyes bored holes in the table.

"We suspect that somehow… by torture or treachery… Silaine was informed that the legend of a sleeping princess was not embellished folklore, but actual truth. A magical bloodline runs in your veins, and could aid a great many dark spells. She had the last of the Aerendel line in her clutches all along, and never knew. And so Silaine sent her *damnsoír* for you at last," Alair finished. "To use you as a weapon in her rebellion against the Fae king. And that is why I believe you woke."

My stomach turned. The key to breaking my curse had been the kiss of Silaine's personal slave. Of course. Well, that explained the kiss.

But not the tenderness behind it.

Alair's story meant that Soren had been leading me to death or enslavement in the guise of being my friend. He'd been so convincing I even believed there was something between us.

I looked over at Rowan. He sat so still, but the knuckles of his clenched hands were white. How selfish I was. I sat here, mourning my life and family like I was the only one who'd been harmed by this. Rowan's family had clearly devoted their lives to me, and now Rowan had lost his father. Because of me.

I had a million more questions. But beyond the confusion, inside the small center of love that was rapidly growing, I found anger. Anger that this was done to me. Anger that nearly everyone I loved had been put to death. Anger that my country had been encased in ice, that my surviving family had spent generations in this wasteland, that my brother had lost his son, and Rowan his father.

But I was awake now. The time for waiting was over.

"So… What are we going to do about Silaine?" I asked.

Rowan looked up. He had an intense face, dark eyes and low-set brows giving him a stormy, brooding appearance. But then he grinned, and his smile lit the room.

Alair's eyes glittered in the darkness. "Now that you've returned, we have a plan to defeat her."

Anything. Anything for my family. "What do you need me to do?"

"Our best hope is to warn the Fae king of Silaine's growing power, and her intention to fight him once more for the throne of Avalon. If he is wise, he will return to Earth and defeat her once and for all before she poses a greater threat. But as our legends tell us, the portals were sealed with the blood of both Fae and human kings, so that only those bloodlines could open the doors between worlds. And though the Fae seal is broken, for humans the seal still holds. There's only one person left on the whole of the Earth who can open it."

I looked at their eyes, their faces turned towards me with warmth and hope. I knew who they meant, the savior they had been waiting a century for:

Me.

Five

I wanted to know more about this plan immediately, but Rowan and Alair assured me there would be time to talk later. The sun was starting to rise as Rowan set me up on a bed of soft furs near the fire. My mattress at home had been stuffed with sweet grasses and lavender, but in Briar everyone used layered furs of the many monsters they'd killed. I didn't recognize any of the furs beneath me, but they were thick, if a little musty. I much preferred this nest by the fire to the gaudy bed I'd woken in the day before.

Rowan helped Alair into a bed with railings on the side that Alair used to support himself as he lay down. With Alair made cozy, Rowan pulled up a chair and they spoke quietly for a while.

I picked out a few words, but it wasn't until the buzz in my own head quieted that I heard them clearly, and by then I was moments away from losing myself to sleep entirely.

"I'm so happy, Rowan. So many years, so many plans. This is just the beginning. You do understand now, don't you?"

A sigh. "I do. I don't like it, but I do. Sleep now. It's been a long day."

"It's been a long life. He's going to come for her, I'm sure of it. You have to be strong, my boy. You must do as I have instructed."

"Yes, Grandfather. I won't let him take her away again. I swear it."

I did not wake until midday. I was still so tired my eyelids hurt to open, but once conscious I wanted to stay that way. Sleep and I were still reconciling.

I threw off the furs and climbed to my feet, slipping on the boots waiting for me by the hearth. The fire had gone to coals overnight, leaving the room in ashy darkness.

"Rose."

I jumped, but it was only Alair, voice coming from somewhere in the shadows. "I thought it best not to wake you. Help me with the fire, and we'll heat some breakfast."

My brother and I waited for both the stew and ourselves to fully warm as Alair told me the story of his life, from seeing the sparkling coasts and colorful port cities of Shalimar, to learning magic, to founding Briar decades ago, and the constant struggle to keep it staffed with men and supplies.

"And these," he said, gesturing behind us to the many shelves, "are the sum of that work." The contents of the shelves were varied: labeled jars, stone, bone, glass, but most of all books and scrolls. "Half I found in the castle's library, but the other half I wrote myself. Magic is a lost art these days. There was only Maeve to teach me, and the erdwitch way with magic could not be quite the same as mine."

"Alair, if I'm really the daughter of the former king, wouldn't I have magic? But I don't. I mean, I don't think I do..."

My brother considered. "I don't remember you ever displaying any sort of power, but you might not have told me." He winked. "It is also possible that the Aerendel line had lost the talent, but maintained the mystique. The erdwitches might know. Regardless, it won't affect your ability to open the portal.

Bloodkeys are sealed with magic but you don't need to be magical to participate in one."

Yes, the doorway to Avalon. The thought of being able to help my family and country lifted my spirits again, but they were dashed when Alair explained the difficulties of reaching the portal. Silaine had assembled her court of Fae rebels close to the portal to Avalon. It existed in an island of normal weather, swarming with Fae and beasts, and surrounded by hundreds of miles of snow.

"It's not a matter of the journey, which will be difficult in itself. It's a matter of reaching the portal without being stopped."

"Can't you just... make me invisible or something?"

Alair smiled. "I could shield you, yes. Make you a shadow, turn eyes away from you. But that won't work near Silaine. Fae and erdwitch magic have a funny way of acting at odds. I have slipped through her enchantments, but her servants have slipped through mine. It's too dangerous. No, I'm afraid our path must be less subtle than that. We shall have to fight our way in. That is why, now that you have woken, we will leave Briar and go to Shalimar. We will make our case to King Egari there and explain how he must help us."

"What if he says no?"

Alair pursed his lips and reached out to take my hand again. "The battle against the Fae will be very fierce. Briar alone would not last ten seconds against them. If we are to free Valeria and prevent the destruction of the rest of the world, then we *must* have an army on our side. We will ask Shalimar first, then ask the same of Adalwin. They are a poorer nation and their army is famously less disciplined, but they have numbers on their side. If both agree, we have our best chance. If one, but not the other, we will still risk it. But we must have at least one."

I swallowed. "What do you need from me?"

"Oh Rose, I waited a hundred years for you!" He patted my hand. "Seeing you again is more than a dream come true. But now I must consider my grandson, who must also make his way in the world. And I still grieve for my lost country. Rose, I do not ask this of you lightly... But you might consider the fact that you are the last of Valeria's true royal line. All other successors, relatives, even false usurpers, are dead. You are the rightful and only heir to the throne."

They had called me princess. They had explained how my birth father was King Stefan himself. Last night I accepted it only as bizarre trivia about my origins. But so concerned was I with the fate of my family and home that I had not considered what the circumstances of my birth truly meant.

A shudder rushed through my body. Me, the ruler of a country? But I hated to stay inside, hated table manners, and wearing uncomfortable clothes. I didn't know the first thing about being royal—or maybe I'd learned, in those months before Silaine destroyed my world. Halen must have been an extraordinary person for me to agree to leave my beloved mountains and join him at court.

Alair jiggled my hand to bring my attention back to him. "Rose... I live on borrowed time. Maeve saved my life when I was a boy, and gave me magic in the process. But it's not mine. Erdwitches grow from the earth, they live, they become weary, and then they return to the earth. Maeve was old when she saved you, and that was a century ago. When last I saw her she was feeble and forgetful. I know that one day soon she will forget us and reabsorb, and with her will go my magic. And my life."

"*No*." I put my other hand on top of his. I knew my brother was old, far older than he should have been. But I had just found him again, and couldn't stand the thought of losing him now.

"I want to see you safe and settled before I go. For so long I have dreamed of what we could do once you returned to us. Think of it Rose—you will take your birth name, Talia, and be received in Shalimar and Adalwin as a visiting queen! You will treat with the Fae King as an equal. And when Valeria is finally free, you will be the leader of a new country. It will be a whole new world, with our family at the helm."

I shook my head. "I'm not—I can't—"

He didn't seem to sense my panic. "As the last surviving citizen of Valeria," he said grandly, "I name you queen, by birth and by blood. Queen Talia Aerendel."

"No!" I stood quickly, chair toppling behind me as Alair made a sound of dismay. "Sorry."

Face heating, I picked up the chair and set it upright. Wringing my hands, I took a seat again.

"Alair," I began, throat swelling painfully. "Yesterday I was *home*. Yesterday I knew who I was. Yesterday Mother and Father—" I tilted my head to the ceiling to keep tears at bay. "You've had ages to think about this stuff. You lost your family years ago. I just lost mine last night."

"Oh, my dear, I do apologize," Alair crooned. He took my hands again and I lowered my head to meet his gaze. "You're right, of course. We can discuss this another time."

Surely he meant his words to be comforting, but they felt like the news of a punishment deferred. It was enough pressure that I was the only one who could open the doorway to Avalon. Was being queen something I could reject or deny, and what would it mean to do so? He wanted me to change my *name*.

Heart sinking, I realized I was already bound by the obligation of my brother's tireless vigil, by my family's hatred of Silaine, and the needs of a snow-cursed land. Last night I fervently promised to do anything for my family. How could I deny Alair this dream when he had sacrificed so much for me? When we'd have a better chance of winning support for our cause if my pleas were voiced by a queen with a crown, instead of a girl from the mountains?

My dismayed reverie was interrupted when a blue glow lit the room. It came from my brother.

"What's that?" I asked, as Alair pulled the glowing thing out of his shirt. It looked like a stone on a leather thong worn about his neck, shining with a hazy blue the color of a clear sky.

"This," Alair said as he rubbed two fingers across it in a pattern that caused the glow to fade, "is an amulet with a spell I've embedded. It glows when it's a good time to go hunting."

Hunting! One of my favorite pastimes. Just me and the forest, away from words and expectations and chores. My hands ached to grip the wood of a bow, to feel a quiver on my back and enter the silent world of pure focus. This room was so dark and insulated, and the glow from the amulet had been so blue. I hadn't seen any real blue since waking, I realized. I wanted the sky, the forest, and the mud of the earth, though I could make do with snow and ice.

Most of all, I wanted to run away from the thought of being queen.

Boots stomped on the porch, then the door opened, revealing blinding daylight. Rowan stepped inside. "Good morning." A wisp of cold air brushed my cheek, invigorating.

Rowan shrugged off a heavy mantle of black fur as he approached. He brought the smell of outside, snow and woodsmoke. "Grandfather." He bent and kissed the top of Alair's head, and my brother's smile further deepened the heavy wrinkles by his eyes. "Rose." No kiss for me, just a grin as he took a seat. "Glad to see I didn't dream you. It's noon. Everyone's hard at work on the feast and wondering if you're still alive in here."

"Feast?" I asked.

"Of course! Didn't you hear that the princess has finally awakened? Grandfather, let me take Rose around Briar and introduce her to our sentries. Everyone's eager to meet her."

I was all for this, but Alair hesitated. "The men should have fresh meat for their celebration. You should go hunting."

My heart leaped. If there was a hunting party I *would* be going with them.

Rowan frowned. "But Grandfather, it's midday, and we have plenty—"

"You should go now. It's a good time for it." Alair's hand crept up towards the lump beneath his shirt.

Rowan glanced at me, then his frown relaxed. "Yes… You're right. We should take advantage while we can."

"Tell Rickard," Alair said. "Have him put together his best team."

"Rickard seems to find himself increasingly busy these days. I can lead the team. Especially if I am to... go now."

I looked between them and wondered not only who Rickard was, but what they were dancing around.

"You know that's not an option," Alair said.

Rowan pursed his lips. "I led the group that rescued Rose last night. I fought off the Betrayer by myself."

"Magic is one thing, and managing Briar quite another." Alair sighed, and pulled his fur closer around his shoulders. "You will lead one day, my boy. But today is not that day. If Ferras were here..."

"Well he's not. And Rickard's acting like he's Commander already when we don't even know if—"

Alair put his fist to the table with sudden force. "You are *not ready*, Rowan."

A moment of hurt silence.

"It's not about that," Rowan said. He looked my way but I averted my eyes. This discussion of leadership was between the two of them. "Rose should come." Rowan's voice was low but I whipped my head back around immediately.

"What did you say?" Alair asked.

"Rose should hunt with us," Rowan said louder.

"Yes!" I stood, ready to go.

"No." Alair glared at Rowan. "It's too dangerous."

"I can protect her. I did it last night."

"No offense, but I can protect myself," I said. "I want to go, I'm good at hunting."

"I remember," Alair said with an indulgent smile. "But the woods could be filled with enemies, and you are precious to our plans. It's safer for you here."

"We'll do the closest circuit, with our best warriors. Between us I'm sure we can keep her safe. Besides, it might help with her memory." Rowan's eyes held Alair's. I could almost feel a taut line of tension between them. "And I know we both want that back as soon as possible."

I held my breath in anticipation. I wouldn't dishonor the request of my elderly brother who had sacrificed so much for me… but at the same time I fairly itched with the desire to escape my new, strange reality and lose myself in the outdoors.

Rowan softened his tone. "She hasn't done anything in a hundred years, Grandfather. Please. I might not have waited as long as you have, but I've waited, too."

It was Alair who finally looked away and deflated inside his furs. I put my hand on his shoulder. "I'll be careful. Besides, I don't think I need permission from my younger brother to go out if I want to." I smiled to let him know I was joking.

"I've raised a son and a grandson since you last walked this earth, young lady… But as long as you maintain full caution—"

I whooped, whirling for my cloak hanging by the fire. I slung it around my shoulders and followed Rowan out of the house with sword and belt in hand. I turned back at the last second and mouthed *thank you* to Alair, who waved resignedly.

The day outside was a thousand times brighter than my brother's house, yet the sky still swirled with gray clouds, parting every now and then to reveal shafts of light. It wasn't what I would call sunny, but perhaps it was the best we would get.

Rowan waited so I could buckle my sword belt. "I didn't think we were going to get you out of the house, honestly. Hey, where did you get that sword?"

My stomach dropped. "Um..." Would he have a problem with me carrying a sword once owned by the Betrayer? "I took it from Soren. Some gargrayles attacked us, and I helped drive them off."

"Gargrayles attacked you? But they belong to Silaine." Rowan frowned. "Why would she attack you if you were with her *damnsoír*?"

I finished buckling the belt and let the sword hang from my hip, keeping one hand on the hilt. "We'd taken a left at a crossroads, but after the attack we backtracked and took a right instead. Maybe Soren was going the wrong way, so Silaine sent the gargrayles to threaten him? Maybe he really was trying to get me to safety."

"Hmph. I doubt it."

Rowan's overt contempt for Soren made me uncomfortable. Deep down I wanted Soren to be innocent of what they accused him of. The connection between us felt true somehow. It shamed me, to be so fooled, and to still hold on to that kernel of belief that he cared for me, in the face of everyone else's anger.

Eager to change topics, I made a show of examining our surroundings. This was my first time seeing Briar in daylight, and it was just as impressive as last night. "I can't believe my brother built all this for me."

"Well, we've had a long time to wait." Rowan's smile was small, but inviting. "When I was little, I probably wished for you to wake up harder than any of them. I thought I'd wait for you my whole life, like my father, and his father before him."

My cheeks warmed despite the chilly air. I felt unworthy of such sacrifice. "Well, I'm here now. Shall we hunt?"

"Yes! Let's go to the stables, and I'll tell you everything about Briar."

I followed Rowan through the village. The ground was mostly frozen mud, but drifts of dirty snow piled against the sides of the buildings. Volunteers called sentries were all around us, moving with purpose but stopping when they caught sight of me. Some carried buckets of snow towards a bonfire for melting, others worked in large forges, and I even spied a few young men on the roofs of the buildings, sweeping off the snow that had fallen overnight. Surrounding everything were the tree trunk fences, their tops sharpened into spikes. Guard towers hovered above them on stilts, surveying the village and the lake of snow surrounding it.

Everywhere we went, peoples' eyes followed me, some with excitement or curiosity, and others with no expression at all, or a vague disappointment. I understood—How could the reality of me measure up to the legend? By Alair's logic I could claim the title of queen. But I was still just a girl from the mountains, wearing plain clothing and reeling from the knowledge that had been plain to these people for generations. Now that I was awake… would all these so-called sentries feel their service had been worth it? What if I declared myself queen, and everyone just laughed?

Rowan repeated the story of how Alair in his youth had spread the legend of the sleeping princess, and even led some adventurous young men through the forsaken snows to the castle to prove the story was true. For a time it was fashionable for Shalimar's young lords to spend their winters hunting vicious beasts and pretending to stand a noble guard for the last princess of Valeria. Alair took advantage of this and sought foreign support to build Briar, growing the fort into a veritable village.

Locked in eternal winter, Briar's survival depended on donations and trade with other cities, exchanging exotic meats and furs for necessary supplies. Briar was also a waypoint for anyone traveling between Shalimar and Adalwin, the only safe refuge in a treacherous land. It made a tidy profit offering lodging and hot meals for merchants and other travelers who didn't care to sail along our southern coast.

"Grandfather devoted his whole life to Briar," Rowan said as we stopped so I could watch a tall, burly man forge a broken sword back together. "He only left to find himself a wife, but even then... The women in our family have always lived separate from the men. We visit of course, but it's not a real life, out here. Not for them."

As I watched his rueful smile a now-familiar guilt stabbed through me. Somewhere out there were wives who'd lost their husbands to the care of a girl not yet eighteen. Maybe now that I was finally awake my family could return home.

I opened my mouth to ask about his parents, but a large hand clapped Rowan's shoulder and we both turned to see Redbeard smiling at us with a toothy grin.

"Good morning," he exclaimed. As I'd noticed last night, Redbeard had an accent different from Rowan, Alair, and I. It was quick and musical, with a way of dropping his *g*'s, and indicated he was from Danaan, an island nation off the coast of Shalimar.

"Good morning, Gile," Rowan said, returning the hard thump on the back.

Rowan was tall, but Gile stood higher by about six inches, and probably carried a hundred pounds more. Now that it was daylight and I stood before him, I could see he had a chest like a barrel and arms thick with muscles.

"And good morning, my lady," Gile said, extending his hand. When I gave him mine he kissed it, mustache tickling the skin. "I hope you do not fear me too much. I tried to be gentle with my grabbing."

"I don't fear you," I reassured him. "I could have gutted you if I really wanted to."

His stunned silence turned into shouts of laughter. "A princess, eh? Gods help us." He touched the corner of his eye as if to wipe away a mirthful tear, while I smiled awkwardly. "Where are you kits off to? Showing Rose the village?"

"Yes, but we also need a hunting party. Grandfather felt we should have fresh meat for the feast."

Gile shrugged. "We have plenty froze up. If you want to stay here I'll swear the meat served tonight were killed today."

"Thanks Gile, but... it's for Rose. She wants to go and I want to take her. You interested?"

Gile's eyes were small and crinkly inside his wide, grinning face, but they darted towards Rowan with the silent question I had seen Rowan ask Alair a few minutes ago. "...Aye," he said, nodding. "I'd love to take the princess out. We'll see if the old man's boastings about her are true." He winked at me. "Has Rickard—"

"Let's leave Rickard out of it," Rowan said. "You can run the team, can't you Gile?"

"Aye." Another silent question. "I suppose I can. I'll meet you at the stables." He half-bowed before striding off through the mud.

"So tell me about this Rickard," I said as soon as Gile was out of earshot. "He seems important."

Rowan made a face, and glanced around to check for eavesdroppers. Seeing several men paused in their duties to watch us, he hurried me through the rest of the village, speaking quietly when we weren't greeting clusters of sentries who came forward to say hello.

"Rickard's a family friend. He and Father fought together in the Fulsyrian war across the sea, and when it was over Rickard followed him here. I used to call him Uncle Rickard. He's always been one of Briar's leaders, but for some reason..." Rowan looked around again. "With Father gone he's acting different," he continued in a lowered voice. "Like he's the Commander now. And we may not have heard from my Father for a week, but that doesn't mean... It doesn't give Rickard the right..." Rowan struggled for words. I waited patiently, and he gave me a sheepish smile. "I'm sorry. It's complicated. I like Rickard. I just don't like that he's got no problem filling my father's shoes when..."

"When you don't know what happened to him," I finished.

"Yes. And I believe Father could still be out there."

"You think Rickard's trying to take over Briar?" I asked.

"I don't know. Grandfather doesn't seem too concerned, but I wonder…"

"Maybe he's just trying to help out," I suggested. "How long is your father usually out of contact?"

"The witchlines are only set one day's travel apart," Rowan admitted. "The team should have checked in every evening."

"Witchlines?"

"It's how we communicate. I'll show you when we get out there."

"Well, perhaps Rickard's taking care of Briar until you know what's happened with your father. My brother clearly can't, and you're not much older than me."

"I'm nineteen," Rowan said with joking superiority. "You're only seventeen."

"A hundred and seventeen," I said with mock indignity.

"Well, you're really more like a hundred and twenty," Rowan said. "Or twenty-one. I forget precisely how many years you were asleep."

Far, far too many. "At least I didn't age while I slept," I said. "That would have been awful."

"Yes. She could have done far worse things to you."

He didn't have to remind me who *she* was. And yes, Silaine could have harmed me physically. But freezing me in time while everyone around me aged and died, while my country drowned in snow, while the memory of my first love faded to nothing…

I shook my head. "No. Silaine took everything, and almost everyone. She took away the only boy I've ever loved. I don't even know what he looked like. And I can't… I can't think of much worse than that."

Rowan didn't answer. When I glanced at him he was looking elsewhere, mouth and brows furrowed. Maybe my loss made him uncomfortable, or perhaps he had a young man's squeamishness with the topic of love.

"Well, anyway," I continued. "Maybe you should talk to Rickard if he's overstepping his authority. If he's really that close with the family, he can't mean harm, right?"

"I don't know. It's just strange."

Rowan finished explaining Briar to me with all its functions and patterns. We cut through the village to the stables where Gile and a group of men tacked up their horses. They laughed and talked amongst themselves, but that stopped when they took notice of us.

"Rose." Gile gestured me forward. "Meet some of Briar's best—Perry, Alyla, Jack, Kipp, Bradley, Dedrick, and Ravinger. Folks, you know the lady."

I nodded in greeting, and several removed their woolen hoods or gave a bobbing bow. My cheeks heated. These men and women were older than me, older than Rowan, even the youngest one called Perry. The men had full beards, most cinched up in smiles. And along with their heavy clothing they carried bows, with quivers of arrows mounted on their backs.

In the dim light of the stables the arrows glowed a faint blue.

Breaking the silence, Rowan took my arm and guided me over to his stallion's stall, where he led out the magnificent, shaggy beast named Garland and asked for my help in tacking him up. We'd had horses in my village, but they belonged to others, and I hadn't ridden often. Rowan explained each piece of equipment and helped me mount my own brown mare, called Clover. "Don't worry, she knows what to do. Just follow me."

"You ready to go, lad?" Gile asked from atop a mountainous piebald. The rest of the group had been waiting for my lesson to end. "We're about to leave you behind."

"We're coming." Rowan mounted up and followed Gile out of the stables.

My mare stepped forward without me needing to tell her to. I fingered the gold hilt of my sword before returning my hands to the reins, wishing I'd asked for a bow before we departed.

That's another thing Silaine took from me—my favorite bow. I'd made it myself, under the guidance of one of the elders of my village. It was lightweight and springy, and with it I was the best shot out of all the men or women. Now it was probably lost to time and winter.

I stayed by Rowan's side as we moved with the hunting party towards the entrance of Briar, the horses' hooves crumbling the frozen mud. Now when we passed others they shouted greetings and gave cries of good luck. I remembered the cheers of my village when we would return with some treasure from our bandit raids. I grinned in the excitement, but it quickly waned when we were stopped at the gate.

Gile spoke to a captain there, asking him to command his men to lower the wooden wall for us, but the captain shifted on his feet. "No one's to go in or out, not with the princess here."

"That's daft," Gile said. "We always been able to come and go. The princess is perfectly safe with Rowan."

I needed to find time to take Gile aside and ask him to stop calling me *princess*.

"I'm sorry, Gile. Rickard's orders."

"Rickard is not our Commander," Rowan called out. I turned to see him glowering. "Even if my father *is* missing. Now let us pass."

The captain looked to Gile, who shrugged. "We're only hunting. What's the harm?"

"It's on your head, then," the captain said, and whistled to his men on the platforms above the gate to lower it.

Rowan was the first over the icy, wooden surface, and I let my mare walk with the others until we reached snow again. The tracks from last night's heist were partially filled in, but we trampled the path anew. Then the old tracks curved away, back towards the palace haunting the distant horizon like a misty tomb.

I shivered, or perhaps that was the cold. Someone picked up the gait and then we trotted over the snowy field while I held on for dear life. Within minutes we were well away from the safety of Briar, and all I could wonder was what dangers awaited us out here in Silaine's snow-cursed lands.

Six

When we reached the trees the men slowed and formed a single line, with Gile at the head and Rowan and I at the tail. The horses moved into a clear path between the trees, and from the front of the line Gile whistled. Rowan whistled back. "Come look at this," he said to me, and dismounted.

Getting off the horse was easier than getting on, but I didn't execute the move any more gracefully. The snow came up to my knees and shifted underfoot. I wondered how truly deep the snowfall was. It had to melt at some point, or else the snow would have been hundreds of feet deep by now.

I tramped after Rowan up the line of men until we reached Gile, who'd paused his mount by a large tree. Its canopy of leaves had frozen together, providing a shelter from the snow that meant the visible ground curved downward near the trunk. Rowan stepped under the canopy and I followed.

"Watch," he said, and touched his hand to the gray trunk, on a carving of a symbol I didn't recognize.

As I looked on with wonder the carving lit with a golden glow, vibrating faintly until it faded out a few moments later. The magic's proximity left me with a pleasant tingle in my chest.

"These are the witchlines," Rowan explained. "It's a series of symbols Grandfather made, on trees, rocks, and what have you. Many are near Briar but some go all the way north to near Silaine's fortress. When we press one, they all light up, and this symbol appears on Grandfather's amulet."

"It's wonderful," I said, and Rowan matched my smile. I reached out and touched the symbol again, waiting for a glow that didn't appear.

"They only work for someone with erdwitch magic," Rowan explained. "It's how Father or I would let Briar know we're safe, and where we are. Each symbol is unique. We'll see more as we go on."

"And you'll touch them?"

"Every one on the way. Just so Briar knows we're all right."

The system seemed simple; all it required was a touch. But Rowan's father Ferras hadn't been able to do that for a week. I followed Rowan back to our horses and wondered how he could keep faith that his father was still alive.

"So what are we hunting for?" I asked as we re-mounted and the line continued forward. "Deer? Rabbit?"

"Gods, no. All the normal animals died or migrated ages ago. Every now and then a confused deer wanders down from the mountain range in Shalimar, but I haven't seen one in years. We're looking for any of Silaine's beasts. Most are edible, though a few stink so bad you'd rather go hungry."

Rowan described the many types of beasts they'd encountered, usually adorned with vicious fangs and heavy, sharp claws. Many were one-of-a-kind, but there were some common types which had held various names over the years, usually more literal than creative.

"Quiet now," Gile called from ahead. "We're almost there."

Rowan winked at me and we fell silent. Wind in the trees muffled the sound of our horses plodding through snow. My hips grew sore, and I shifted in the saddle. My brown mare tossed her head as if to rebuke me.

Gile called a silent halt with one raised fist, and the line stood still. Rowan dismounted and I followed suit, realizing belatedly that no one else had. Rowan didn't seem to mind, but he gestured for me to stay close.

I tailed Rowan through the trees. The ground beneath us sloped up slightly, and by the trees in the distance I could tell we were on a short ridge. Rowan lowered to a crouch and I copied him, snow scooping into my boots as we moved forward, and I twisted my mouth in displeasure.

A hand on my arm called a halt. Rowan put a finger to his lips and belly-crawled through the snow as if it didn't bother him, up to the edge of the ridge. Gritting my teeth I lay belly-down too, dragging myself through the drift.

We peeked over the ridge and my eyes widened.

Below was a hollow devoid of trees. In the center stood a wooden post, stained dark with old blood. A chain hung from it, leading to a mutilated carcass, more a collection of bones than a juicy piece of bait.

The reason for the picked-over skeleton was clear: surrounding the post in the pink-stained snow stood three beasts whose shapes I did not recognize. Their bodies reminded me of bears, with that peculiar hunch in their shoulders and sloping backsides, but instead of hair they had tough, gray skin. Their ears and tails were like boars, with similarly large heads sporting lolling tongues and teeth as long as my fingers. As they paced and sniffed at the carcass I noticed their warty skins were splotched with different shades of gray. One had tufts of white hair on his head and a short, scraggly beard, like Alair. The comparison did not cause me any amusement. Was Rowan serious about killing and eating these monsters?

He pulled the crossbow off his back and notched an arrow. I stared at it in envy. Now that I was inches from one, I could see that the arrow's faint glow resulted from tiny markings. *Runes*. Magical inscriptions. What were they for, and who had magicked them?

Rowan moved his head closer to mine. His breath was warm against my ear as he whispered, "After I shoot, run."

I nodded, legs tensing already. Rowan's mouth pursed in concentration and I held my breath until he let the arrow fly, then his eyes met mine with mischief.

Twang.

The arrow sped towards its target, taking down one of the beasts with a perfect shot to the sweet spot just behind the foreleg. His target cried out and stumbled, and the other beasts whirled, wicked jaws curling up into slobbery snarls. They barreled towards the ridge.

"Come on!" Rowan shouted, grabbing my hand and pulling me up, dashing for the safety of our hunting party.

The trail where the horses waited might as well have been miles away, and the beasts tore through the snow behind us. I ran as fast as I could to keep up with Rowan. Behind us one of the beasts growled. The hair on my neck shot straight up.

We burst through the tree line. I spun and watched as the gray-skinned beasts leaped into view, barreling towards the men and finally falling under a hailstorm of faintly-glowing arrows.

Twang! Thump!

The creature with the beard let out a terrible, hissing whine as the arrows found their marks, and it slumped into death with a groan.

Some men whistled or cheered softly, and Rowan stepped up to my side, panting hard. "What did you think of that?" He asked, grinning.

I put a hand over my racing heart. Adrenaline still surged

through my system. "A little warning would have been nice. I thought they were right on top of us!"

He made a flippant gesture. "Aww, these guys are harmless. We do it this way all the time. Besides, you're new here—I had to fit a little hazing in."

The grin he gave me was positively wicked. I shoved him playfully. He shoved me back, so I tackled him and we tipped over into the snow. We wrestled, rolling around in the icy cold and then I was laughing, and so was Rowan. He overpowered me and rubbed my head in the snow, but I bucked him off and lay panting on the ground.

For a moment I forgot everything I'd lost, everything I still had to do. It was a moment of pure freedom, unburdened by grief and guilt and dread.

Gile cleared his throat. "Are you quite finished?"

Rowan offered me a hand and I took it, seeing once again how his smile lit up his whole face, and turned him from harsh to handsome.

"Out here we have to do what works," Rowan said, brushing snow from his clothes. "It's not like traditional hunting, no. Silaine's beasts are smarter than deer. Usually they attack first, and we don't often get a chance to sneak up on them. Graydogs are an exception. They're so greedy we can lure them."

Gile guided some of the men in loading up the dead beasts. Rowan didn't help, instead tracing our tracks back to the ridge. I followed.

He slid down the embankment and approached the graydog he'd shot first. I watched as he picked up the beast and slung it over his shoulders, hunching slightly at the weight. Rowan staggered back up the hill, and I gave one last glance at the carcass tied to the chain, the empty eyes of its skull staring at me blankly.

"Was that a graydog skeleton?" I asked as Rowan made the top of the ridge, his face red with the effort.

"Yes. They eat their own."

My swallow came hard, stomach unsettled at the beast's tongue wagging with Rowan's steps. I didn't like these creatures, not like I enjoyed deer—their delicate faces, long, graceful legs, dark meat delicious in a sauce of berries… I sighed, longing for venison. "What do they taste like?"

"Slightly worse than chicken, believe it or not."

"That good?"

He gave a short laugh under the weight of the beast. "It's good when it's all you've got. These aren't from our world, you know. They're not, strictly-speaking, meant for us to eat."

I frowned. "Where are they from, then?"

We made the trail and Rowan dumped the carcass onto the ground with the others, then rested an elbow on the saddle of his horse. "Silaine," he answered. He wiped one of his hands on his cloak, then tapped his temple. "From her head. She makes them with magic. That was her job in Avalon, before she got kicked out, to make monsters for the Hunt. Here, look at this."

He took out a knife and slit open the belly of the graydog. Some of its innards spilled out onto the snow and I crouched down to get a better look. Meat, blood, and organs were a grayish white. Instead of blood they excreted a pale pink slime.

"No hearts," I said. "No lungs."

"Very good." Rowan wiped his hands and knife on the snow, drying them with his cloak. "But then again, Fae have no hearts, either. Ready for the next one?"

I was the last mounted, but one of many to carry a beast on the back of my saddle. We walked slower through the woods this time, and more quietly, but the next trap was devoid of prey.

"I thought we were hunting, not trapping," I grumped to Rowan.

"You're right," he said. "Hey Gile, let's take Rose to the Corridor and have some real fun." The rest of the team smiled or laughed.

"What's the Corridor?" I asked.

"You'll see." Then, to Gile, "I'll check the rest of the traps and meet you there." Rowan kicked his horse and galloped off into the woods without waiting for a response.

My horse took a step towards where he'd gone, and I pulled her back. "Should someone go with him? He shouldn't be alone out here."

"He'll be fine," Gile said. "Come on princess, we got a real treat for ya. Bet you never had this where you're from."

I followed the rest of the team, looking back at the shadows Rowan disappeared into, but of course there was no hint of him. Why would they let him go check traps alone, when it took the whole party to take down the beasts found there? The customs of Briar baffled me.

Gile told me about the Corridor as we rode: it was a stretch of open snow across what had once been a lake. It was the nearest open space for miles, except for the land around Briar, and the men used it to lure beasts out into the open.

"What kinds of beasts?"

"All kinds, princess. Like throwing a lure in the river, you never know what you'll get."

When we entered the trees we slowed to a walk, and after a few more miles descended a gently-sloping bank shielded by trees. We peered out over the Corridor. It was a full mile of virgin snow, portions of it blinding as the turbulent clouds swirled above us. In the openness I could see mountains to the far north. For a moment, my heart filled with the ache of longing.

My home was lost forever. I would never go home again.

The men had taken extra effort to be quiet as we approached the Corridor, and now Gile spoke in whispers. "Who's on our fastest horse?"

"Me," Perry said. "I'm up for it." He unstrapped his bow and quiver, handing them to me.

As he clucked at his mount and moved forward I put on his rigging and drew an arrow from the quiver, lost in the muscle memory of the draw. I used to save up forest treasures to trade for new strings in town, and make my own arrows from river stones and goose feathers. The muscles in my right arm remembered the resistance, and how to lock in my strength so the bow held steady.

I sighed happily, then relaxed to focus on the hunt.

Perry rode straight and tall, inching out across the snow at a slow walk. The men around me were tense, watching the sides of the empty lake. One hundred paces… two hundred…

A noise behind us.

We turned, arrows drawn, but it was just Rowan, trotting up on his black horse. No beasts were tied to his saddle, but the packs on each side were bulky and strapped shut. Perhaps he'd raided traps aimed at smaller beasts. He brought his mount up to my side. "What did I miss?"

Before I could answer, a low, keening sound rang out over the meadow, like a creature whining and yawning at the same time.

"What was that?" I asked.

Rowan frowned, trying to recognize it, then his eyes widened. "No!"

Out of the tree line to the right burst a creature bigger than I ever imagined possible. Taller than two men, it was at least four times as wide, a huge, muscled, rolling mass of flesh covered in tangled white hair. Galloping forward on six stubby legs, it moved fast despite its size, rolling shoulders as large as my horse's hindquarters.

"God's mercy," Gile breathed, then yelled, "Perry, lad! Ride!"

SEVEN

The group of horses bolted into the open, my mare drawn along before I could consider the wisdom of joining the chase. Out on the frozen lake Perry turned his horse to the left and kicked it, fleeing across the narrow width of the lake for his life.

"What are we doing?" I yelled as we sped towards the marauding beast.

"Saving Perry," Rowan yelled back, letting his horse's reins lay loose as he swung the bow from his back. "That beast isn't supposed to be this far south. Be careful, it's extremely dangerous."

Aside from its size, the creature didn't look so deadly to me. No large claws, no whipping tail, not even any noticeable teeth. "Why is it dangerous?"

Just then an opening appeared in the beast's otherwise seamless round head, exposing multiple rows of jagged fangs. Its jaws were so wide they nearly met at the back of its head, and my own mouth dropped open in surprise. The beast let out a high-pitched, ear-deafening shriek as it barreled towards the terrified Perry.

As we got closer arrows started flying, trying to distract the beast from its prey. Enraged, and with two arrows now embedded in its haunches, the creature skid to a stop and reversed direction to chase us instead.

"Split up," Rowan yelled. "Rose, with me."

The men took off in different directions, and I urged my mare toward Rowan, glancing over my shoulder as the beast headed for what was directly in front of it—us. Rowan and I barreled across the narrow field, the huffing breaths of the beast far too close, while the rest of the men doubled back to assault it again.

"Have you ever killed one of these before?" I shouted to Rowan.

"No!"

Wonderful. The beast shrieked again, and I looked back to see it less than ten paces from us. The men chasing it were only hitting its meat, and the size of its muscles were so large, and the arrows so short, they'd never penetrate whatever organs needed to be punctured in order to kill it.

We were coming up on the tree line.

"Left," Rowan screamed, and we turned east, kicking at our mounts though they were already running in terror. "Keep going," he yelled to me. "I'm going to double-back and aim for its face."

"Wait," I shouted, but he had already turned. The beast continued straight, and I leaned down to my mare's neck to urge her to more speed.

I dared to look back, and the monster was still gaining. Rowan's stallion couldn't keep up, and he was launching arrow after arrow into its side, but unable to get a good shot at the head. I had to do something.

I pulled the quiver of arrows off my back and squeezed it and the bow to my chest. I slipped my boots out from the stirrups, gave the mare a vicious kick, then tumbled off her into the snow.

My world exploded into ice and cold. I made myself roll

despite the impact, grateful for the thick snow which broke my fall. By the time I sat up and got my bearings everyone from the monster to the men had already shot past me. I'd thought the white beast would continue after the horse, but it swung wide and turned around.

The horsemen were not far behind, and the beast bellowed as it saw us in front of it again. It picked up speed and the horses parted, launching arrows as fast as they could, but all missed or bounced off their hard skull.

I was next.

The bow's wood was cool and firm in my left hand, and I notched the arrow with my right. One shot. What could I do against a charging beast with only one shot?

"This," I whispered, and as the white beast opened its jaws wide to shriek or gobble me up whole, I let the arrow fly. It pierced that gaping mouth and came halfway out the neck. White liquid gushed from the wound like a fountain.

The beast stumbled and fell. I dove out of the way as it crashed towards me, and drew my sword, sapphire shining in the sun. When the beast's forward movement stopped, I swung the sword down onto its stubby neck. The blade felt so good in my hands, so strong and sharp, that I hacked at the neck again and again as the beast gurgled and died, spewing forth that same slimy white fluid as the graydogs.

Rowan arrived first and leaped off his horse, rushing over and grabbing me by the shoulders. "Are you all right?" he yelled.

"I'm fine," I said indignantly, pushing off his hands. "The jump hurt, but I'm fine."

"You killed it, girl," Gile said with an immense grin, dismounting and clapping me on the back so hard I thought I heard something crack. "You're the first one."

"That was very, very stupid," Rowan said, ignoring the whooping cheers of the horsemen as they arrived. His tan face had gone white. "I told you to keep running."

"I'm stupid? You started this! It was gaining, and you fell behind. He would have caught me anyway. This way it was on my own terms."

"Not like we was much help either," Gile said with a grin, oblivious to Rowan's anger. "Excellent shot. Right through the throat. Dead as a doornail."

Rowan stood as if deaf to the exclamations around us. "Grandfather was right. If something happened to you…"

Chagrined, I remembered Alair's reluctance to let me go with the hunting party. His fears seemed more rational now. I could have been killed, and his hundred-year sacrifice would have been for nothing. Adrenaline faded to shame.

Before I could say more to Rowan, Gile pulled me away to finish beheading the beast, loudly retelling the story of the fight. I wiped the blade of my sword on the snow to rid it of the white mucus and slipped it back into the sheath at my side.

Gile held up the beast's head though he could barely get his arms around it, shouting in admiration as the jaw felt open to reveal no less than 4 rows of serrated teeth like short, white triangles.

"Come on," Rowan said, touching my arm. "Let's go get your horse. We need to talk."

I wanted to see the butchering, curious about the color of the muscles, and what the men thought could be done with the pelt, but gave in to Rowan's consternation.

He led his stallion, and I kept pace at his side as we walked toward my poor mare staring suspiciously at us across the field.

"This is why Grandfather says I'm not ready to lead," Rowan

said, voice thick with self-derision. "I'm too impulsive, and I don't think things through. I shouldn't have convinced him to let you come hunting, I was just angry that he—" Rowan bit off his words.

"You said these creatures aren't usually so far south," I offered after a minute of silence. "You couldn't have known it was here."

"No, but I still shouldn't have been so careless. Rose… if you die, we might as well surrender to Silaine. I have to do better."

"I see. I'm just a means to an end to you," I teased, but for some reason I wondered for a moment if it was true.

"Don't be ridiculous," Rowan said gruffly. "You're family. But the world needs you, not just Valeria. It's the only country snow-cursed, but as Silaine expands its control, other countries and people could be affected, too. And if her rebellion actually succeeds, the whole world will be stuck with a dangerous, bloodthirsty Fae who cares nothing at all about sharing the Earth with humans. Things could go back to the way they were before the portals were sealed—Chaos and violence, and humans helpless to stop it."

"I understand," I told Rowan. "I really do. I just… don't want to be treated like I'm made of glass." Like I'm a queen already, a symbol to be preserved, not a girl who still loves running wild outdoors.

"We don't always get what we want, unfortunately."

I sighed. "I won't tell Alair if you won't."

"He'll find out anyway."

"So tell him how well I managed to handle the situation myself."

"You got lucky."

"Well," I said with fake indignation. "I don't think a shot like that, in my weakened condition, can be called *luck*. That was definitely ingrained skill, despite a hundred years of sleep."

"No, you were lucky." But the corner of his mouth lifted in a half-smile.

"Maybe we'll need to put this to a wager. I assume you *do* practice your archery, don't you?"

"There might be a few targets I could scrounge up when we get back to camp. Some entertainment for the sentries before the feast."

"Perfect. Me against your finest archer."

"Why, I'd be delighted to beat you in a contest."

"*You're* the finest archer in the village?"

There was a grin in his voice when he spoke again. "It must run in the family."

But there would be no time for our archery competition. When we trampled back over the slippery wood of the gate, we found a small welcome party waiting for us, and they did not look happy.

"Rickard," Gile called in cheerful greeting.

So this was Rickard. He stood with arms crossed and brows furrowed, five others at his back with similar expressions. He wore his hair long, with two small braids framing his cheeks. His beard came down to mid-chest, chestnut brown with the beginnings of two white streaks under his mouth.

We pulled our horses to a stop. "Greetings, princess," Rickard said, inclining his head. "It is good to meet you at last." His seriousness made me nod instead of smile. "Better get your horses settled quickly, lads. Alair has called a meeting in the great hall. Rowan, might I have a word?"

Rowan's mouth thinned. "Of course." Then, to me, "Go on.

I'll meet you at Grandfather's house."

I left with the other members of our hunting party. Looking back, I saw Rowan had dismounted and stood speaking with Rickard, brows bunched together.

Gile insisted on taking care of my mount, so I returned to Alair's house to wait for Rowan and learn what this meeting was about. Alair sat on a rocking chair on his porch, wrapped in blankets and cuddling heated stones for warmth. I had just begun to tell Alair about our adventure that afternoon when Rowan returned, and I let him tell the rest while I went inside to enjoy the shallow tub of hot water that was waiting for me within.

With sharp-smelling soap I scrubbed every square inch of myself, taking the opportunity not only to clean but become re-acquainted with the body that had been hidden under thick clothes and cloaks for the past two days. I found a mirror on the mantle and peered into it to check that the face shown there matched the one in my mind.

Blue eyes, narrow chin, and a smattering of freckles. "Hello you," I said, and smiled, raising one pale eyebrow at myself.

I was missing six months or so of my memory. Six months during which I'd fallen in love, agreed to be married, and traveled to the capital city. My face and body had lived through these events, and I didn't think it was my imagination that they both seemed slightly different than I remembered. Sharper. Evolving further into adulthood.

I pulled my hair over my shoulder and re-did the braid of pale orange hair, starting at the base of my neck. I checked the mirror once more, satisfied. There. That was me, more or less. That was the face Halen had fallen in love with, and Alair had looked up to. The face Rowan saw when he grinned at me and winked.

Alair had laid out a nice dress for me, simple but finely made. At home I'd worn similar dresses for special occasions, but they were all hand-me-downs with minor stains and mended tears. This dress was a thoughtful gift, dark blue and thick for winter, with leather laces through the forearms. With a grateful heart I put it on, then joined my remaining family on the porch.

"Rose. Don't you look nice," Alair smiled.

"Yes," Rowan agreed solemnly, and I felt myself color.

"Well, I feel much better, so thank you," I said to Alair. "The dress is beautiful, and you are so kind. Come, let's get you inside. It's freezing out here."

"I appreciate your concern, sister, but I think we'd better take ourselves to the meeting hall. I believe we're already late."

"Would you like your chair, Grandfather?" Rowan asked.

Alair waved his hand. "No, that would not do. I can still walk to my own meeting hall."

Rowan gave me a look, and I merely shrugged. We helped Alair take ginger steps down the porch, and he held Rowan's arm as we picked our way through the frozen mud.

The great hall was a long rectangle with no windows and only vents on the roof to let out smoke and circulate the air. Two women passed out hot stones at the entrance to warm our hands. Torches and candles attempted to brighten the darkness inside but did little to beat back the shadows. Rough-hewn benches stood in neat rows, save for one long end of the rectangle where a small, mounted stage waited.

Two chairs stood upon the stage, and Rowan and I guided Alair up into one of them. The other remained empty.

I followed Rowan to a bench reserved for us in the front row. The walls rumbled with conversation, and the air grew hazy with pipe smoke. So many bodies in one area beat back the frigid cold but also added the unpleasant odor of unwashed bodies. I wrinkled my nose, grateful I'd been given a chance to bathe.

After a few minutes, the stream of sentries through the doors dried to a trickle, then a full stop. By then all the benches were full, and latecomers stood against the walls. I shivered, wishing I'd taken a heated stone. Rowan slipped off his heavy mantle and wrapped it around my shoulders. I whispered my thanks, the gesture warming me from within.

With no fanfare, Alair pushed himself up from his chair, arms shaking. He walked to the edge of the stage with his cane and held up one hand for silence. It warmed my heart to see the respect with which the people listened, for their conversations ceased instantly.

"Sentries of Briar." Alair's voice boomed over the audience, magically amplified. "After a hundred years, our watch is complete. The sleeping princess—my sister, Rose—has awakened."

My very bones shook in the roaring and stamping that met Alair's words. Lights flickered as the sentries' cheering rattled the torches and candles. Rowan bumped his shoulder to mine while he clapped, smile somehow brighter than the very flame.

Alair continued when the noise died down. "Some of you have been with us for years. Others visit now and then. Most we see only once. It does not matter. I say this to you now as I wish I could say it to anyone who ever lent Briar their sword, their sweat, or their coffers: Thank you. From the bottom of my heart, thank you for sharing the watch with my family. Thank you for giving me back my sister. Thank you for preserving a future for Valeria."

A tear slipped down Alair's cheek, and he wiped it away with a gnarled hand.

“Though we rejoice tonight, there are those who should rightfully be with us, yet are not. Two weeks ago, we sent some of our finest men, my son Ferras included, to spy on the Fae sorceress and report on her developments, as we have done every few years. It was a dangerous mission, as always.”

Beside me Rowan tensed. I looked over to see his hands gripping the bench so hard his knuckles looked white even in the shadows. I touched them and he relaxed, then grabbed my hand, squeezing once before pulling away. I left my hand lying awkwardly between us in case he wanted to take it again. For comfort.

“It has been over a week since their last communication. At this time...” Alair paused, cleared his throat, and changed tack. “Now that the princess has returned, we have several important decisions to make. For this we must choose a new leader from among you. Let he who wishes to bear that burden come forward now.”

The hall erupted in discussion. I turned to Rowan, but he was staring at Alair with an inscrutable look. They were replacing his father. I opened my mouth but didn’t know what to say to this distant cousin of mine, my new friend.

By this time some of the crowd were chanting, and a cheer broke out to the right of us. I craned past Rowan to see a man striding through the sea of benches, and then the name in the chant became clear.

Rickard took the stage.

EIGHT

I didn't have to look at Rowan to know how this development affected him. He ground his boots into the wood chips at our feet and whispered something I didn't catch in the din.

Rickard shook Alair's hand and they exchanged a few quiet words. My brother did not seem surprised by the crowd's choice. "So be it," he said in that booming voice, and everyone quieted again. "Rickard, I think—"

"Wait!" Rowan leaped to his feet, his own voice magically projected throughout the hall. "We don't even know for sure that my father is dead. How can you replace him as Commander?"

For Rowan's sake, I was relieved to hear several in the crowd voicing support for his protest.

Alair's bright eyes now seemed stony at being questioned. "We are not replacing Briar's Commander. We still hope for the return of Ferras and his men. But right now we need someone to speak for the sentries of Briar and decide… what needs to be decided. I defer now to your chosen leader." My brother took his seat.

Rowan did not clap or cheer when Rickard stepped forward. Rickard did not have Alair's magical, sonorous voice, but he spoke loud enough for everyone to hear. "I thank you for your confidence, sentries. As Alair said, I hold this post only in waiting for Ferras, who has led Briar with wisdom for many years." He paced about the stage, addressing one corner of the room, then the other. "It is Ferras we must think of now. Two weeks he and his men have been gone. One week of messages relayed through the witchlines. One week of silence. A rescue party would be two weeks gone, at minimum, and we do not know what they might find. I will put it to you, Briar—Do we spare the men and supplies for a rescue, or do we mourn our fallen and look to the future?"

The response was a mess. Whistling, hissing, cheering, booing. I wanted to cover my ears. I wanted to freeze my heart. They were deciding Rowan's father's fate. How could he stand it?

He couldn't.

He leaped to his feet again. "Grandfather, how can you let them choose if my father should live or die?"

"Rowan," Alair pounded his cane against the floor. "We will discuss this later—"

"Answer me!"

"I cannot ride with you, Rowan." Alair's voice betrayed a deep frustration. "Briar has been in family hands for a hundred years, but we are dependent on these people for its survival. I will not send them into danger for the sake of my son unless that is their wish. I will only ask, and we will abide by their decision."

Rowan turned and looked out over the seated crowd. "People of Briar," he said, voice as near as if he spoke into my ear. My scalp prickled with the use of magic. "Sentries. Guardians. My father never gave up on any one of you. He spent his whole life here, not just for Briar, not just for Rose, but to stand against the Fae, who will overrun all our countries if we let them. Do not abandon him now, I beg you."

From the middle of the room, a woman rose. She had the

strong, tough look of a fighter. She removed her fur cap, revealing a coil of dark braids. "It has been a week since they touched the witchlines. I'm sorry, boy, but if we find anything left of them out there... it'll be their bones."

No one spoke as she took her seat. Rowan stood still for a moment, then raised his chin. "I will go, then. Any sentry who does not fear the cold and the danger is welcome to ride at my side. Now have your vote."

My brother's toothless mouth bunched up in displeasure, and Rowan sank to the bench, nearly vibrating with righteous anger. I was glad I was not expected to vote, because I did not know which way my voice would have fallen. To give all for family, with no man, not even his body, left behind? Or to keep the rest of us safe even if it meant never knowing if our kinsmen could be saved?

In the end, Briar overwhelmingly decided there was no use to a search party, though several spoke of what a fine man Ferras was, and how it was none too fair for the land to claim him. Rowan stormed from the hall, leaving me alone on the bench, and my heart ached for him. Gile went after him, so I didn't. He wouldn't let Rowan do anything foolish.

"We will mourn Ferras and our fallen on the morrow," Rickard said. "Tonight is for feasting. But I cannot in good conscience send you off to celebrate with no indication of our future here. The princess has awakened. Briar's purpose is complete. Her family is leaving soon, and we must decide our next course of action."

My waking had far-reaching consequences I couldn't have imagined. Would Briar be abandoned, or maintained? Who held the right to run it, or draw profit from it? This little village was far more complicated than I'd thought. I listened as the sentries debated, their concerns revealing the very tangled threads of trade, class, and patriotism.

Briar wasn't just Alair's stakeout. It was a waypoint between Shalimar and Adalwin, a haven for merchants and travelers who would rather journey by land than by sea. It was a legend, a hobby, and a tradition for others. Young nobles wintered here to prove their toughness. Others merely liked the idea of fierce warriors defending a beautiful princess… Although maybe they felt differently now that said princess was walking around without a fairytale-caliber face.

Briar was also a bloodline of communication. Both Shalimar and Adalwin routinely made gifts of supplies and weapons in exchange for news that could travel between the capitals faster than the waterway in the south separating the north countries from Fulsyria. Occasionally Briar even hosted exiles, or other people the government wanted to keep out of the way for a time.

Briar may have been founded by my brother, but now that he was abandoning his claim to it, Briar's future ownership seemed caught between Shalimar and Adalwin.

Unless, of course, the kingdom of Valeria rose from the snow and reclaimed its territory.

"What's to be done with the girl now that she's awake?" A young man with a wispy beard shouted out of turn.

"That matter will be discussed later," Rickard said. "In private."

"We gots a right to know! We guarded her, didn't we?"

"Shut up Gareth," another man called.

"If she's the princess, then it's her land, and her town. Let the girl decide."

The hall was thrown into an uproar. I froze in my seat. Alair's proposal for me to rule had somehow spilled into the open, far too soon for me to know what to do about it. I didn't want to make any decisions, to be responsible for so many lives.

As the debate raged, Rickard turned to Alair as if asking a silent question. My brother gave a nod of assent and eased himself up from his chair. Rickard fell back as Alair waved for a quiet that soon came.

"Regardless of whence you came, or your interests, you know why Briar exists." My brother pointed at me, and I winced. "For this girl. And now that our watch is complete, we turn to our next purpose. The reason we waited for her. The reason this land is covered in snow, and your homelands are bursting with people whose ancestors were forced across your borders just to survive… The Fae."

His words ignited a curious reaction, charging the chilly air with something dangerous. I peeked at the folks behind us. Some wore rapt expressions, chins firm and raised. Others muttered darkly or wore the wry smirk of skepticism.

"I reveal to you now a secret my family has kept for a hundred years, a secret told to me by an erdwitch herself."

The quiet turned to breathless silence.

"My sister—my *adopted* sister—is the last surviving member of the ancient Aerendel line."

Exclamations of surprise or disbelief raced through the room. I gripped the edges of the bench to stay calm even as my stomach roiled with anxiety. We hadn't discussed this. I wasn't ready!

"Saved from the Usurper's murderous coup by that same erdwitch, my sister is the only one who can open the portal to Avalon and warn the Fae king of the threat growing in our lands. She is our solution to this curse, and our best chance of sending the Fae scourge back to the world where they belong."

The cheering was slow at first, as the surprise and brilliance of Alair's plan sank in, but it quickly rose to a stream of whistles and cheers.

"Hey, princess, is it true?" The people behind me called out their questions, and I nodded awkwardly, igniting a new wave of speculation and excitement.

"What we need from you now," Alair spoke over the din, "is your petition. Support from your governments. They have allowed, and at times encouraged, Briar's existence. They took in Valeria's citizens and integrated them with their own. But they have not acknowledged, or lent us any aid, to resist against the Fae threat, which grows by the day. Shalimar and Adalwin *must* help us now. They *must* give us the armies to slip our dagger—" here he pointed at me again, "into the heart of the sorceress Silaine. We must help the princess reach the Fae king in Avalon, or else the Fae will one day spread over our world like a plague, destroying everyone regardless of borders. We have waited long enough. Silaine must be stopped!"

The crowd roared, ignited by my brother's passion. He seemed to vibrate with power, shaking on his cane but as determined as a zealot, and my name was his battle cry.

"Do what you will with Briar," Alair said. "It is a greater fight that concerns us now. You want to know what will be done with the princess, Gareth? She will be the arrow flown to the heart of the Fae sorceress. She will be the key in the lock to our freedom. She will be our emissary to Avalon, and return with a Fae army to destroy our enemies."

He gestured, then Rickard was in front of me, pulling me up by my arm. I stumbled after him onto the wooden platform, where Alair took my hand and raised it high in triumph.

I did not feel like an arrow, or a key, or any of those things.

Alair promised victory, but I didn't know how to open a portal or talk to a Fae King, let alone convince him to raise an army to fight his rebellious sister-in-law.

From the stage I could see the whole crowd, so many faces filled with hope or concern, clapping, whistling, or cheering wordlessly. I swallowed hard and looked to my ancient brother. The skin hung from his bones, and he trembled where he stood. But his eyes were bright, gleaming fiercely from the recesses of his skull. He gave me an encouraging nod.

There was no one else to carry this torch. I wasn't ready, and I wasn't a real princess, let alone a queen.

But I'd have to be.

I raised my other fist, and feared for a moment that the cheering would bring the building down around our feet.

For the sentries here. For my lost country. For the people of this world who did not know or believe in the danger. And most of all for my family, to avenge the dead and create a new future for the living. I would claim the crown. I would fight for my country.

I would find the portal to Avalon, and I would make Silaine pay.

NINE

The meeting adjourned. I waited on stage with Alair and Rickard as many came forward and voiced individual concerns. I felt like I was floating outside my own body, nodding numbly along with whatever my brother said. Finally, the last of the crowd trickled out the door, leaving the three of us alone.

Rickard turned to Alair. "I want to thank you for your support. Ferras was—is—my great friend. I don't wish for anyone to think I take this role with anything but a heavy heart."

Alair nodded. "Rowan will be all right. If he took a single moment to use the magic his erdwitch powers afford him, he would see your heart is true. One day he will realize it was the right choice. Now run along and eat with your sentries. They'll want to celebrate with their new leader. Rose and I will be fine on our own."

Rickard departed and I escorted Alair through the twilight. "You knew Rickard would take over, didn't you?" I asked. "And you wanted him to."

"Yes. He is a good man, and will be a good leader."

"So you've already given up Ferras for dead."

Alair was silent for a moment. "My son has never failed to send word of his safety before. I have no doubt in my heart that he is truly gone."

Sadness pelted me like rain. Family was a strange thing, if I could mourn someone I'd never met simply because they were part of it. "Then why did you send him on such a dangerous mission? He was your son, and Rowan's father. You both need him. Why let him risk his life like that?"

"Ferras understood what was at stake, and we should honor his sacrifice. He did his duty, as you must do yours."

"What if I can't?" It was a reasonable question, but my composure fell apart the more I spoke. "What if I can't convince the other countries to fight Silaine? What if we can't find the portal? Or the Fae king won't help us?"

"Shh, shh." My brother patted my arm, and I tried to calm my rising hysteria. "You don't need to know how to do those things today. I have planned this mission for decades, and we are weeks away from trying to meet with King Egari in Shalimar. You have time to learn what you must. No, don't cry, dear one."

But I did cry. I wanted my old life back, my parents and my sweet younger brother. I never could have imagined the little boy I loved and fussed over as if he were my own would push me into this strange, new role.

I did not truly know him, I realized, choking back my tears as we walked to Alair's house in stiff silence. My brother was a man grown old, and a century of absence lay between us. I knew as little of him as he likely remembered about me. We were family, by love if not blood, but also strangers.

And somewhere in all those long years, Alair stopped seeing me only as his sister. I was a game piece now on the political playing board, one he seemed eager to use. We dealt with the fate of kingdoms, not just our tiny family.

I would stop feeling sorry for myself, I vowed as I helped my brother back into his house. People had died to give me this opportunity. I would try not to feel so unworthy and focus instead on what I needed to do.

But when Alair brought out the tiara, I still blanched.

"I can't," I said immediately. "I'll look like an ass."

"You will look like what you are, which is royalty."

Alair held a thin, silver tiara in a velvet-lined box. It was unadorned, thank the gods, no jewels or crafted flowers like the tiara I woke with. But this one felt just as wrong. If I still lived in my village, an item like this would never be mine. Even if we seized it from a wealthy merchant, it would be sold, and the money spent on tools, supplies, and livestock.

"People need to see you wear it. Much of the power of royalty lies in appearances. This will help them believe in your true identity and grow support for our cause."

I swallowed hard and dared to touch the band of silver sparkling in the candlelight. It was smooth and cold, like ice.

"We'll have a coronation ceremony soon, of course. The ceremonial crowns of the royal family are with Rowan's mother, for safekeeping, but I had this made for you. I figured you'd want something simple and easy to wear."

I stared at my brother like he had begun speaking gibberish, and he smiled at my wide-eyed shock.

"Here, try it on."

Remembering my promise to myself, I clenched my jaw to keep from protesting and let Alair lift the tiara and set it on the literal crown of my head. A perfect fit. At my brother's suggestion I undid my braid and spread the wavy hair around my shoulders. "Behold," he said, gesturing to the mirror on the mantle, "a princess."

I eased the image of myself into view, as if it might flee like a frightened deer. My eyes were still red, mouth pursed with tension. I took a deep breath and tried to relax.

"See?"

I touched the tiara, adjusting it. It was warming with the heat of my head and didn't feel nearly as heavy as it first did.

"Well?"

I had to say something. "Thank you. It's… Thank you."

My brother beamed. "Now go, go be among your people."

"You're not coming?" I ignored the sense of relief I felt.

"I'm tired. One of the cooks will send along a plate. But enjoy yourself. Celebrate. The adventure has finally begun."

I kissed my brother's cheek dutifully, then fairly fled from the house. As soon as I was outside, I pulled off the tiara and stashed it in my cloak pocket. Embracing my circumstances was all well and good, but as my mother used to say, you can only eat a sow one bite at a time, and I'd eaten enough today. One more mouthful and I might choke.

"Ahem." I jumped, but it was just Gile, waiting below the porch. "I'm to take you to the feast," he said grandly, offering me his arm.

I took it gladly, hoping he didn't ask me about the tiara. "Where's Rowan? How is he?"

"Ehh… Rowan wasn't feeling festive. He's taken a shift on one of the watchtowers."

The news disappointed me. I'd hoped Rowan and I could expand our growing friendship by comforting each other in our private and painful woes. He had been by my side almost constantly since I came to Briar, both guide and guardian. It felt strange to face a celebration of sentries without him.

The feast took place in an open square with a bonfire at the center. A central kitchen provided roasted beast, fermented drinks, and sweet pastries. A group of musicians played on a raised platform to one side of the square, and others sang along in harmony. I heard a familiar *thwack*, *thwack*, and noticed an archery course set up past the square near the great, spiked fence.

The gathering seemed more festival than feast. It was much smaller than the ones we'd enjoyed in Lorensile, with vendors hawking trinkets, tables laden with food, dancing floors, and colored lanterns strung from the walls. Lorensile had been the city nearest to my village, but now it was gone, too. There would be no more festivals along its cobbled streets.

Gile fetched slices of meat and roasted potatoes from one of the serving tables and led me through the square as we ate. We greeted everyone we passed, and Gile whispered little stories about who was an exile, who had come to Briar to escape prison for petty theft, who was a rich lord playacting as a humble soldier, and who truly believed in Valeria, and me.

When I recognized a tune, I pulled Gile closer to the singers. It was a sad song, one of mountains, changing seasons, and being far from home. Several members of the nearby audience joined in. When I was sure I remembered the words I, too, raised my voice, spilling out my homesickness and grief to the smoky air. As the final notes of the song faded away the people nearby clapped politely, and I turned around to—

My eyes met only Gile's, and I paused.

Who was I looking for? The moment would have been perfect, but someone was missing. I kept searching for a particular smile, a certain set of eyes in the crowd.

"What is it, princess?" Gile asked.

"Nothing, I just… For a moment I thought I remembered…" I shook my head. "It's nothing."

As Gile and I claimed seats among the benches and tables I tried to place this feeling of absence inside me. Flickers of memories returned like stars glimmering in the night sky, as if spurred forward in the wake of the song.

Was the missing presence motherly in nature, smelling of

sheep's wool and fresh-plucked sage? Or my bear of a father, his figure so similar to Gile's wide chest and girth? Or maybe the sweet presence of my younger brother, back when he was truly younger than me?

No, it was none of those.

The mystery of the missing presence loomed in the back of my mind, a persistent itch even as I chatted with the sentries who flocked to my table. They were enthralled by the fact of my existence, but ultimately we had little to say to each other. I came from a world that no longer existed, and faced a future of unknowns. Eventually I took on the role of attentive audience, listening to everyone's best stories of hunting or encounters with the Fae. And still I worried the question of who was missing, like rubbing a stone in my pocket.

As the answer grew clearer, the crowd of boisterous sentries became overwhelming. I excused myself to visit the privies and steal a few moments of solitude.

Though I couldn't picture his face, my heart remembered the joy of his presence: The kidnapped nobleman with the grain bag over his head had somehow become someone with whom I was inseparable. Someone I would leave my family and home for. I didn't know him, but I missed him.

Halen.

I closed my eyes, replaying last night's dream of running with him in the forest, but I couldn't see his face. Frustrated, I squeezed my eyes shut and lowered my head, digging deeper and deeper into the memories still hidden from me.

The only memory of romance and tenderness I could recall was the ghost of the kiss that woke me. Disgusted, I pushed the image away and left the row of stinking outhouses. It was so unfair that I couldn't remember the person I had loved.

Again I wondered why I, out of all the others present, was cursed by Silaine to endless sleep. Why me, in everyone's eyes a rough-mannered peasant girl, who by a stroke of luck managed to become engaged to the crown prince? Why not the prince himself, or the king, or any of the other members of the Usurper's court? No one knew I was born Talia Aerendel when it happened, not even my family. Was the cursed sleep a side effect of my royal ancestry?

I sighed and drew my cloak closer as a biting wind blew through the buildings. If only Alair could tell me more of Halen, more of what happened on that deadly day when Silaine slaughtered the castle's inhabitants and cursed me to sleep. Unless I recovered my memories, the only other person who had been there and still lived to tell the tale was… Soren. The Betrayer.

I'd had enough of feasting and crowds, but didn't want to return to my brother's house. I asked Gile to find out which tower Rowan occupied. His post was near enough that I insisted Gile didn't need to escort me, and left him happily pounding mugs on a table with a group of other men slurring a drinking song.

The guard towers were built up against the vertical logs surrounding Briar. I walked along the defensive barrier, lost in thoughts of Halen and my uncertain future. Eventually I realized I'd forgotten to count the towers, and couldn't be sure which one held Rowan. I turned back, annoyed at retracing my steps, when—

Rose.

My whole body shuddered, thrown into the memory of the moment when my name filled the tower's room with hope and longing. How could Soren have pretended he cared for me, and shown devastation when he thought I didn't remember him? Was he here, now, like Alair feared, to steal me from—

A brief, high whistle rang out above me. "Hey, Rose!"

I looked up and around, spying movement from one of the watchtowers nearby. A hand waved from over the tower's guardrail.

I took a step forward and squinted. "Rowan?"

His voice was as close as a whisper. *It's me. Come up?*

My shoulders sank in relief. I must have confused Rowan's magical whisper for Soren's. I climbed the icy ladder and Rowan pulled me through the square hole in the watchtower's floor. I steadied myself by the brazier of hot coals while he replaced the trapdoor cover and bolted it shut.

"What are you doing out here, alone?" he asked. "Gile was supposed to watch you tonight."

"Am I a child, to be nannied after?" I scoffed. "I thought I was safe in Briar."

Rowan chuckled. "Safe from the Fae, maybe, but… Not every sentry in Briar is here from the goodness of their hearts. Never mind the criminals and exiles, any of the nobles from Adalwin or Shalimar might sense a profit in riding off with the heir to Valeria."

"Oh." Politics. Of course. My mouth twisted as I turned to take in the view. The night was cold but peaceful, and the snow on the fields beyond Briar was unblemished. "I suppose I'll have to learn to think like that."

Rowan stepped up beside me. "I know what you mean. If Father is… gone… then I'm a Duke of Shalimar now."

"Wait, what? Your father was a Duke?"

Rowan laughed. "Didn't I mention that? My mother was a Duchess, first. Father married her after the Fulsyrian war. It was a bit of a scandal, honestly."

I joined in his smile, until it faded.

"When we go to Shalimar and talk to King Egari, he'll expect me to swear loyalty to him," Rowan said. "But I can't."

"Why not?"

He stood a little straighter. He was taller than me by almost a hand. "Because I want to be a member of *your* court, obviously. A citizen of New Valeria."

The weight of the tiara in my cloak pocket suddenly felt very heavy. "I don't know how we can make a country out of deserted lands and no people," I confessed.

"Oh, you'll have people. Immigrants, like me. Descendants of Valerians, and anyone who wants a fresh start."

"Won't Shalimar or Adalwin just claim the land for themselves? We have no army."

"Grandfather says we'll make alliances, and use erdwitch magic to hold our own."

"Ah. He's got it all planned out, doesn't he?"

"Well, he's had a long time to think about it." Rowan leaned over the railing, so I did too, the warm brazier at our backs. We looked out at the quiet, frozen land. "You know, I keep thinking, if they hadn't left when they did, if Father had waited just a little longer... He would have been here when you woke up. He waited his whole life, just to miss you by a week."

"I'd have woken sooner if I could," I said bitterly. Again I thought of the kiss that brought me back to consciousness.

"It's not your fault," Rowan said. "If I were older this wouldn't have happened. In a few years Father would be too old to fight, and he'd pass the leadership down to me. He was going to take Grandfather back to Shalimar, to my mother, so they could know a little peace in their lives. Rickard shouldn't have given up on him. Not ever. But especially not now that you're finally here."

"I wish I could have met him."

Rowan's teeth flashed in the darkness. "Father would like you. And he'd know what to do about all this. I wish..."

I imagined I felt his grief like a tangible force between us. Without his family, Rowan was adrift. I knew that feeling. Wind blew through the tower, and we turned back to the brazier.

"Tell me more about your father," I prompted.

"Like what?"

"Anything. I don't know who his mother was, or where he was born, or how he came to be here."

Rowan told me of his grandmother Emmaline, passed away now. Another regret—I would never meet the woman Alair chose to marry. They'd met after Alair founded Briar. He traveled back and forth from Shalimar, learning from Maeve and making money as a healer, even though Shalimar had outlawed magic and erdwitches by then.

Rowan made a noise of disdain. "Might as well outlaw rain, or the changing seasons."

Emmaline was younger than Alair, and made him a father at sixty. Ferras was hot-headed and rebellious as a youth. Against Alair's wishes he joined the Shalimarian army when they went to war against Fulsyria."

"What was the war about? I thought Fulsyria was just deserts and barbarians."

"Hardly," Rowan said. "Shalimar and Adalwin were trading in Fulsyria, and trying to establish new cities. They fought each other, then the Fulsyrians themselves. Eventually the Fulsyrians kicked us northerners out and now they're independent."

Ferras was a war hero, summoned to court to receive

recognition and compensation. He met Rowan's mother, and they married. Rowan was born not long after, but Ferras spent most of his time in Briar.

"It drove Mother crazy. Said she wouldn't give him any more children if he was just going to abandon us all the time. I don't think she's forgiven me for leaving her, either. When she hears Father's dead…" Rowan trailed off, sorrow biting us as sharply as the wind.

"How long have you been here?" I asked.

"Since I was nine. After one of his visits I stole a horse and followed him out of the city. I caught up to him at the border. Father said I'd inherited the family stubbornness, and if I wanted it that badly I might as well grow up around the family legacy and learn to use my powers. Briar's been my home ever since."

"So you spent almost your whole life here," I said. "In the snow. Fighting monsters. Surrounded by adults."

"It was fun! What little boy wouldn't want to ride horses and shoot arrows and learn to sword fight? I wanted to be a warrior so badly…"

"Has that changed?" *Please say yes*, I begged him silently, hoping he wanted to escape from Briar. Something good must come from my waking, at least.

Rowan sighed. "Grandfather spent his whole life here, and so did my father. Just… waiting. I hate Silaine. I want to stop her. But it looked like you'd never wake up, Rose. I'm not sure I wanted to waste my life waiting, too. Or expect my children to follow me."

My heart swelled with sympathy and affection. I touched his arm. "I'd have understood," I told him. "You deserve your own life."

Rowan grabbed my mittened hand, like he'd done at the

meeting hall, but this time he didn't let go. "Let's just say I'm glad you woke up when you did. What comes next is far more exciting. Taking down Silaine. Starting a new country. That's something I can spend my life doing. For you." He looked up at me through a shock of black hair and smiled.

Rowan's excitement was infectious. I'd been so focused on the weight of my responsibilities, but he made them sound like the adventure of a lifetime. Battling Fae like the heroes of old. Rebuilding Valeria, and ruling how I saw fit. An essential and oppressive responsibility, yes, but also, perhaps… one of joy?

But an instant later Rowan's smile fell. He squeezed my hand, and let go with a heavy sigh. I wished he hadn't, but like a good friend, I waited for the words that must be coming.

"He's not dead, Rose," Rowan whispered. "I just... know it."

"Through the magic?"

"No. By this." He put a fist over his heart. "He's still out there. Maybe captured, maybe enslaved. Waiting for us to come save him. But we're not coming."

I didn't know what to say. It wouldn't be okay. It couldn't be fixed. Even Alair believed Ferras was dead. And no matter how much everyone insisted they were glad to have waited for me, the fact remained that my curse indirectly caused whatever happened to Ferras.

"I told him not to go," Rowan continued. "It was so dangerous last time that they decided never to make the journey again. But for some reason this time he wanted to. Said he had to. And then he hugged me like he'd never see me again. Like he knew. I think..."

"What?"

But Rowan shook his head, mouth pursed. "Nothing, it... nothing."

I opened my mouth to protest, but a yawn came out instead. I turned away, but Rowan saw. He stood up. "It's late, and you've had a long day. How about I walk you back?"

"Aren't you on duty?" I asked.

"We'll only be a minute." He bent down to undo the trapdoor. "You first?"

Rowan helped me get my footing on the ladder. I climbed down rung over rung, pretending I was only a few feet from the ground instead of twenty or so.

By the time I steadied myself on solid ground again Rowan had jumped the last few feet and we set off. I expected Alair to be asleep, but as we got closer to his house the door opened. Gile was just leaving, calling a musical goodnight to my brother. He gave a shout of greeting when he saw us. "Princess! There you are. Had enough for one night?"

"It's been a long day," I admitted. We met at the base of the porch.

"It has," Gile said gravely. "You'll be getting back to your post now, won't you?" He asked Rowan.

"Of course, just making sure Rose got home safely."

"Have a good night then, princess. And welcome back." He bowed on unsteady feet, and marched back towards the celebration.

Rowan gave a low chuckle. "Now there's a man fond of his drink. But seriously, try not to go anywhere without an escort. Just listen—" he said as I opened my mouth to object. "I'd dislike it too if I were you, but we've already talked about this. You're too important to let anything happen to you, Rose."

The only answer I gave was grudging silence.

Rowan grinned, and gave my arm a gentle nudge. "Get some sleep, and I'll see you in the morning."

"Goodnight," I said as he walked away, then when no one was watching I pulled the tiara from my cloak and put it on. I mounted the steps, relieved to enter the warm house.

Alair sat by the fire, slumped over as if sleeping, but when I opened the door he roused himself and met me with a smile. "My dear Rose. Come and sit with me a minute."

I hung up my cloak and sword, and reluctantly took a seat by my brother. I held my hands out to the fire and rubbed them together.

"Gile tells me your memory may be coming back," Alair said.

"Umm…" I was startled to realize Gile had pulled himself away from the celebration to report my little wisp of a memory to my brother. "It was nothing really. I just thought maybe, for a moment, I would remember Halen, but then it was gone again."

"Has there been anything else?" Alair pressed.

"No. Nothing yet. Why?"

He nodded thoughtfully. "Rose, it's very important that you tell me any memories you recover. Anything may give us some clue that could help destroy Silaine. But also, so much happened back then that didn't make sense until later. If you should remember something… confusing, promise you will bring it to me so I can explain."

"I promise," I said hesitantly. "Is there something in particular you think would be confusing?"

"No," he said quickly. "But with the Fae, you never know. Things are not always as they appear.

"I understand," I said, though I didn't, really.

"Good. Now if you'll help me up, perhaps we can both see some sleep before this night is over."

I got Alair settled into bed, and his soft snoring wafted

through the room before I was even undressed. The tiara went back in its velvet box, and I exchanged my fine dress for a sleeping gown, then sank onto the furs by the fire. I closed my eyes with resolve, preparing to face my private enemy, sleep. Snippets of scenes from the day danced before my eyes, and I replayed the moment by the fire over and over again, trying to grasp another kernel of memory.

Where was my lost love? Where was Halen's face in my shadowed memories? All I could bring forward was Rowan, then, as I drifted away, Soren. He mouthed a word and I heard it in my mind a moment later, like an echo across a dream:

Rose.

TEN

Shouting woke me. I was really getting tired of that.

I leaped from the furs and opened the door to reveal sentries rushing by in the streets outside. Great drums boomed from the watchtowers, repeating a signal I didn't know the meaning of.

Alair was just waking as I grabbed my cloak and sword and slipped from the house. He called to me but I shut the door like I hadn't heard him, and leaped down the porch onto the street. If we were under attack I wasn't going to stay holed up in the house waiting for enemies to come find me like some… princess. Even if I was only wearing a nightdress under my cloak.

People ran every which way in a frenzy, carrying not just bows and spears, but swords and axes, as if expecting hand-to-hand combat. Criers stood at each intersection, chanting directions.

"Archers to your towers! Footmen to the front gates! Chargers, tack your horses! Boilers, start your fires!"

Defenders mustered to their rallying points, so I headed for the front gates where the offensive force and leadership must be. One man fought the current of people, splitting the crowd like a rock jutting from a river. It was Gile, and when he saw me he called my name, gesturing me to his side.

"What's happening?" I demanded.

"It's the Betrayer. He's outside the gates, asking to speak to Alair or Rowan."

My heart pounded with strange excitement. Soren was here, and with him the opportunity to answer so many of my questions. I longed to see him again, to reconcile what my heart and my family had told me about him.

"Rickard sent me to find you, and keep you safe," Gile said. "Come on girl, I'll take you back to Alair's house."

"No, I want to hear what Soren has to say." I pulled my arm from Gile's grasp. He looked uncertain, as if he didn't expect my resistance and now didn't know what to do. "I deserve to know what's going on," I insisted. "Take me to the front, and if any fighting starts we'll retreat somewhere safe."

Gile finally nodded his assent. "All right. But stay with me."

We jogged through the rows of buildings and joined the anxious crowd pooling around the front gates. Their attention was focused on one of the guard towers where Rickard stood, arms crossed, glowering over the walls at our unexpected guest. Another figure climbed the ladder to join him—Rowan. He conferred with Rickard, posture equally stiff with anger.

Finally Rowan gripped the outer wall of the tower and spoke, his magically magnified voice like a rumble in the mountains. "Traitor. What do you want?"

Even unseen beyond the wooden wall, Soren's answer felt as close as if his breath tickled my neck. By their glowering expressions, the sentries around me felt it, too. A single word reached us, *Rose*, said with such wistfulness I feared the magic would make flowers bloom from my ears.

"She's not here," Rowan thundered. "With any luck, she's far away by now, and you will never find her."

Soren's voice, now merely magnified, was weary and resigned as he replied, "We both know that's not true."

"I can't see," I hissed to Gile. "I'm going to a tower."

"No, wait—"

But I was too fast for him, slipping through the sentries until I reached the guard tower opposite Rowan's.

"Listen, all of you," Soren said while I climbed the ladder. "There need not be bloodshed tonight. I know what you think of me, but I beg you to hear my offer."

The three archers in the tower did a double-take as I joined them, but made no objections. Their bodies hid me from Soren's view, and I peeked between them to look over the wall. My heart leaped into my throat.

Soren wore white, his cloak of shadows swirling around him as if in a high wind. His pale skin shone, tawny hair gold in a magical light that glowed from his body as if he were the moon.

It stunned me, to see the boy who had been so close, and so dangerous. The boy who I trusted because of something that lived between us, something he wouldn't tell me about and everyone else denied. But seeing him again, I knew it was real.

There was something about Soren that wouldn't let me go.

"I know of your plans now that Rose is awake. You want to bring her to Avalon, to beg the Fae king to crush Silaine's rebellion and end her curses. I serve Silaine because I must, but I share your goal. I want to see her slain and Valeria restored as much as you do."

I shuddered to hear him confirm the terrible truth Alair warned me about. Soren was *damnsoír*, slave to Silaine both body and soul. Was it possible for him to defy her, to long for her death despite their enmeshment?

"You lie, Betrayer," Rowan said. "Everyone knows you sold yourself to the Fae. Your pretense is laughable."

"I deserve your poor opinion of me. I won't deny that. Under Silaine's command I have done… unforgivable things."

My heart ached for him, for the pain he must have endured. I couldn't understand why he would choose to join the Fae in the first place. He must have had a good reason. Everything I knew of him told me so. If only we could talk, just the two of us, perhaps all would be made clear.

"But there are ways around her orders, sometimes," Soren continued. "You know of what I speak. Fae bindings are literal. Silaine has erred, and left me an opportunity to defy her. If you let Rose come with me, I can take her straight to the doorways between worlds."

My breath stilled. If this was true, it would save countless lives, and months—perhaps years—of time. I wouldn't have to be a queen and beg the kingdoms of Shalimar and Adalwin to volunteer their armies to attack Silaine's forces. This terrible curse of winter could end. I might even be able to bring Alair back to our village, if any part of it still stood. We could go *home*.

"We will take her there ourselves, *damnsoír*," Rowan replied. "We don't need your help, and wouldn't trust it anyway."

"You think a human army can stand against the Fae?" Soren shook his head. "You have no idea the power she holds, Rowan. It will be a slaughter. I've seen enough of those. This is our one chance, and it's closing. If you don't release Rose, I have orders to destroy Briar."

Rowan spoke above a ripple of uncertainty that ran through the sentries on the ground. "My grandfather says we've killed you before, and you always come back… eventually. But I've never tried my hand at it." A few jeers from the crowd punctuated his words.

"Why is the boy bothering to argue with him?" One archer

whispered to another.

"He's just buying time," came the reply. "This is gonna be a fight to the death, mark my words. Make peace with your gods, brothers." He lifted a charm hung about his neck, and kissed it.

The first man grew pale and wide-eyed, fear rolling off him like fumes. He turned to me with a wordless plea, and my stomach twisted like I'd taken a punch. If they died it would be because of me.

Soren's sigh reached us like an errant wind. "Rowan, the Fae have never attacked this stronghold, not because they could not take it, but because there was no reason to. That's changed now. Please don't make me do this."

"I think we can stand against one man, even one tainted with Fae magic."

Soren's shoulders slumped. "Foolish boy," he whispered, but everyone heard it. Rowan's face grew dark with anger, but before he could reply Soren snapped his fingers and unveiled his army.

The snow beyond the walls suddenly teamed with monsters. They looked like a mix between panthers and wolves, big as bears, black as night, and pacing with wicked feline elegance. My mouth went dry. The beasts panted, exposing sharp fangs through which hot puffs of breath rose white in the freezing air. I didn't think their claws could tear down the walls, but if they could jump like cats they wouldn't have to.

The men at the peepholes of the gate made cries of alarm, and soon word passed through the crowd of the beasts at Soren's side.

"Last chance, Rowan," Soren said, sounding defeated. "Please think this through. If I meant Rose any harm, why would I have let you take her from me? Yes, I *let* you have her, to defy the orders Silaine gave me."

I remembered how the gargrayles appeared to punish us for straying from the path that must have led to Silaine. It hit me like a splash of water to the face—Soren was telling the truth. Whatever the bonds of his servitude, Soren was trying to do the right thing.

Rowan shook his head, disgusted. "With every breath, you lie."

"Oh, I'm the liar?" For the first time, anger colored his words. "Ask your grandfather about Rose's lost memories. Did you blame that on me? It was no Fae magic. How have you explained *that* to her?"

A terrible feeling washed over me, like all my blood had turned to ice.

Could it be true? Had my own brother taken my memories, and lied to me about it? Little things he'd said or done over the past few days—things I'd ignored for the sake of loyalty—suddenly coalesced into something terrible.

Rowan spluttered. "You can't turn us against each other," he finally said, but it was a weak riposte.

My heart sank. Rowan knew. The trust I'd had in him, in my brother, shattered like a pane of glass.

What were they hiding from me?

I hugged the cloak around my body and shivered. The safety I believed innate to our relationship as family suddenly didn't exist. The little brother I knew would never do this to me, never take the memories of the boy I loved, and whatever other secrets hid in those missing months.

But he wasn't my little brother anymore.

All that talk about sacrifice for the love of his sister made a pretty story. But that's all it was. Asleep, I was his rallying cry, a symbol of resistance against Silaine. Awake, I'm a tool to be used. The key to a locked door. A crown with which to seize power. Never mind my resistance, or my need for time to come to terms with it. And if my memories were inconvenient? Banish them. Cut a piece from my heart while it bled from everything else the curse had cost me. My family. My home. My identity.

I had never known betrayal like this.

"People of Briar," Soren said, "you won't survive my attack, and then I'll have your princess anyway." His voice cracked, desperation bleeding in. "Please. For your own sake, just give her back to me." I felt his sincerity, and the truth of his feelings for me when he said, "Rose, if you can hear me, I swear by all the gods, on my soul and every part of my being. I will get you safely to Avalon."

I believed him.

"Give him the girl!" A lone man called. The people nearby hissed for him to shut up, but similar cries echoed around the crowd. It was not an army, after all, but a militia of myriad loyalties.

"Silence," Rickard admonished from the tower.

"I'm not dying for her!" the dissident shouted louder.

A new and tremulous hope dwindled into nothing. These people didn't believe Soren. They just didn't believe in me. In what Alair promised I would do.

"Then leave," someone else yelled, and the sentries erupted in murmurs and arguments.

"Keep order," Rickard bellowed. "Remember your training!"

Gile called to me urgently from the ground, "Girl, get down from there!"

But I was stuck, frozen in the wake of Alair's duplicity. What could he have hidden that might disrupt his plans or weaken my loyalty if the truth came to light? What could be so bad that he feared I'd turn on my own brother?

The only other person who might have answers… was Soren.

"Hold fast!" Rowan's anger thundered in our ears, louder than before. "This is what you came for, to protect the princess. Sentries of Briar, attend me!"

"Please." Soren's plea was faint, lost under the sudden roar of the crowd.

I swayed on my feet, and backed up to a railing for support.

Below, some fled the impending fight, while others surged forward. Rickard made a flurry of hand signals over the side of the tower. Runners took off, the remaining sentries milling before the gates lifted their weapons, and the archers beside me nocked their arrows.

It was all happening so fast. There was no more time to think, no pause to weigh the dangers.

This was going to be a slaughter.

"Wait!" I cried, but I had no magic to amplify my voice. No one heard me. No one listened.

"Archers!" Rowan roared. "Fire at will!"

The archers raised their bows, and the panther-wolf creatures sprinted toward the walls. Hissing like snakes, arrows fell.

But there were too many creatures for the archers to stop. They came over the wall like a tidal wave, black shapes landing amongst the sentries and felling them with swipes of their claws like scythes moving through wheat.

No arrows reached Soren. He fired red streaks of magic that exploded against the gates, loud as thunder. The towers rattled, and chunks of wood splintered from the walls.

“Soren, no!” I shouted, and below me Gile bellowed my name.

Rowan’s own magic joined the fray, bolts of red lightning streaking toward Soren and falling short, then turning on closer enemies. Archers sent shot after shot into the massacre below. The battleground was a horror, a nightmare of flashing lights, torn limbs, and spilled blood. The screams of men and beasts formed a singular cry of rage and pain.

I had to stop this. People were dying down there, in my name. It was all so wrong, so pointless.

My body seemed far away. Ignoring the height, I slipped one leg over the tower’s railing, and wavered there, unsteady. I could climb down the scaffolding and reach the outer wall. From there I would drop to the layer of defensive spikes at the base. They pointed outward, so I would only land on more logs. With any luck I wouldn’t break an ankle, and could leap clear of the spikes down to the snow.

“Rose!” Rowan must have caught sight of me. His magical scream rang over the cacophony of battle. “No! Wait! Gile, get her!” The tower shook as Gile charged up the ladder.

Rose.

Soren’s whisper let me know he saw me, too. If I came to him, there was no more reason to fight. The roar of the battle shifted. The great beasts flooded back over Briar’s walls, drawing premature shouts of triumph and the wretched cries of the injured and dying in their wake.

My heart was glad, even as I hardened it against Rowan’s desperate pleas for me to stop.

The walls of Briar were formed by upright logs bound together. Their ends were sharpened into points, but they were only wood. One hand around each spike, I hung from the wall and dropped to the logs below. It was a bad fall, bruising my knees and scraping my hands, but it didn't matter.

I hauled myself up the icy logs of the defensive barrier, jumping from the tops of the sharpened wood to the soft snow of the ground. I shook as I rose to my feet.

The remaining panther-wolves swirled angrily in front of Briar. I brushed snow from my night dress and walked slowly toward them. Green eyes glared, and many jaws licked red blood from their chops, but the beasts parted.

"Open the gate! Open the gate!" Rowan commanded, but he couldn't stop me now.

My breath came in cold and hard, my ears rang, and my skin tingled. This was either the bravest thing I'd ever done, or the stupidest.

I raised my eyes to meet Soren's, and my fears fell away.

He looked at me with hope and relief. As I watched, his smile grew, contorting the fine scars on his face, and his tensed shoulders relaxed. His smile said he knew me, and found the same thing looking at me as I did when looking at him.

Soren held out a hand. "I promise, Rose."

"You lied to me, too," I reminded him.

Behind me the gates fell open. I heard boots treading the wood. Some of the beasts faced Briar and growled, but Soren made a gesture with his outstretched hand, and they quieted.

"I did," he admitted. "I wanted to save you from knowing the truth about me. I'm ashamed…" He looked away for a moment. When he looked back, the light in his eyes had died. "And I'm guilty, and I'm hollowed out inside." Weariness aged him. Sorrow flooded the space between us. "Rowan is right. I'm sworn to Silaine and I must obey her, but I fight it every chance I can. And we have a chance, right now, to stop her."

Rowan called my name again, a howl of despair.

"What if she makes you turn on me?" I asked.

Soren winced. "She could. But that's why we'll go quickly. She'll sense us approaching, and think I'm bringing you to her, but we'll go to the portal to Avalon instead."

"And you'll tell me the truth?" I pressed. "About everything?"

"I will. Gods help me, I will." He held out his hand again.

I stepped forward.

"NOOOO!"

A man's terrible howl rose behind us. I turned to see Alair staggering through the gate in his brown nightdress, barefoot, eyes aflame with power and anger. I gasped to see him so animated, moving with the strength of a younger man. His voice boomed through the night. "Get back, Betrayer! By blood and magic I demand you leave this place!"

A wave of power radiated from Alair and pushed against us like a strong wind, but Soren stood firm. He gritted his teeth, and I felt a different flavor of power flowing from him into the beasts around us. Their mouths parted and they growled as one.

"I am leaving, Alair. And I'm taking Rose with me. She'll be safe, I swear to you. It's the only way."

"I'll come back," I called to my brother, voice so small compared to his and Soren's magical roars. Rowan stood behind Alair, pale and wide-eyed. "I'll convince the Fae king, then I'll come and find you."

I turned to Soren, hand outstretched—

A heart-rending shriek rang over the snow, so violent the black beasts flattened their ears and hissed in its echo, and the men behind us raised their voices in alarm. Every hair on my body flaring, I turned and gasped to see Alair, my brother, with a dagger lodged deep in his heart.

His own hand held the blade.

"No!" Rowan screamed, but all eyes were on Alair, still standing, speaking words in a voice not his own. Inhuman words, magical words. A red mist rose from his heart, and the amulet about his neck floated in the air before him. His body glowed with unnatural light that grew brighter and brighter, illuminating the field like daylight. The beasts closed their eyes and cowered before the power that thrummed louder and louder until the ground shook and my bones quivered like jelly.

With a terrible flash, a burst of energy pushed Soren and his black beasts away, tumbling them about like paper dolls in the wind. A power so strong it knocked me back into the snow and the village behind Alair creaked, moaned, and collapsed with his body.

The sleep I feared took me again.

ELEVEN

After spinning and wandering for countless ages, something appeared in the emptiness to ground me. Something so familiar I felt surprised I'd forgotten. It would have been easy to find my way out if only I had remembered this.

Soren held out his hand, then a shadow crossed his face. His eyes looked past me, and widened in fear. Then it was Rowan's face, and Rowan's arms who grabbed and shook me.

I woke fighting. Someone held my arms, pressing me to the ground. I screamed and kicked, until I recognized the voice urging me to stop.

"Rose, you're okay! It's me!"

Rowan.

I stopped thrashing, panting as if I'd run for my life. But when he released me I grabbed him. "Don't let me go," I gasped, voice cracking. "Don't let me sleep again."

"You're awake now. You're fine." His voice was not comforting, but bitter.

After a few moments I let go of his arms, and pushed myself to a seated position. I lay on a fur spread over a board, and Rowan kneeled beside me. It was morning, the early daylight harsh and unforgiving. My stomach dropped as I surveyed the wreckage around us.

Briar was demolished. Its walls had fallen like they'd been blown outward. The buildings that hadn't collapsed sagged on broken timbers, and debris was scattered everywhere. Blood darkened the mud, and the bodies of several beasts lay where they'd fallen.

The memories of last night came back in a rush. "Alair." I turned to Rowan. "Is he—Did he really—?"

Rowan's mouth was curled, eyes dark and accusing. "Grandfather's dead. He used his death to curse Soren away. Why, Rose? Why did you do that?"

My heart seized in my chest. "I didn't know Alair would—I was trying to—" I put a hand to my mouth as a sob wracked my body.

My brother was dead. And it was my fault. I curled into a ball, shaking with grief and horror.

If I had known Alair would be driven to kill himself to protect me, I would never have gone to Soren. But the battle was agony, seeing people maimed and killed because my family couldn't give Soren the benefit of the doubt. I *knew* he was telling the truth. He could have taken me straight to Avalon, in defiance of his mistress. He was bound to her, but he was on our side.

"Why," I croaked, wiping tears and snot from my face. "Why did Alair take my memories?"

"What are you talking about?"

I sat up, shaking. "Soren said the Fae didn't do it."

"Soren said—" Rowan's face darkened. "Has he bewitched you? How can you trust *anything* he said?"

"You're lying!" I cried. "I know you are! What are you hiding from me?"

"He is the *Betrayer*!" Rowan shouted. "What is wrong with you?"

"He wants to stop Silaine, too. He's trying to help us!"

Our shouts were attracting stares from the surviving sentries.

Rowan took a deep breath, and put both hands on my shoulders. He spoke quietly and firmly. "Soren cannot ever be trusted, no matter what he says, or what he makes you feel. He is *damnsoír*."

"I know what a *damnsoír* is," I said, wiping fresh tears from my face.

"Do you?"

I held my breath to stop the sobs that still wracked my body. Rowan repositioned himself so we sat side by side, then he put an arm around me. It felt forced, but I took the comfort anyway, leaning against him as Rowan spoke, low and urgent.

"*Damnsoír* means dancer. In the old days, Fae would capture men and women with their music, and make them mindless slaves. For work and entertainment, or even as prey in the Hunt. But there was another type of slavery for those the Fae liked best. They used magic to bind Fae and humans together, and the humans became... Other. Undying. Incapable of defying orders. Closer to their masters than a lover, or a pet." Rowan pulled away and turned my chin to face him. His gaze bored into mine, unblinking. "Soren is one of these, bound to Silaine. He must do as she commands. But this is a bond that can only be entered into voluntarily. He had to *choose* to link his soul to hers. He wasn't captured, he wasn't enslaved. It was a choice. He *chose* to become a monster."

I shook my head. Why would Soren give up his freedom for such a horrible mistress?

Rowan explained. "In return he is immortal. He can be killed, but always comes back. Soren is invested in making sure Silaine wins because he sits at her right hand. Why would he long for her death when it would kill him, too? Because he lies. It's what he does. During those first days, when the snow fell and everyone in Valeria eventually had to leave or die, Soren lured people into Silaine's clutches. Whole villages, Rose. They believed he was telling the truth, too. Then he led them to their deaths. They became slaves, or food and practice for Silaine's beasts and followers."

My stomach turned. Villages, like mine. Families, afraid and freezing in the unexpected winter, following anyone who said they knew of a safe haven. But all that waited for them was death, and worse.

"So you see, Soren could have been ordered to trick you. To be charming, to sow doubt. After all these years, he's very good at it," Rowan said bitterly. "He's probably the one who took your memories. Because if he didn't, you'd remember what he did, and know you couldn't trust him. Do you see now?"

I nodded, but my feelings were a vicious tangle. Had I truly been so horribly fooled? Was Soren's sincerity a practiced facade, his tenderness an act, his kiss a perversion?

Rowan took my hands in his. "Promise me, Rose. Whatever happens. You won't believe his lies again. Or my grandfather killed himself for nothing."

What could I say? "I promise," I whispered, miserable. "Rowan, I'm sorry. I'm so sorry."

He pulled me into him as I sobbed again, and held me until I could calm my heaving breaths. When I finally pulled back his eyes were wet, too.

We were alone now, the two of us. All that was left of our strange family.

He took me to see Alair's body, laid out amongst other fallen sentries in a clear space. Nearby, some men already stoked a bonfire, the only way to handle our dead with the ground frozen solid.

Someone had removed the dagger from Alair's heart. His

ancient body was a crumple of bones, hands curled into claws. I couldn't recognize anything of my brother in that husk. Still I knelt, and smoothed back the hair from his cold head, saying my silent goodbyes.

I had started to resent his plans for me, feeling like a chess piece instead of a loved one, but in the end he gave his life for me. I regretted my doubts fiercely.

Maybe if I'd followed Gile back to Alair's house, Briar would have won the battle. Or maybe Soren's beasts would have slaughtered everyone. Maybe Alair still would have sacrificed himself to banish the Betrayer and his minions, to keep Soren from me one last time. Maybe I'd still be here, saying goodbye forever to my little brother, and none of it would have been my fault. But we'd never know.

Rowan removed the amulet from his grandfather's neck, and placed it around his own. The torch had passed. Alair's experience and wisdom was gone now. The dream of freeing Valeria and saving the world from Fae brutality was a dream Rowan and I must carry.

We joined the teams culling supplies and belongings from the wreckage. Without walls to act as a buffer, the wind was fierce, but at least there was lots of firewood for the cooking fires.

Some people packed up their things and fled in ones and twos. Most stayed, to care for the injured, to attend the funerals planned at sunset, or to wait on the departure of the mass groups that would eventually leave for Shalimar or Adalwin. There was safety in numbers, a reassurance to sticking together.

Rowan and I were bound for Shalimar, of course. To deliver the news of Ferras's death to Rowan's mother, and leverage her connections at the royal court to meet with King Egari. I dreaded the trip, both its dangers and destination, but looked forward to leaving the icy chill of my once-homeland.

I helped Rowan pick through the wreckage of Alair's house. He was particularly interested in his grandfather's collection of books and scrolls. All of Alair's knowledge of magic was there, too precious to be abandoned in the snow.

We packed the scattered library into crates. I couldn't help but flip through some of Alair's journals, marveling at the diagrams and symbols. If I performed these actions and read these words, would the magic in my Aerendel bloodline awaken? Or was the magic of humans different from erdwitches?

Rowan explained that magic was like cooking with limited spices. You could make certain dishes with no problem, others would be a little off the mark but passable, and there were some dishes you couldn't recreate no matter how hard you tried. The similarities and differences between the flavors of magic inherent in Fae, erdwitch, and human all overlapped and contradicted each other in a confusing kaleidoscope of possibilities.

Alair's research and observations documented decades of knowledge of his hybrid erdwitch magic. They would be invaluable for Rowan, who was now the last carrier of Maeve's shared powers, and had no more teachers.

"What about Maeve herself?" I asked. "She was in Shalimar after the curse, to teach Alair. Don't you know her?"

Rowan shook his head. "Maeve wanders. We haven't heard from her in years."

"She didn't wander when I knew her. She lived in a cave near our village."

"That's because she was watching over you. Erdwitches

don't normally stay in one place for long. They go where the earth pulls them. I feel it, too, sometimes," Rowan confessed. "The urge to follow traces of energy, a pull toward imbalances that need to be set right. It's easier to bear it here in Valeria. Everything is wrong, so it all feels the same."

Our frozen land was a gaping wound. Humans disturbed the flow of energies and elements with our cities and destruction of natural resources, but only the Fae could violate the earth like this. It was wrong, a spell wrought from death and blood, a deviation from nature's rhythms.

"We'll save Valeria," I said, trying to sound determined, but falling flat. "Somehow."

Rowan just looked at me with his mouth in a flat line. "We have to."

I found the tiara, safe inside its velvet box, and tucked it once more into my cloak.

As the sun set, casting vivid reds and purples across the snow, we surrendered our dead to the blazing pyres. Almost everyone spoke, naming the lost and praising their courage. A rare barrel of brandy was cracked, and everyone accepted a portion. We lifted our glasses to toast the sacrifice of the dead, and wished them well in their journey to the shadowlands where all dead spirits gather.

One of the few women present lifted her voice in a farewell dirge. Only the gifted singers among us joined her. Tears streamed silently down my face as the beautiful music wrapped us in sorrow and perseverance.

The crowd took a long time to disperse. Some stared at the

flames for hours, mourning lost friends or loved ones. The rest of us trickled over to the cooking fires and began the business of continuing to live despite our grief.

Word of my defection to Soren's side during the battle had spread among the survivors, but interpretations of my actions varied. One man thanked me for being willing to sacrifice myself to save them. I overheard others wondering if they could trust me, or if, as Rowan suggested, I was bewitched by the Betrayer.

I didn't feel bewitched. Just confused, and resigned to maintaining my vow to disbelieve Soren if he appeared again, no matter what my heart told me. Apparently it couldn't be trusted.

The full impact of Alair's death-spell was unknown to us. Rowan strongly suspected the spell was centered in Alair's stone amulet, which was already connected to whatever conditions allowed it to detect when beast-hunting would be fruitful. Although why Alair would be responsible for receiving and transmitting such a message didn't make sense to me. Perhaps it was simply the way things had always been done.

From one of Alair's journals, Rowan believed the amulet now acted like a reverse magnet, pushing away the Betrayer and perhaps any creature carrying Fae magic. But that remained to be seen.

"Princess." Rickard approached Rowan and I as we ate while seated on a log that used to be part of the meeting hall. "We need to rally the men. We should remind anyone with a connection to the Shalimarian throne of their obligation to support our appeal to King Egari. For the nobles still with us in particular, we should secure their alliance. Will you come speak to them?"

I sighed. Politicking never rested, not even on a day like this.

Rickard was right to think of these things. All too soon, it was time to start practicing being a queen.

And I didn't want to do it alone. "Rowan, do you want to come with us?" It hadn't escaped me that perhaps this was Rowan's responsibility as well.

But Rowan seemed resigned to Rickard assuming the mantle of leadership over Briar. He demurred in favor of continuing to study some of Alair's notes that might shed some light on the new powers of the amulet.

I followed Rickard as he moved among the groups of sentries. He seemed to know everyone's name, and their respect for him was palpable. Rickard spoke grandly of duty and the global threat of the Fae, but I was more of an accessory. I nodded thoughtfully at his words and thanked everyone for their support, accepting bows or curtsies as they were given.

People *bowed* to me. It was strange every time, and all I could do was smile and nod.

My eyes found their way back to Rowan time and again. I hoped he would change his mind and join Rickard and I, but he only got up after Alair's amulet glowed blue. Rowan stalked off toward where the horses were penned. Was he seriously thinking about going *hunting* now, all alone, at night?

By the time I could politely extricate myself from the current conversation, Rowan was already urging his stallion across the snow toward the tree line. Was he trying to get himself killed?

In a fury, I haltered a horse at random and led it to some wreckage I could use to climb onto its back. But the damned beast kept sidling away from my attempts to mount it.

"Whoa there, princess." Gile appeared, and claimed the horse's halter. "Where are you off to?"

I pointed. "Rowan went out there all by himself. He could

get hurt, or attacked!"

"So you thought you'd charge into the same danger, all alone-like?"

"*Someone* needs to go after him. If you don't want me to go, then you do it!"

With every second, Rowan got further and further away. But Gile just looked at me with an inscrutable expression.

"He's all I have left, Gile, *please*."

"Rowan's a smart boy," Gile eventually said. "If he's got business in the woods then it's none of our concern." He clucked to the horse and led it back toward the pen.

I stomped after him, appalled. "*Business*? What do you mean, *business*?"

Gile released the horse to its fellows, and turned to me with one eyebrow raised. "Alair used to have business out in the woods alone. Then Ferras did. Now Rowan does. And if you remember anything about cats, my girl, you'll know that curiosity frequently gets them killed. The same could be said for princesses." From any other man, it might have been a threat. But Gile's tone was friendly, and he winked. "Now come along, you're wanted back at the gathering."

He offered his arm, and I took it, bewildered.

When—if—Rowan returned, I would make him tell me what this was about. The same doubts and fears from last night reared their ugly heads, but with an effort I pushed them away. Rowan would explain. I had to trust him.

There was no alternative.

Gile led me back to the fires, passing me over to Rickard like caretakers exchanging a child. One of the Shalimarian nobles had generously offered to house myself and any attendants. I attempted to affect an air of quiet dignity as I thanked him, but I misliked the way he looked at me. I suspected his offer was a gamble on elevating his own fortunes rather than selflessly looking after mine. But what else could I expect?

The romanticism of Briar's purpose had the cadence of a fairytale. The valiant dedication of its sentries in service to the lost princess of Valeria was a pretty story to fire the imagination and swell the heart. But the reality was that no one truly belonged to Briar except my family. Everyone else had a home in other lands. These nobles would return to the courts of Shalimar or Adalwin. Outcasts, exiles, and nomads would move on to other pursuits. Merchants and messengers would find other routes to travel. Even those who hinted they might want to return to Valeria or join the court of the awakened princess, once the minor problem of the Fae was rectified, hedged their bets.

Rickard spoke confidently of the eventuality of exorcizing the Fae presence and returning Valeria to greatness, but it must have been an act. Still, I felt gratitude toward him, and understood why Alair was pleased with Rickard taking up the mantle left behind by Ferras.

We were finally running out of people to speak to when a cry rang out from those at the edge of the wreckage. "The beasts are back!"

Everyone still in the common area turned toward the commotion. A dark shape hurtled toward Briar across the snow. Those with weapons bared them, but it wasn't a monster returning to finish the battle.

"It's Rowan!" I proclaimed, relief spreading through me.

The stallion flew, Rowan leaning over his neck for greater speed. Men dove out of the way as he thundered to a halt amidst the clustering sentries. I could have sworn the bags on either side of his saddle were empty when I spied Rowan heading into the trees, but now they were bulky. A faint blue glow flickered under the flaps.

Rowan leaped from the stallion's back and strode toward Rickard and I, though he only had eyes for me. "The witchlines!" he crowed, grinning ear to ear. "Father touched the witchlines—he's alive!"

TWELVE

Rowan and I clutched arms, shaking each other with giddiness. Questions and cheers erupted from those who'd heard him. Noise spread easily across Briar's now-open air. The excitement drew others back from their various tasks around the wreckage.

Rowan pulled away and leaped onto a bench so he could address the growing crowd.

"My father is still out there," Rowan announced. "He's not dead! Who will join me for a rescue party?"

Conversations erupted, friends and fellows consulting each other or exclaiming at the news. A few folk moved forward, and I was glad to recognize some from our hunting party the day before.

But beside me Rickard crossed his arms, brows furrowed. His question was low, yet seemed to carry. "You sure, boy?"

Rowan turned to him. "Of course!"

"And you're the only one who saw the amulet light up?"

Rowan's grin fell. "What are you saying?"

A deadly quiet spread outward from them. In the sudden silence, Rickard said, "I know you miss your father, lad. I know you wanted to send a team to find him. But is there any chance you misinterpreted what you saw?"

When Rowan spoke his voice held a tingle of power. "Are you calling me a liar?"

I froze in the sudden tension.

Rickard inclined his head, as if in apology. "No. But we've made our decision already."

"You think I'd lie?" I shivered at Rowan's tone. "I'm not making it up. I *saw* the signal. Only one with erdwitch powers could activate the witchlines. It's my father. He's alive."

"It's too late, Rowan," Rickard said softly. "Briar is gone. We aren't prepared to go north. And we have the princess to think of. Our path leads to Shalimar. It's what your father wanted."

"Rose, you believe me, don't you?" Rowan demanded.

Even if I hadn't, I couldn't imagine denying him after I caused the death of Alair. I owed him this, and more. "Of course."

Rickard shook his head. "No. I won't have it, boy. Your father would want you to follow the plan."

"My father touched the witchlines," Rowan shouted, turning to appeal to the listening crowd. "He's counting on us. Any true sentry of Briar will go with me to find him."

No one moved for an agonizing moment. Then one man cleared his throat. He wasn't one of those who came forward initially. "Rowan, I have to wonder… Why couldn't Ferras touch the witchlines before tonight? It could be a trap."

"No," Rowan said stubbornly. "Father wouldn't touch them unless he wanted us to know. He's waiting for us."

But doubt had infected the crowd. I saw it in the exchange of knowing glances, and the solemn shaking of heads.

Rickard tried again, tone gentle with sympathy. "I promised Ferras I would watch over you, son. Don't make me break my word."

Rowan met his eyes with a steely gaze. "We all make our choices. I'll give your regards to Father."

I winced as Rickard's face betrayed a flash of hurt. He didn't deserve that. Despite Rowan's resentment, all I'd ever seen in Rickard was a good leader with a good heart. But now his expression darkened, and his voice grew cold. "And I'll give your regards to your mother. It's the last she'll ever hear from you."

Rowan's face went white, and his nostrils flared. He opened his mouth and my heart already broke for the further shattering of bonds that would come with his acidic reply.

But Gile—blessed Gile, always there at the right moment—stepped between them and held up his hand. "I'll join your team, Rowan."

Rickard put a hand on Gile's shoulder. "My friend, *no*. You know this is folly."

"I gave my word, too," Gile answered. "And now you can keep yours, knowing the boy is with me."

They stared into each other's eyes, a potent yet silent communication passing between them. Finally, Rickard nodded, but he had one more card to play. He turned to me. "Tell them not to go, princess. There's only death out there."

I opened my mouth, but nothing came out. I looked at Rowan, who looked back with a plea and a challenge.

It was an impossible situation. I couldn't tell Rowan to leave his father to die… but I also couldn't go to Shalimar without him. I couldn't pretend to be a queen without my family to fight for. He was all I had left, my only friend in the world. Without Rowan I was truly alone.

"How many days will a rescue take?" I asked.

"Father's in Lorensile. It will take eight days to get to him, then another four east to the border of Shalimar."

Lorensile. The city closest to my home. Its name ignited

homesickness, and resolution. "I'm going with you."

Rowan frowned, but before he could respond Rickard jumped in again. "Absolutely not! Throw away your own life if you must, Rowan, but not the princess'."

"He's right, Rose," Rowan said reluctantly. "You're the only one who can reach Avalon. It's too risky."

"Then we'll need more volunteers." I stared down the crowd. "Rowan is the only one with magic to rival the Fae. My brother's—" I forced myself to say the word, "—death… paid for a spell that repels them. Rowan carries it in his amulet. I am safest at his side."

It was a slight exaggeration. Rowan didn't truly know the full effect of Alair's curse. But he still fished out the amulet from under his shirt and held it aloft. In his hand it glowed with a golden light. An awed silence held until the glow faded.

"Well what about us?" A man with curly blonde hair asked. He stood on makeshift crutches. "That leaves us to go on our way without that same protection. Lots of monsters about, these days."

"The Fae will be tracking the girl," Rickard said bitterly. "You'll make the journey unharmed. I'd bet my life on it."

"You will be! And betting ours, as well."

Rickard ignored him. "Princess, if you die, we lose our chance to summon the Fae King. That means Shalimar and Adalwin—and hell, Fulsyria too, if we can convince them—must combine their armies to try and defeat Silaine. Thousands of soldiers will die."

"They have to fight anyway to get Rose to the portal," Rowan said. "But…" A new idea lit him from within. "Maybe a smaller team could succeed where an army can't." He locked eyes with me. "We'll be so far north, anyway. We can make a run for it. My magic can hide us."

The plan ignited a fire of certainty in my heart. No pleading from a powerless position with foreign kings, or navigating the treacheries of their courts. No sending soldiers to die against the might of the Fae. And no pretending to be queen of the country I still called home but never dreamed of ruling.

"We could end it." I nodded, enthusiasm growing. "In just a few weeks, it could all be over."

I felt the tide of opinion shift as the idea took root among those listening, and bloomed.

"Volunteers, to me!" Rowan stepped down from the bench. Gile, myself, and those who believed in our mission followed.

The crowd flowed into two groups, those at Rowan's side or Rickard's. Ours was much smaller, but bigger than I'd anticipated. Finally the lines were clearly drawn, and Rowan glowed with triumph.

Rickard sought my eyes, confrontational and pleading, but I looked away. "Fine then," he said bitterly. "Those of us with sense will beg support from our respective kings. We must assume you'll fail in your quest, so our ask will be for war."

Rowan nodded, arms crossed and chin lifted. "That's fair. And you'll know by the melting snow that your armies are not needed."

One of the men in our new party whooped, and smiles broke out all around.

"I hope so, Rowan." Rickard's eyes were dark, and his words were bitter. "I really do."

The new plan had wide-ranging consequences to the

distribution of supplies already divvied up by the survivors. Rowan and Gile spent the rest of the evening directing the team in assembling what we'd need for a long journey in the snow.

With Briar's buildings flattened or uninhabitable, safe and comfortable bedding was at a premium. Rickard had directed that priority be given to the injured, of course. Temporary shelters sprung from the wreckage. Two women invited me to join their lean-to, but as much as I wanted their company I had business with Rowan when he was available.

I settled down in the area our team chose as a base of operations. Tables from the common area were stacked around a fire to insulate us from the wind. I curled up in a nest of furs, laying part of my cloak across my face to save it from the cold.

I dreaded sleep, but I dreaded being alone with my thoughts more: guilt over Alair's death, second-guessing the journey ahead, and the claustrophobia of everything everyone wanted or needed from me. Thankfully, exhaustion ruled, and I drifted off before the maelstrom in my mind had a chance to truly begin.

Rowan's arrival woke me. I didn't know the hour, but the circles under his eyes were dark as he slipped into the saved pallet at my side.

I turned toward him, and whispered, "Where were you earlier? You left, and brought something back."

"What? Oh, just a new batch of arrows. You've seen them, with the blue runes?" Rowan put his head on his arm and closed his eyes. "It makes them deadlier to the Fae."

I frowned, pondering his answer. "You can only make the runes in the woods?"

He shrugged. "That's the way it is."

It must be something to do with erdwitch magic that I simply didn't know about. "Well, don't go off alone again," I grumbled, curling into my own arm.

"Were you worried about me?" Rowan's eyes were closed, but his lips turned up in the barest hint of a smile.

"Of course."

He opened his eyes and we stared at each other for a moment. It seemed crazy that I'd only known him for a few days. So much had happened, so much had been lost. We were all that was left of a legacy written in blood and magic. Only Rowan remained to fight with me toward a desperate and uncertain future.

"Can you forgive me?" I whispered.

"I already have."

I closed my eyes, a single tear gliding down my cheek. Rowan brushed it away, and smoothed a strand of hair from my forehead. "Get some sleep," he whispered. "We leave at first light."

I nodded, and turned over. Sleep found me quickly, but so did the nightmares. Emotions I repressed and bound in simple facts during the day re-emerged as the body's visceral horror. My family's murder, the loss of the world as I knew it, Alair's heart-piercing dagger, the violence of battle, the guilt of knowing it was all my fault, all of it. I should have died with them. I lived a coward's fate, deserving death but fleeing it, no matter who was swallowed up behind me.

I cried out in my sleep, and Rowan woke me from the nightmares, twice. Finally he kept a hand on my shoulder, ready to jostle me awake if needed, but his anchoring touch brought peace and easy rest.

When dawn finally broke I found my hand wrapped around his. I let go as Rowan woke and stretched. The touch had soothed parts of me, but made others ache with longing.

I wanted my mother's hug, my father's firm hand on my

shoulder, Alair leaning on me as we whittled. And I wanted something else, something family couldn't offer.

I had no direct memories of it, but my body missed the closeness of a partner. Hands on my hips, a chest pressed against mine, being held, and the taste of a familiar kiss. My heart knew what it was like to kiss him. My body remembered his touch, even if my mind couldn't summon his face. Would I ever fully remember Halen? And if I did, would I ever be able to love again?

As Briar stirred, I broke the ice on a bucket and splashed my face with cold water. Cold was what I needed, the cold of determination, and perseverance. Not this hot, bleeding ache.

I followed Rowan, helping where directed, and all too soon our party was ready to go. Six of the twelve volunteers had changed their minds or been gently rejected by Rowan and Gile. Those remaining were proven fighters and trusted team members.

We took Rowan's stallion, and a chubby pony named Crackers who would pull the sled of supplies. Crackers was a mountain breed, compact and hardy, with a thick coat. Rowan would use Garland to scout ahead and behind, concealing our passage with his erdwitch magic as much as possible. The rest of us would walk. It would have been nice if we all had mounts, but the amount of grain we'd have to haul with us to feed the horses would necessitate more sleds, and more horses, only compounding the problem.

The other groups leaving for either Adalwin or Shalimar had much more to prepare before they could depart. Our team said their final goodbyes, and gathered at the far side of Briar.

Rickard came to see us off. He didn't ask us to change our mind, but his glower spoke for him. Rickard shook hands with our volunteers, bowed to me, then he and Gile embraced, pounding each other on the back. The way their gruff hug lingered revealed a mutual pessimism in the success of our journey.

Gile never expected to see Rickard again, either.

The thought chilled and saddened me. Did all these men believe we were leading them to their deaths? Perry, the youngest man here besides Rowan, who had run from the snow beast. Dedrick, also from that hunting party, short and stout like a black-haired Gile in miniature. Two mustached brothers from Adalwin named Effer and Bremmer, who made their coin by sourcing beast hides and trophies to buyers back home. A rangy, seasoned soldier called Wes, who was missing two fingers and an eye. And lastly Fitzsimmons, always smiling, who wore a case for his lute across one shoulder.

None of them seemed like they had a death wish. Were we all fools, or did Gile know something we didn't?

Rickard didn't attempt to shake hands with Rowan, who was already mounted atop Garland. They nodded at each other briefly. "If you do find your father," Rickard said, and I tensed for some final rebuke. "Tell him… tell him it was an honor."

"I will."

Rowan met my eyes before turning his horse and riding across the field of snow toward the kingsroad in the distance. Merry little Crackers, led by Dedrick, fidgeted like he wanted to race after the large stallion, but was kept at a brisk walk. The rest of us shouldered our packs and set off after them.

I looked back at the wreckage of the stronghold both built by my brother and destroyed by him, all for my sake.

The sacrifice Briar represented must not be made in vain.

THIRTEEN

We walked straight north on the kingsroad, passing empty towns with buildings collapsed or else frozen into blocks of ice. Every bridge we saw had crumbled, but the rivers were frozen solid, making for an easy but often slippery crossing. This land was hilly, but Gile assured me the going would be easier once we reached the farmlands, then much more difficult as we crossed mountain ranges.

Rowan switched between riding ahead and riding behind, either setting spells to alert him to the presence of Fae magic, or wiping the tracks of our passing from the snow. I longed to speak with him, or witness his magical workings, but he rarely pulled up his horse to walk beside us.

We couldn't hope that Soren, his beasts, or other minions weren't watching us. Rowan could erase our tracks, but do little to guard against spying eyes, especially as our path took us so frequently into open spaces. Nevertheless, he did not sense any Fae presence that morning.

Gile called a brief halt at midday, and we ate a meal of the more perishable items culled from Briar's supplies. I was already exhausted. I thought myself athletic, and no stranger to hiking in the snow. But this unnatural winter was different. There were no deer trails to follow, no traffic to flatten the kingsroad and clearly mark its trail. We followed the path as best we could, but still waded through snow, sometimes as high as my knees.

After our meal, Effer led the pony and Gile and I fell back to let others cut through the snow, walking more easily in their trail. We'd been cautioned not to make unnecessary noise, but Gile broke up the endless miles by whispering stories of the Fae to me. I knew all the old tales, of course, but Gile's accounts were recent, and more accurate.

"I've seen 'em seven feet tall, and heard they can be any color under the sun," he recounted. "They have ears like deer, and no eyelashes. And their eyes... No whites. Can't tell what they're looking at. They don't have to work, like we do. All they do is eat and drink and hunt."

"That doesn't sound so bad," I said. "I wouldn't mind doing that myself."

"Heavens forbid, princess. They ride the Hunt, their sacred game. They track the hind, the bear, the beast, or worse. In fearsome revels they have even hunted humans."

"And they dance," I added, that terrible word repeating in my mind. *Damnsoír.* Dancer.

"Oh, aye. You must be wary of hearing music in the forest. We've had some folks just vanish on patrols. I have to wonder if a Fae tune was the last thing they heard."

I thought about it for a moment. "It can't be true. If it were, the Fae could just charm us all into surrender."

"Possibly. Or maybe there's only some as can do it. Or perhaps it's a frail magic, only working on those who can't easily fight it. Some men wear iron, or garlands of the plants said to repel them. Bunch of nonsense, to my mind. The Fae bear weapons like we do, and what would a creature of the forest have against ivy, or boxwood?"

Gile's tales were interrupted when unevenness on a ridge tipped the sleigh over, spilling supplies and dragging a frightened Crackers down the hill. We all rushed forward to untangle his traces and set the sleigh to rights. Rowan rode back to us, worry furrowing his brow.

"There's Fae about," he announced before dismounting. "Be on your guard. Rose, with me."

We all carried some sort of weapon, but the heavier ones had been stored in the sleigh for convenience. With a surge of anxiety, I joined the men retrieving their battle weapons. I'd been allotted a bow and quiver full of arrows, which I strapped to my back. The shafts of the arrows glowed with tiny runes. Something about them still filled me with misgiving, but there were bigger problems to worry about.

On impulse I grabbed my sword, and the belt for it. I felt an odd affection for the blade I'd taken from Soren. I wanted its comforting weight on my hip more than the inconvenience of dragging it with me through the snow.

My father might have told me I was likely to do more harm than good, wielding a weapon I wasn't experienced with. But I'd done all right with the gargrayles. I was still primarily an archer, but reserving a weapon for close combat seemed like a good idea.

I walked at Rowan's side while he led Garland through the snow. Rowan wore the inherited amulet outside his shirt, and held it with a bare hand.

"What does it tell you?" I asked.

"Many things. It's just a stone, but Grandfather often used it as an anchoring point. It's part of the witchlines, and it can act like a… like a warning bell, ringing when certain conditions are met."

"Except it doesn't ring," I pointed out.

"No, the ring is silent," he agreed. "You'd have to have

erdwitch magic to sense it."

"What does it tell you about the Fae nearby? Are they beasts or actual Fae? Or… the Betrayer?" I used Rowan's preferred term for him, another brick to help secure the friendship between us. Rowan said he forgave me for how my actions caused Alair's death. I wasn't so sure I forgave myself.

Rowan shook his head. "Not him. And real Fae don't usually come this far south. It's a beast, like as not. But I'd hoped we'd have more time before facing any real danger."

"At least we'll find out if Alair's curse deflects all Fae, or just the one."

We walked in thoughtful silence for a minute. The open fields we'd passed all morning were transitioning to wooded lands, the natural domain of the Fae. It seemed we walked toward danger, but we had no choice.

"Rowan, what do you think happened to your father?"

"I can imagine a thousand different fates," he admitted. "Perhaps there was a heavy snowstorm, and the team holed up somewhere until it passed, then the witchline was hidden and difficult to find. Or perhaps they were attacked, and retreated to some defensible position, waiting until their attackers grew bored and left." Rowan ran his thumb across the amulet, lost in thought. "I fear, of course, that he was gravely injured. Dragging himself toward the witchlines to call for help. It's killing me that I didn't go looking for him earlier. But everyone insisted…" Rowan paused, frown deepening. He clutched the amulet tighter. "I think—"

"Mavens!" The cry came from behind.

Rowan swore, and looked up, searching the skies.

I turned to see Perry pointing toward the trees ahead, the others gathering around him, clearly not seeing what he saw.

"What's a maven?" I asked Rowan urgently.

"Murderous raven. Where there's one, there's more."

Cries of recognition rang behind us. "Make for the tree line!" Gile shouted. "Or they'll swarm like flies!"

"Garland, kneel," Rowan urged, and the great stallion *woofed* his displeasure before sinking to one knee. Rowan helped me on and mounted after me. Garland rose with an uneasy stagger and Rowan kicked him into action.

Rowan wrapped one arm protectively around me, and we galloped toward the trees ahead as a flock of birds took flight. But these weren't starlings, or crows. They were the size of Garland's head, and when they screeched in an awful, hair-raising cacophony, their beaks parted to reveal sharp teeth.

The flock rose from the trees like an ominous cloud. A few broke from the murder and dove toward the nearest prey—us. We bent over Garland's neck, and Rowan whipped his cloak over my head just before a maven raked its claws across us. Garland screamed a war cry and Rowan hissed, blood drawn even through his sleeves.

We made it to the trees and dropped from the stallion. Garland's ears were pressed back and his eyes ringed with white as Rowan pulled him off the road. Behind us came Crackers, Wes perched precariously in the sleigh. A few mavens chased us under the frozen canopy, but the bigger problem was the murder we left behind.

Our men charged as fast as they could through the snow, but the mavens would be on them in seconds. My bow was drawn before I even thought about it, loosing as fast as I could at the storm of murderous birds. I could pick off a handful, but there were dozens, maybe hundreds.

"Cover your eyes!" Gile yelled, and our poor men ran as if

pelted in a hailstorm, but this hail had teeth and claws.

The mavens latched on to arms and hair and clothing, slicing and biting anything within reach. One of the brothers, Effer, paused to throw his attacker to the ground, but before he could stomp on the flapping body another collided with his face.

"Don't stop!" I cried, felling another terrible bird. "Over here!"

A stream of hot, red light blew by me. I ducked and yelled in surprise before realizing it was made by Rowan. The magic blasted through a layer of mavens and helped the last of our team cross the field into the tree line.

The frozen canopy prevented the mavens from falling on us like a plague of locusts, but they streamed through the trees, weaving through branches and dive-bombing from all directions. I was in a panic, swirling and shooting as Rowan helped the others get free of any mavens clung to their clothes like burrs. The mavens were quick as cats, fighting like bladed whirlwinds.

Garland reared and screamed, more dangerous than the birds if he kicked or crushed us. Crackers was tangled in his harness, sleigh caught between two trees. Blood ran from a myriad of scratches on Effer's face, one gash on his forehead streaming into his eye.

"We'll never get them all," I called in dismay.

"You don't have to," Gile panted, pulling out his war axe. "They'll start to eat their own, and we can move on."

"Archers, circle up," Rowan ordered. "Back to back! Protect the horses."

I took my place in the circle, along with Rowan, the brothers, Perry, and Fitzsimmons. A comforting chorus of *twangs* and *thuds* joined the terrible song of the mavens' screeching. Gile,

Wes, and Dedrick were our hunting dogs, killing the maimed and retrieving arrows.

"Slow and steady now," Rowan urged. "Stay in your section."

We settled into a rhythm. The adrenaline didn't fade, but my anxiety did. I took deep breaths and quickly found that place of quiet focus. Sight, pull, aim, release.

Slowly we pushed back the tide of incoming mavens. True to Gile's prediction, soon most weren't even interested in us, instead dropping to the ground like starlings after a rain and pulling apart the flesh of their dead kin. Their blood was black and sticky, mixing in the snow like a foul oil.

Dedrick sorted out Crackers, and Rowan calmed Garland. We moved on slowly, Rowan walking his prancing stallion with Perry and I on either side to clear the way. Then came the nervous pony and sleigh, flanked by the rest of the team. We made our way down the road, doing our best to pick off any mavens following overhead or hopping tree to tree. We couldn't get them all. Even hours later I spied wings far overhead, or the glitter of an angry eye peering at us behind a tree trunk.

We paused to clean our wounds and bandage Effer's forehead. I was the only one without injury, though my arm ached terribly from the strain of the bow. I wondered silently if my luck was a combination of Rowan's protection and simple good fortune, or if Soren had influence with the mavens. If he could control them like the wolf-panthers, perhaps he'd ordered them not to hurt me.

Perhaps Silaine wanted me brought to her unharmed.

Rowan continued to scout ahead and cover up our tracks behind. It may have been a futile precaution, but we couldn't be sure. Rowan didn't sense any more Fae presence beyond what already tailed us. We were disappointed to find Alair's curse didn't deflect all Fae magic, but Rowan felt confident it still worked against the Betrayer.

The sun had set and the gray clouds above were quickly darkening when we reached the first checkpoint on the witchlines. It was a knee-high stone alongside a narrow, frozen creek. Just beyond it stood a barn, which was to be our lodgings for the night. Workers from Briar had kept it in good condition, for expeditions such as ours.

Rowan kneeled before the stone and touched the carved symbol, which lit up in a golden glow. A corresponding symbol shone on the amulet. Elsewhere in Valeria, the other witchlines lit up in unison, perhaps even one by Ferras. If he was still at the Lorensile witchline he might press it, too, sending a signal back to his hopeful son.

I waited with Rowan while the others entered the barn to stable the horses and unload our supplies. Minutes dragged by. The heat of constant movement faded from me, and I shivered. The symbol remained as dark as an extinguished candle.

Finally I touched Rowan's shoulder. "I think we'd better get inside. If he touches the witchlines you'll see it on the amulet anyway."

"I know," Rowan said as he stood. "I just…" The worry of what might have befallen his father hung thick in the air. Rowan shook his head as if to clear his thoughts. He met my eyes. "How are you? Holding up okay?"

"Oh yes, I'm just grand," I joked as we walked to the barn. "Warm, well-rested, full up on entertainment and safety. If only I had my memories back, I'd be golden."

"Rose..." Rowan paused outside the doors. "What if you get your memory back and it's awful? There's a lot Grandfather couldn't tell you about because he wasn't there. When your family was killed. And Halen. What if it's a blessing not to remember?"

"It's better to know," I said without a moment's hesitation. "It's always better to know. I'd rather know what I've lost than—than live like Halen didn't even matter. I was going to *marry* him, Rowan. And I don't even know what he looked like. He was so important to me, and now he's just… erased."

Rowan shifted uncomfortably. He didn't like me talking about my first love.

I sighed. "How can I know who I am if I don't know where I've been? Who I've loved? If you were me... would you really rather not remember?"

"But you're still you. Just like how Grandfather always told me. You hunt and fight, and you're stubborn—" I smiled ruefully, but he was staring into the distance. "And if I knew somewhere in the past I'd watched you die, or—or something worse—"

My eyes narrowed. "Like what?"

Rowan seemed to remember himself. His eyes jumped to mine and then away again. "I don't know. I was just saying—"

"Like *what*, Rowan?" My voice was so sharp the muffled flow of conversation inside the barn faltered for a moment.

The look Rowan gave me was tinged with hurt. "Hey," he said softly. "I'm sorry. I don't know what it feels like to not remember parts of your life. I thought maybe it would be easier if you didn't want to remember, but clearly that was stupid. Grandfather always made it sound like your village didn't die easy. He wasn't there of course, but the bodies..."

A chill that had nothing to do with the wind started at my scalp and moved down to my knees. "Where are they buried?" I asked. "My family, I mean. And Halen. Or did the Fae..." I couldn't ask it.

Rowan thought for a moment. "Silaine buried the bodies at the castle. She used them to grow the thorns."

I remembered the terrible wall of thorns Soren and I passed under. How they parted for us and vanished as we left, like now that I was awake their purpose had been fulfilled. My nose stung. "Oh," I said. So I'd already seen my family's graves. They'd been protecting me, too, in their way. And I hadn't even known to say goodbye.

Rowan embraced me and I clung to him, head fitting in the crook of his neck. He held me for a minute, sadness and comfort flowing between us. "Come on," he finally said, and pulled open the door to the barn. "It's been a long day."

We joined the team. Perry worked the firepit, coaxing flames from twists of ancient hay and sticks of seasoned firewood stacked in one of the stalls. Gile showed me how to care for the horses, cleaning their hooves, rubbing liniment where needed, brushing their coats, and applying blankets for the night.

The brothers cooked slabs of frozen meat and boiled snow for tea. The rest of us laid out sleep rolls, or plugged chinks in the walls with more twists of hay. Between the fire and body heat the barn warmed slightly. It couldn't be called cozy, but compared to the icy air outside it felt almost tropical.

After filling our bellies with warm food and drink, the team settled down to complete small chores before dropping off to sleep. I mended the tears in my cloak that still hadn't been repaired from the gargrayle attack with Soren. Wes rubbed oil into Crackers' traces to keep them in good shape. Fitzsimmons strummed his lute, humming softly. Rowan and Gile recited a history of other expeditions, and the dangers they encountered.

“We’ll reach the mountain pass in three days,” Rowan said. “It was infested with gargrayles on the last run.”

“Not the last run,” Gile reminded him darkly. “We do not know what the last run found.”

“If Father’s in Lorensile, they made it through. We can, too.”

I yawned, and joined several others already tucked into their sleep rolls. Wes gave a loud snore, and Dedrick shoved him to turn over.

“We’re almost out of runed arrows,” I heard Gile say quietly after I finished arranging my blankets. “The mavens took most of our stock.”

Rowan sighed. “I’ll do what I can. Until then we’ll have to make due with regular arrows.”

I wondered how Rowan would manage to rune more arrows if we were constantly on the move. The process was still unclear to me—how long could it take to apply the symbols to the shafts, and let the blue glow of magic fill them? If they couldn’t be made with other people around, Rowan would be hard pressed to find the space, time, and safety to go about his mysterious task.

Conversation dried up, and Gile and Rowan joined the rest of us on the floor. With nothing else to do I concentrated on summoning up the stored thoughts from my mind that didn’t want to be found. My memories were as shards in a bowl, and I sifted through each broken piece with care:

Running through a forest alive with light. Pine needles on the ground. Slippers made of deerskin. I could feel rocks through them, and roots. They kept my feet clean but I could still move, nimble and graceful. The person with me was not so capable. He stomped through the forest, but he had city boy’s boots, shiny and new. He chased after me.

Laughter.

I opened my eyes to stare at the vented apex of the barn. A dying echo rang in my ears. Halen's laughter. We were always laughing. I closed my eyes and nestled into the blankets further.

If only I could see his face. Then I would remember everything. If I could only recall the one person who had been so important to me, I could—

Rose.

I flinched awake, having almost dropped off with the half-seen memory floating in my head. Wind moaned against the barn's walls. I waited, body tensed, for that whisper to come again. Was Soren outside, here to lure me away with more confusion and empty promises?

Nothing happened. It must have been the echo of a dream. I pulled the blankets over my head, willing myself to sleep and remember only good things. My first, young love, and the summer we met. Laughing together, and running in the woods. The closeness we must have felt, the feel of his mouth on mine.

The only kiss I could remember still haunted me.

"Are you Halen?"

"No," he said, eyes full of honey and sadness. "But I wish I was."

Why not say yes? Why not pretend to be the prince I fell in love with? Why would Soren tell the truth about that one thing among all the other lies he spun?

I pulled my thoughts away from the Betrayer, and begged myself for more memories.

None came.

FOURTEEN

The next day was far worse than the first.

My hips and legs ached, unused to walking so many miles at once. A storm rose, pelting us with ice. Under hats and hoods we wrapped scarves around our heads, and my eyes squinted closed against the driving sleet more often than they were open. The sleigh stuck frequently in uneven drifts, and digging it out was a thankless chore.

Conversation was impossible, so there were no distractions from the misery. Any reasonable creature would hole up and wait out the storm, and perhaps they did. We encountered no beasts that day.

As night approached it became clear that we wouldn't reach the next checkpoint on the witchlines without slogging through darkness. Even though the storm had stopped, we were exhausted from fighting it. Rowan found a hut built into the side of a hill with a lean-to nearby for the horses. Gile chopped through the ice coating the door, and we filed in gratefully.

Inside was a time capsule, a home abandoned after the family fled Silaine's curse of winter. I touched the earthenware cups and plates left behind, and smelled the mummified wreath of garlic over the window. It could have been my family's home. I wondered what would be left if I ever saw it again.

The next day temperatures rose, and the fresh snow turned porous and crunchy. Water dripped like rain in the trees, running down grand icicles. When freezing winds came again, everything that melted would become ice.

We had left the land of fields and farming behind. The kingsroad wound through forest, passing villages and the rare city before diving into woods again. The change in weather made it easier for us to move around, but gave the same advantage to our enemies.

Sometime after our midday meal, Rowan returned from scouting ahead. He rode past Gile and Fitzsimmons, currently escorting Crackers, and pulled Garland up at my side. Rowan showed me the amulet, pulsing with a red glow like a heartbeat.

"It's the Betrayer," he said, voice tight. "He's near."

My heart jumped. Soren. Would he show himself? Would he speak to me? I looked all around us as if I could spy him lurking in the forest.

"Rose…" I looked up at Rowan. His brow was furrowed. "You'll remember your promise?"

"Of course," I said, stomach twisting. The guilt of Alair's death was a bruise on my heart, always there, always aching. I wouldn't abandon Rowan for Soren. No matter what he said.

Someone cried out.

Rowan and I looked at the men trailing behind us, who had also turned to see what caused the cry. Wes was the last man on the road, nothing behind him. But that was the problem.

"It's Perry!" Wes shouted. "He's gone!"

Rowan spurred Garland to a trot, and I ran to join the others gathering around Wes. He pointed to a spray of red blood on the snow in the ditch.

"Something… something grabbed him."

The brothers, Effer and Bremmer, pulled out hunting knives and dove into the trees. Wes and Dedrick followed, and I would have, too, but for Rowan. He'd dismounted, and grabbed my arm. “Wait,” he hissed. “We don’t know what’s out there.”

Between the drifts and branches laden with snow, our men were soon lost among the trees. I drew my bow, heart in my throat. We heard a scream, and shouts of fear and anger. Sudden movement in the shadows made me raise my bow, but it was Effer and Bremmer running back to us. Dedrick and Wes followed, but Wes was limping heavily.

“Move, move,” Effer shouted. “It’s big! Get some distance!”

We backed away, but before we turned to run I saw the thing tailing Wes.

“Hold!” I called, notching an arrow. “It’s here!”

Wes gained the road, and the monster followed. It was as tall as three men, coal-black, and shaggy. It walked on two feet, with clawed hands like a man. The beast had the face of a goat and the snarling snout of a wolf. Twin horns spiraled from its head. The stench of carrion blew towards us on the wind. Alien, red eyes looked up from its quarry.

It saw me.

I released an arrow. It should have hit the creature square in the chest but it somehow… missed.

The creature bellowed, and with a few quick steps it gained on Wes, and swiped a claw across his back. The one-eyed man sprawled forward, blood streaking the snow. The monster stepped over him, red tongue lolling.

It was looking right at me. It wanted me. And I knew, deep down, it was sent to capture me.

I shot another arrow, only to have another bewildering miss. A blue-runed arrow flew from my left, but it just grazed the creature’s shoulder. As it screamed in rage, someone pulled me backwards. I hadn’t realized I’d stopped retreating, or that everyone else was behind me.

"Rose, run!" It was Rowan, and as we fled the men closed ranks after us, bows drawn, weapons out.

"I couldn't hit it," I yelled to him. "We need more blue arrows!"

The creature's bellow mixed with a shout of human pain. I looked back—Dedrick lay crumpled on the side of the road as if thrown. Effer loaded a crossbow as Bremmer slashed at the creature with a short sword, but he could only ward off those grasping claws. His blade might have been made of wood for all the damage it did.

Gile and Fitzsimmons had reached us now. Gile ran past Rowan and I, axe in hand, as Fitz sighted a runed arrow. He hit the creature's shoulder, but it only gave another bellow before pulling the arrow out. Effer was so close his crossbow couldn't miss, but his non-magicked bolt only glanced off the creature's chest.

"Rowan, get them blue arrows," I shouted. "It wants me—I'll distract it!"

"No, wait!"

But he couldn't catch me. I sprinted to the sleigh and pulled my sword from the back.

As I ran past him again, Rowan shot an arc of red magic at the monster. It took no notice, backhanding Bremmer and grabbing Effer, quick as a spider. It lifted him in one hand and reached the other toward his head—it was going to rip his head off!

"Hey!" I yelled, waving my arms and the sword sheath in the air. "I'm over here! Look at me!"

The monster looked up. Red eyes met mine.

I pulled my sword free, and the blade seemed to flash in the light. I dropped the sheath so I could use both hands. "Come and get me," I called, backing off the road into the ditch.

The monster dropped Effer and stepped toward me, slaver dangling from its jaws. Gile circled, waiting for an opening.

"Blue arrows!" I called. "Only use blue!"

I couldn't spare a glance to see if the others took heed. Those red eyes held mine as if the creature were entranced. It loomed over me, knees bent and arms spread, like a child cornering a rabbit.

Suddenly it darted forward and reached as if to grab me about the torso. I slashed down with my sword and it howled, pulling back claws dripping black fluid. Unlike Bremmer's blade, mine could actually cut it.

Thunk, thunk. Two blue-runed arrows hit the monster above its right hip, one right after the other. It bellowed, back arching in pain.

I saw my chance.

Before the creature could recover, I ran forward, piercing its shaggy belly and drawing my blade sideways. Wormy gray guts spilled, steaming, to the trampled snow. The monster screamed.

Its left hand swiped my shoulder as it grabbed for its wounded stomach. I stumbled, falling sideways to the ground, where I dragged and kicked myself forward to get out of the creature's reach, pulling my sword along one-handed.

The monster fell to its knees and keened. As I climbed to my feet another blue-runed arrow sunk into its shoulder. It made a pitiful bleat of pain. Those red eyes locked with mine as it fell to its unharmed side. Black, shaggy arms stretched out to me, claws still grasping. It panted, whining with each breath.

I circled around those arms as the others ran up. Gile slammed his axe against the back of the creature's neck, but it only whimpered. There was something special about my sword that let it harm this creature when regular blades couldn't. Perhaps it was magicked, same as the runed arrows.

Both hands on the grip once more, I stabbed the sword down through the monster's neck. It gurgled, hands convulsing, then was finally still.

I tugged my sword free. The sapphire on the hilt had turned gold, and gently glowed. My confusion at this was interrupted when Gile clapped a hand on my shoulder, and by the time I looked back, the sapphire was plain blue again.

"That's another one, Princess," he panted. "You must think we're great bloody fools if we need *you* to rescue *us* all the time."

"No, it's just… it wanted me," I tried to explain, but then Rowan was there.

"Are you all right?" His dark eyes searched my face, hands on my cheeks, then my shoulders. "Are you hurt?"

"I'm okay," I nodded, but as the adrenaline faded I felt a handful of small complaints. A scratch on my cheek, a bruised hip from the fall. "Nothing serious. The others…?"

Dedrick lay in the snow like a thrown doll. Bremmer and Effer were ambulatory, but there was no sign of Perry.

Gile strode toward Bremmer's body, but when I tried to follow, Rowan held me back. "I…" He seemed at a loss for words.

"Are you mad?" I suggested. Once again I hadn't listened to him, exposing myself to more danger instead of retreating. But if I hadn't, then who knows how many more bodies would be laying in the snow?

"Yes. No." He shook his head. "I have to accept you're good in a fight. How did you know it wanted you?"

The compliment warmed me. "The way it looked at me. I

just knew."

"And your sword…"

I held up the blade, its end dripping with dark fluid. "It must be enhanced like your arrows, to harm Fae."

Rowan pursed his lips, considering. "Lucky we have it, then," he finally said. "I didn't know Silaine could make creatures my magic couldn't touch."

I remembered how his streak of red energy washed over the monster harmlessly. There was something interesting there, a thought I couldn't quite harness.

"I'm just glad you're okay." Rowan's eyes searched mine, and I wasn't sure what he was looking for.

"Come on," I said, pulling his arm to follow me. "Let's regroup."

I cleaned my blade and recovered its dropped sheath. Gile determined Dedrick was still breathing, just unconscious. Wes was scratched deeply on his right leg and across his back, blood staining his shirt and trousers red. The brothers thanked me for saving Effer's life, and searched the woods for Perry.

As Fitzsimmons guided Crackers back toward the scene of the battle, Bremmer and Effer returned, dragging Perry between them.

He was dead.

"Ah, lad," Gile sighed, closing Perry's unseeing eyes. The monster had broken his neck. A quick death, everyone said, but that didn't make it any better. I liked Perry. He was young, easygoing, and eager to please. And now he was dead because he'd chosen to follow Rowan and I. Because he believed in us.

I tried to repress my tears like the men around me seemed able to, but they fell anyway as Gile and Fitzsimmons loaded Perry's body and an unconscious Dedrick onto the sleigh. I leaned into Rowan, who wrapped an arm around me until Gile began helping Wes remove his layers so they could treat his wounds.

"I have to go," Rowan said regretfully. I followed him to Garland, to give Wes some privacy.

"Be careful," I said as he mounted up, wrapping my cloak around myself. "There could be more monsters about. Do you want my sword?"

"No, I'll be okay. You keep it. Protect the others." He winked, and I gave a small smile.

Secretly I was glad to keep the sword at my side. It had been a good friend to me. I was starting to suspect the sword was enchanted with more than just an ability to harm Fae creatures. I wasn't an experienced sword fighter, but three times now the sword had helped me kill a monster. When I wielded it my arms seemed to know what to do. I felt powerful, I felt… safe.

Rowan galloped off to begin another cycle of scouting. I pet Crackers and calmed his nerves until Wes was bandaged and dressed in fresh clothing. Dedrick woke up, pupils dilated and complaining of a headache. Everyone agreed he wasn't out of danger yet, but he refused to ride on the sleigh with Perry's body.

We trudged away from the scene of the battle, trusting that Rowan could follow our trail to catch up with us. He was away for longer than usual. Dark anxiety spread like a vine in my chest, but eventually he rode out of the wood, saddlebags full again with the mysterious blue-runed arrows.

He passed the bags to Gile before approaching me. "I need to show you something," he said, expression dark.

Perhaps he would finally reveal the secret behind the Fae-killing arrows.

Bremmer gave me a knee up. I climbed aboard Garland,

taking my now-familiar place in front of Rowan. One arm curled around me, and I held it in place while my other hand grasped Garland's withers. By the time the trees broke to reveal a small town at the base of a hill, our fingers had entwined.

The buildings were half collapsed with snow and ice, but a little church still stood at the top of the hill. Garland carried us up the spiral path, back over tracks he'd laid earlier. We dismounted at the church, and I saw how the hill looked down over the road where we'd fought the monster.

Rowan pointed. Boot prints lined the snow, fresh from some pacing stranger.

"It's the Betrayer," Rowan said quietly. "He's following us."

FIFTEEN

That night we settled in a snow-ravaged village, gathering any dry wood we could find to collect enough for Perry's funeral pyre. He burned on the furniture of folk long gone, wrapped in the ancient bedding of strangers.

In the absence of a suitable building we slept in tents. I went to set my sleeping roll beside Rowan's, only to be turned away by Gile. "You'll sleep alone, princess," he stated with a knowing smile.

"That means I have to heat a tent all by myself," I protested.

"We'll load you up with hot stones," he said. "I'm a man of propriety."

"Rowan's *family*," I grumbled.

Gile raised one auburn eyebrow. "Not by blood."

I turned away before he could see how that made me blush, and stomped off to find an unoccupied tent. I threw in my roll and lay down my sword. There. That was all I owned in the world.

After a somber dinner I gathered the hot stones I was promised and arranged them around my bedding. I nestled down and tried to sleep, but Gile's comments returned to torment me.

He was right—I called Rowan family, but there was no blood tie between us. We hadn't even grown up together as cousins might. Instead we were bonded by complicated and overlapping ties of duty and shared dreams. Many people cared for each other in those ways.

But I couldn't convince myself that my feelings for Rowan were completely chaste and platonic. He was too interesting to look at, tall and dark and brooding. He was powerful, and passionate, and dedicated to me. I had found comfort in his arms, and safety. Our hands kept finding each other. Each time it felt pure, a simple meeting of the hearts… or perhaps I was fooling myself.

I called him family. But what were husbands and wives, if not family? It didn't have to mean blood. It could mean love, and connection. A shared history. A mutual passion.

I had planned to be family with my lost beloved. It felt disloyal to explore romantic feelings with someone else when my first love remained unrecovered. Perhaps when I remembered Halen I would be aghast at these feelings.

Surely my heart broke when I lost him. That heartbreak was still mine, a terrible possession I longed to hold. I needed it to fly home to me, to claw open my chest and resume residence in my body.

Unknown, I was incomplete.

I traced the sapphire on my sword's hilt and begged the gods for my memories of Halen. I fell asleep with my prayers unanswered.

Rose.

The word rushed through my mind like a perfumed wind. I felt the need behind the call, the pining loneliness, the tender ache, but I couldn't answer. A force kept my eyes glued shut, and for an instant I feared I was trapped in sleep again, but then the air changed. There was warmth and the fresh, unbelievable scent of roses. I floated.

My eyes finally opened and I found myself in a dream. I stood by a pool of dark water in a grove of willow trees. Their canopies were lost in the shadow of night, but tiny lights glowed in the grass at their feet. I watched in amazement as the lights rose from the ground and flew about, bright orbs that lit the grove like candles in a room.

I moved as if swimming in honey, body distant and slow, mind foggy. A thought drifted lazily by—this was an enchantment. I clenched my eyes shut and screamed in my head, but could not make it go away.

Then came the sudden awareness that I was not alone.

My heart beat loud as a drum, and all thought faded as Soren emerged from a curtain of willow branches.

He was *here.* The murderer who attacked us today. The Betrayer so terrible my brother killed himself rather than see me fall into his hands. He wore a red and gold tunic, shadowy cape ruffling behind him, and his face... On his face he bore no scars.

Soren walked toward me. I stepped backward and the world tipped over as I tripped and fell in slow motion to the grass. The long, lush blades pushed between my fingers, but I snatched my hands away.

"What have you done?" I asked, unsure if I spoke aloud or not. "Send me back!"

"You haven't gone anywhere." He smiled with sad, golden eyes. "It's a dream. The only way we could meet."

"End it," I said with as much force as I could, jarring the grove's tranquility. "Let me go."

"I will, but I have to talk to you first. I want to help you."

He continued to approach. I rose to my feet easily, noticing the dream had placed me in a red velvet dress.

"Help?" I echoed, panic and anger silting away against my will. "You tried to kill us today."

Soren nodded sadly. "I was ordered to. That's what I'm trying to tell you—Rose, you mustn't continue north. The chance I once had to save you is gone now. Silaine has given me strict orders, to kill your men and take you prisoner. Every step you take makes it harder not to do that."

He was so calm, his eyes so earnest. This was the boy I had trusted, who made me doubt what my family told me. I mustn't fall for the same trap. Not when I'd promised Rowan. Not when I knew what he'd done, what he *was*.

"You're a liar," I said, reciting Rowan's words. "My brother is dead because of you."

Soren's mouth firmed. "Alair did that to himself. I didn't want him to die. He could never accept that I want to help you. That I *can*."

I struggled to recall the terrible things Alair and Rowan told me about Soren. "You haven't done one thing to help except wake me up. And that was only so you could take me to your mistress."

"Just listen." Every few moments he took another step closer, and I was too disoriented to keep retreating. "You can't hope to sneak into Avalon on your own. I'm the only one who could take you safely to the portal. And only when the time is right. You believed me at Briar, can't you trust me again?"

At Briar… I shook my head to clear my muddled thoughts. "No. Alair told me what you did." The lights in the grove flickered. I used the words Alair had spoken. "You were a coward. You betrayed everyone."

His golden eyes darkened. "Rose, please. I can explain—"

I thought of Rowan, and held on to my promise. "You killed

your country, and brought your own people to slaughter."

The shadows around us grew darker as the lights dimmed. "Please, don't—"

With every ounce of strength I had, I defied him. "You sold the world for your own pathetic life."

"Lies," he said, a storm growing on his face. "All lies!"

Every floating light vanished. Suddenly the grove was a desolate, terrifying place, and a rushing filled my ears.

Soren grabbed my arm as the dream disintegrated, shouting across the wind, "It was for you!"

I jerked awake with a gasp, blankets tangled around my neck. I tore free and grabbed my sword. It shocked me like a static pulse and I cried out. The sapphire in the hilt glowed gold for a moment, then faded.

I stared at the sword in the dimness of my tent, at the gem that had glowed like… like the lights in the grove. Like Soren's eyes. I tossed it away from me and took deep breaths.

It was for you.

I tugged my boots on, slung a blanket across my shoulders, and ventured out into the night. The cooking fire had quieted to orange coals. In the distance, Gile's silhouette stood before the blazing funeral pyre. I snuck around the other tents until I reached Rowan's.

"Rowan?" I crouched at the entrance and tapped on the oiled animal skin. "Rowan, are you there?"

A cough. "Yes. Hold on." He untied the flap and pushed it open, eyes bleary with sleep. "What's wrong?"

"Let me in. I need to tell you something."

Rowan scooted out of the way and I crawled in beside him. The air was musty from blankets, faintly humid from Rowan's breathing.

"What is it?" he asked. "What's happened?"

"I had a dream. About Soren." Between us, a tensing of the air. "But it wasn't really a dream, it was… like an enchantment, or a vision. Soren said he wanted to help, that he had to tell me something—"

"What have I told you about listening to him?" Rowan demanded in a fierce whisper. "You promised you wouldn't—"

"I *know*," I hissed. "I'm just telling you what happened. *Listen*." We both took a breath to temper our frustrations, and I started again. "Soren said he's been ordered to kill everyone and take me prisoner, but he doesn't want to. He said we should go home now before it's too late."

"Did you tell him our plan?"

"Of course not! But he guessed half of it. He said there was no way we'd sneak into Avalon, and he was the only one who could take me, but only when the time was right."

"And what did you say?"

"I... I told him I didn't believe him, and I reminded him of all the things he's done, and he got mad, and the dream ended."

"Rose." Rowan rubbed his face. "This is very bad. How could he bring you into an enchantment? I wouldn't even know how—The amulet should have—"

I swallowed, but kept my silence. Maybe I should have mentioned the glowing sapphire on my sword, but I didn't want Rowan deciding I had to stop carrying it. That sword was one of our only reliable weapons against Silaine's beasts. It probably had nothing to do with Soren, and just lit up whenever it detected Fae magic.

Rowan finally gathered his thoughts. "Well, I don't know what game he's playing at, but if he doesn't want us going north then there's nothing else I'd rather do."

I didn't feel as certain. "Rowan…" I bit my lip. This was going to be a hard conversation, for many reasons. But I had to know. "When I first woke up, Soren thought I'd remember him. He seemed devastated that I didn't. He treated me like he knew me, like he cared about me. I even asked him if he was Halen because he felt so… Familiar."

I closed my eyes, remembering the energy between us. The clarity in my heart that said I could trust him, despite everything I'd been told.

"Why didn't he just lie, and say he was Halen, or pretend to be him from the beginning? He tried to take me somewhere, and Silaine sent the gargrayles to correct him. Why would he do that if he weren't trying to help? He could have led me to her like a lamb to slaughter, but he didn't." I opened my eyes to meet Rowan's sorrowful gaze. "I'm not going to break my promise. My loyalty is to you. But I have to know. Who was he, before? Did I know him?"

Rowan took my hands, holding them between us. He looked deep into my eyes. "Soren is what we told you. A noble who chose to become *damnsoír.* A Betrayer who helped Silaine kill thousands of people."

My heart broke just a little bit more. "Is it so impossible that he could be trying to help us?"

"Maybe he is," Rowan allowed. "But we could never be sure he wouldn't turn on us in an instant. We can't trust him."

I nodded, and Rowan released my hands. "Okay. But is he right about the portals? Are you sure we can get to them without Silaine finding us?"

"No," Rowan admitted. "I'm not sure. Just as I'm not sure we can make it to my father alive. We know very little about Silaine's domain. She's built a fortress, and the portals are somewhere outside its walls. It may take everything we have to find them. Everything," he emphasized. "And everyone."

The gravity of our mission fell on me harder than ever before. The journey to the portals had been vague in my mind, something to be undertaken after we survived the rescue for Ferras. I'd been counting on Rowan's magic to hide us, or at least him and I. But we had recently seen that his powers had unexpected limits when it came to the Fae.

"Rowan, why did the runed arrows work on the monster when your magic couldn't? Isn't it all erdwitch magic?"

He shifted uncomfortably. "It's complicated. Remember that Maeve shared her powers with Grandfather. We have erdwitch power, but it lives in human bodies. It's a hybrid magic, the first of its kind. Grandfather studied it his whole life. We use our powers in ways the erdwitches don't, or at least won't."

His answer was interesting, but Rowan's reluctance to discuss specifics regarding the blue-runed arrows still bothered me. "How do you make the arrows, anyway?" I asked casually. "You don't just apply runes to regular arrows. You leave, and come back with bags of them. How is that possible? What are they made of?"

"They're… It's…"

I waited while Rowan floundered, consternation growing by the moment. "Why won't you just tell me?"

His sigh held notes of both frustration and defeat. "It's complicated. I made a promise. It has nothing to do with you, though," he reassured me quickly. "I swear. It's just… dangerous, and I don't want you involved. Can you trust me on this?"

I pushed down the panic that came with the knowledge Rowan was keeping secrets. *Could* I trust him? Rowan had never misled me, except on this issue, and apparently that was due to a prior promise. Who would have made him promise? Alair? But to what purpose?

Rowan waited, silently giving me space to process my thoughts. I took a deep breath, considering my options. I could demand he tell me anyway, or order him to, as his future queen. I discarded both strategies as childish, unworthy of our friendship. He said it had nothing to do with me. Who could I trust, if not Rowan? There was no one else.

Finally, I nodded. "Does it hurt you?"

The tightness in his shoulders eased. "No," he said softly. "It doesn't hurt me."

"Good." I tried to recall the point I'd been working toward before the secret of the arrows distracted me. "Soren keeps saying a human army can't stand against Silaine. Even your erdwitch powers may not be able to help. But my… my birth father, the old king… he was raising an army to fight Silaine. And she partnered with the Usurper rather than face him. He had the magic of the Aerendels, right? Magic she must have feared."

Rowan looked confused as to my point. "I suppose… Her forces were smaller then, though."

"Oh, right. But the Aerendels were still supposed to have magic, so… shouldn't I have it, too?"

Rowan tilted his head. "I don't know. Grandfather never mentioned it."

"Isn't there something you can do to help me find my powers, if I have any? And teach me to use them? We may need them to reach Avalon."

“We can try, I guess.”

I didn’t understand his reluctance. The idea that I may have magic of my own, magic that could help us, lifted my hopes, and filled me with excitement and purpose.

“But even if you do have human magic, I may not be able to help you with it. It could end up being more dangerous than useful.”

I nodded quickly. “That’s okay. I just want to know.”

“If you do have any powers, the first thing we should try to figure out is how to stop the Betrayer from contacting you. He can’t get near you physically because of the amulet, so he’s going to try to convince you to go to him.”

My heart sank a little. “Oh. I wouldn’t—I mean, I promised—”

“I know, but… If he starts to sway you, you must tell me, Rose.” He put a hand on my arm. “Just tell me what he said and I’ll tell you why he’s wrong. Promise?”

It was the same thing Alair asked of me, to bring him my doubts and confusions. I knew it was right, but I still dreaded to betray the truths I felt inside me, no matter how misguided Rowan professed them to be. Reluctantly I said, “I promise.”

Rowan sat back. “Good.”

For half a minute we sat in silence. My eyelids grew heavy. I wanted to stay with Rowan instead of walking back through the cold to my own chilly tent, but Gile’s shift would eventually end, and he’d need his bed back. Just as I opened my mouth to tell him goodnight, Rowan spoke.

“Rickard was right, you know.” Rowan’s voice was quiet and low, a confession only enabled by the darkness. “Grandfather would be so disappointed if he knew what I’d done. Changed his plan. Risked you on this journey. Sometimes

I wonder if this is the biggest mistake of my life. But I know what I saw. I'm sorry Rose, but I can't... I can't sacrifice my Father. I know I should, but I just… can't."

"Don't apologize to me. Family is everything. What kind of person would you be if—" The words caught in my throat.

"If I chose you over him?" Rowan finished my thought. "If I chose my duty over my personal feelings?"

It was what we should have done, with the stakes this high. A proper queen would choose the longer, safer path, over this impromptu rescue plan with a nebulous bid to save the world tacked on the end. But I wasn't queen yet.

My hand found Rowan's, almost of its own accord. "I chose this, too."

His other hand brushed my cold cheek like a warm ember. "Yes. So stay with me, Rose. Trust me. Keep choosing me."

My heart fluttered. "I will. I promise."

Then it was time to go. Before my heart could add another complication to its tangled web of desires and loyalties.

I rushed back to my tent, breath leaving plumes of fog in the wintry night that faded into nothingness. A natural kind of magic. And tomorrow, perhaps I could make my own.

Maybe then I would find out where those runed arrows truly came from.

SIXTEEN

The next morning Rowan and I rode Garland ahead of the group to find a place where we could have some privacy until the others caught up.

We peeled off the kingsroad onto a snowy inlet by a frozen river. After dismounting we stood by the ice, hemmed in by trees and the high bank on the other side. The little pocket of space must have been lovely in summer. Trees shading the river, tall grasses swishing in the wind, and a lazy river with cool, fresh water to wade or swim in.

I was thoroughly sick of winter. Today's clouds were high and thin instead of low and pregnant. A few dry snowflakes floated down, but I pointed my face towards the ground. I would not let them touch my lips, would not feel that phantom kiss again. Not when I was near Rowan.

We faced each other, awkward and uncertain. Rowan bent down and packed a snowball between mittened hands. He rolled it over and over while we talked, sometimes tossing it lightly in the air before catching it again.

Needing something to do, I snapped a stick from the frozen bushes and worked at peeling off the bark.

"Let's begin. You can do sums in your head, right?" Rowan asked.

I raised an eyebrow. "A few."

My mother knew her letters, but had been determined that her children wouldn't struggle at reading like she did. She made

Alair or I read to the family nearly every night, and we swapped books and pamphlets with other villages and during the festival at Lorensile. Even Maeve brought us books, come to think of it. Tales for children, and histories, and treatises on sums.

It startled me to realize Maeve had quietly ensured her secret princess would grow up somewhat educated.

"You know when you have two numbers, and you add them in your head, and when you get the answer you *know* it's correct?"

I nodded hesitantly.

"That's sort of what using magic feels like. It's *knowing*. It's… Imagine raising your right arm. Don't do it, just imagine it. You *know* how to raise your arm. Thinking and doing are different things, but you still know how. And then when you actually want to…"

Clutching the stick in my left, I lifted my right hand up in the air.

"Exactly. Make sense?"

"No," I admitted. "I don't know how to go from knowing to doing."

Rowan pursed his lips. "I'm sorry. It came so easy to me. It's another sense, another limb. Invisible, untouchable, but… there."

We frowned at each other, seeing the distance between us, yet unable to cross it.

"I've never felt anything like that," I admitted, discarding a strip of bark to the snow. "If it's an extra arm, I've never moved it. Not even accidentally. Is that possible?"

"Perhaps… Sometimes using magic feels easy. Natural. Like moving your eyes to look at something, or sneezing. Other times it's like whistling. Do you remember learning to whistle?"

I brightened. “Yes! My father was an expert. He could imitate almost every bird, and we could hear him whistle to call us home from miles away.”

“But when you were learning, I bet you couldn’t do it immediately. You had all the right parts, and the right motivation, but you still had to practice to make the right sounds.”

“You’re saying my magic might be a skill like whistling. Some could figure it out on their own, but others may never know they have the ability until someone teaches them.”

“Exactly.” Rowan grinned.

I was less enthused. “So now I just have to figure out how to whistle without ever hearing someone else do it.”

“Let’s focus on a specific action,” Rowan suggested. “Try to amplify your voice. It feels like…” He trailed off, at a loss for a comparison.

“Shouting?”

“No, it doesn’t happen in my throat. It happens…” He gestured vaguely. “Out there. I tell the air to be louder. No, that’s not it. I tell anybody listening to hear it louder.”

“...That doesn’t help me.”

Rowan scuffed the snow at our feet, and tried again. “It’s like reaching out with invisible arms and *pulling* the air tighter. But in everyone’s ears, all at once.”

“Got it. So if I were trying to do it now, I should picture two invisible arms pulling the air tight by your ears. Which is definitely something regular arms can do.”

Rowan laughed at his inadequate metaphors. “Try this. Come here.” He stepped forward, and my stomach fluttered as he pulled off my mittens. He took one of my hands and placed it on his throat. The other he held to his heart. “Close your eyes.

Try to feel this."

I did as he asked. I concentrated on detecting any change beneath my palms, any new sensation in my fingers.

"I'm doing it now," he said. His voice was louder than normal, but not painfully so. I shook my head. "How about now?" A whisper, as if sighed into my ears.

It reminded me of Soren, and I pulled my hands away. "It's not working. Sorry."

Rowan demonstrated different displays of magic, but nothing brushed against my senses in a way that gave me insight into replicating his abilities. I could feel magic, sometimes, like the tingle when he lit the witchlines, or the pressure when Alair stormed out of Briar to confront Soren. But it was like watching someone dance when you were born without legs. I recognized dancing when I saw it, but couldn't step to the beat myself.

"What if I don't have any magic?" I asked after another failed attempt. I meant it to sound casual, but desperation quavered in my voice anyway. "What if I can't go through the portal to Avalon? What if all this has been for nothing?"

"As long as you're a child of the Aerendel line, you'll be able to use the portal," Rowan reassured me. "And Maeve says you are. So even if you didn't inherit any powers, or there were none left to inherit, you can still reach Avalon. Do you want to try again?"

"No," I sighed. "It's pointless."

Rowan had tied Garland to the trunk of a thin tree. The stallion lipped through the nearby bushes, seeking anything edible and finding only ice and dead stems. I walked to his side and patted his flank. Garland's ears flicked back to me once, but he was intent on his futile search.

I leaned against his warm haunch, and sighed. It was time to return to our party and continue the journey north, but I didn't want to. It was nice to spend time with Rowan, working on something together. Tension and sadness filled too many of our conversations lately.

"Isn't there anything you can do to check if I even have powers?" I asked as Rowan undid Garland's ties. "You're part erdwitch. Can't they sense magic?"

The stallion pushed his nose against Rowan forcefully, and Rowan patted his head. "Hold on, boy. Stay here a minute." He draped the reins over a branch and gestured for me to step away with him. "That's an excellent question. I can sense Fae magic, so why not human magic?"

I nodded hopefully. Rowan studied my face, but his eyes were unfocused, reaching for something inside himself. He lifted a hand, tentative. In answer I closed my eyes, and leaned into his touch.

Rowan ran his fingers over my face. Up into my hair, down the sides of my cheeks, his hands on my neck sliding out to my shoulders. His palm pressed to the space just under my collar bones, and I wondered if he felt the wild pace of my heart.

"There's something there," he murmured. "Something…"

I opened my eyes. Rowan's were closed, face tilted up as if listening for a tune on the wind.

"Here," he said, and slowly turned me around. My breath caught as he stepped up behind me, chest pressed against my back. Rowan lay the left side of his face against my right cheek and temple. "Don't be afraid," he whispered, warm breath tickling my neck. His hands ran down my arms and left goosebumps in their wake. "I'm only going to show you what's inside yourself. What you do with it is up to you."

"You trust me?" I asked, voice shaking as he took my hands

and lifted them. He folded our arms across my chest and pulled me close. I smelled the wool of his cloak, the foresty musk of his skin.

"Yes," he said, and then a miracle happened.

Heat bloomed in my chest and flushed through my whole body. The blackness behind my eyes turned white for one shining moment. Something moved through me, then out of me, and it was everything Rowan described—an invisible limb stretching forward, a song finally sung, a knowing both intuitive and certain.

I cried out, and then it was over. Rowan's arms released me, and with him left the magic. My vision cleared in an instant. "What happened?"

"Look down."

Where I stood, the snow had melted. A vibrant layer of lush, emerald moss sprouted in a circle around my boots. A handful of tiny pink flowers bloomed on delicate stalks no thicker than the lines on my palm.

"Oh," I breathed and sank to a crouch to observe my personal garden.

They were the first living green things I'd seen since awakening. I wanted to scoop up the spot and carry it around in my pocket. I touched the flowers with petals thin as breath. Already the cold stole their life away. But I'd made something green. I'd transformed the cursed snow into something good.

I had magic.

"That was... strange," Rowan said. Stepping carefully away from my miracle, I turned to see him regard me with squinting eyes. "I could pull power through you, like water through a straw, but there's no opening for you to spill the water out yourself."

I reached for that hot core in my chest, tried to stretch that previously unknown limb… and found nothing.

My hand clutched at my chest as though I could take hold of my heart. I tried to remember the *knowing*, but it was like thinking of a sunset versus seeing one. I couldn't summon the colors, the brightness, the awe. There was just… nothing.

Devastated, I asked Rowan, "What's wrong with me?"

He shook his head. "I don't know. Maybe Grandfather would have some idea. Maybe when we get to Shalimar we'll find something in one of his books that explains it. I'm sorry, Rose, I just don't know enough."

I nodded, trying not to feel heartbroken. I had magic, after all. That was a victory. And even though Rowan said it didn't matter, I felt reassured that if—when—we got to the portals, they would open for me.

Rowan had brought a single journal of Alair's with him, more by accident than planning. He gave it to me that night, hoping it might help me understand the context of human magic within the overall system of existence.

I read by the light of the cooking fire, perhaps later than I should. My brother's handwriting was elegant and steady. No inkblots marred the pages. I grieved for another part of my brother I would never know—the philosopher, the historian, the sorcerer.

This world was made by dreams of the gods, his journal told me, and magic is the name we use for the substance of those dreams. Magic is the force knitting the world together. It is in everything, and everyone, but only certain beings can channel it.

Fae were the first children of the gods. More like nightmares, in my opinion. They used magic as a toy, but had small capacity to carry it, and little reason to use it. It was in the nature of the first Fae to play and gambol, to dance through the world that was their playground. Only later did they become powerful, their souls expanding in knowledge and increasing their capacity to pull magic from the universe itself. And, of course, they had many more years of life to study it.

Then came the erdwitches. Alair hypothesized their creation was a reaction to the Fae, a byproduct of nature balancing itself. Erdwitches are not, strictly speaking, creatures like the Fae or humans. They emerge from the ground fully formed, with all the knowledge of those who came before. Alair likened them to shearing a piece of rock from a mountainside—the rock was part of the mountain, and once separated is considered its own entity. But unlike rocks, erdwitches can rejoin their metaphorical mountain. They live for a time, pulled to balance energies and set right various wrongs in the flow of creation, then eventually merge back with the earth. Because they are the byproduct of the dreams of the gods, some consider erdwitches to act with the gods' authority.

This was the magic running through my brother and his descendants. Maeve gave part of her essence to Alair as a way to save his life. It had never been done before, and Alair wasn't entirely sure he understood why she did it. But Maeve's powers were only on loan. When she reabsorbs into the earth, Alair suspected his family's powers would go with her.

And perhaps their bodies, too.

He wrote it so factually, a simple sentence describing the potential death of his entire line. How had he committed the possibility to paper without the ripple of a single fallen tear on the page, or a shakiness in any evenly-spaced letter? The knowledge hurt me like a punch to the gut.

I looked at Rowan over the fire. He sharpened his belt knife across a stone, the *swick* of it forming an almost musical beat. The thought that he could die at any moment was intolerable. I'd already lost everyone else. Would I be forced to lose Rowan, too? I returned to my reading, praying Alair's theory was wrong.

After the erdwitches and the Fae came humans. Alair hadn't found any records of how we got magic, or who gave it to us. It wasn't instinctive, like the erdwitches, or inherent, like the Fae. It was a modification to us, and we paid for it in ways the others didn't have to: the use of magic literally sucked up our life from the inside. It was possible to use so much magic that the practitioner died from blood loss or faded away to skin and bones.

But things were different in the world by that time. The Fae had figured out how to bind magic for their purposes, attaching results to certain words or actions. A nonsense word, spoken just right, would yield the same result over and over. Magic isn't like fire, which burns out, or water, which evaporates. It's always there. It never expires or dies or slips away. If bound to something, it always stays.

Alair's notes indicated he believed the Fae gave humans magic first, because it was certainly them who taught us how to use spells. Later humans grew so powerful they were able to learn on their own, even create new spells. That was where the conflict came between our races.

Then, somehow, after the portals to Avalon and Shadelorn were created, magic started dying out in humans. There was no explanation for this, either. The most powerful bloodline, my bloodline, had kept it longer than any other, but Alair suspected our powers were not what they once were. My powers, if I had them, would probably not compare to those of my ancestors.

Alair's journal went on, but nothing in his writing prompted any revelation or insight. Whatever challenges we faced in the future, it seemed we must conquer them without help from my magic.

SEVENTEEN

I smelled roses in my sleep just before the dream came again. Roses, roses, and underneath them something darker. Something sweet and metallic. Blood.

Then the grove.

This time the tiny lights already floated between the trees, illuminating the dream with soft shadows and shades of yellow. It would have been lovely if I weren't so angry and afraid.

I stood in the red velvet dress, fists clenched at my side, waiting for Soren to appear. When he didn't, I closed my eyes and wrapped my arms around myself, like Rowan did earlier. With everything in me I tried to unlock the hidden magic at my core, and use it to leave this place.

"What are you doing?"

I opened my eyes. Soren stood at the edge of the grove, wearing the same red and gold tunic and ever-present shadow cape as last time.

"Trying to get out of here," I answered, heart beating like a rabbit's. "Let me go."

"No." He walked towards me. "Not until you hear what I have to say. I told you to go back."

"I'm not talking to you," I said, stepping into the curtain of willow branches. They parted with a soft susurration. Inside the globe of green leaves Soren was mostly hidden from me, and I from him.

Glimpses of his red tunic told me he approached, but he

stopped outside the willow's branches. "You must go back, Rose," he said. "Even if you never let me take you to the doorways between worlds. If you continue on this path, I'll have to take you, and kill your companions. I'm doing everything I can to delay it, I'm sending you only beasts you can handle. But eventually Silaine's patience will run out and my hand will be forced."

I tried to remember what Rowan would expect of me. "You can't fool me with your lies."

"What could I be lying about? Why would Silaine send me to discourage you traveling north? Every day you get closer to her, closer to being captured."

I couldn't deny his logic, so I stayed silent. Surely even Rowan would agree that at least in this moment Soren was telling the truth.

"You can't possibly hope to fight your way to the portal to Avalon. If Rowan thinks you can, he's wrong."

Silence was my refuge.

Soren sighed. He ran his hand through the waterfall of branches, but didn't try to part them. "We know they're giving you weapons."

My attention was piqued. Did he mean the blue-runed arrows?

"Both sides pretend it's not happening," he continued. "Avalon won't take action until they absolutely have to, and Silaine knows it."

My thoughts moved slowly in this enchantment. I reviewed his words carefully, parsing out the implication. If 'both sides' meant Avalon and Silaine, then Rowan's magicked arrows came from—

The Fae.

Rowan routinely had contact with the Fae. That alone was enough to bend my mind in half, but what Soren said next truly shocked me.

"What Avalon doesn't know is that Silaine isn't just recruiting rebel Fae. She wants to open Shadelorn."

Shadelorn—the repository of all the magical beasts too terrible to be left on Earth. Even through the molasses of the dream, my heart skipped a beat. All those terrible beasts from ancient history, the monsters that only Fae warriors had the strength to defeat, would be released from their prison and used to devastate the world again.

It was a fantastic story. Potentially catastrophic, if true. But I remembered Rowan's warnings, and tried to hold on to skepticism. "She can't open the doorway to Shadelorn." I spoke aloud, to anchor my thoughts. "She would need royal blood—"

I gasped, realizing the final piece.

Soren's voice was bathed in misery. "Why else do you think Silaine sent me to fetch you out of the castle? She found out you were the last surviving member of the Aerendel line. Her last hope for breaking open the doorways between worlds. She's tried every other option for decades."

"How did she find out?" I had to know.

"Some of Alair's men were captured recently."

My heart sank. His words confirmed the suspicion Alair shared with me at Briar.

"They were tortured," Soren admitted. "If I'd been there I would have found a way to end it, given them a quick death. But I wasn't. Alair's son, Ferras… He told them who you really are. Silaine was furious."

I parted the willow branches an arm's length from Soren, and walked through. I had to know. "Is Ferras alive?"

Soren's golden eyes were filled with sadness. "Not anymore."

My heart broke for Rowan. He would be devastated.

"Silaine sent me to get you as a punishment," Soren continued. "I knew the secret, you see. All this time, I never told her you were the lost Princess Talia Aerendel. Please believe me, Rose. I'm doing everything I can to help you succeed. I don't want Silaine to destroy the world. That's why I became *damnsoír* in the first place—I had to live long enough to see her stopped."

His words streamed over me in a wash of sincerity. What he said made sense. Soren was on our side, in spirit at least.

"If there's an opportunity for me to take you to Avalon, you must let me," he pressed.

I shook my head, unable to agree.

"Please just think about it. I'll find a way to reach you when the time is right. But listen, there's some force keeping me away from you. If you can find a way around it, if you can come to me… I'll hide you, walk you right through Silaine's lands with no one noticing. I'll get you through the portal to Avalon. If you can warn Avalon—"

"What's the point, if they already know she's raising an army against them, and they don't care?"

"Because they'll want to know she's trying to access Shadelorn," he said. "Perhaps that will rouse Oberon to action. With or without you, she'll find a way in eventually. Fae live a very, very long time."

The light in the grove darkened. I took a small, hesitant step towards him. "Even if I believe you, I can't trust you. Silaine could order you to change your plans at any moment."

"She can only give me orders in person," Soren assured me.

"If I ever appear and first call you Talia, not Rose, then you'll know I've been commanded to betray you."

"Will such a simple trick work?"

"I believe so. Names hold a lot of power to the Fae. Now that she knows who you really are, Silaine refers to you by your true name, the name you were born with."

I shivered. "It's not my true name. Not to me."

The corners of his mouth lifted in a soft smile. "Not to me, either. That's why it will work."

A breeze wove around us, bearing the heavenly scent of petrichor. I inhaled deeply, missing green, living plants, and the smell of the earth.

Soren watched me. Sadness limned every angle of him, weariness in his features even when he smiled. How could anyone perform such sadness? Who would ever want to?

The questions I'd longed to ask him finally burst free. "Why did you lie to me when I woke up? Why didn't you tell me who you really are, what you were really trying to do?"

"Because I was ashamed," he whispered. His eyes held mine captive. "How could I explain that I belong to the being who cursed you, that I was sent to fetch you so your blood could be used to destroy this world? But I was always on your side. Always."

He stepped forward. Breathless, I let him take my hands, light forming where our skin touched.

"You must find a way to break the force that keeps me from you. And if you don't, soon... no one will survive."

"We knew each other before," I pressed. "You have to tell me. Please." My heart fluttered in my chest. On my lips danced the ghost of a kiss. "Who are you?"

To my dismay, Soren shook his head. "To explain would

take more time than we have. But if you come to me, I can show you. There are ways, but not in this place."

The grove appeared to be going black, or was it my dream eyes? Everything faded. My next words were a struggle. "So I won't know if I can trust you or not until it's too late."

His voice came distant, yet his breath touched my ear. "I think you already know. You woke up knowing."

It was so dark now. Soren and I were merely two shadows standing next to each other. The stuck-in-time feeling began to fade, the sound of the grove and its earthy scent winding down like a dying echo.

Break the spell. Wait for me. Soren's voice in my ear. Did he stand close to me or fill the whole grove? *It's the only way.*

Then I was alone with the nothingness, until the nothingness became my own mind.

I opened my eyes and found myself back in my tent. The sapphire on my sword's hilt glowed gold again, but faded to nothing as I watched it.

I lay back on my cold pillow and two hot tears of frustration welled up in my eyes. Outside the enchantment I could pick apart Soren's possible motivations. It was highly suspicious that he kept insisting I break Alair's spell keeping him from me. Rowan would say Soren was trying to lure me away, enlisting my unwitting help in dooming us all.

But when I was with him… I believed him. If the certainty in my heart and gut was just an enchantment, as Rowan feared, wouldn't I trust Soren with no hesitation? Instead my trust was an agony. It lived in defiance of logic, and my promises to

Rowan.

I should have brought him news of this encounter with Soren immediately, but I needed time to sort out everything he told me: First, Ferras was dead. Second, Silaine was trying to access Shadelorn. And thirdly, somehow the Fae were giving Rowan weapons to use against her.

Some of what Soren said could be verified. We would reach Lorensile in two days and finally discover Ferras's fate. Rowan could confirm his contact with the Fae. If Soren was right about those two things… maybe he was right about all of it.

If I went to him, he would explain the connection between us. He could take me to Avalon without risking the lives of Rowan or our men.

The only thing I couldn't reconcile was something Soren said at Briar. That it wasn't Fae magic binding my lost memories. Was he lying, or simply wrong?

If the Fae hadn't taken my memories, who had?

EIGHTEEN

The next morning, I approached Rowan as he prepared Garland for the day ahead. He met me with a smile that made my stomach flip, then sink. "I need to tell you something. Can we walk ahead a bit?"

Sure enough, his smile fell. "Do you want to ride?"

"No, let's just walk."

Rowan led Garland out onto the road. We had left the kingsroad and followed smaller paths winding up the foothills toward the mountains. The sight of my mountains in the distance might have been balm to my soul, but the task ahead was joyless.

"You had another dream," Rowan said flatly.

"Yes."

He sighed. Garland tossed his head, as if reading Rowan's dismay. "All right. What lies did he tell you?"

I bit my lip. I had my fears, my questions, but there was only one rightful place to start. "He said your father is dead."

Rowan's composure broke for a moment, but then he shook his head. "No. I know what I saw. My father touched the witchlines. Unless he just...?"

The sudden panic on Rowan's face made my heart ache. "No, Soren made it sound like it's been a while."

"Good. Then he's only lying."

"He said it's the reason Silaine finally woke me up. Because your father… told her the truth about me. That I'm the last Aerendel. Soren says he knew as well, but kept the secret all this time. Why would he do that if he wasn't on our side?"

"He's only pretending he knew," Rowan insisted. "What else?"

"Soren said he's been sending us beasts he knows we can handle, but if he keeps failing, Silaine might take matters into her own hands." I used one of Soren's arguments. "Why would he deter us from going north, if it's just bringing us closer to Silaine?"

"I could think of a million reasons why. Maybe her false court turned on her, and there's no one guarding the door to Avalon. If he doesn't want us going north it means they have something to hide. He's *damnsoír*, Rose, you know that. Why do you insist on believing him over me?"

I flinched. "I never said I believed him over you, I just think we should consider—"

"You don't have to say it. It's all over your face! Grandfather was right."

"What does *that* mean?" But he shook his head and refused to elaborate. Anger ignited within me. "You ask me to trust you, Rowan, but when will you trust me? If Soren is telling the truth, we don't know what we're walking into in Lorensile. And everything in me tells me he can help us."

Rowan stopped walking to pierce me with an accusing stare. His expression was a storm cloud. "You promised," he growled.

"I'm keeping my promise, by telling you what he said! You're supposed to convince me he's wrong, but you can't. Soren says the Fae are giving you those runed arrows, Rowan. The *Fae.* What the hell are you doing talking to the Fae?"

Rowan's features expanded with true shock. "Soren says—How does—" His hand jerked towards the amulet hanging beneath his shirt, then he swore, and wheeled Garland around.

"Where are you going?" I demanded, following as he trotted back toward the rest of our men.

"Rose, I have to do something, and you need to stay out of it."

"Tell me what's going on."

"I will, later, but you have to give me—"

"No, *now*," I shouted, grabbing Garland's reins. Rowan slowed to a stop so we didn't hurt his horse's mouth by fighting. "Soren says we have to turn back or he'll be forced to attack us."

Rowan glared. "We're not leaving until we find my father."

I let him pull the reins out of my hand and trot ahead of me. He made straight for Gile, whose frown deepened and deepened as Rowan whispered to him. When I caught up, I marched right up to both of them. "Tell me what's wrong," I said flatly. "Tell me how we're somehow in league with the Fae even though we're fighting against them."

"Shh," Rowan hissed. "Give me one minute, for the love of—"

"Boy," Gile warned, and Rowan fell silent. "There's no reason she shouldn't know."

Rowan's jaw was clenched so tight I would be concerned for his teeth if I weren't so angry. "That is not your decision to make."

We stared at each other in mutual hurt and anger. The others were approaching, and they would also want to know what was wrong. Rowan sighed, and his shoulders slumped. "Look, it's not you, we haven't told anyone—"

The amulet began to glow blue through his shirt. Blue like the runes on the arrows. Gile and I watched in silence as Rowan yanked it from beneath the cloth and ran his fingers over it, ending the signal.

"I want to go with you," I said before anyone moved.

"Absolutely not," Rowan replied. "It's too dangerous. Stay with the men, Rose. Gile and I have to go, but we'll catch up, and I'll tell you everything, I promise. Please?"

His words reminded me of someone else's pleading just hours before. I shook my head. "No. We have to leave before it's too late. Silaine wants you dead and me captured. We have to go."

Rowan handed Garland's reins to me and I took them, confused. He wrapped a scarf around his mouth, signaling he was done talking. They were going to walk off and leave me here.

I turned to Gile. "Listen to me. We have to leave Valeria. Soren's been warning me in my dreams. I know you want to find Ferras, but Soren says he's already dead."

It was as if my words meant nothing to them. Gile only looked at me with somber eyes. Rowan instructed me once more to wait with the others, then strode off toward the trees without a word of goodbye or reassurance.

Gile waited, and I thought for a moment he'd listened. But he only leaned close and sighed. "It's not for Ferras's sake we're here, princess."

Then Gile strode off, too, leaving me standing in the road, holding onto a horse but otherwise alone with my outrage and helplessness.

Rowan and Gile disappeared among the gray trunks. Garland tugged on the reins, wanting to follow his master. I held him back until Bremmer caught up, leading Crackers and the sleigh, with the others not far behind.

"What's happening?" Wes asked, examining my face with his good eye. "Why'd they go off together?"

Because they're secret-keeping idiots, I wanted to say, but channeled my frustration in a different way. "Take these." I held out Garland's reins to Effer. "Everyone wait here."

I ran after Rowan and Gile, following their footprints through the forest. The trail took no special skill to follow, but what started to concern me was how long it went on, and how straight. They weren't tracking anything. They weren't following some hidden path. They were just walking, aimlessly.

What on earth were they doing out here?

I slowed when I thought I must be catching up and paused to recover my breath. It was dark and silent beneath these frozen trees. The land was craggy, concealing any line of sight. I could almost believe the footprints in front of me would wind through the forest forever.

Taking care to move quietly, I picked my way through the snow. Not a minute later I came to another ridge in the land, and instinct made me sneak up until I could peek over it.

Sure enough, in the resulting hollow stood Rowan and Gile, speaking quietly to each other. I couldn't hear what they said, but Gile stood with fallen shoulders and Rowan paced in tight passes. I crouched down into the snow and waited with them.

Wind whistled among the rocks and treetops. My left hand gripped the hilt of my sword for comfort. The run had warmed me, but kneeling in the snow soon brought me to shivering.

Gradually, I realized the wind's whistle was becoming music. Haunting and teasing, its quick, low notes danced in and out of hearing. Below, Rowan and Gile's conversation ceased and they stood at attention like dogs with their ears pricked forward. Laughter sailed on the breeze.

A Fae strode into the clearing.

My mouth opened to finally see one of the legendary beings

that had so disrupted my world. True to Gile's stories, he stood at seven feet tall, skin as pale and blue as snow in moonlight. Pointed ears poked through his long, white hair. His face was narrow, angular, and utterly beautiful, with eyes so bright and blue they seemed to shine in the shadows.

He dressed as if for style rather than protection against the cold. His boots and trousers were black, his belt silver, but all else was white as the moon: an embroidered tunic cut low on his chest, and a thick mantle of fur topping a floor-length cloak.

In his arms he carried a thick bundle of the special arrows, runes glowing blue as the summer sky.

So Soren was right. The magicked arrows we depended on were hand-delivered by the Fae.

The Fae man inclined his head by way of greeting. "Rowan. You are far more greedy than your fathers, witchling." His voice was musical and mocking.

"Darian." Rowan bobbed his head once, too, but his voice was full of contempt. "It's not your arrows I need this time. You have a traitor on your side."

Darian threw the bundle to the ground like it meant nothing. "A traitor? To the *king*?" His smirk was a paragon of contempt. "Oh, he won't like that. How is it you've come to know of this traitor?"

Rowan glanced at Gile, who stood firm and silent, respectfully looking at his feet. "Through the one you call *damnsoír*. He's been plaguing us at every step. Now he says he knows Avalon's giving us weapons."

Darian laughed, beautiful and condescending. "Well that's hardly difficult knowledge to come by. You think Silaine wouldn't notice after all these years exactly how you put down her nasty, little creations? I expect she's known for some time."

“So tell your king to give me better weapons. Swords, shields, spears—”

Darian shook his head. “No. Arrows are all you get, and all you need. If you encounter something too strong for arrows then it’s your own fault. You should not be here.”

“We are busy taking care of *your king’s* problem since he’s too cowardly to do it on his own! The least you could do is give us decent weapons.”

Darian wagged his finger like Rowan was a naughty child, and clucked his tongue. “Firstly, you’re obviously *not* here to blot Silaine from the Earth once and for all. Not with that ragtag army. If you manage to one day get your dull-witted neighbors to come together for what’s good for them, then perhaps we’ll talk. Second, much as you and I may not agree with King Oberon’s tactics, I’d hardly say cowardice is the reason behind it. Shame you didn’t inherit your grandfather’s brains along with his magic.”

Rowan glowered, but made no reply.

“Third, you *do* have a Fae sword among you, for all the use you seem to be getting out of it.”

Rowan’s eyebrows raised. “What?”

Darian laughed again. “Poor little witchling. You don’t even know what you don’t know, do you? How your kind ever managed to overrun mine is one of the greatest examples of incompetency in my people’s history.”

Rowan was silent against the insult but I could see his mind working. I held my sword tighter.

“Be that as it may,” Rowan said, “if you let us die out here then who’s going to stand against Silaine once we’re gone? You need us, Darian. Tell your king *that*. He’d better protect us if he knows what’s good for him.”

Darian waved a hand about. "Yes, yes, your petty human threats will put him right off his feasting. I'll be sure to pass the message along."

"I am not human, I am *witch*, damn you. In the old days, the Fae listened to erdwitches."

"You use erdwitch magic, but you are not an erdwitch. You're just another parasitic human, taking others' magic for your own pleasure. Erdwitches provide balance. You have only ever sought our destruction." Darian nudged the bundle of arrows with his foot. "Here, take your weapons, *human*. Use them well."

He turned away as Rowan leaned down for the bundles, but then turned back. "Oh, and tell the girl on the ridge to keep an eye on that sword. I don't know where you got it, but it's the last Fae sword you'll ever get from us."

Then he was gone. Stepped behind a tree and disappeared, leaving Gile, Rowan, and I alone in the middle of the woods. Rowan and Gile were frozen in shock, but then they both turned to where I crouched.

I sighed, and stood up. They waited while I walked down the ridge. Rowan's fists shook at his sides, and Gile's bunched mustache betrayed ill-content.

When I reached them I took a deep breath and held up my hands. "Look—"

"I'll meet you back at the road," Gile interrupted. He picked up the pack of arrows and trudged toward the hill, leaving Rowan and I alone.

"I know you're mad," I said quietly as he turned away from me. "But I'm trying to figure out why you'd hide from me that our arrows come from the Fae. Do we have an *alliance* with them, Rowan? What—"

I gasped as Rowan whirled towards me. "Do you have any idea what you might have done?" he shouted. I stood frozen as he stepped forward and grabbed both my arms. "I told you to wait for me! If Darian knows who you are, he'll tell the Fae king. And then he'll come back, and he'll kill you, Rose!"

A bolt of fear cut through my anger. "Why?"

"Because of what you can do." Rowan released my arms but didn't move away. Our breath mingled in the chilly air as he spoke quietly. "The King knows Silaine's raising a rebellion against him. He sends us arrows because it's easier to arm us against Silaine than fight her himself. But he doesn't want to be told about her officially, in front of his court, because then he'd have to do something about it. If he kills you before you reach him, then he may never have to act."

"Soren says Silaine will find a way—" I stopped myself, realizing I hadn't yet told Rowan about Silaine planning to use me to get into Shadelorn. Maybe now wasn't the best time. "That she'll find a way to defeat him anyway, with or without me."

"Well it won't be with you, I promise you that." My breath hitched as he wrapped his arms around me. "But you have to trust me, Rose."

"You kept this from me," I said into his shoulder.

"We kept it from everyone. If the others knew we were working with the Fae, they wouldn't understand." He let me go, and looked deep into my eyes. "I can't lose you."

"So don't," I said, eyes blurring. "Leave with me. We shouldn't be here. Soren says it, Darian says it. Even the men know it."

"Rose..." He sighed. "Have I told you about the first time I saw you?"

"What does that have to do with anything?"

"I was nine," he pressed on. "It was the year I followed Father out here. Grandfather said I should know what I was choosing, so he and Father took me up to the castle to see you. I was nine," he repeated. "But I saw you, asleep on that bed, and you were so beautiful..."

My chin trembled.

"You are everything I dreamed you'd be. You're tough, and fierce, and you believe so strongly in what you think is right. You're the queen that was promised."

My tears finally spilled over, hot and then instantly cold in the freezing air. I leaned into Rowan and he wrapped his arms around me again.

"I shouldn't have let you come with us," he whispered. "We should have stuck with Grandfather's plan. But we're so close now, and I can't leave until I know what happened to my father. Just one more day, and then we'll go. I promise."

I nodded against his shoulder. We could survive one more day. Soren would have to make it work.

As we walked back through the woods, Rowan told me how Darian had been our Fae contact since Briar's inception, appearing one day to Alair and offering King Oberon's self-serving goodwill through the magicked arrows. He had treated with Alair, then Ferras, and now Rowan. For all those years the family had managed to keep this secret from Briar, feeling it wise not to disclose we were in contact with the Fae. Only Rickard knew, when Ferras was Commander, and then Gile, out of necessity.

We emerged from the woods and found our team waiting with patient silence. I remembered what Gile had told me not an hour before: *It's not for Ferras's sake that we're here*.

Had these men known they signed up for a doomed quest?

Did everyone but Rowan realize his father was already dead?

That night, in the dark, with the wind whipping around and our fires low and sputtering, I truly feared for our lives for the first time. We might never make it out of this snow, and everyone except Rowan seemed to know it.

That night's camp was pitched near a petrified farmhouse and collapsed barn. The witchline symbol was engraved into the stone wall of the farm's well. Reverent yet joyless, Rowan knelt by the well and pressed his hand to the symbol. Just like the past several nights the symbol lit up with golden light, then faded out. But as Rowan stood and walked away the symbol flared into life once more.

I shouted, pointing and leaping up from my seat by the fire. Everyone looked, and I know some of them saw what I had.

The witchline had been touched, and not by Rowan. I'd seen it with my own eyes. Men's cheering ignited the night and Gile grabbed a stunned Rowan to knuckle his head. Among the ecstatic troupe I alone stayed silent. Tomorrow we will reach Lorensile, and learn the truth.

Soren said Ferras was dead. Either he lied, or something terrible summoned us north.

Nineteen

The symbol flared twice more that night. By morning Rowan was in a frenzy to be back on the road, and we left as soon as the sky lightened enough to safely let us travel. The road remained steep, but we moved faster than ever before. For once the sun shone in a pale blue sky, transforming our endless white waste into a sparkling winter wonderland.

The day's brightness clashed with the dread I carried. Our frantic pace spurred anxiety but quelled thought. I couldn't begin to imagine what would happen when we reached Lorensile.

Finally, as the sun began to wane, we crossed a ridge and beheld the city spread out before us. The sight squeezed my heart. We were so close to my own village now, just another day's ride away.

For a moment I saw Lorensile as it used to be: red-tiled roofs, waving flags, fires in the watchtowers, colorful pennants strung between buildings, and crowds of people ambling over the cobbled streets. But then I blinked, and it was just another empty city, ravaged by a hundred years of winter. Its signature red roofs were hidden by snow or bleached pale by the sun. No lights shone from its haunted windows. No pennants waved in the frozen breeze.

We stumbled down the hill. Rowan's frenzied energy infected Garland, who danced side to side or had to be spun in circles to wait for the rest of us to keep pace.

It was evening, though dark had not truly begun to fall. The city's tall buildings loomed above us, the stillness at every window unnerving. Its towers were riddled with crumbling walls and collapsed roofs. The river that ran through the heart of the city once boasted a dozen bridges, but only a few stood now. One wooden door of the front gates had fallen, and the other hung loose from its hinges.

As we rode through the entrance, the enemy struck.

A maven dropped from the sky like a rock, unfurling its black wings at the last moment and raking Gile's head as it swooshed by. "Why, you filthy, little—"

The sky, which had been so empty before, now filled with mavens as they took flight from hidden crevices around the city, pouring out like ants from a red nest.

"Hurry," Gile said, blood dripping down his face. "Into the city!"

Rowan led us inside and quickly found cover in a dilapidated stables. He dismounted, and the archers among us strung our bows. The cloud of mavens hovered above the city, a swirling storm of wings and teeth.

"I've never seen so many," Gile said, almost reverently. "What are they doing here?"

"If they're here, it's likely something else is, too," Rowan said. "Probably around the witchline. Preventing us from getting to it, or guarding—" He broke off, and the possibility hit my mind at the same time.

"Rowan, no!"

But he abandoned us, dashing into the street, sword out like an idiot who didn't know one trip could get him impaled on his own blade. Gile and I looked at each other, at the mavens, and at our exhausted men and horses huddling under a snow-laden roof.

"Gile, I—"

"Go," he said. "We'll come after you when we can. Keep him alive, princess."

Rowan was already out of sight. I followed his boot tracks down the wide main road, until they cut into a side street. Now there were overhanging roofs, and one lonely line of frozen laundry above me. I chased Rowan's winding trail until I no longer knew in which direction I ran. Nothing looked familiar, until suddenly everything did.

I plunged through a shadowed alley into an open courtyard with a great fountain in the middle. The water had frozen in sheets and curls like a spiky, white flower. I could see the witchline symbol at its base, lit up in gold from Rowan's hand touching it.

Above us, the cloud of mavens sang their murderous song.

"Rowan?" I walked forward, lungs heaving.

He removed his hand and the symbol faded. There was no one here, and no response on the witchline.

"Rowan, I'm sorry," I said. "But let's go back, we've left Gile—"

"Shh," he said, and held out his hand. I stopped walking. "Look."

He pointed. Faint on the snow at his feet were two small shadows, and they led in an alternating pattern out through the opposite end of the courtyard.

Footsteps.

A maven fluttered down and alighted on a glittering branch of the silent fountain. It regarded me with its head tilted to the side. Its gaze was not curious like any other raven, but malicious.

"*Caww*," it cried, revealing those unnatural teeth. More mavens landed on the flagpoles in the courtyard and the rooftops surrounding it.

"Rowan," I said quietly. "Don't run. Just wait for me, and we'll go together. All right?"

He stood, and the maven on the fountain hissed at him. I walked forward as quickly as I dared, but the way Rowan stared at the shallow footprints scared me.

"Rowan, look up," I said. "We have to get out of here."

He extended his left foot forward to sink into the nearest footprint. His boot overwhelmed it, crushed it. Whoever made these footprints was smaller and lighter than either of us. I was near enough now to almost reach him.

"Rowan..."

I glanced at the maven, and as we made eye contact it screamed.

With a *whoosh* the creatures around us took flight. I grabbed Rowan's arm and we plunged after the footprints, but we had a hundred feet to go and a thousand mavens at our backs. We didn't make it halfway before claws sliced my neck.

Rowan jerked me to a stop and with a few shouted commands we stood back-to-back, swords drawn, slashing wildly into the foray.

Bodies dropped around us, but there were too many of them, a cyclone of cutting claws. Legs tangled in my hair and teeth bit my hands as I pulled mavens off me. I couldn't see, didn't dare open my eyes.

Rowan grabbed my arm and we fled, one hand holding each other and free arms blocking our faces. We ran and ran until the sound and light changed, and I looked up to find us in another alleyway.

Mavens still dove at us, but in fewer numbers, either distracted by the cannibal feast in the courtyard or because we were no longer in an open space. I sheathed my sword and pulled out my bow, loosing arrows at the mavens as we followed the faint footprints. How would we ever get rid of the angry murder? Where were we going, and what would we find there? What if—

A loud, deep sound made me stumble. We looked behind us to the crossroads we'd passed, and for a moment I didn't understand what I was seeing.

Something big and black, with thin jaws longer than my arm, had snapped into the mavens tailing us and crunched down on a handful. Some still wiggled in its mouth, and as Rowan and I watched in horror it gulped them down while the rest of the murder hissed and cried in anger.

It ignored them and turned its eyes to us. Then it eased around the corner, revealing a thick, reptilian body, wings with curving talons, and four feet that clung to the brick. It walked towards us along the faded red wall, using its wings for balance. Tendrils from its chin dripped black with the mavens' blood.

Rowan spoke, but it took several moments for meaning to find me. "Run," he was saying, "Rose, just run."

We ran.

The creature howled, a high-pitched noise as thin as a needle, and crashed through the city behind us. I carried my bow in one hand and an arrow in the other, but didn't dare stop to try and get a shot off.

"We have to hide!" I shouted to Rowan.

He didn't respond, still chasing those small footprints. With no choice I followed… right until they led us to a dead end.

We realized it before we got to the end of the alley, but by then it was too late. The beast behind us knew it had us trapped. It clung to the entrance and *snickered*, a hideous, guttering sound from its black belly.

I aimed a blue-runed arrow and took a shot, but it bounced harmlessly off the creature's armored skin. It snapped its jaws and advanced toward us by leaping to the other wall, clinging like a reptilian bat.

Notching another arrow, I whispered, "Rowan, do something!"

The monster shrieked and flapped its wings before slamming its spurs into the brick walls, sending chunks of rubble to the cobblestones.

I loosed the arrow but the monster ducked, then took another leap forward while I notched a third. This one pierced its thick wings but went straight through. The hole oozed, but the creature didn't seem concerned. I reached back into my quiver and groped blindly, feeling nothing.

Rowan pulled me behind him. I threw down the bow and drew my sword. We faced the monster as it crawled toward us, almost in range now. Its tail lashed the air like a whip, and snapped forward to strike. Rowan swung, too slow.

The creature leaped forward on the wall and lashed its tail again, but we were inching backwards, and the strike fell short. But we couldn't retreat forever. Eventually we'd hit the alley wall and be forced into a close-quarters last stand.

"Rowan," I said, but could think of nothing else to add. This could be the end. I didn't know if this creature would kidnap me or kill me, but Rowan wasn't going to make it out alive. The lizard before us was too big, and too fast.

"If we attack at the same time…" Rowan couldn't finish his thought, either. Every strategy seemed hopeless.

I moved around him and up to his side. The creature's eyes followed me. They were orange, with slit pupils like a cat.

"Maybe it's like the one that got Perry," I whispered.

"Maybe I can distract it."

"No—"

The creature charged forward.

We raised our swords and its jaws opened, but then the lizard's eyes moved off me to something… behind me.

Wings flaring, the creature stumbled to a halt. It hissed, and scuttled backward along the wall. Rowan took a step after it but I stayed frozen, petrified with fear.

A shadow was rising along the wall, darker than the gloom in this forgotten corner of an abandoned city. Something terrifying grew behind us until the lizard fairly scurried out of the alley and ran away, shrieking and crashing through the streets.

When Rowan saw the shadow he whirled, and I closed my eyes, cringing from the killing blow the new monster behind me would surely make.

But nothing happened except for Rowan's gasp.

I peeked open one eye to see him drop his sword to the snow, eyes wide and unbelieving. "Maeve?" he breathed.

I turned.

The erdwitch's hands lowered, and the darkness vanished on the walls.

"Rowan," she said. "You've come at last."

TWENTY

Rowan rushed past me as I stood, stunned. "Maeve! What are you doing here?"

Maeve the erdwitch was a grandmotherly figure, short and stocky, with a puff of gray hair. She had human features, and though she bore no wrinkles, something about her face always implied great age.

She held out her hands and Rowan took them, dropping to his knees before her. "Ah, Rowan, my boy." Her face lit up in a gray-toothed smile. "You're so grown. Humans grow so fast."

"Maeve?" I asked, almost not believing. When I last saw her she was shrewd in mind and expression, definitive in her actions. The erdwitch before me was a shadow of her former self. Her skin, once grayish-green, was now merely gray, the color of ash. She swayed on her feet, and both her eyes and movements were slow.

Maeve turned to me, pleasant confusion forming on her brows. Her eyes wandered around my face. She let go of Rowan's hands and reached for mine. The instant we touched, understanding finally dawned.

"The princess," Maeve said. "Dear Rose. So you are awake." She closed her eyes and smiled. Magic ran from her to me, exploring, penetrating, but there was only kindness to it, like the firm yet gentle caress of a cat licking a recovered kitten.

"Rose doesn't remember what happened after meeting Halen," Rowan blurted.

"Yes." Maeve opened her eyes and dropped my hands. She shot Rowan a sharp look. "I can tell."

"Can you fix me?" I asked, heartbeat quickening.

"You are fixing yourself. Something Fae breaks the spell."

My sword! Rowan's eyes and mine glanced off each other. Soren had been right about this, too. But if Fae magic could wear away whatever kept my memories hidden, then what kind of magic had locked them up in the first place?

There were only three types I knew: Fae, my own... and erdwitch.

"What are you doing here?" Rowan asked Maeve, oblivious to the sudden horror in me. "Are you all right?"

"Alair," Maeve said, as if just remembering. "Alair is gone, and so is his son. I knew you needed help, but I couldn't find the way."

And so is his son.

But my own revelation overpowered this news. "Maeve," I said, panic growing, "Do you know—"

"Not here," Rowan interrupted. "Look at her, Rose."

Maeve shivered, leaning against Rowan for support. "I'm sorry, children. I have a place, somewhere out of the wind. Follow me..."

But Rowan had to support Maeve as we left the alley. My thoughts raced as we followed her slow, faltering steps through the icy wreckage of the city.

The erdwitch led us to a shop with a broken door. The inside was cold and dank, but it did shield us from the wind. Ancient straw lay in a lumpy nest in one corner, and Maeve sank into this gratefully. My heart ached as she hacked and shuddered, Rowan at her side every moment. I could see on his face that he wished he'd pushed us harder, fought longer to come here. To be with her.

Maeve was dying.

Or dying as much as erdwitches could truly die. She lay still as a stone, glittering black eyes the only alive thing about her.

"My father," Rowan said. "Did you say...?"

"He's gone, dear one. When I felt Alair leave as well I knew you would need me, but I will soon be gone, too. I'm sorry, Rowan. I've just been in this body so long."

"It was you who touched the witchlines," I said, realizing, and her eyes turned to me.

"I was lost," she said. "I used to know every inch of this land, but now, in the cursed snow... I called you. I waited for you to come. Rowan?"

"I'm here," he said, leaning over her. His face was arranged in a terrible fury, but I knew it was only stubbornness against the pain inside.

"You know what will happen when I leave."

"Yes. The magic goes with you."

Maeve touched his cheek. "You must help me, my boy. We have to undo what I did to the princess."

"What did you do to me?" I asked, panic rising.

"I saved you," she said simply. "You have the last drops of magic in human blood, but it had to be a secret. I hid your powers from you. To protect you."

I sank to my knees at her other side. Rowan and I shared a glance of understanding. That was one mystery solved, at least. Rowan would lose his powers soon, but we would have mine. I would get us to Shalimar safely. I had to.

"Rowan." Maeve held out her hands, and Rowan took them, swallowing hard. Their fingers slipped around each other, hers gray and stubby, his bronzed and long. Family formed by magic.

Maeve bid me lay my head on her chest, where I did not hear her heartbeat, but only the faint inner workings of her erdwitch's body. Her dress smelled like dirt and moss, and the calming scent of stone. For an instant I lost my sense of direction, feeling somehow a depth in Maeve that ran leagues deep, into the earth itself.

Maeve closed her arms around me, and Rowan's hands warmed my back. The moment was peaceful and warm with love, but then something grabbed me on the inside, and then Maeve's arms were a cage.

It felt... like a scab tearing open in my heart, a pain that spread through my whole body. I whimpered, but it quickly faded to waves of relief.

A new awareness rose in me, sprawling and confusing, a limb I couldn't control yet. It wasn't overwhelming, but soft and subtle, like the warmth from a swallow of liquor. It felt like looking at an object you'd seen a thousand times, and finally noticing its immaculate beauty.

"Rose?" Rowan's voice, fearful.

I sat up from Maeve's now-limp embrace and nodded. "I'm all right. I—"

Maeve's gasp for breath banished my thoughts. She grabbed on to both our wrists and held tight, wordlessly voicing what might have been prayers or curses.

"She's going."

"No, wait," I cried. "Maeve, stay! I have so many questions."

Her hands clung to us so hard, fighting to stay together. It was a struggle for her to speak, and the words came out as if ground through gravel. "What you fear is true," she said to me. "But you will know all. If the spell does not break, then he will show you. I gave him the way, long ago."

"Just tell me why," I breathed, our eyes locked to each other "Why me? Why did I sleep?"

"It was the boy," she said, eyes widening. *"Damnsoír!"* Maeve coughed, and struggled to form words through gasping breaths. "It was better—you slept—than lie dead. Alair never—forgave him, but you held us—to this world. I swore—I would not leave—until you'd woken."

"Don't leave now," Rowan whispered, voice tight with grief. "We're not finished. I need you."

"There will be—others. When the snow melts. They will know—what I know. This body is—worn. It is time." She turned to me and pulled her hand from Rowan's to touch my cheek. "Forgive him. He—tried so hard."

I nodded, though I knew not who she meant.

Then Maeve leaned back, and with a sigh lay still on the ground. Her body crumbled into dust like it had never held another form, and only her worn dress remained.

Maeve was gone.

Beside me Rowan looked wan and lost, and I wondered if he felt the same change I had, except his was a closing, not an opening.

It was too cruel, to have found and lost Maeve so soon. If we had taken another day, another hour... I might never have known why I couldn't use my magic. Never gained it back. But Maeve had left behind more questions than she'd answered.

Fae magic ate away at the spell that hid my memories? *Soren* chose me to sleep?

What you fear is true.

My eyes turned to the last of my kin, but his devastated expression erased my questions. "Are you all right?"

Rowan's breathing was ragged, but his eyes were dry. The

look on his face chilled me.

"It's over," he said, and stood. "I shouldn't have brought us here." He took off Alair's amulet and dropped it to the ground. "It doesn't matter now, does it?"

I grabbed the amulet and stood as well.

Rowan looked straight ahead, eyes empty. "And my father..."

I touched Rowan's arm, expecting him to look to me for the same comfort he'd given me so often.

"He's dead," Rowan said. "My father is dead, my grandfather is gone, and I'm the only one left." I didn't realize the quaking in his voice was anger until he turned and smashed his fist against the wall. "You haven't even figured out the worst part, yet."

"What?" I whispered, afraid.

Rowan's eyes were dark, and he smirked grimly. "Grandfather knew Maeve was approaching her time. She was old when she saved you, and that was more than a century ago. She was feeble-minded—you saw her. And when she finally reabsorbed, Grandfather's power would have gone with her, as my power did. So he couldn't wait any longer. He had to force Silaine's hand."

My eyes searched his face, struggling to put it together. "You're not saying he...?"

Rowan let out a cough of laughter. "Yes. Grandfather sent my father to die. To have the truth pulled from him in the torture pits of the Fae, so Silaine would send for you at last. That's why you woke, Rose. Your brother killed his own son to free you."

Something irreplaceable shattered in my heart. "You must hate me," I breathed, tears pooling in my eyes.

"No. I can't hate you. Loving you has been my family's

obsession for a hundred years. I'm as trapped in it as they were."

Trapped. His words were another stab of despair.

"Father must have gone willingly. He would have told Rickard before he left, that's why—" Rowan put both hands to his head. "Rickard was right. We were never meant to be here. He tried to tell me... What have I done? Gile knew. He stood by me. Oh Rose, I've brought these men to their deaths."

"No," I said, wiping my tears away. "Maeve gave my magic back. I can protect us. We'll get everyone home." Even though I didn't know how to use these powers. Even though the threat of Silaine's forces hung over us like a growing storm.

"Rose, I'm sorry, I'm so sorry." Rowan sank to his knees. His eyes were on the amulet dangling in my hand. "I can't even undo it now."

"You *can*. We'll make it to Shalimar."

"Grandfather made me promise. He said it would keep you safe."

I placed the amulet back over his neck, where it belonged. "You have kept me safe," I said.

His eyes closed as the weight of the small stone settled against his chest. Two tears slipped down his cheeks. "But they're all gone now," he whispered.

"I know." I knelt, and hugged Rowan to me. "I know how it feels. But you still have me. We'll get through this."

"Rose, don't. I don't deserve—"

"Shh," I said. "You did what you thought was right. Everyone will understand."

Rowan's arms crept around me. We held each other for a long minute, and when he pulled away we stood up. He cradled his gloved hand shamefully.

"Here," I said, holding out my own hand. "Let me help."

Maeve had removed whatever restriction there was on my magic. I could feel it. What better way to test my powers than to make something better in this place of despair?

Rowan pulled off his glove, revealing bleeding knuckles. I touched them with my bare fingers, reaching for the center Rowan himself had shown me by the riverbank, a place I'd touched just moments ago, when Maeve set my soul to rights.

Heal, I commanded, pushing the heat deep inside me onto Rowan's injured hand. Blood seemed to rush from my head and I swayed, seeing twinkling blackness for a moment before recovering.

His knuckles were healed. Rowan looked at me with admiration and sadness, but even in this moment of triumph all I could think about was Maeve's warning: *What you fear is true.*

I couldn't think about it. Not now.

"We'll go back," I said, talking over my treacherous thoughts. "We'll tell the men we're returning home."

Rowan gave the barest of nods, and I led him from the decrepit building. We made our way through the maze of Lorensile with the wind nipping at our heels. Above us the skies were clear.

Rowan did not speak, not even when we found the main road and followed it towards the gates. By that time strength had mounted in me, the weight of responsibility settling over my shoulders like a heavy cloak. Our men waited where we left them, dead mavens scattered around the stables.

Gile greeted us with a shout, hair standing up like he'd been running a hand through it. "You're all right! What happened?"

When I spoke my voice rang with power. I wanted it, and it was there, making me just a touch dizzy. "We found who touched the witchlines." All eyes, all ears, focused on me. "It was Maeve, the erdwitch. Ferras is dead, and Maeve has reabsorbed. Rowan's powers are gone, but mine have returned. We leave for Shalimar in the morning."

There was nothing else to say. Gile took Rowan on a walk as the rest of the men made camp inside the walls. We cooked food and ate it. Fitzsimmons played his lute and sang a funny song about a farmer's daughter. One kind of tension had left the group, but another took hold. Rowan wore his dismay like a coat, and said nothing.

He went to bed early, and I found a nearby building in which to privately practice my new magic, but struggled to produce anything that would help in a fight. Every use of power made my head spin, and I felt more weary than ever as I dragged myself to my tent.

"You were right," I whispered to the silent sapphire on the hilt of my sword, its blue a jewel of black in the darkness. "I need to see you. Please."

Yet I lay atop my blankets wide awake, the sword hugged against my chest. *Wear away at me*, I told it. *Break the spell.*

Alair sent Ferras to his death so I would finally wake. How could my brother do that to his only son? What else was he capable of?

Maeve's words continued to repeat in my mind: *What you fear is true.*

What I feared? That Soren was everything Rowan claimed. That we would not leave Valeria alive. That I would never remember the lost year of my life. That I did not have the strength or the power to guide us home. That I was no princess, no one's sister, and nobody's friend.

And most of all, I feared it was Alair who stole my memories. The knowledge was a knife in my soul. I'd been living in denial. Soren told the truth at Briar, and Rowan lied about it, using my guilt at Alair's death to make me doubt myself.

But Maeve also said all would be revealed. *If the spell does not break, then he will tell you.*

He... I knew who *he* was.

I gave him the way, long ago.

I slipped into sleep, and the dream rose to meet me.

TWENTY-ONE

The grove had changed. Small flowers dotted the lush grass, tiny pink petals on delicate stalks. Perhaps my newly-revealed powers meant I could influence this enchantment.

I tried to sense its shape, to understand what made this dream and controlled it, but the syrupy muddle defied my efforts. Still, when Soren arrived, I felt it.

I looked up from the flowers. He stood by the bank of the pool, watching me silently. I walked toward him. "Hello, Soren."

"Hello, Rose." He winked, but his small smile was sad. The use of my name meant he could speak freely.

"You were right," I said. "Rowan gets arrows from the Fae. Ferras is dead. We came here looking for him, but found Maeve the erdwitch instead." His eyes widened. "But she's gone now. We're leaving Valeria, like you wanted."

"It's too late. You need to break the spell that keeps us apart and come to me now. Silaine won't let you escape."

"I can't do that, Soren. You've held her off this long, you can keep it up until we're in Shalimar."

He shook his head. "Silaine isn't contained by the snow. She can go wherever you go, and so can her forces. So can I. Once she tires of my defiance, she will come for you with everything she has, no matter where you hide. Please. This is our last chance."

“Maeve told me about you,” I blurted out. The grove quivered, power rippling like a pond struck by a stone. “She said you were the one who chose me to sleep.”

“I won’t deny it.” Did he look hopeful as he asked, “What else did she tell you?”

“Nothing,” I said, voice betraying frustration. “Except that you could tell me everything. So do it. If I can really trust you, then tell me why. Why did you pick me? Why—How—did you keep it from Silaine? Who *are* you?”

“I... I knew you to be a daughter of the former king. I couldn’t let Silaine kill you, not when I knew what your blood could do.”

“So out of gallantry you became this... monster.”

He closed his eyes for a moment against the word. “I loved my country. I loved my people. Silaine would destroy everything I held dear. There was no other option.”

“Then why did I sleep?”

“A punishment. For me.” He walked to the boulder by the pool and sat down, looking up at me plaintively. “I asked that she let you live. It was the condition of my servitude. But Fae are cunning, and cruel. Silaine made you sleep. Alive, yes. But still taken away, like everything else.”

I stepped closer. “And you put me in the tower?”

“No. That was Silaine. A joke of sorts. She thought you were a peasant, so she dressed you in a fine gown and placed you in the King’s bed. I brought the roses. Before the snow came.”

Soren stared at the ground, lost in the past. The scars I’d forgotten resurfaced on his face. A fretwork of pale lines spread on his skin and collected under his neck.

He looked up with those strange golden eyes. “Your brother hated me because I kept you alive, but not living. Because I sold my soul to the enemy. Because as a slave I have been commanded to do… terrible things. Almost everything they told you about me is true." His voice cracked with bitterness. "I'm a murderer, and a betrayer. But they got the *why* all wrong. It wasn't selfishness. It wasn't greed. It was a fear of what would happen if you were gone. I don't have love anymore, but I remember what it was to love. I remember needing you to survive."

His sincerity flooded me like always, a tide of agony and sorrow. I floated with it, drowned in it, heart bleeding for this boy I believed but didn't dare trust.

"Please, Rose," he whispered. "I've waited a hundred years in hell to save you. Let me."

A moment went by, then another. The grove was so quiet, everything listening for a response I couldn't seem to give. I had to think of Rowan, and our men, and of getting them to safety. I had to plan for a future where my magic was a force to be reckoned with, where I could truly fly, as Rickard predicted, like an arrow into the heart of Silaine's rebellion.

Gently, I let my words out. "I'm sorry... I can't." At my feet, the flowers shriveled. "If you care for me at all, then keep your monsters away from us as we go."

The grove began to fade. Soren stood, desperation lining his features. "If you come to me I can restore your memories."

I shook my head. "I'm finding them on my own." Maeve said something Fae wore away at the spell, and it had to be the sword. I would keep it close to me. I would leverage my new powers to unlock the missing year of my life. And then I would finally know what everyone was hiding.

"When you remember," Soren said as the grove blew away like the wind, "You'll want to find me. Break the spell keeping us apart. I'll be waiting."

In the inky gray of first light I woke with the sword in my arms and a dream of roses slowly fading from my mind. Glowing, heavily-perfumed, large and soft and blindingly crimson. Roses on vines, in fields, and across the mantle. Roses in my heart.

Rowan walked with the rest of the team as we traveled west, toward Shalimar. He had no more magic with which to guard our travel. Garland sulked, tied to the back of the sleigh, and Crackers trotted merrily, elated to finally be the one in the lead.

No monsters found us, but I only wondered vaguely what Soren had to do to keep us safe. I held the Fae sword in my arms, sensing its slippery magic humming against my own. *Remember*, I told myself as we walked on and on. *Remember*.

And slowly… I did.

Halen picked a bouquet of roses for me from the wild ones growing by the river in the woods. Small blooms, viny, with thorns so big they cut his hands, and I wrapped his thumb with bandages, my fingers burning with surprising heat each time they touched his.

I remembered his eyes, blue, with gold around the pupils. This was important, because I also had blue eyes, and it was a rare color in the mountains. At the time it felt like a sign.

I remembered the way he made me feel seen. He wanted to know everything about me, all my thoughts on life and a myriad of topics he raised, like I was more than a girl with a bow and a dirty dress. Like I was a forest, deep and beautiful and worthy of exploring.

We made camp, and Rowan talked quietly with the men, but there was no tension in him anymore. He did not stalk the perimeter, or look into the woods as if he wished to be further ahead. Rowan had found what he came for, and was sated, though the truth was a bitter draught.

I stared into the flames of the fire, among friends, yet alone. I wanted to live in my memories instead of worrying how we would get out of Valeria. Lost in my head, I tried to let the coals hypnotize me and reveal what I could not see, replaying what memories I had and begging always for more.

I remembered the red and gold on the pennants of King Cynric's knights that day they came to claim Halen. I felt the echo of my shock, the sinking in my heart that everything I had put my faith in was going to be torn away, the look on Halen's face—

His face.

With a jolt that shocked my whole body, I finally remembered the face of my beloved. And I remembered that special night, under the light of the full moon, when we kissed for the first time.

Familiar. Intimate. The kiss that woke me.

"No," I said aloud, the truth thundering in my mind. Impossible. A trick of my overworked brain, providing fantasy in response to my demand for memory. But this was not my imagination.

How could everyone have lied?

I dove into my tent with the sword clutched in my arms and willed myself to sleep, using magic or stubbornness to summon the enchantment again. I faded into the darkness and the dream came…

I stood in the meadow, more alive in this dream place than I'd ever been, the pool quivering as if reflecting vibrations from deep underground. The trees shifted, whispering secrets on the breeze.

It wasn't long before he joined me. By then I'd whipped the wind into a frenzy and the pool lapped against the edges of its banks. Pink flowers infested the grass, but they all closed their blooms as if preparing for a storm.

His jaw was set with concern as he stepped into view. His shadow cape swirled behind him, for once matching the movements of the wind. "What's happened?" He rushed towards me.

"Why do I see your face in my memories?" I asked, loose hair whipping around my eyes, voice about to break. He reached me, and grasped my hands. "Why do you have the same face as Halen?"

A moment hung between us, the gap of silence filled with the storm of the grove, mirroring the storm in my heart.

Soren pulled me close. "Because I am Halen."

I sank into him as we kissed, unable to resist for a moment longer. His arms, his scent, his mouth... The boy I loved wasn't dead, he was *here*. He had never left me.

Drums or earthquakes shook through our world, and I knew I would lose him in a moment.

Find me. I heard the whisper in my heart and mind, then—

"Rose!"

Rowan was in my tent. He had me by both shoulders and was shaking me awake.

"What?" I gasped, squinting in the light.

"You're bleeding magic all over the place!"

I sat up, Rowan's face not inches from mine, and found vines and flowers bursting through the base of the tent, pushing through blankets when they had to and climbing up the poles.

"You," I snarled, and punched Rowan in the chest.

He exhaled forcefully, and his eyes widened with shock. I swung at him again but he caught my arm, and we tumbled onto the blankets and vines, crushing their stems beneath us.

"You liar! *You're* the betrayer," I cried, swinging wildly.

Rowan pushed me off him but I came back, landing on top of his chest and straddling his torso to keep him from moving. Our arms battled.

"Rose, stop it! What are you talking about?"

"You knew that Soren is Halen, you bastard! You knew the whole time!"

Rowan bucked me off and I whirled for my sword. A cluster of vines wrapped around it, pink blossoms facing the sapphire that burned gold as I dreamed. The sword was stuck fast.

As Rowan approached I kicked at him while my fingers struggled with the sword. "You were lying to me, you and Alair both!"

"We were trying to protect you," he shouted, admitting the truth at last.

"I didn't need protection. Soren—Halen—was able to save us the whole time."

"You're bewitched," he yelled. "Let go of that sword. I'm destroying it today."

"No," I cried, finally pulling the sword from its sheath. I twisted around to stop Rowan as he came for me again.

We paused in a standoff, the blade between us.

"Give me the amulet, Rowan," I said, chest heaving.

"Rose, you don't—"

"*Now*." My voice rang with power.

He fumbled in his shirt and yanked the stone over his head. He tossed it to me, and with the sword I gestured him back into a corner of the tent. I retreated to the other corner and held the amulet in my fist, feeling for the first time its threads of magic. In my hand the amulet began to glow red.

"Just listen to me, first," Rowan was saying. "Listen."

But I wouldn't. The amulet was all that stood between me and Soren—Halen. I had to end the spell, had to escape this snowy hell and find him before it was too late. He'd warned me, he'd pleaded, and I hadn't listened. Why hadn't he just told me who he was?

The amulet was erdwitch, and my sword was Fae. Maybe one could break the other. I lowered the blade to the stone and sliced along it.

"Rose!"

I sawed at the rock, tears blurring my sight. Halen!

"No, Rose, wait—"

The stone split open, a faint blue mist rising from its hidden heart.

Rowan and I stared at the silent rock, and a terrible noise filled my ears. A thundering, beating cacophony descending to destroy us, only after a moment of horror I realized the sound was in my mind.

What Soren told me was true. Silaine had not stolen my memories along with everything else. That crime belonged to my brother. The amulet Rowan had worn around his neck all these weeks not only held Alair's death-curse, but also the bind on my memories.

The spell broke apart inside me.

My mind unlocked.

The terrible magic that guarded the knowledge from me like mist on the mountainside melted away, revealing the forest of memories waiting below. My family hadn't died at the castle; they died in front of me at our village, at the hands of Silaine as she spilled their blood and grew monsters from their deaths. Before then we'd been to Maeve, asking her blessing to marry, and she confessed the truth of my birth. My bones still rang from the shock of learning I was a princess.

And before that, the summer months I'd spent with Halen, at first mocking him for being a rich man's son, then the bewildering shock of falling in love with him. His hands, his eyes, the way he rushed to me after returning with his father's permission to marry me. The joy, the hope before the day that killed everyone I loved. My village, my people, my family, and Halen, Halen, Halen—

I stood, bending under the ceiling of the tent. My sword pointed at Rowan's neck, his eyes watching me with growing panic.

"Please," he whispered. "Please understand. I didn't know, not until it was too late."

The tip of the sword quivered as my hand shook. I spoke through the terrible ache in my throat. "How—How could you?"

"I promised."

"You did this to me." The cracking of my heart would break open my chest.

"I didn't know." Rowan scrambled to a sitting position. "Grandfather didn't tell me he'd hidden your memory until after we'd brought you back. I hated it but he made me promise—Rose, please!"

"No. Stop it." I jabbed the sword at him until he lay on his back with palms up. "After all this, after you knew what he'd done, you still lied to me. I trusted you and you *lied.*"

My brother hid my past from me. He kidnapped me from my love and let me believe there was no cure for what I'd lost. My life. My *heart.* He looked me in the eye and *lied.* And Rowan, my only family, my closest friend, had let me live that lie for weeks, even after Alair had gone, even after he discovered Alair's betrayal. I couldn't tell whose lie hurt more.

"Why?" I demanded. "Why would you do this to me?"

"Grandfather believed you'd trust the Betrayer no matter what we said. You didn't know what he'd become, you trusted him when he wanted to kill you—"

"He never wanted to kill me, he wanted to save us!"

Rowan's eyes darkened. "And you proved Grandfather right. You chose Soren over us at Briar, and Grandfather killed himself to keep protecting you, to keep you from knowing, because once you knew..."

"What?" I growled. "Once I knew, I'd choose the only one who could help us? The only one who hasn't held a grudge for the past hundred years?"

When Rowan crawled to his knees this time I let him. "How many times have we told you? Soren is *not* Halen. Halen died when he became *damnsoír.* He's not trying to help you, he's only following orders."

"He sacrificed himself for me. He saved my life."

Rowan lunged.

Even furious, I wouldn't do it. I moved the sword so he wouldn't impale himself, and Rowan crashed into me, tumbling both of us to the ground.

"He is *damnsoír,*" Rowan shouted as we struggled and he

pinned me down by the arms. "Do you think he's doing anything Silaine doesn't know about? Do you?" He shook me. "Soren may have saved your life, but he's *hers* now. If she ordered him to kill you, he'd have to. If you trust him you're going to wind up dead, and the rest of us with you!"

The truth burst out of me in a wave of anger and frustration. "No, *you* don't get it. Silaine's trying to open Shadelorn."

Rowan froze. "What?"

His momentary shock was enough for me to get a hand free and grab the dagger at his side. He reached for me but I got the blade to his neck first.

We froze. The tip of the knife dented the soft skin of his neck.

This time I would not flinch.

"Listen to me," I said, trying to calm my breathing. "Silaine needs my blood to get into Shadelorn. That's why she sent for me after all these years. Soren *did* know who I was the whole time, and didn't tell her."

Rowan stayed silent, staring at me with those black eyes, as cold as the stone they resembled.

"Soren was going to sneak me into Avalon, same as you. Only he actually has the power to do it. Even if we could somehow convince the other kings to help us now, we might never get close enough."

"We'll tell Darian what she's trying to do the next time we see him."

"You taught me better than that, Rowan. The Fae King will just have me killed so Silaine can't get her hands on me. And that won't solve our problem. She'll get into Shadelorn eventually, and then we'll all be gone."

"If that's the case, then they'll kill you in Avalon," he said through gritted teeth. “Just to stop your blood from ever being used to open the other door.”

“I’ve got to take that chance. If I can tell enough of them, or announce what Silaine’s doing publicly somehow, or—”

“You still don’t have a way to get there.”

“Yes I do. I’m going with Soren.”

“No!” Rowan moved suddenly, but I did not flinch with the dagger.

A thin trickle of blood slid down his neck.

“You don’t know what happened that day,” I said, steeling my heart against the sight. “But I do. I’m going with Soren. Take your men and go home. Go *home*, Rowan.”

Keeping the dagger at Rowan’s throat, my left hand reached around and picked up the sword I dropped in our scuffle. Rowan and I circled each other until my back was to the tent entrance. I fumbled with the ties while he watched, face clouded with anger and disappointment, but then I was free, and it didn’t matter.

Our fight had woken the others. Gile, Dedrick, Effer, Bremmer, Wes, and Fitzsimmons all stood in the circle of our tents. They must have heard everything.

“Your work is done,” I said, head spinning. “Go home.” I walked through them, sword in one hand, dagger in the other.

Rowan burst from the tent and watched me leave. I couldn’t meet his eyes. As soon as I was safely beyond the fire’s light I sheathed the dagger and ran through the woods. I wore only my cloak against the elements, and carried only my sword. Soren’s cloak. Soren’s sword.

Halen’s girl.

Perhaps a shouting grew behind me but I plunged and floundered too recklessly to tell, charging through drifts and breathing hard. In truth I was an inch away from crossing the line into sobbing or hysteria.

He waited for me not half a mile outside the camp, black cape swirling on a non-existent wind. I fell into his arms, home for the first time.

"My Rose," he whispered, voice breaking. "I should have told you sooner. I'm so sorry. I thought you'd hate me."

"Never," I said fiercely. "I could never hate you."

He wrapped his cape around me and the ground disappeared beneath my feet. The cape was as substantial as darkness, but it covered me completely, cocooning me in a nothingness centered only by Soren's warm body. I clung to him, breathing in his spicy, magical scent as he rode the winds. We covered ground it would have taken a week to travel by foot, and as the sun rose he set me down on the peak of the last mountain.

A magical fire awaited us next to a bed of Fae-woven blankets, burning bright and warm despite the winds and lack of fuel. No snow covered the ground here, though the heights were cold. The land before us was dark in the shadows, not white or gray. We had reached the end of Silaine's curse.

The scent of snow was on the breeze, but also the spice of trees, and the heavenly smell of living earth. I stared over the edge of the peak, hungry for the shades of dark green in the distance. I grieved for my snow-covered land and tried to pretend I wasn't grieving for Rowan as well. For leaving him. For the things I'd said.

I turned back to Soren, pushing away thoughts of the men I'd left behind. Rowan hid the truth from me. All I wanted now was to cover myself in memory and prepare for what must happen next.

Soren drew me down into the thick, soft blankets. We lay side by side, hands clasped together, and stared at each other, two lovers finally reunited after a century apart. The blue eyes I'd adored were gold now. I missed them, missed *him*.

"I remember," I whispered. "Everything until my family died. Until you… made the deal with Silaine. Tell me what happened after."

Soren sighed like he bore a grief so heavy it might kill him. "I could tell you. Or I could show you."

He pulled his hands from mine reluctantly, and we sat up. Soren retrieved a small bottle from a pouch at his side. The liquid inside glinted in the firelight. Maeve's gift.

The potion was cold as ice, but on my lips it turned warm, leaping into my mouth and then drying, coating my throat with ash. I gasped for air and Soren grabbed my shoulders as I thrashed, falling into another dream world where my body disappeared like the moon turning black.

And then I discovered that the truth is more horrible than any lie.

TWENTY-TWO

ONE HUNDRED YEARS AGO

I saw through Soren's eyes, and felt with his body, my own self lost in the wake of the memory.

Soren woke in a hut shared with two other bachelors, and crept out into the morning. But of course, he was not Soren then. He was Halen. Blue eyes not yet golden. Skin unblemished. Heart still pure.

Halen walked through the village of huts, their occupants beginning to stir. A baby squalled. A rooster crowed. Halen smiled. He'd grown to love this simple, quiet village. Life was slow, and peaceful, so different from the cutthroat culture of his father's court.

Mist covered the river that morning. He splashed some water on his face, then picked a rose from the vines that spilled over the banks to dangle in the water. He met my past self at my door with it, but in the vision I crushed the bloom between us as I leaped forward to hug him.

Today was a special day. Today we would go to the erdwitch and visit my little brother Alair, still recovering from his illness. But we had a second purpose. According to village tradition, we would ask Maeve for her permission to wed. She would give it, then we would return to the village and a great celebration before leaving tomorrow for the palace, where we would be married under the watch of the royal family.

On this day, my past self chose to let my hair hang loose in waves of orange. I wore a special dress of undyed wool, representing new beginnings, a blank canvas upon which we would paint a new life together. It was the same dress my mother wore at her wedding, a little too big for me, but the way it draped made me look like a priestess, holy and pure. Halen couldn't wait to take it off me.

We set out that morning under the approving smiles of my parents. Halen observed me be so careful not to dirty the dress, holding my hand to help me over logs and up the steeper hills. The erdwitch's home was half a morning's walk away, and we talked and laughed as we went. Halen told me again how his father reacted to Halen's declaration that he had fallen in love with a peasant and intended to marry her. Cynric had hoped for an alliance with Shalimar, but one of Halen's brothers or sisters could fill that role just as well. We felt only slightly guilty for this.

"And what did you tell them about me?" My past self asked.

"That you'll be a terrible princess," he said, and I laughed. "That you climb trees and hunt deer. That you wear deerskin and go barefoot sometimes."

"You didn't!" I gripped his arm tighter.

"That you bathe in the river with the men—don't give me that look, I know what I saw! And that you are brave and beautiful and kind, and we could live in the palace with their blessing or we could live in your village without it, because I am never leaving you."

Then we kissed. Halen put his hand in my hair and pulled me closer, in love with the joy of being around me. This was that fabled thing called love he'd witnessed courtiers risk everything for. Now he understood. He was willing to give up his home, his family, and his title for me, his wild mountain girl.

We made it over the foothills and ascended the rocky slope to the erdwitch's cave. The entrance was tall and wide enough for any type of man to go through, but beyond the opening lay a darkness too black for the bright day around us.

I'd told Halen that Maeve said I was welcome any time. She hadn't met Halen, as I'd carried Alair inside myself when he was dying, and Halen waited outside. But he didn't recall this long shadow. There was only light and warmth inside the cave, so why couldn't we see it?

I took Halen's hand and walked boldly into the opening. We groped around in inky blackness, and the sun at our backs vanished. Then the dark cleared from our eyes like mist to reveal what had greeted me before: a cozy interior room filled with candles, herbs, and furs. My brother lounged on a pile of animal skins, still bedridden. He jolted upright in surprise.

"Rose," he cried, and I ran to him.

Through Soren's eyes I saw myself embrace my little brother, his tan skin and dark hair so at odds with mine. Alair was eleven years old and still a little boy who idolized his older sister. But when he saw Halen over my shoulder he pulled away from my arms. "Why is *he* here?"

Halen and I exchanged glances. "Alair, where is Maeve?" I asked.

"I am here."

We turned, and saw her. Maeve looked much the same in Soren's memory as the last time I'd seen her in Lorensile, but she bore no smile, and her eyes were alert and focused. She stood as still as a tree, gaze locked on Halen.

I pried myself from Alair's hands and returned to Halen's side. I stepped in front of him. "Maeve, what's wrong?"

But she spoke to Halen. "You are the son of the Usurper."

"I... am the king's son," Halen faltered. "I'm not proud of how my father became king, but by the old laws his claim is rightful."

"No one can rule this land without the magic in their blood," Maeve said, advancing. Halen and I backed up. "Rose, my darling girl, why do you bring this boy to me?"

"We..." Halen's eyes and mine darted to each other again. "We came to seek your blessing. We wish to be married."

Behind us Alair gasped. Maeve closed her eyes. "Oh my child. Dear, sweet girl. How I have failed you."

"What? Maeve, I don't understand."

Maeve took Halen's hand and then mine, leading us towards the warm alcove. She sat us down on the furs and Alair scooted closer to my side. I placed one arm around him, but my other hand entwined with Halen's.

"It is time you knew the truth," Maeve said. "I wanted to wait until you were old enough for this responsibility, but it seems fate has moved for me."

"What truth?"

Maeve closed her eyes, and as she spoke the air swam before us until her words wove a misty dream to accompany her tale. She showed us the great crack of magic as Silaine was cast out of Avalon into our world. She told us of Silaine's growing power and followers, and how she used the blood of murdered villagers to create her terrible beasts.

Silaine had offered peace to Valeria's King Stefan, if he would only let her use the north as she saw fit. He refused. His army prepared for battle. In the mist we observed the features of King Stefan, his eyes blue like mine, his beard bristling with gold. Another man appeared in the mist, with a familiar face. Halen's father.

As Maeve spun her tale, Halen's mouth grew dry, and his grip on my hand tightened. His father had never been kind or patient, but Halen never knew the truth about Cynric's rise to power. It turned his stomach to know his father had made the wicked deal with Silaine.

Maeve's visions in the mist spared no detail. She showed us the cut throats of King Stefan and Queen Briallen, and the blood of their little children. Then the erdwitch's gray hands sank into a cradle and pulled forth a newborn babe with reddish-blonde hair. She quieted its cry with a touch of one finger. Princess Talia.

Lord Cynric overturned the bassinet and searched the room, but Maeve crept through the shadows, made invisible by her erdwitch magic.

With the entire royal line dead, Cynric received the crown amidst a sea of whispers, but Silaine's magic compelled all to raise no weapon against him.

"That child, the last of the great line of Valeria, carries the strongest magic left in human blood," Maeve explained. "She is the only heir to the blood seal on the portals between worlds. The only one who could open them again."

Halen glanced at me, but my face betrayed no suspicion, just rapt attention. His palms grew sweaty.

In the mist, Maeve disguised herself as a human, and placed the redheaded girl child into rough hands that cradled her gently. It was my mother.

Then my face shone from the mist.

Halen's blood chilled, and my hand squeezed his tight. A golden glow surrounded me in the image, and a silver circlet appeared on my forehead.

"Princess Talia," Maeve pronounced, and the mist dissolved,

revealing her strange face behind it. "Though her village calls her Rose." Her black eyes were bright with love and hope. She took my sweaty hands in hers. "You, my dear."

It took a long time for the shock to fade. Over the months he spent with us, Halen saw my pride in my village, and my love for my family. To learn I did not belong with them... to learn they were a placeholder until I could reclaim my true ancestry... He saw it break me open.

The knowledge beat in his head that his father had killed my father. That Halen's family was fundamentally at odds with the girl he loved.

"This can't be true," I insisted, pacing before him. "I'm not a princess. I'm not magical."

"You are," Maeve said, voice leaving no room for argument. "I carried you from the palace. I gave you to your parents to raise as their own. I have lived in this cave, waiting until you became a grown woman and could take on the burden of your responsibility."

"What responsibility? How could you not tell me?"

"To keep you safe. To keep anyone from discovering the truth." Maeve advanced on me. "Silaine grows powerful on the blood of your people. She will destroy us if she is not stopped. Only Avalon's King Oberon could challenge her, and as the last of the royal human line you are the only one who can open the portal, who can go to the king, who can plead for mercy—"

"Plead with the Fae? I would never."

"Rose." Alair's voice was quiet, but Halen knew the power he had over me. I immediately attentive to him. "You have to.

You're a princess now. You can save us, I know you can."

"Alair." I sank to my knees at his side. "I don't know how."

"Maeve will teach you," Alair said. "She's teaching me. See?" He clenched his eyes shut and held up his hand, from which a golden light began to glow.

I touched his hand, and Halen saw my chin set. I turned back to Maeve. "What does this mean for Halen? When he is king... can't he undo the agreement made with Silaine? Can't we fight her then?"

Halen opened his mouth, but didn't know how to say that he was ashamed of his father. That he would stand by me. That he felt everything he wanted slipping away from him.

"The Usurper made a blood oath," Maeve said. "It's possible it could be undone, yes, by one of his blood. But by the time Halen ascends the throne it will be too late."

"You can't marry him now, Rose," Alair said, tugging on my arm. "You can't."

Halen bit his lip. "He's right. You're the true ruler of Valeria. I can't ask you to marry the son of your family's murderer." He hated the words as they left his mouth.

When he could bring himself to look at me, my eyes were filled with tears. My chin trembled. "And I can't ask you to fight against your father. He's your family, Halen. No matter what he did."

"You of all people should know that family is made of more than blood. I love you, Rose. And I will do everything in my power to fix what my father did."

I looked at him for a moment, eyes bright and mouth firm. "Maeve, do you give your blessing?"

Alair looked to Maeve with panic, but the erdwitch smiled and held up her hands. "If you know the truth and still choose each other, then I will bless your union."

Halen and I embraced. He held me in his arms, shaking with relief. For a moment there... for a moment he thought he'd lost me forever.

We made promises to return soon, to plan and learn, and Maeve swore us to secrecy about my true identity. Halen waited while I kissed Alair, ruffled his hair, and told him to get well and strong. He clung to me and sniffed hard but didn't cry, and glared at Halen when I wasn't looking.

But there was time for that to change. As Alair grew older he would realize that his sister loved him and would always be there for him. We might even need to use his powers one day, though he was still such a small boy.

Then we exited the cave into the bright sunshine, and set off down the mountain. That was the last time Alair spoke to his sister for more than a hundred years.

We heard the screaming from a mile away.

We had nothing with us—no bows, no swords, not even a knife. That didn't stop me. I ran toward my village with Halen struggling to keep up, begging me to slow down, to wait, to *think*. He caught up with me at the ridge overlooking the hollow where my village lay.

All was carnage.

Beasts with snarling fangs and terrible claws smashed our homes. The bodies of our men lay scattered on the ground. Giant Fae guarded what remained of my people, shoving forward one at a time to die at the hands of the mistress who orchestrated the massacre.

Silaine.

We knew the tales, but had never seen a Fae. They were tall and angular, with lithe bodies and long ears. Some were green or pink or burnt umber, but Silaine was white as milk. Power rippled from her like heat around a flame. Her hair was black as death, hanging down to her waist and braided with beads and bone.

She wore a crimson dress made wet with splattered blood. Fae soldiers threw another victim at her feet, and Silaine bent to cut the poor woman's throat. As her blood spilled Silaine raised her arms, and with a string of dark, musical words, something began to sprout from the blood.

It puffed up like a mushroom from a pile of manure. As in birth, the large, meaty head came first. Then claws scrabbled at the dirt as if it could pull itself from nothingness into existence. The puddle of blood it grew from vanished as its body filled out with a hunched back and fat, stubby tail. The creature roared through its fangs but shunted sideways as Silaine reached for her next victim.

The drained body was now a colorless husk. A Fae seized and threw it onto a pile of bodies burning in the bonfire that was to be used in our celebration that night.

Halen forgot himself, forgot me, so horrified was he by the slaughter below us. There was nothing we could do. It was too late. Silaine had almost finished with the villagers—my family, my neighbors, my friends.

Neither of us heard the Fae soldiers that crept from behind and seized us by the arms. Halen stood still in shock, but I twisted like a mad cat, unleashing the wild scream Halen couldn't seem to voice himself.

Restraining me easily, the Fae dragged us down the ridge

and threw us into the mud at Silaine's feet. I launched myself at the nearest Fae, but he backhanded me and I fell to the ground. We were going to die. There was no escape. And our blood would be used to birth more monstrous creatures for Silaine's terrible army.

Halen stared at me on the ground, my sacred white dress soiled with muck and blood.

A feeling bubbled in his bones. It was love and anger and overwhelming clarity. It was an absolute refusal to let the girl he loved die in this massacre and become another nameless husk turned to ash. The refusal was stronger than anything he'd ever felt, stronger than his love for me, and crystallized by the knowledge that it wasn't merely the anger of the doomed. He had the power to save me. Maeve had given him the key.

He stood to face Silaine.

In one hand she held the dripping knife, but what frightened him most was her face. Her expression was peaceful, joyful even, as if her work were virtuous and rewarding. Her eyes were large and slanted, mounted in an unusual face too angular and fine to be human. But it was her mouth that drew him in, that stunned him. The mouths of the Fae men he'd seen were thin and regular, but this one was different. Silaine's lips were full and red, split on either side like someone had taken a knife and widened her smile. A monster's mouth.

The look she gave him was cruel and beautiful, those terrible, thin darts curving upwards in amusement.

Silaine raised the knife to slit his throat. He could not speak, not even to object at his impending death. But as the knife descended Silaine's arm seized, and her eyes widened in shock and pain.

The knife fell to the ground.

Silaine clutched her arm in one hand, and looked down at Halen. "Why can't I kill you?" Her voice was husky and musical, yet disinterested. As if this turn of events was nearly beyond her notice.

Determination rose in him, made him defy the Fae with his glare. "I am the son of King Cynric. You made a blood oath to never harm him or his descendants. To support his rule. To only work in the northlands."

Silaine eyed him. "That is so. Leave then, prince. This harvest does not concern you."

She turned to me. Halen leaped between us. "I won't," he said, planting his feet in the mud. "I wish to renegotiate the blood oath."

"No," I cried, but Halen didn't take his eyes off Silaine.

For an instant she looked surprised, but then her gaze sharpened upon him. "What do you require?"

"That you spare her life." Behind him I climbed to my feet, one hand reaching forward to touch his back. To anchor myself.

Silaine's eyes looked past him, to me. They roved up and down my body before switching back to Halen. "What is she worth to you? You have much I desire, young prince. My price will be steep."

"Name it," he said through gritted teeth.

"Halen," I said. "Don't do this."

"You will dissolve the restrictions on my movements. I will have full access to all of this land."

"No," I begged.

"Yes," Halen said.

Behind him I charged one of the guards but he was too quick

for me to steal his sword. He grabbed me. Instead of throwing me back to the mud, he held my hands behind my back so I couldn't attack anyone again. I screamed and thrashed, but the guard shook me until I stopped. Halen ached to comfort me, to even look at me, but didn't dare take his eyes from Silaine. Behind him I sobbed in defeat.

"You will dissolve the protection against your family, and my defense of your father's rule."

"...Yes."

"You will agree to become my slave, to serve me forever and a day, to advise me on matters of this earth."

"Halen, no," I cried behind him. "Don't do this. Don't give it to her."

He knew what she was asking. He knew what it meant. But a world without me in it was not only intolerable, but a death sentence for every human. There would be no one left to warn Avalon, to make them return for the horror they'd inflicted on us. In the end it was no choice at all.

"Yes."

Silaine smiled so wide even her slitted lips parted. I screamed and screamed until Silaine approached me herself and sang a tiny melody that made me lose consciousness.

Then she bound Halen with Fae-magicked cord that held him immobile as Silaine's new beasts surrounded her and began to sing. Amidst a chorus of howls and barks she lifted her arms to the evening sky and danced. In an instant everyone scattered into the woods, and as his captor darted between shadows and light, Halen too lost contact with this world.

He woke on a stone altar with the ceremony already pulsing around him. Night had drawn across the sky, and small fires lit the darkness in concentric circles surrounding the stone. Silaine stood at his head while Fae chanted and danced. In the intoxicating music, his mind swam. He moaned on the stone in the grip of this terrible dream, and choked down a cup of bitterness poured into his mouth.

Then the true nightmare began. He slipped in and out of consciousness. The only voice became Silaine's, thundering in his ear, spelling out the points of their agreement while he cried his consent. Then another cup. One of blood.

He cried out for me but never heard my voice or saw my face. He felt lips at his throat, but they were cold, not warm like mine. They bit, they hurt, they drank from him.

And everything went quiet.

He went to a deeper place, where he saw the borders between himself and the magic that whirled about the world, but was not his to channel. Another being hung there, this one bright and glowing with the power he could feel but not grasp. It came to him, absorbed him as one fish will gulp another in the depths of the darkest places. And then the light was in him, too.

It hurt. It shone through bonds never meant to bear this brightness. The universe shifted as if swinging on a hinge, and Halen belonged to himself no more.

A roaring grew in the distance, and shook him back to his own body. Silaine lay next to him on the great stone, her mouth red with his blood, holding him to her like a mother clutches a newborn babe.

He felt different. He was no longer in possession of his own soul—everything he was belonged to Silaine now. Her voice shook his world, her words became unbreakable law.

He pulled from Silaine's arms and examined his hands, now smooth and white, and hairless as the Fae. He saw differently, as if he had walked around with eyes unfocused his whole life. He heard more, smelled more. He could smell the blood spilled between them, but when he touched his neck there was no wound.

Silaine's eyes opened. She smiled. He was not afraid of her, only of what he had done. He was not human now, but Other. A being whose sole purpose was to serve. Not to die, not to betray, but to submit within the bounds of his Mistress's law.

But he still loved me.

"What am I?"

"*Damnsoír*," she pronounced. "My dancer. And what shall I call you, dear prince?"

The name rose unbidden to his lips. Not his own, for he was not himself. It was a name of thunder, and of being set apart. "Soren," he said.

A name of sorrow.

"Where is Rose?"

He staggered after Silaine as they returned to her half-castle in the pale morning light. It was a stunted thing, built of rock and mud and magic. Silaine showed him to the cell where my sleeping body lay on the hard floor.

He rushed to me, shook my body in its stained dress crusted with blood and mud. My chest rose and fell. My heart beat. But I would not wake.

"What have you done?" he cried, rocking over me.

"You love her, slave of my soul?"

"Yes. Please, let her go. You promised."

"Your blood and my blood made a promise. And all we agreed was that she would live." Silaine crouched near my body, though Halen wanted to scream at her to get away.

Silaine began to hum, and ran her long fingers through my orange hair. Bruising and tear marks stained my face. "A beautiful child, *damnsoír*. I will keep her for you."

"No," Soren said. "Just let her go. Please, just let her go."

"You misunderstand. This girl will age and grow old while you serve me, as beautiful in a thousand years as you are now. Wouldn't you rather keep her just how she is?"

"No! I want her to live."

"She does live, my prince. I will keep her safe. My gift to you."

"Please—"

"Do not anger me, slave." Her voice turned vicious in an instant. Her will vibrated through him like sound through a bell. "Now, kiss her."

"What?"

"Kiss her. Kiss her now." The command came over him as an uncontrollable urge. He wanted to kiss me. He *must* kiss me, but feared the look in Silaine's alien eyes.

As he bent his head over mine, Silaine hummed her haunting tune and touched my arm with one finger. Where she touched the skin glowed gold before fading, and as Halen's lips touched mine he felt that magic inside my skin, felt his kiss finish the spell like pulling a knot tight.

"There now," Silaine said. "I give her to you, my prince. Eternally young. Eternally beautiful. You hold her in your kiss. And I tell you now, you may never kiss her again, but that I give you leave."

What was left of his soul felt torn asunder. Even Silaine must have sensed it, for the indulging smile fell from her face.

"You," Halen said, voice deep and terrible, eyes on me, but they both knew to whom he spoke. "You are a monster."

Silaine's eyes flared. "I am Fae!" She yanked Soren to his feet.

"No," he screamed. And screamed. And screamed. Until Silaine had to issue a thousand commands to keep him silent and still.

"You will learn quickly with me, slave," she said, voice low. "I chose you because you are a prince, and a fine *damnsoír* to have in this dirty, little world. But remember now that all you have is mine. You are mine. And if you do not learn to be a good companion, you will see how fast your golden cage becomes one of bone."

When Silaine released him from his stillness, Soren followed her without a sound.

In the coming weeks he learned much about his new life and role. He was a different person now, tempered by power and slavery, and his new education concerning the Fae. He learned their customs, their hierarchies, and his place among them. He was born human, a lesser being, but now inseparable from the Fae sorceress who had bonded with him. Lesser Fae deferred to him wherever he went, and he spoke with his Mistress's authority.

All that remained of the boy Halen was his love for me. He felt the most like his old self when he visited my lifeless body, stroking my hair and cleaning the dust from my brow. A thousand times he tried to kiss me, to end the spell of sleeping, but any time he brought his lips near mine an invisible force kept him from me. He could no more unite the sun and moon than kiss the girl he loved.

Silaine envied this remaining sliver of his old life. She threatened to bury me alive until Soren vowed to let me be, but because she had not commanded his avoidance of me he found he was still able to slip into my cell. It was the first seed of disobedience he would nurture into an entire forest.

Perhaps she sensed the rebellion growing in him. She could not hear his thoughts, but perhaps some part of his desperation made her choose to separate us further. And so when she mounted her attack against Valeria's capitol she brought my body along for the ride.

Silaine's Fae warriors and blood-born beasts ravaged the villages and inner city crouching at the foot of the castle. Her forces moved so swiftly the royal court was left in a panic, unsure of who attacked them, refusing to believe it could be the fabled and reclusive Fae.

Silaine sent Soren to penetrate the castle.

It was simple. He still looked like himself, despite the ethereal smoothness of his skin, and the strangeness of his new, golden eyes. He wore fine, Fae-spun clothes, looking every inch a proper crown prince. With ease he passed through each gate, eliciting cries of joy, and walked among the battlements, playing a curious, small wooden flute. He blew a funny tune, eyes deadened like every movement was made without permission of the being inside. As he passed, the defending guards fell silent. Their eyes closed, and they sank to the ground, dead asleep.

Arrows ceased to fall. No spears flew from the high, stone

walls. Hot oil boiled away in cauldrons untended. A thousand terrible beasts broke through the gates.

Soren blended into the fleeing crowd, flowing through hallways he had known since he was a child. His family cowered in the royal apartments. Even the heavy wooden doors leading to the inner sanctums stood unguarded. His family watched in terror as he stepped from the shadows into the light.

"Halen," his mother screamed, and rushed towards him. He let her cling to him without moving to hug her or push her away. His little siblings, the two princesses and his toddling brother, followed their mother's lead and clustered wide-eyed around him. They cried in terror.

Halen's eyes flickered to his father. King Cynric stood as if frozen, skin waxy and hands trembling. The heavy crown hung too low on his brow. The Usurper looked Halen up and down, stumbling away from him. "What happened to you, son?"

"How could you?" The whispered words fell on their ears like a curse. Halen took his mother's hand. "Follow me," he said, and with blind trust led his family out into the fray.

Everyone rushed in the same direction, called by an unseen host of musicians. They played merrily, as if to calm the shrieks and shouts of panic, but there was something compelling about the music. A few of the courtiers' feet tapped in a nervous step as the crowd flowed on and on.

And Halen led his family at the very tail of the mob. Through the corridors with rich tapestries, down the stairs lit by smoky torches, along the main hallway boasting suits of armor and other fine human creations. Into the magnificent, long throne room.

Where Silaine waited.

Fae guards separated the men and women onto two sides, like they might have stood at court. A carpeted pathway lay from the entrance to the King's throne where Silaine stood on the royal dais. And Soren knew what it was to behold her in the full glory of her Fae beauty and heritage.

She wore another dress of red, fitted everywhere but the calf, where it spread along the floor like a puddle of blood. Gold scales accentuated the fabric and swirled around her skin. Behind her stretched two magnificent wings of white, not flesh but decoration. She was an angel of death, a goddess of destruction.

If the Fae court was filled with naught but those like Silaine, he dreaded ever having to see the sight of it.

"Oath-breaker!" Soren's father broke the spell of horror and awe. "Oath-breaker!" He stumbled down the carpeted path, rage purpling his face. "We have a blood oath!"

Even in a moment like this a chorus of shocked or smug whispers echoed around the chamber.

"A blood oath. Oh, yes," Silaine said, her voice ringing from the rafters. "But you forget the laws of blood. And I've made a new oath."

Soren couldn't bear to meet their eyes, but his mother's gasp was forever imprinted on his mind. His father rushed at him in rage and was flung back by two Fae guards.

"You have done well, servant," Silaine said to Halen. "So I will spare you from the next. Leave us now, and bar the door."

The crowd screamed. He saw their faces, so many faces, as the men struggled and the women cried. Fae warriors guarded Soren as he retreated up the carpet to the tall double-doors.

Though he wanted to rage against her command, his will was no longer his own. With all his strength he pulled the doors shut, Silaine's orders the only thing forcing him to function. But once the doors were barred there was nothing to stop him from collapsing on the cold stone.

Screams of the people inside filled the night. Silaine's voice rose over them, powerful and deep, shaking the walls and calling to blood, enticing it to spill. A thin stream trickled out of Halen's nose as the cacophony turned to silence.

Blood flowed out from beneath the double doors. Then stopped. Then sucked back into the room as a great roaring grew in the distance, and wind swirled around the castle in a tempest under command of Silaine's curse.

At last, all was peaceful. The Fae warriors broke down the doors from inside and exposed Soren to the aftermath: a sea of bodies scattered about the room, pale as snow, bloodless as the husks of insects. Silaine shone from her seat on the king's chair, vivacious in the afterglow of her magic.

Soren stumbled towards her, praying not to see the bodies of his family. He fell at her feet. "What have you done?"

Silaine only smiled. "You will soon know what I am capable of. But now I have prepared something special for you, my prince. Go to the tallest tower, and there let your lovely prize comfort you."

Soren rose and fled the hall of death. Silaine's warriors gathered up the bodies and threw them into the courtyard below. Her beasts were set free, and they raced through the halls, tearing apart anyone who remained hidden in the corners.

Outside the sky darkened, and the winds grew cold.

Soren climbed the tall, tall tower as the first snowflakes fell.

In his arms he carried freshly-cut roses from the wilting gardens. Their thorns dug into his skin, but he never noticed his blood darkening the petals. Outside, Silaine's beasts buried the bodies of the courtiers in a ring around the castle, and Soren feared what evil she would coax from their graves.

As he passed each window the wailing from the villages in the distance grew louder, and he heard the church bells tolling, tolling...

Then silence.

Finally, he reached me. In the uppermost room of the tallest tower my body lay on a bed meant for a king. The frame shone with gold leaf laid over the intricate carvings of a hundred roses. Pale bedding draped from my body in ripples of the finest silk.

Silaine had ordered me dressed in the gown of a princess, priceless jewels adorning the bodice. The tiara set on my forehead belonged to one of Soren's dead sisters.

I was the bride Soren was never to have, the peasant with which Silaine thought to defile the royal bed. Only Soren knew I was finally where I belonged.

He lay the roses around me one by one; the only gifts he could give me now. He touched my hair and tried to kiss my lips once more, but Silaine's orders held him from me as surely as her curse kept me sleeping.

Soren wept.

He stood at the window, heart as cold as the cruel winds that brought in the storm. He watched the land sink beneath endless waves of snow. Then Soren stepped onto the crumbling ledge and leaped from the tower out into the great, white, empty world.

No longer human, no longer free, not even Soren's death was his own.

His body pieced itself back together in a matter of minutes. Silaine stood waiting when he opened his eyes, her skin white as the snow, her gown red as the blood that made it. When she smiled even the slits on either side of her lips parted.

She held out her hand. "Come, *damnsoír*. You will not be rid of me so easily."

Soren despaired.

In the confusing months following the endless snowfall, more and more refugees gave up and fled Valeria. Where once Silaine's forces would have captured the crowds, now she sent Soren to lead them astray. Bound by his curse, he had no choice but to lure countless families into death and slavery. Silaine either broke their backs in labor, finishing her great and hideous castle, or else spilled their blood to bring forth more of her monsters, growing her army of beasts to the count of legions.

During this time Soren learned more of the Fae, and Silaine in particular. He learned that entertainment was their highest law, dancing and music their finest sports, that they held all things Fae as sacred, and all things non-Fae as disposable. They were a proud, vain species, ruthless because they lacked empathy, murderous not out of cruelty, but because they did not see their actions as wrong.

In this way he came to understand them.

After the massacre at the castle, Silaine returned to her base in the north, a lone bubble of life amidst the desolate, snow-covered lands. Soren slipped away the first instant he could. He snuck past the Fae warriors at their music-making, and went the long way around the slave cages so he would not have to witness their despair. He wondered if Silaine could sense this disobedience, or if she could track him by the magical cloak, but nothing impeded his escape.

The cloak had been a gift, woven from darkness and moonlight. It allowed Soren to move as the Fae did, darting through shadows and slipping between fey lines that took him farther and faster than he'd ever run before. He stepped into the moonlight in front of Maeve's cave, his boots leaving the lightest imprint on the snow.

The cave's entrance was half-covered with drifts, and as dark as before, but something was different. With new eyes he looked over the magic of the erdwitch, noticing for the first time how the darkness *shone*. Would he even be allowed entrance to this safe place?

Soren pulled enough snow away to slip through the cave's opening into the shining darkness. For a moment all was still as he groped along the rock. A tendril of fear wound its way up his heart. What if he wouldn't be allowed in? What if he'd wander here forever in the black? Worse, what if Alair and Maeve had been killed, or abandoned the cave?

Then the mist cleared and Alair ran to him.

"Halen!" The little boy rushed to Soren, but as soon as they reached each other, he gasped and drew back, afraid.

Soren felt it, too—the strange current between them as their skin touched. Soren wondered if Alair fully understood, or if the new magic in him simply sensed something cursed in Soren's heart.

"What's happening? Where's Rose?" Alair blurted.

My name was a dagger, and Soren didn't know how to begin.

Maeve rose from her stove, and Alair retreated to her side. "*Damnsoír*," she said, the word rough in her mouth, not melodious as when Silaine spoke it. She pushed Alair behind her and Halen thought he would die of shame. "How did this happen?"

He had to find the words. "Silaine attacked the village. Everyone is dead."

Alair's eyes flooded with tears but he wiped them away furiously.

"She tried to kill Rose, but I—I couldn't... I made a deal, her life for mine. And Silaine—"

"Rose is alive?" Alair tried to lunge forward but Maeve held his arm. "Where is she?"

"I traded my freedom for her life," Soren said. "I should have made a better deal. She's safe, Alair. But she sleeps. At the palace."

"What do you mean?" Alair yelled even as Maeve tried to shush him.

"She won't wake until I kiss her. And I can't. I'm—I mean, I..." He couldn't say it.

"Halen belongs to the Fae now," Maeve said. "He must obey the commands of his mistress."

If Soren's heart hadn't already been broken, Alair's tiny fury would have done the job. He broke free from Maeve and ran howling towards Soren, who accepted the pointless beating, not even trying to hold Alair from him.

"I'm sorry," he said, but Alair wouldn't hear it.

"You killed them," he screamed. "I know you did. I hate you. I hate you. I wish *you* had died." He collapsed into Maeve's arms and she whispered to him until his eyes grew heavy with sleep.

"Help me with him," Maeve said, and together they carried Alair onto the soft blanket of furs in the inner recesses of the cave.

Soren was grateful she did not shun him. He knelt and smoothed Alair's hair from his forehead. "He'll never forgive me."

Maeve didn't argue. "Did you really become *damnsoír* to save Rose? Does the princess truly live?"

He rose and nodded. "Her sleep is sealed with my... kiss. And I've been forbidden to ever kiss her again. Please, is there any other way? Can't you do something?"

"The binds of a Fae curse are outside my reach. Rose is bound by the rules of the curse." She touched the place where his heart still miserably beat. "As you are bound."

"Can I reverse it? Any of it?"

"No. If your kiss is her seal, then only your kiss will wake her. And to be *damnsoír* is to be forever changed. There's no going back."

He hadn't dared to hope anyway.

"I'd rather she sleep than lie dead," Maeve said, her voice gentle. "Alair may not understand, but I do. This was a great sacrifice you made. You must never speak of this to anyone. You must keep it from Silaine at all costs."

Soren nodded, two tears coursing down his cheeks. "Yes, I know."

"And the winter... I assume it belongs to her as well?"

"Yes. Until she gets what she wants."

"I see."

"What will you do?" Would she trust him with this?

"We will go to Shalimar," Maeve said. "Alair is very young and has much to learn of his magic. We will wait. Gods willing, there will come a time when the princess wakes again."

"And then?"

Maeve's black eyes met his with pity. "We will hope it is Silaine's death that has ended her sleep."

Soren left with Maeve's blessing and crept back to his new home. He would not see Alair again for over a decade. What few bonds of friendship had existed between them would remain irrevocably broken.

A scant year after the first snowfall, Silaine pit her meager troupe of Fae warriors against a battalion of her hand-created beasts. It was a glorious day; the weather calmed for the battle. Piercing gargrayles, lumbering behemoths, and slithering dragons marred the virgin snow. Soren stood at Silaine's side, her hair embellished with war beads, her body covered in robes of gold and red. She blew a Fae horn and the battle raged. Warriors yelled, beasts screamed, and in the distance the noise unleashed an avalanche from the mountain.

In the end, the warriors slayed the beasts. Soren sensed Silaine's anger growing, her smile darkening to a glare. She threw her ornamental sword to the ground and stormed off in a spit of sparks. Soren smiled. Her beasts would never be enough to withstand the force of Avalon. They were copies, good for sport in Avalon, but no more able to kill true Fae warriors than a rabbit could overpower the hounds. Silaine needed an army of real power, an army that could stand against King Oberon himself.

That night, as Soren stood the only unharmed object in the path of her rage, he witnessed her epiphany. If she could not create an army then she would find a better one.

"It's simple, *damnsoír*," she said, running her hand through Soren's hair as he sat at her side by the fire. "We shall open Shadelorn."

In the old human legends, Shadelorn was a dark and terrible place, filled with beasts cursed from our world by the uneasy truce between Fae and humans. But the Fae had a different version of the story. One in which Shadelorn was not a prison, but a sanctuary.

Fae history spoke of an agreement made between Fae, human, and erdwitch after centuries of conflict. Earth was already covered with humans, so they could keep it. The Fae would retreat to a world of their own making, their fabled utopia Avalon. Any other intelligent beast—magical or other—that sought peace would enter a third world of endless forests, where they could live as they'd always wanted to.

For protection, for solitude, for permanence, the portals were sealed with blood so only a few could pass back and forth between. As the generations of humans continued, stories about the beasts faded, until we remembered them as murderous monsters, and the Fae as our somewhat mischievous partners in helping us rid our world of their threat.

Why would the denizens of Shadelorn want to help Silaine? Perhaps they were as weary of their utopia as the Fae were of theirs. Perhaps they wanted revenge on King Oberon for slaying thousands of them years before. In any case, forming an alliance with Shadelorn was Silaine's last hope, and she set about entering that lonely kingdom.

But first she had to find the doorway. Human legend held it was buried deep in the earth so the beasts within would never claw their way out.

Silaine's human slaves began to dig.

Soren visited the old palace every chance he had. He'd learned to find the loopholes in Silaine's commands with the cunning of a Fae. Unless specified, her orders didn't have to be completed immediately. He chose his little rebellions with care, selecting each one with the intention to surprise—and therefore entertain—his Mistress. As the novelty of having a *damnsoír* faded, he worked to maintain his value. He became not just a mindless slave, but a confidante. An advisor.

An opponent.

His humanity—his defiance—amused her. Her power over him was so great that she could not fear him. Her commands grew less and less specific. He suspected she delighted in the ways he could surprise her.

But she was not without surprises herself. Their games gave him the freedom he needed to return to the palace, and the first time he dared the journey he found another of Silaine's workings:

Surrounding the palace was a ring of thorns. Vines as thick as his waist surged from the earth and tangled their millions of branches together. Needle-sharp, foot-long thorns pointed in a thousand different directions, their tips tinged a deep red as if dipped in blood.

So this is what Silaine had done with the bodies of the courtiers. They were rose vines grown monstrous, with every petal of tenderness and beauty stripped away. They made a wall so thick Soren hadn't the faintest hope of squeezing through. Except the thorns moved away as he approached. The vines and trunks bent and creaked, arching out of his way and forming a gateway for him to pass through.

He feared they would seize him in an instant, holding him trapped yet unable to die as their thorns pierced him over and over, but Silaine's evil fence did not so much as shudder as he passed beneath its boughs.

Soren continued to visit often, weeping over my body and trying to break his curse and kiss me. In the endless snow he didn't realize how much time had passed until, for the first time, he found someone else in the tower when he arrived.

It should have been impossible. Terror gripped his heart as he hadn't known in years. How could someone have broken through Silaine's magical fence, let alone someone like this? It was a young man, wrapped in armor and thick fur. He hummed with what Soren could now recognize as magic, but it wasn't like the Fae. Soren had felt it once before, in the first days of his new life. In the mountains. In a cave dark with secrets.

In an instant he saw the little boy in the man before him. Alair. Full grown and with a portion of the erdwitch's power. Alair stood over my bed, fist clenched at his side. Soren cleared his throat and Alair whirled.

They stared at each other for a moment. Alair stood taller than Soren by several inches, his strength evident even through the heavy furs he wore against the cold. His dark hair was short on top, with a small braid in the back. He looked like his grandson would years later, but stockier. Rougher.

Alair spoke first. "You."

The air seemed to crackle between them. Soren recognized the terrible feeling lurching inside him: envy. Alair had grown, matured, *changed*. Soren was the same. For a moment he thought it would come to blows, but Alair only turned back to the girl laying motionless before him.

"She seems so much younger now. I am older than my older sister," he said with wonder. "You were both like giants to me."

Soren felt naked in a way Silaine had never yet managed to make him feel. Not for the first time, his seventeen-year-old body was a prison, not a blessing. "How did you get in?" He asked.

Alair made a noise of disgust. "I am witch. We walk through Fae magic as easily as cobwebs." My brother touched my hair and fiddled with the silver tiara. "Maeve taught me that. She also told me what happened. That you were there, at the village. She told me what you became."

The hope in Soren's chest turned cold.

"*Damnsoír*," Alair continued, the word bitter on his tongue. "Slave. Companion. Do you kiss the Fae like you kissed my sister?"

Soren reacted, but in his heart he wanted the pain. And so he didn't struggle as Alair slammed him against the stone wall, as he didn't struggle years ago when Alair beat him with small fists. Now my brother lifted him up, magic sparking as Fae and erdwitch powers were set at odds.

"How could you do it?" Alair snarled. "How could you do this to her?"

"To save her," Soren managed to say, his sole defense

sounding as tired aloud as it had in his mind.

"And everyone else? Do you know what you did to Valeria?" The veins stood out in Alair's neck. "Thousands who lost their lives, and the rest homeless. Outcasts, foreigners in a land that never wanted them. You destroyed us!" He slammed Soren's head against the stones again, then let him drop to the floor. "I should kill you for what you did."

"Please," Soren whispered. "Do it. If you can."

The squint in Alair's eyes lessened only slightly. Soren picked himself up, the pain in the back of his head making the room spin.

"There is a legend now," Alair said, watching as Soren checked his scalp for bleeding. "A demon who lures travelers astray in the snowy lands. Whole villages never made it out. What defense do you have for that?"

"You know what Rose is. Did Maeve never explain it to you? The only way to stop Silaine is through that gate between worlds, and the rest of us don't have a key. What else could I have done?"

"You could have died," Alair bellowed. "You could have faced death like a man, not cowering before that monster and begging for your life!"

"That's not how it happened. You weren't there. I had to save her."

"Yes, and look how you've *saved* her. She's a breathing corpse in a ruined kingdom—"

"No—"

"When she wakes, she will have nothing left but me. And *you*... the boy we thought loved her... You swore loyalty to her enemy and destroyed her birthright. You have been a far greater foe than Silaine ever was."

Anger moved through Soren's chest into the tightness in his jaw. "Would you have let her die, Alair? Would you have stood there, safe, and watched Silaine draw a blade across her neck?"

"I wouldn't have sold myself to that demon. I wouldn't have become this—this *monster* that you are."

Monster. The word hurt unexpectedly, deep inside. A monster, made from blood. Just like Silaine's terrible beasts. *I am one of them.* Soren sank to his knees.

"If you care about her at all," Alair said, though Soren hardly heard him through the pain of his realization, "then when the day comes that you are given leave to kiss her again... you will flee before she opens her eyes."

Two tears squeezed from between Soren's clenched eyelids, hot and stinging. He turned away and shoved both fists against his mouth to keep from crying out.

"But I will be here waiting for her. And when she asks for you... I will tell her you are dead."

Soren hid his face from the world and took a shuddering breath. Then another. He lowered his hands and looked Alair in the eye. "We should not be enemies, Alair. We both want the same thing."

"Aye. But when that bitch Fae tells you to wake my sister with a knife at her throat, what you *want* will mean less than nothing. You betrayed her, *damnsoír*. Never think it was something different."

Soren watched Alair's boots clink on the stone floor as he walked back to my sleeping body. A pause while Alair kissed my forehead. Then Soren listened to the footsteps echo down the long spiral staircase. He did not rise again until he could believe that Alair was wrong.

It took a long time.

Meanwhile, Silaine's human slaves dug for months. Dug until their hands were useless with sores. Dug until their backs gave out. Dug until they collapsed. And every time a slave died Soren supplied a new one to take their place.

After the portal was finally located, Silaine thought her blood would be enough to open it. After all, her sister was the Fae Queen. She gave Soren the honor of piercing her hand, but as she held it to the portal nothing happened.

Silaine raged.

She had tricked King Oberon to break open the portal from Avalon to Earth. He could not be fooled in that way again, so there was only one option left. The family she had so carelessly helped Halen's father slaughter those years ago turned out to be the key to her dreams. Silaine gave Soren a special task, that of locating any of Valeria's remaining royal line.

And so Soren brought my every distant living relative to the slaughter, from old men to newborn babes. All in vain. All while knowing the solution to this violence. But he stayed silent.

In the years that came, the boy I loved sought his death with the devotion of a religious zealot.

He threw himself off cliffs, then mountains. He sank to the bottom of frozen lakes. He burned himself in great bonfires. Each time, his body knit itself together again, and his unconsciousness during the false death was no more refreshing than a terrible night's sleep. But the deaths were not without consequence. A landscape of fine scars sprouted on Soren's skin where it had broken apart, scars that would never fade.

Silaine met his suicides with amusement and did not forbid his futile deaths. It was not in the Fae nature to be self-destructive, and his death-wish fascinated her. "Do you love me so little, *damnsoír*?" She asked once after he bled out through his wrists.

"I can't do this," he said, voice breaking as the blood slithered back into his veins no matter how he tried to shake it out. "Please. Please, I'll do anything. Just let me die."

"My poor dancer." Silaine pulled him into her arms. "So weak. So cowardly."

Not even his pride stung him anymore. Only the pain. "I was not meant for this. I'm only human."

"In that you are wrong. You are no longer human, my pet, but not Fae. Immortality was not meant to be carried on human shoulders, and so you stumble under its weight. But I am not too cruel a Mistress. This, too, we can fix." She touched a finger to his forehead.

Soren bowed under her will. "Anything," he whispered, "just make it stop."

That was the night she cut out his heart.

Silaine was many centuries old and had learned many spells. Spells to part the skin, spells to stop the bleeding, and spells to remove the heart and leave it beating.

"Shall I tell you what I'm going to do with it?" Silaine asked, turning his heart over and over in her hands as it quivered like a frightened pet.

Before her, Soren lay chained to a stone table, his chest sealing up with a jagged, white scar. He did not answer, only turned his head away and let the last tear fall from his eyes.

After that day, everything changed.

It was inevitable. Soren had already lost his family, his love, his country, his free will, and now his connection to his heart. He was inextricably bound to a violent, cruel Fae, privy to her plans and secrets through virtue of his servitude. And with his heart hidden somewhere kept secret even from him, Soren's pain lessened. The guilt that strangled him like ivy on an old tree withered and fell away. The murders that once turned his stomach now left him numb. The desire to die that had raged in him like a hurricane now only throbbed like a sliver deep in his chest.

He pushed down the memory of murder—his family's, his countrymen's—because the guilt on his shoulders would have broken his back otherwise. And so all that remained was the memory of the girl he loved.

Me.

Now not only his personal agony, but also his deepest secret. Whatever wrong Alair might have made him face, the evil was already done. To make his sins excusable his gambit *must* succeed.

Aside from the erdwitches, Soren alone knew I was the lost princess of the royal family. Had Silaine ever suspected, she would have had the truth from him in an instant. But her Fae pride blinded her, and she could not begin to comprehend that the peasant girl she locked in a tower—the one humans now called a princess—was the key to her triumph.

And so Soren sacrificed my distant relatives on the altar of Silaine's ambition, watching silently as she annihilated the last line that might have yielded a spark of human magic. He put those innocents to death because he knew I was the last chance to stop Silaine. The key in my blood was a double-edged sword—I could open Shadelorn, or enter Avalon and initiate Silaine's death. The end to his suffering. The end to his guilt.

A hundred years passed from the day Silaine had cursed me with sleep. And then another year, and another. Soren lived now only to protect the body of the girl he once loved. The key to his salvation, and the world's.

Until.

They were linked at the soul, and he felt her revelation at a distance, her anger a searing heat crippling his mind. And beneath it, his own fear. *She knows.*

Come!

The silent command carried him through the compound to her throne room. She stood, magnificent in her fury, every ounce of Fae pride and self-righteousness emanating from her like heat from the sun. How could she know? Who could have revealed this deepest secret?

At her side knelt a Fae warrior, tunic splattered with the blood of humans, and then Soren knew. One of Alair's men. Someone they'd entrusted the secret to, who they'd stupidly let be captured. Men were weak, as Soren knew well. Whoever's blood covered the warrior's hands had doomed them all.

Soren fell prostrate at Silaine's feet, and she bared her teeth. "You *foolish* boy," she thundered. "How dare you keep this from me? How dare you think to deceive me?"

He stayed silent, a terrible tendril of pleasure writhing up in his soul. Their shared pleasure. His at her finally knowing he'd managed to keep this most powerful secret all these long years, and hers at his resilience demonstrated yet again. Oh, what terrible games they'd played, and he'd proven a worthy opponent. It made her victory that much more enjoyable. It made her sadism that much stronger.

"Kiss her, then, slave," Silaine ordered, sinking back onto her golden throne. Her command rang in his bones like always. Her smile was terrible to behold. "Kiss her, and tell her what you've done. Then bring her to me."

His worst fear and greatest hope all rolled into one. *Yes*, he thought as he fled the castle. *Yes, but not until after she's set us free.*

And then, the memory still fresh and biting, he climbed the tall, tall tower as the snow outside continued to fall. The room was not perfectly preserved. Part of the wall had fallen away, and a thin frost covered the weathered stones. The roses were even more pitiful, mummified by the cold, turned ashen like the sky outside. Even Soren's young face was scarred and tightened by his curse, but mine was the same.

In his distant heart he knew it. I was the sacred center. His refuge. His absolution. Silaine's command ached in his bones, and for once their wills were not at odds. Despite his bitterness at having failed after so long and so much sacrifice, he felt the relief of finally beginning the end. Gladly he let the command overwhelm him.

He rushed to my side. He touched my unresponsive face. Here I was. So close now. Alair's words stung him across the decades, but he couldn't let me wake alone and defenseless. Alair was old now, too old to fight and protect me. His son, Ferras, lay dead, and the boy was too young. They'd never make it.

One final game.

"Forgive me," he whispered. His lips touched mine.

Beneath their lids, my eyes began to stir.

TWENTY-THREE

When I returned to myself, my eyes had already bled salty streaks down my face. With shaking hands I unbuttoned Soren's white shirt and found the scar on his chest where Silaine's knife had cut out the heart of the boy I loved.

"No," I sobbed. "Why?"

"You saw. You understand now. I wanted to die, Rose," he said, gently pulling my hands away. "I wanted to not feel anymore. I would have gone mad, otherwise."

"No!" I jerked my hands from his. "Don't you dare be grateful. Where is it? What did she do with it?"

"I don't know." He spoke calmly to my hysteria. "Don't think of it, Rose. Please. Putting it back wouldn't change anything." My tears sprang forth again. "I am what I am. I have done wrong, but I did it for you. Please... forgive me."

Were those Soren's emotions or mine swirling inside me now? Guilt, shame, regret, and enduring strength. Love.

Alair was wrong. Soren made the sacrifice no other could. He had bought our potential freedom with his life, but the cost... body, heart, soul... Having been there, having felt it with his skin, I knew he had paid enough. I brushed the tears from my eyes. "I forgive you. Of course I do."

I loved my brother, but he shouldn't have handed down his hate to Ferras, and then to Rowan. How could they have believed Halen would betray me? Look what he suffered for me.

Though we were trapped in this winter land, facing down a

near-undefeatable enemy, at that moment I was unconcerned. We would make it. We had to. And then we could go back to the way it was, to the cluster of huts where roses grow over the doorways and my feet know the trails through the woods as intimately as the lines on my own hands. He had waited a hundred years, and now I finally knew where I belonged.

I leaned over to kiss him. Our lips brushed against each other, fire and magic, but Soren pulled away.

"No. We shouldn't. I am very old, Rose," he whispered in the night. "And you are still a girl of seventeen. Somewhere out there is a heart that loves you, and always will, but I'm not that boy. Didn't you see? I'm a monster—"

"No."

"I am *damnsoír*, Rose. A choice that cannot be unmade. It can't be how it once was, and even if it could... I am weary. Seeing you again is a miracle, but I have lived a hundred years without you. And when this is over, I'll be gone. I'm ready. Do you understand?"

Even as my tears blurred his face, I understood, and all my hopes came crashing down. The world I could now remember so clearly was gone, completely and forever. Its last remaining member had lived a life that took him far away from the person he once was. Even I did not belong. We were ghosts of the past.

"So. Now you know. Don't be too hard on your family, Rose. Can't you understand why they wanted to keep it from you?"

"No," I said stubbornly. "It's my choice, my right to know. They shouldn't have hidden it from me."

"As I did? To keep you safe, to keep you free from fear or worry. To escape our sins... If you hate them, then you must hate me, too."

I held my hands to my mouth and tried not to cry out. I would *not* forgive Alair for what he did. I would *not*.

"We should go," Soren finally said to my silence. "If you're ready."

How could I be? Soren's revelations, his memories, might take a lifetime to process. But there was no time. I had everything I needed—my memories, my love, and the way into Avalon. But I had lost hope.

What was the good of saving the world if I had no home in it? And who was I saving it for—Rowan who hated me, Soren who could not love me as he once did, or myself, who had reclaimed her past only to realize she has no future?

The sun had risen over the horizon by the time we stood. I filled my eyes with the sight of green trees in the distance.

"Over that hill," Soren said, pointing, "is the castle. You can ride in my cloak. I can get you close to the portal. After that it's up to you."

"How does the portal work?"

"The other Fae just walk through. I imagine you can do the same."

I turned toward him, to see the face so beautiful in my dreams, and so exhausted in the daylight. "You're not coming with me?"

"If we're lucky you can make it with no one seeing you. I'll need to present myself to Silaine, to, ah, explain your continuing absence."

"Will you be all right?"

"Her punishments are much the same as they were a hundred years ago," he said dryly. "What more could she do to me? I'll be fine."

We spoke at length about Silaine's castle, its rhythms, the

Fae world, and their customs. Eventually there was nothing else to cover, no more advice Soren could give me.

He stood. "Are you ready?"

My breath caught with a sudden flare of nervousness, surprising since I thought myself to be empty inside. I nodded, and he took my hand.

If we were lucky, the next time I saw Soren the Fae would be attacking Silaine's compound. These might be the last words we ever exchanged. The morning wind whipped around us, but the sun was bright. The green lands before us gave me courage. I wanted that freedom for my winter-cursed country. It was depending on me.

"Let's go."

Soren held me delicately in his arms and permitted me one final kiss. With it I said farewell to the boy I loved, and the shattered soul still wearing his body.

Then I slipped beneath his cloak and was lost to darkness. Muffled sounds made their way to me, first the almost silent thump of Soren's feet leaving the ground, then the wind whistling as we flew. It wasn't long before his feet touched down again, and I heard voices, so many voices.

Some were light and beautiful as chimes—those must be the Fae. Others moaned in agony, clearly human in their cries. Snarls wound through the cacophony like snakes. Blades crashed against each other and animals lowed. We had reached Silaine's compound.

Soren's boots sometimes crunched through gravel, other times squelched through mud. Some of the Fae called out to him in mocking voices. Some of the humans cursed him.

He walked onward, never saying a word, despite how some threatened to kill him and others threatened that Silaine would do the job for them. How could such beautiful voices say such cruel things? We left the noise behind, and I rested my head on his back for comfort, feeling the weariness in his body like a tangible thing.

There was so much left to say. I should have said more, back on the mountain. I should have made him wait, begged for one more day with him.

"We're almost there," he whispered, voice tickling my ears in the magic of his spell. "Be ready."

My stomach leaped into my throat. I nodded though he couldn't see me, still wrapped in shadows and nothingness. Eventually Soren came to a halt. In an instant the cloak fell away and my feet touched earth again. Blinking at the sudden light, I found us in the middle of a small grove of trees.

I turned in a circle to establish myself in the world. Behind us was a dirt path, gray towers rising over the treetops. And in front of us stood the portal.

Having never seen a portal before, I wasn't sure whether to be impressed or disappointed. It was a wall of shiny black stone, wide as two men laid end to end but only as tall as one. The top curved in a smooth arch. Nothing shone or shimmered. There was no magic here. None active anyway.

I turned to Soren, a question on my lips. He reached out a hand and touched the stone, sliding his fingers over the glassy surface. It showed a reflection, but not his. Only the forest around us.

And, strangely, me.

I stepped forward, seeing myself move in the reflective rock, but the stone looked through Soren as if he weren't there. When I touched the surface, the place where my fingertips made contact glowed white, ringing like a chime pulsing faintly in my ears.

"It recognizes you," Soren said. "It was sealed with the blood of your ancestors."

I brushed my hands along the stone, leaving trails of white that faded in moments. "How do I use it?"

"Just push."

I placed both hands on the smooth, cold surface, and gave it my best. Nothing happened, except that the glow increased.

"Hmm," Soren frowned.

I fought the urge to laugh hysterically. What if it didn't work? What if all our sacrifice was for nothing?

"Give me your hand."

I didn't flinch when he drew a knife and pressed the tip into my palm. A flawless ruby welled up from my skin. Soren pressed it to the black stone at a point above my head, and then the gate opened.

A fizzle of light trickled down from the spot of blood. The stone melted away like a curtain drawing open, and beyond the opening—darkness.

A dank and musty smell slithered from the opening, moist like earth but also old and decayed. On the Fae side, the portal dwelled within a tunnel beneath the king's gardens.

My nose wrinkled, and a sudden fear gripped me. I might never return from this place. I groped the sword at my side. I'd already killed gargrayles, two huge beasts, and countless mavens. Whatever came, I would face it, and fight it if need be. I could do this.

I turned to Soren. "Thank you," I said. "Whatever happened before, whatever happens next... Thank you for everything."

He didn't speak. The weight of a century of suffering filled the air between us. My thanks could never be enough. I stepped forward, wanting to be near him one more time, to bask in the memories and pretend everything was all right.

He kissed my forehead. "Go, my love. Go... and come back."

An unexpected tension released in me, like throwing off a heavy mantle. I hadn't forsaken Rowan for nothing. Soren did what he said he would. Somewhere deep inside was the ghost of the boy I had loved. Halen hadn't let me down.

I turned, taking a deep breath and preparing to enter the darkness.

"Stop!" A voice rang over the clearing, strong and beautiful as a waterfall. Fae.

We whirled to see three Fae men on fanged mounts standing at the edge of the tree line. All three held bows aimed at us. "Move and die, human."

I grabbed Soren by the arm and plunged through the portal.

Twenty-Four

The portal fought me.

Soren wasn't of the Aerendel line. He wasn't supposed to go through. But I clung to him, trapped between two worlds, refusing to let go of his arm. Blood boiled in my veins, simmering, crying out for release. I demanded entrance. The portal yielded.

Soren and I collapsed to the hard ground, and the portal closed behind us. We were in a different world now, someplace dark and cold that stank of stones and worms. The only light came from the sapphire of my sword glowing in the presence of magic.

My stomach heaved and my brain went fuzzy. There was something wrong with the world of the Fae. The lines of the tunnel slanted wrong, as if my two eyes weren't enough to make sense of the universe.

Soren grimaced and held his stomach. He swore. "Rose, what were you thinking? Why did you do that?"

"I saved your life," I said, too sick for anger.

"I could have stopped them. Now Silaine will know we're here. We have to keep moving. After Silaine broke the portal with the king's blood, Fae can pass through it at will. Those three won't risk it alone, but once they get others... Avalon runs slower than Earth. They'll be here before long."

I nodded, and put my hand on my sword. "Let's go, then."

We stumbled through the tunnel. It was tall, to better

accommodate the Fae, and rent with a strange mixture of roots and veins of rocks. Sometimes a fleck of mineral glittered. Other times the walls around us moved, and I realized they were covered in beetles and other crawling creatures.

My stomach settled as I learned how to make sense of Avalon and figured out a new way to focus my eyes. The ground sloped upwards, and temperatures increased. Finally a glow appeared ahead.

We exited out the mouth of the tunnel through a hanging curtain of flowered vines, and stepped into paradise. In front of us was an immense, three-tiered fountain twice as tall as me, filled with water that sparkled like no other water I'd seen. A carpet of lush grass covered the ground, running up to the edges of flower beds and colorful trees. Everything bloomed with vigorous life, in a rainbow of colors. Soren and I were shabby in comparison to such beauty. I suspected we had entered a forbidden place, dirtying things with our muddy boots and sweaty faces.

The perfume of nectar floated around us on a faint breeze, washing away the scent of earth. A flock of silver birds winged by, calling to one another with pretty trilling.

Then I noticed the walls.

So pale I thought them part of a distant sky, the gardens, though vast, were contained in an ivory structure, so tall the tips seemed to meet in the far distance. We were inside the King's castle, the forbidden center of Avalon.

"Which way?" I whispered to Soren.

He shrugged. "I don't know. Straight, I suppose."

We wandered along the paths, admiring trees dripping with mouth-watering fruit, and bushes bearing flowers so bright they seemed formed out of jewels. Just when I thought the maze of paths would never end and we'd be trapped in Avalon's garden forever, a pure note rang over the greenery.

"A hunting horn," Soren said. "They know we're here."

"Are they hunting us?"

"I think it's more a call to arms."

I gripped the hilt of my sword to steady myself. We moved to the center of the nearest grass-covered courtyard and waited for the Fae to arrive.

They came on foot, a squad of six wearing filigreed white armor from which sprouted iridescent dragonfly wings. The color of their skins varied from brown to green, but they shared braided hair and long, pointed ears. Each was almost two feet taller than me, and I shuddered to imagine fighting them. Every eye glared, every lip curled to reveal canine teeth.

But it wasn't these warrior-Fae who concerned me. I was more distracted by their leader.

"Darian?" Soren and I said his name at the same time, and glanced at each other with unease.

How did Soren know him? His expression asked me the same question.

Darian raised his eyebrows but said nothing.

The last time I'd seen him he wore beautiful clothes of white and black, perfect for slipping through frozen lands unnoticed, even his white hair blending in with the snow. But today he wore the white metal armor of the others, one shoulder draped with an emerald half-cape. The others carried spears, but Darian's hip sported a sword whose sheath matched his intricate armor.

"You are trespassing in the King's gardens," one of the warriors growled. "This crime is punishable by death."

"Don't be a fool, Nazall," Darian said, eyes running over us. "These are humans. The *damnsoír* of She Who Was Cast Out, and... another." His eyebrows lifted as he realized the truth, and he looked at me with new respect. "You know the rules. Only one from the bloodkey line can pass through the Earthen Gate." My mouth opened as he bowed at the waist. "It is our honor to welcome human royalty to Avalon."

As one, the warrior Fae also bent at the waist towards us. I looked to Soren, unsure what to do, but far from being pleased by this development, he glowered, crossing his arms over his chest. With a drop in my stomach I remembered the silver tiara tucked into the pocket of my cloak… which I'd left behind when I ran to Soren.

Darian rose. "How shall we address you, oh fair one?" The tiniest hint of sarcasm accompanied his words.

Now was the worst time to realize I hadn't bathed in over a week, and wore the dirty, practical clothing of long travel. Speechless, a flaming blush swept up my neck and over my cheeks.

Thankfully, Soren jumped in. "This is Her Royal Highness, Princess Talia Aerendel of Valeria." He sounded as haughty and demanding as any courtier ought to be.

Darian adopted a satisfied smirk. "Your Highness, please allow us to escort you to His Majesty's palace, that you might rest and... refresh yourself."

I lifted my chin, feeling absolutely ridiculous. "Yes, please," I said. "And then we wish to see King Oberon." If we weren't going to be killed immediately, there might be some hope that this could go as planned.

"We will discuss all matters of importance later," Darian said airily. "Please, come with us."

It wasn't a request. Darian led us through the maze, with all six soldiers following closely behind. I attempted to talk to

Darian as we walked, but Soren touched my arm and shook his head.

The palace was even more beautiful than the gardens, though seemingly devoid of life. Darian led us through ornate halls in ivory and gold, and up endless grand staircases. The legs of the Fae never broke stride though mine began to ache and slow. Finally they deposited us in extravagant guest quarters, rich beyond anything I had ever imagined.

Marble floors spread to white walls decorated with live plants and flowers. The room contained a gigantic bed framed by translucent veils, and a clear pool set into the very floor before floor-to-ceiling windows looking out over the King's gardens.

"Please rest," Darian said as I looked about the room in wonder. "Someone will return for you shortly."

Before I could object he closed the door. I rushed towards it but there was no handle, and no matter how much I pounded and yelled, no one came to open it.

"What does this mean? Are we guests or prisoners?" I asked, turning to Soren, who stood as still as a statue. "And how do you know Darian?"

"He's one of Silaine's advisors," Soren said. "I didn't know he was a spy. Rose… I don't know what this means."

My heart dropped into my stomach before I remembered my own truth. "That can't be. He's the one who's been slipping Rowan weapons."

Soren looked up with surprise. "What? That was Darian?"

"Yes. I saw him give Rowan the rune-marked arrows."

Soren pursed his lips. "If he's been helping Rowan, then he might be on the king's side after all."

"So is he going to help us or hurt us?"

"I don't know."

My breath came rapidly. I couldn't enjoy the sweet smell of honeysuckle permeating the room. They hadn't taken our weapons, but what did an entire city of Fae have to fear from one human girl? Even if I did have my magic back, I didn't know my limits or capabilities, and certainly not if I was even powerful in comparison to the Fae.

"Rose." Soren approached and put his hands on my shoulders. "Whatever happens, I won't let them harm you. I carry extensions of Silaine's power. I can fight them if need be. Enough for you to get away."

"No," I said. "I'd never leave you behind. And I can't go without speaking to the king. He'll help us. He has to."

Soren took his hands from me, and sighed. "No, he doesn't."

"If he won't then we'll keep fighting," I insisted. "There must be another way to destroy Silaine."

It was inconceivable that so much time and blood had been spent only for this mission to fail at the finish line.

"I don't know any. She's too strong now. It would take all the human armies of the world to defeat her."

"If that's what it takes, then we'll do it."

He gave a thin smile. "I believe you'll try."

"You'd be with me. You can't go back to her." The corners of my eyes stung.

"I… can't hide from her. Not truly. We're a part of each other. She can always seek me out. But I pray I'll get to stay with you until the end."

The end. My mind cast around desperately for another solution. "If King Oberon won't help us, perhaps we can open Shadelorn ourselves, and use it against her before she can use it on us."

"Perhaps," he said, turning away again. "Or perhaps Shadelorn would destroy us all. But it would be best if Oberon simply agreed to stop her. Look, I don't know what's going to happen, but we can at least make the best of it. Let's bathe. It won't do us any good to go before the king stinking of fear and sweat."

"I'm not afraid," I protested. Or I prayed I wasn't showing fear, anyway.

Soren took off his boots. How could he be so calm at a time like this? I leaned against the alabaster walls and tried to take deep breaths, but the perfume in the air dizzying.

"Rose, come on. We're safe for now. Let's get you cleaned up."

Squashing my frustration, I nodded and took the hand he offered. Soren waited in another room while I stripped off my clothes and sank into the strange Fae water. Bottles and powders on the side of the pool scrubbed off dirt and sweat with bursts of orange, lavender, and the sweet shock of rose.

Finally I felt clean, and explored our rooms while Soren took his turn in the water that refused to grow dirty. I found robes in a closet, made of satiny white fabric embroidered with vines and flowers. With nothing else to wear, I put one on and tied the belt at my waist. It felt like a casual garment, something to wear between bathing and donning real attire. It was better than the dirty clothing I'd worn here, but hopefully we wouldn't have to appear before Oberon wearing what was basically a fancy towel.

After his bath Soren donned one of the robes as well. I realized how much better he fit in with this Fae world than me. The changes wrought by becoming *damnsoír* made him ethereally beautiful. Aside from the scars, his skin was smooth as porcelain. His tawny hair curled perfectly, and his golden eyes were as captivating as they were inhuman.

My heart ached to look at him. The boy in front of me resembled Halen, but he wasn't that person anymore. He wasn't even a boy at all. I would give anything for him to be flawed and human again like me.

The Fae persisted in ignoring us. I stood by the wall of glass and looked over the lush gardens. Shimmering butterflies gamboled around the flowers. Colorful birds flew from tree to tree. Everything was perfectly manicured, not a brown leaf or drooping blossom anywhere.

"Why is it forbidden to enter the garden?" I asked Soren, who reclined on a white couch.

"The Fae are very different from humans. They have much more strict social customs, and they live in hierarchies. The king is the highest position. He's afforded certain luxuries most don't have. It's his privilege to keep the gardens for himself."

I harrumphed. What good was a garden as beautiful as this one if no one could use it?

"Additionally, it holds the portal to earth. Probably wise to keep other Fae from mucking about with it."

"Silaine did. And the rebels who joined her."

"Well, they're banished now. Even entering the king's gardens is a crime, unthinkable by most standards. To cross the portal is the same as renouncing Avalon."

"Do you think Silaine has sent warriors after us by now?"

"If she has, they won't look for us beyond the tunnel. I don't think we have to worry about her yet."

I turned back to the window. "Why would they even want to leave this place? It's so beautiful. It makes Earth seem... well, not dull, but certainly less... less..."

"Perfect."

"Exactly." I wouldn't trade Earth for anything, especially not this land that belonged to my enemy, but Avalon was indescribably beautiful.

"Perfection has its costs," Soren said. "Boredom, for one. The Fae hate to be bored. That's mostly why Silaine is doing this."

"Boredom?" I raised my eyebrows. "She ruined my life, killed thousands of my people, and cursed my kingdom because she was *bored*?"

Not to mention what she did to you, I thought. *What she turned you into.*

Soren's eyes were dead inside. He'd only looked weary since we arrived in Avalon. "I've lived with the Fae for a hundred years," he said. "I know their ways. When Oberon led them to Avalon, it was their chance to make the world how they thought it should be. Paradise. Perfection. But there was no prey any longer for the Hunt. No sacrifices for their festivals. No sport. That was Silaine's role here. She created beasts for entertainment."

I remembered the beasts we'd fought, and their gooey, gray insides. They were made from blood but could not stand against true flesh and blood.

"But with a lack of external danger, everything became... dull. The customs and ceremonies that rule Fae culture became all-consuming. Life in Avalon turned into a series of monotonous chores. Bowing to the king, singing to the king, dancing for the king... Silaine realized the Fae must return to Earth, or lose their souls. Oberon would not listen. But Silaine is of the Higher Fae. She is the queen's sister. She doesn't feel the same desire to be loyal and obedient to royalty. So she decided to take Avalon by force. They put down her rebellion and chose to speak of her no more. But her idea—her revelation—was cancerous. Fae defect to her side all the time, a slow trickle. She's not just motivated by power, you see. That's what makes her so dangerous. In Silaine's eyes, she is fighting for the very soul of her people."

I swallowed. "It sounds like you admire her."

He blinked. "I'm part of her. I can't help but... understand. To the Fae her cause might be noble, but I have known her too well to wish her anything but dead. Because of what she would do to humanity to save her own people."

Soren joined me at the window and stared into the king's garden. I glanced at him, at the web of scars covering his skin, physical proof of the hell he'd suffered. I reached out a hand. He turned to me and I touched his face, with my fingertips tracing the lines that marked every escape he'd failed to make.

"I still love you," I told him. "Whatever was done, it could never take that away."

He grimaced under my touch. "Don't say that."

"You got me here," I insisted. "Alair said you would only harm me, but you managed to do what had to be done. I'm only sorry I made it so hard for you."

"Please," he whispered. "Please don't."

"Don't forgive you? Don't love you?"

Soren took my hands and pulled them from his face. "Rose, I can't let you love me anymore. I've lived too long and done too much evil. That's what I tried to tell you on the mountain. I am so far gone from the boy you knew. I don't deserve you."

I closed my eyes, remembering his lips on mine, wanting to be near him again... and that feeling like stones in my stomach when he told me it could never be.

"The boy you loved is dead. I'm only Soren now."

“I don’t care,” I said, opening my eyes. No matter what he’d done, no matter who he’d become, I’d always look for the part of him that was still good.

Soren studied me, eyes shining. His mouth twitched, and he raised a hand to brush his fingertips across my hair. “No,” he said. “Of course you don’t.”

He pulled away. My heart sank lower with every step.

Day turned to night in Avalon. Two moons hung in a purple sky amidst a glittering court of stars. Blinking lights floated through the garden. The darkness exposed shimmering dust in our pool, each particle glowing and softly illuminating the room.

Soren and I sat in our beautiful prison, not speaking, just waiting for the end, and watching the magnificently-carved clock in the corner slowly tick away the time.

News arrived when the clock struck thirteen.

TWENTY-FIVE

Darian slipped into the room.

Soren and I leaped to our feet, but the Fae bore an amused smile on his face, and held his hands out to show they were empty. “Relax, *damnsoír*. I won’t hurt the princess.”

Darian wore cloth boots, dark blue trousers, and a high-necked white kirtle sashed at the waist, heavily embroidered with green and blue. His manner and dress struck me as oddly casual, and I suspected this was an unofficial visit.

“Are you a traitor?” Soren demanded.

“Undoubtedly.” His blue eyes glowed faintly in the dim lighting. “I’d be very interested to know what *you’re* doing here, *damnsoír*, with the last human bloodkey. As I recall, Silaine was rather keen to keep her on earth.”

“And I was rather keen to get her to Avalon,” Soren said sharply. “What do you want, Darian?”

“To help.”

“Help how?” I asked, and his blue eyes turned their attention to me.

“It’s obvious you know nothing of Fae customs, even with the guidance of Silaine’s little pet. She never had the temperament for refinement, and her ‘kingdom’ is as barbaric as the humans’.”

I bristled.

“If you don’t know what you’re doing, you’ll get yourself killed, and the stand-off with Silaine will never end.”

"Why do you care?"

Darian studied me for a moment, and I wondered if he'd even say. "I have spent much time on Earth. I have seen the threat Silaine poses. If we do not act soon, all worlds will be hers. This I cannot allow."

Hearing it from Rowan, who had grown up hating Silaine, was one thing. Hearing it from a Fae countless years old who had seen both sides was entirely another. My heart quivered. "What should we do?" I asked.

"An envoy will come to ask you to state your intentions. They are from the king, though they will not announce themselves as such. You must ignore everything they say and demand a royal assembly. It is your right, as recognized royalty, and an emissary from Earth, to petition the king before his court. Whatever you say will spread through all of Avalon, so think carefully, human. Make them respect you." He looked me up and down, lip curling in amusement. "I'll send over some appropriate attire in the morning. It would offend the court to see you thus."

"Thank you," I said with as much dignity as I could muster. It wasn't my fault I had to sneak into Avalon without the benefit of a royal entourage and all the riches and planning that should go into a formal visit.

Darian swept into a bow, but managed to make it look sarcastic. "Your Highness," he said with a wicked glint in his eyes, then left us locked in our rooms again.

Soren and I shared the bed, on opposite sides of its magnificent breadth. In the morning breakfast awaited us on one of the glass tables, though we neither heard nor saw its deliverers. Pastries light as air, rich cream spreads, and assortments of strange fruit filled my stomach. They included a bowl of flowers that Soren told me were edible, a delicacy in fact, but I didn't touch them. It seemed so wrong to me, to eat flowers. The Fae cannibalized beauty.

After breakfast we heard a muffled sound, like a door shutting, and a pure, high note rang briefly from the closet. I opened it to find outfits for both Soren and I. Soren's clothing featured a tailored surcoat of sapphire, with gold embroidery to match his eyes and hair. Both the pattern and off-center buttons were in the shape of blooming roses.

My gown was rose-themed as well, but in soft pink. A layer of embroidery hung over the skirts and curled up the tight bodice. Fresh roses garlanded the waist and capped the shoulders, where gauzy fabric fell to the floor, like a train for my arms. A necklace of buds and blooms gathered in frail netting would drape over my collarbones. A crown of white roses waited, too, a nod to my status without the loan of an actual crown or tiara.

"I'll give Darian credit," Soren said, admiring the gorgeous outfits with me. "This was well done. He might be on our side after all."

We donned our new clothes, and Soren used a small collection of provided creams and powders to put a faint blush on my cheeks, and a pink tint on my lips. We left my hair loose, in its natural waves, and Soren placed the crown of roses on my head.

"You look perfect," he said as I inspected myself in a mirror. "Like a princess. Like a queen."

The gown fit me wonderfully. It gave me a feminine shape,

and indeed I had never felt more beautiful. Or more like an imposter. “I’m nothing compared to them,” I grumbled. “But now I won’t completely embarrass myself.”

“I disagree. Fae are only beautiful on the outside. You are beautiful from within. Nothing outshines that. They’re painted statues, and you’re a living flower.”

I met his eyes in the mirror, and his expression broke my heart anew. The longing between us was for a time impossibly distant, when our love was young and his soul unsundered. I was still the girl he’d known. But the boy I loved died a lifetime ago.

Soren held me while I pressed my palm against his empty chest, bitterly ruing our fate. “Wherever my heart is, it’s still yours,” he told me. “But death is all I long for now. Knowing you are safe, and Silaine is defeated… That would finally bring me peace.”

I nodded, holding back tears. It hadn’t escaped me that if my gambit in Avalon was successful, the end of Silaine would mean the end of Soren.

The envoy came at mid-morning.

A Fae woman led, three men and three women following her like a flock of colorful geese. Each wore a distinct color that complimented their skin or hair. The leader was lavender, with aubergine hair and a violet gown. It clung to her waspish waist, gauzy sleeves gathering in bells around her wrists.

The decadent outfits Darian had provided were still conservative compared to the style of the envoys. These Fae glittered with jewels and touches of gold or silver. Flowers decorated them, sprinkled over their elaborate hair and on the clothes themselves. If this was the style, the court must go through acres of flowers a day just to stay freshly attired.

The leader of the group glowered at me with pale green eyes in the shape of teardrops. She had a mouth like Silaine, plump lips that drew out to slits at the sides. All the women present had such mouths, painted in bright colors as if to draw attention to the fact that they could go from pout to snarl in an instant.

Despite my Fae gown, next to them I felt like a short, squat toad. Even the men were more beautiful than the prettiest human woman, with their symmetrical, angular features, and long hair worn in complicated braids, or loose yet perfectly curled.

The leader spoke as I gaped at them, in a haughty tone that instantly shamed me. "We have come to see the wretched prisoners and hear if they will confess their crimes."

"What crimes?" I stammered.

"Trespassing in the king's gardens, an offense punishable by death," the speaker announced, tongue lingering between her teeth on the last word so she almost hissed like a snake. Those slits on either side of her mouth crept upward.

"Perhaps for Fae—" I began, but she interrupted.

"If you confess your crimes and beg leniency, perhaps His Majesty King Oberon will graciously consider ordering your execution to be quick and painless."

I raised my eyebrows, but Soren stepped in. "You idiots," he said, lip curled and disdain dripping from every syllable. "This is Her Royal Highness Princess Talia Aerendel of Valeria, come to remind your king of his duty to destroy the heretic Silaine before she in turn destroys us all."

I schooled my features to indifference, attempting to look cool and imperious.

The Fae party flinched at Silaine's name. "She Who Was

Cast Out is no threat to the court," the leader snapped.

"You are embarrassing yourself," Soren pronounced, lifting his chin as though he could look down at them. "Did you not hear me? This is a princess of Valeria, last of the Aerendel line. Bow, or disgrace your king with your boorish manners."

"The Aerendel line has ended," the leader sniffed. "We do not bow to impostors."

Soren turned to me and made a respectful obeisance. "Your Highness, please take pity on these ignorant wretches and demonstrate your power, thus proving your royal heritage."

The Fae turned their eyes to me, and I felt the blood drain from my face.

My magic was unpracticed, untested. Would it even work in the Fae realm? If I couldn't rise to Soren's challenge, perhaps they'd deny my claim and just kill us. For a moment, the fear overwhelmed me, and my knees weakened. But I clenched my teeth. We'd come so far. It would just have to work.

I closed my eyes and reached for that warm center inside me. To strengthen my efforts, I thought of the place where my magic had felt strongest and most powerful. I imagined Rowan's arms around me, the tenderness with which he held my hands and placed them over my chest. I reached into my heart and revealed the startling truth:

I missed him.

My eyes flew open, and white light burst from my hands onto the floor before me, forming an arrow with runes that glowed blue.

A Fae-killing arrow.

The Fae party flinched again, leaning away one critical inch, and I stepped forward though the blood rushed from my head. "I am Princess Talia, and I demand to see the King of Avalon before the royal assembly."

The eyes of the speaker narrowed, and flicked to Soren before something amazing happened:

The men bowed, and the women curtsied. Skirts poofing around them, arms spread, waists and knees bent, the Fae lowered their heads before me.

"Your Highness," the speaker said, eyes downcast. "Please forgive our doubt. We will relay your wishes at once. Allow us to assemble the court, and then we shall return for you."

"Thank you," I said, a rush of exhilaration coursing through me.

The Fae did not even glance at me as they exited, bowing again before backing out of the room. Soren picked up the arrow on the floor and traced the glowing runes before looking at me thoughtfully. He did not question what made me produce such a thing, and I turned away as my cheeks flushed.

Rowan…

The thought of him still angered me. He was complicit in Alair's betrayal, and his stubbornness almost cost us everything. I wavered between blaming him and understanding his reasoning. Whatever he'd done, I hoped my appearance at the portal to Avalon had pulled Silaine's attention away from him and the others. If Rowan was smart, he'd be half-way to Shalimar by now.

But when had Rowan ever listened to me?

"One more trial passed," Soren said, breaking my train of thought. "Just one more to go."

"I hope," I said. "What if Oberon doesn't listen?"

"If you tell the whole court Silaine is trying to access Shadelorn, he'll have to listen. The battle is practically won."

But I didn't feel triumphant.

"What do I do after?" I asked. "Alair wanted me to be queen. But…"

All I wanted was to go back to my village. That was my happy ending: rebuilding my home, and running through the woods, bow strapped to my back. The only time I'd ever considered leaving home was to be with Halen, and we'd never begun the journey to the capital. I had never received a single instruction in how to be a proper princess.

"You can do anything you want," Soren reassured me. "Let Shalimar and Adalwin fight over Valeria, or split it down the middle. Join Rowan at his family's holdings on the coast. Or hell, you could sail to Fulsyria. Become a trader, or a dancer, or a healer."

I made a face. It should have been nice to have such freedom. But something tugged at me, something that persisted despite my denials.

It was my magic, and the truth of my Aerendel blood. It was the ghost of Valeria, a lost country only I could revive. The Usurper's crimes against my birth family would be rendered pointless if I took back the throne. My ascension would be a conquering of the past, a restoration of the natural order Silaine sought in vain to disrupt. It was my brother's long-held dream, and Rowan's, too.

It would be hard. As hard as the struggles of the past few weeks. But it was a challenge I could dedicate a lifetime to, a life of building, and protecting, growing my family and my home into something strong, something no one could break again.

Soren must have seen the decision settle in my heart, sensed the determination rising in my spirit. He dropped to one knee, took my hand, and kissed it. He looked up with those golden eyes, faith pouring out of him into me.

"My queen."

It felt like he said my name.

TWENTY-SIX

The Fae returned not long after. Maybe they were naturally quick, or maybe the court was already semi-prepared after hearing that humans were found in the king's gardens. Maybe Darian had something to do with it.

This time four warriors marched ahead and behind us, led by the lavender-skinned courtier. The gleaming hallways betrayed more signs of life than when we'd come in from the gardens. Beings Soren whispered were of the Lesser Fae fluttered around corners and peeked at us from crevices and niches. They were small, the largest only coming up to my waist. Most had wings like birds or insects, and they flitted about, blinking huge eyes. Tiny creatures Soren called pixies, no bigger than my hand, glowed in shifting colors and followed us through the halls like a trail of living flowers.

We came to an antechamber. The ceiling here must have been a hundred feet high, each story lined with decadent trim, the layers between carved with images of the Fae. A handful of marble steps rose to a platform before two doors as tall as the ceiling. The procession led us up the steps, those giant doors opened, and we entered the court of the Fae King.

It was massive. I quickly closed my dropped jaw as I looked up the impossibly-high walls. Alcoves dotted them like honeycomb, all occupied with seated Fae staring down at us with thousands of steady, unblinking eyes.

A woven carpet of green ran along the black-veined marble

floor until it reached a dais with a silver throne. Seated on that throne could only be King Oberon. A flock of pixies blew past us and dispersed about the court like floating glitter while I took in the sight of the king.

Even seated, I could tell he was almost twice as tall as the other Fae, and muscular where they were slender. His skin and hair were green, and also unique among Fae he wore a magnificent beard that fell halfway down his chest. His eyes glowed with power, a strange and beautiful color, white with a touch of teal.

To his right, on a smaller throne, sat a beautiful Fae woman who could only be the queen. Her red hair shone like a fiery sunset, so long it pooled at her feet. She looked like her sister, cruel about the eyes and mouth.

The Fae who escorted us peeled off to the sides, and only Soren's momentum behind and slightly to my right kept me moving forward. I could barely feel my feet as we approached the royal couple, in awe of so much beauty. I prayed I would not stumble, and that my voice would not shake as I spoke.

When we were approximately thirty feet away from the silver throne and its royal occupants, Soren touched my arm and we stopped. He swept into a bow and I curtsied, though my ankles wobbled and I prayed they wouldn't think me the world's biggest fool.

Soren stepped in front of me. "Your Grace, may I present to you the once-lost Princess Talia Aerendel, future Queen of Valeria."

I curtsied again because it seemed like the right thing to do. The Fae king observed me with hard, glowing eyes. I cleared my throat and opened my mouth, but while I gathered my thoughts he spoke instead.

"Your Highness. Be welcome in Avalon. To what do I owe this inaugural visit from the human royal family?" His voice was deep and loud, thundering over the court and seeming to shake my bones.

"I come to beg justice," I said in a rush, after a moment of panicked silence. My voice was small and weak compared to his.

I steeled my resolve and willed whatever power was in me to flow and *serve.* When next I spoke my words breathed into the entire room.

"Your exile, Silaine, has cursed my kingdom with endless winter, and tormented my people with murder and slavery. I demand that you retrieve her immediately."

The voices of the Fae court filled the room like a symphony of silver flutes. Their king's eyes narrowed. When he spoke they fell silent.

"She Who Was Cast Out was exiled from Avalon for treason and heresy. She spreads unnatural ideas and creates abominations with her gifts."

"I agree," I said. "I have seen this firsthand."

The king studied me for a moment. "Earth is no longer our concern. Your ancestors made certain of that."

"On this we disagree." I grit my teeth. "Silaine is not content to torment the human realm. She has gathered other traitors and heretics to her side, and she hopes to conquer Avalon with the might of Shadelorn."

The court erupted into concerned whispers and the buzz of agitated wings. The noise fell away in a matter of seconds, all eyes returning to the king. Fae had an unnatural talent for stillness. In a court that seated thousands, not a sound could be heard above my own breath.

The king leaned forward, his glowing eyes staring into mine. "How could she do that?" he asked, his whisper loud enough to fill the whole hall. "As I recall, only royal blood can open the doorways between worlds. And if you are the last of the royal human line, then it seems our solution is clear."

My heart stilled in my chest. This was our worst fear. If they killed me now, Silaine would never have my blood, and Oberon would never need to face her.

A roaring grew—was it in my ears, or the world itself?

"Silaine will find a way," Soren said, shouting into the deadly silence. "I am Silaine's *damnsoír*, and I testify to her ambition. With or without a bloodkey, Silaine will open the door to Shadelorn."

"I doubt that, *damnsoír*," the king said, voice dripping with thinly-veiled disdain. "I placed those wards myself."

He sat back in his chair, and ten armored Fae soldiers appeared from behind his throne. They grinned, revealing teeth sharpened to a point.

My eyes widened. He wasn't going to listen to reason. He wasn't going to help us. This was my death, and Valeria would be lost with me.

Soren carried my sword at his waist, and he ripped it from its sheath, sapphire already shining with golden light. I lifted my hands and sucked in a breath, summoning magic and preparing to meet death fighting.

Then the world toppled.

Commotion was all I knew, a whirl of color and noise I couldn't make sense of. Wind screamed in my ears as the roar of the court fell away, the king's powerful shouts echoing in my bones.

Someone carried me. Through my panic I realized what had

happened: Darian held me in one arm and Soren in the other, as easily and carelessly as if we were dolls in the arms of a child. He flew through the halls of Avalon, so fast his feet couldn't be touching the ground, and burst out a window into the king's gardens.

We plummeted from the high walls in a shower of glass and impacted the earth so hard I thought my neck would break. Then he ran again.

Through the garden's trails we whipped past trees and flowers and fountains until we reached a familiar courtyard. Darian slowed and dumped us from his arms. "Run, humans!"

Soren lurched towards me, as dizzy and floppy as myself, but we clasped hands. "Let's go!"

We plunged through the curtain of vines down the dark earthen trail. Behind us we heard the buzz of wings and a clash of steel. Was Darian fighting other Fae to give us a few more moments to escape? I couldn't understand his suicidal sacrifice.

The tunnel seemed longer than before, but at last we reached the black stone. Soren nicked my palm again, with no time to be gentle. I smeared my hand across the reflective surface, pleading aloud for it to open.

Light burst outward, sparkling down from my blood in a familiar arc. I closed my eyes against the glare, held onto Soren, and jumped through.

The smell of dirt and decay faded away, leaving sweet grass and fresh air in its place. I gasped for breath, scowling in the light and letting my eyes adjust. The portal closed behind us. We were safe. We'd made it.

I heard a noise, like a horse's hoof stamping the ground. I pried open my eyelids.

Before us stood an entire army of Fae on mounted beasts. At

their head sat a Fae woman both beautiful and terrible, whose face I had seen in Soren's memory, whose sister I had looked upon in the throne room of King Oberon himself.

This was the enemy who had been pursuing me since I was born. Looking at her now I remembered my own version of those final minutes before she cursed me with sleep. I remembered her alien face, arched brows with large, dark eyes, and hair as black as night. Now it was swept back in a mound of braids, a black crown holding it all in place.

Silaine's mouth curled, red and wet as blood. I could see in her eyes that she could wield magic better than I could ever hope to. She was large, untouchable, and undefeatable.

But I had her *damnsoír* on my side. Someone who knew her most intimate secrets, who had managed to defy her for so long. He had to have a plan for this. We'd come too far to give up now.

I turned to Soren, waiting for his cue. He stood still as a statue, staring wide-eyed at the army before us. His entire body shook, subtly at first, and then like he was freezing to death.

"Well, my prince," Silaine called, amusement adorning her voice. "You've avoided it long enough. Bring her to me. *Now*."

"No," I cried.

His shaking ceased as Soren gave in to the command. Hands that once held me with tenderness now captured my arms with a grip of steel. Even now, I would not raise my sword against him. I couldn't. Surrounded by a hundred Fae, what could I do anyway? It was too late.

"Please," I still begged, as Soren dragged me forward. "Please don't do this."

His golden eyes flashed, his web of scars stood stark against his skin. "I love you, Talia," he said. Then he pushed me to my knees at Silaine's feet. She grinned. Soren swirled up into his magical cloak and disappeared.

Like Alair said he would… Soren betrayed me.

TWENTY-SEVEN

Silaine's so-called castle stood in defiance of beauty or practicality. It sprawled, a disjointed mix of stone, brick, and wood, as if levels and expansions were added as needed, with whatever materials were most convenient.

Two Fae soldiers marched me through the compound, past the misery I'd missed while hidden in Soren's magical cape. Human slaves—men, women, and even children—toiled in the courtyards, toting water, forging weapons, grinding grain, braiding rope, and a thousand other tasks. Their clothes were unwashed, and their hair matted. But worse were their eyes, dim and uncurious, kept docile either by misery or enchantment.

Then we disappeared into the darkness of the stronghold itself, and descended a staircase plunging into the earth.

They were taking me to the dungeon.

Defeat and betrayal overwhelmed me so much that I couldn't feel anything else, not even fear for my own life. The truth thudded into me with each step: Rowan was right. No matter what Soren felt, or how much he wished to help, he was powerless to protect me when it really mattered.

What would Silaine do with me now? Tales from both Rowan and Soren echoed in my mind, warning of torture and pain for sport. Would Silaine kill me outright or extend my agony? It didn't matter. She would use my blood to access Shadelorn and defeat King Oberon, destroying or enslaving our world in the process.

I had failed.

I barely noticed when we reached the end of the stairs. One of the guards pushed me into a metal cell in the cold, dank dungeon. The stench of human waste filled the air, and a stinging, ephemeral note I could only call misery.

The guards held me down and chained me to the wall, rusty manacles binding a leg and an arm. They locked my cell and took the torches with them, leaving me in complete darkness.

No—after a moment I noticed my manacles glowing faintly. I examined them and made out tiny runes, like the ones on the arrows.

Great. Magical manacles.

I slumped against the wall and put my head on my knees, finally allowing tears to fall. I heard a cough in the darkness, then a whisper. "Who's there?"

I lifted my head and peered into the black so complete I couldn't see my own face in front of my hand. "Rose. Who are you?"

"Rose?" A clink of chains. "What are you doing here?"

I recognized that voice! "Rowan?" I scrambled to my knees and crawled forward as much as the chains would let me. "What are *you* doing here? I told you to go to Shalimar!" A frantic feeling rose in me, anger mixed with panic. "Why didn't you listen?" Now he was here, too, and soon we'd both be dead.

"You left with the Betrayer," Rowan said furiously. "Maybe we were trying to save you."

"I didn't need saving!"

"Then how did you end up down here?" he demanded. "What happened to your gallant prince?"

"He did what he promised," I snapped. "We got into Avalon."

Silence.

I gave a frightened spasm of breathing that was almost a laugh. It was just minutes ago, but already our time in Avalon seemed a distant dream, its beauty the fantasy of an unstable mind. Only the Fae dress I still wore proved Soren and I actually met with Oberon. Pulling the crown of roses from my head, I buried my nose in their blooms, and for a moment escaped my reality.

Rowan's voice was less accusatory and more curious when he finally asked, "What happened?"

I sighed. My time with Soren in the alabaster palace was the culmination of generations of sacrifice, and the execution of a political strategy a century in the making. How many people had died to give me those few moments before the Fae King's throne?

And I'd failed. The dreams of my family were dead, rotted into regrets.

I told Rowan everything about Avalon. While I spoke I explored my cell, seeking any frailty in the chains or bars and finding none. I relayed what Soren told me about the reason for Silaine's exile, and how the Fae culture stagnated in a routine of ceremony and tradition. We talked about Darian, his double-crossing espionage, and defying the Fae King. Perhaps my escape would stir Oberon to act. Perhaps not. Perhaps it was already too late.

"How long have you been here?" I asked. "And where are the others?"

"Not long. The others are dead... or enslaved. She chained me here because they still think I have magic. These chains..."

"I saw. And Gile?"

"Enslaved, I hope. He wasn't killed in the initial skirmish, anyway."

"Good," I said with relief. "Do you know how long she plans to hold us?"

"No. They bring food and water once a day, or at least I think it's once a day. The guards don't talk to me. I thought I'd go crazy with no one to talk to. I'm grateful for company, I'm just sorry it had to be you."

Silence found us again. Somewhere in the dungeon a drop of water plinked into a puddle.

Rowan cleared his throat and sounded contrite when he said, "So you were right about the Be—about Soren."

"Yes and no," I whispered. "You were right, too. In the end... Silaine ordered him to bring me to her, and he did. He had to."

I waited for Rowan's reprimand, or gloating, or exasperation. The terrible ending he and Alair warned me about had indeed come to pass. But Rowan surprised me. "I'm sorry, Rose. I can't imagine…" There were too many ways to end that sentence, so he didn't.

Haltingly, I told Rowan about the memories Soren shared with me. The desperate bargain, Silaine's cruel twists, a century of unforgivable crimes and unquestionable loyalty. I shared the devastation of recovering my first love only to learn he died a long time ago. Soul fractured, heart cut out—Halen was gone. Only Soren remained, a ghost haunting the body of the boy I once loved.

"Where do you think he went?" Rowan asked when my tale was done. "You said he brought you to Silaine, then vanished."

I wiped tears from my cheeks. "If at all possible, he'll be trying to free us. But I can't imagine Silaine will give him that chance." Fatigue and defeat surrounded us, thick as the darkness. "What is she waiting for?"

"Who knows? Perhaps an auspicious star sign. Or maybe they're throwing a wild celebration, and they'll fetch you after everyone's sobered up."

More silence. Dripping water. The clink of chains.

"This might be the last time we ever talk to each other," I said slowly. "I want to say thank you, Rowan, for everything."

"Rose—"

"—And I'm sorry for abandoning you. And I'm sorry I couldn't save us."

"No," Rowan said, voice cracking with pain. "That part isn't your fault. You did everything right. If we'd trusted you, if Grandfather hadn't held such a grudge… If he worked with Soren instead of shunning him, perhaps you could have woken much sooner. My father didn't need to die. Everything could have been different."

I forced the tremor in my voice to stillness, pretending to be brave. "I'm glad I got to know you, though."

"Me, too. Rose, I—"

The door to the dungeon opened.

In the dim light from the stairwell I could just see Rowan crouched in a cell diagonal from me. He was pale and bedraggled, eyes red from the tears we'd both spilled. I drank up the sight of him, and he watched me with the same hunger.

Equal to my dread of losing a single instant of being able to see him was my dread at our approaching jailer. Then my hope surged—Soren! But the figure quickly approaching wasn't him, or Silaine, or even one of her soldiers.

It was Darian.

I squealed his name but he silenced me with a gesture. "Quiet," he hissed, and unlocked my door.

"We worried you were dead," Rowan said, gripping the bars

of his cell.

“I survived.” Darian unlocked my manacles and I kicked them away, glad to be free of their heavy weight.

Darian unlocked Rowan as well and we embraced each other with joyful relief. Rowan’s body was solid and warm, and a giddiness overtook me. We were being rescued! We would live to fight Silaine again.

Our liberator led us up the stairs, pausing to peer around every corner. There were no guards. Was it possible we’d been left unattended this whole time? Soren was right about the level of Silaine’s arrogance.

“Where are we going? What’s the plan?” I whispered urgently.

“A reckoning is at hand,” Darian said enigmatically, but soon he paused at the end of a hallway. “Rowan, if you go that way you’ll find yourself near the human pens. You can free them. Take this.” Darian slipped him a dagger, runes glowing faintly along the blade.

Rowan accepted the weapon with a raised eyebrow, but didn’t leave. “Where are you taking Rose?”

“First, for a bath and a change of clothes. You both smell like swine, and I refuse to accompany such a dank companion. After that, we’ll see you outside. Liberation dawns.”

Excitement, fear, and relief ran like fire in my veins. “I’ll be fine, Rowan. Free the others. We’ll find you soon.”

He nodded, and we parted. I chased Darian as he rushed through the primitive castle. We encountered no one else as we climbed staircases and twisted through a maze of corridors. Finally Darian ushered me into a room where a tub of cool water waited.

“Clean. Quickly.” He ripped off my ruined Fae dress despite

my cries of protest, wilted petals falling in flurries, and picked me up naked to dump me into the water.

"I can do it myself," I yelled and grabbed the washcloth before he could. Darian snorted and peered out the window while I scrubbed off the dungeon as fast as possible so he wouldn't feel the urge to turn around and help.

When I was finished he braided my wet hair so fast my scalp hurt, and threw a red, velvet dress at my feet. "Hurry, princess, we haven't much time."

I stared at the dress. I'd seen it before. I'd *worn* it before, in the dream grove with Soren. This was the dress his mind chose for me.

As I slipped on the gown I looked about the room for the first time, taking in the details and personal items scattered throughout. There was a simple bed in the corner, and a standing wardrobe. A bookshelf leaned by the window, and the titles were in my language. Was this Soren's room? Was he collaborating with Darian?

Heart stinging, I tugged on a pair of sensible boots Darian nudged my way. I didn't even have time to see what he was looking at through the window before we rushed back into the hallways, descending to ground level. My sense of direction had fled. I couldn't guess how many turns we'd taken or where we were going to end up.

Darian put his hand on my shoulder and strode towards a set of arched double-doors. Sunlight snuck through the crack where they met. My stomach leaped. I was almost free.

Darian's hand tightened, so hard it hurt. He pushed open the doors and we walked into the blinding glare. I heard gasps, and angry shouts. I opened my eyes to find we weren't at ground level at all, but on an elevated stone walkway extending away from the castle into a crowded, muddy field.

At the end of the walkway stood Silaine, hair gleaming in the sun, sword glowing in her hand. Beside her stood Soren, eyes heavy with despair.

"No!" I tried to run away, but Darian had a firm hold on me. He picked me up as I thrashed like a fish out of water, like a snake in the talons of a hawk, like a girl in the arms of her captor.

He threw me at Silaine's feet.

TWENTY-EIGHT

Silaine said to Soren, "Now, dear one," and he sank to his knees before me, eyes wide with fear and sadness.

Everything hurt.

"Soren," I cried, voice low and desperate. "*Halen.*"

He flinched. "Talia," he whispered, throwing a silver cord across my legs. Darian crouched on my other side, and between them they bound me more quickly than I could focus to summon any magic.

Darian pulled me to my feet and Soren tied a cord from my wrists to a metal loop in the stone. We kept our eyes on each other the whole time, mine begging, his confessing his wretchedness.

He called me Talia. He was lost to me.

Silaine addressed the crowd before her, but I couldn't process her words. I searched my surroundings, looking for any way to escape.

The elevated walkway stood tall enough that a jump would be painful, but not deadly. It stretched right to the edge of an enormous pit, perhaps fifteen feet deep but hundreds wide. Surrounding the pit were Silaine's rebel Fae, dozens of them, but they were outnumbered by human slaves.

Their faces blurred. So many, covered in rags and mud, watching Silaine speak with a blankness I identified as hopelessness. In a way, they were all here because of me. I scanned for anyone familiar but under the common mask of misery recognized no one.

These were the slaves who built Silaine's castle, who had baked her bread and dug this pit. I'd seen it before in Soren's memories, and I stood just close enough to Silaine that I could look past her into the pit itself, onto a black stone wall laying flat in the dirt. It was twin to the one in the grove except its veins were red, not white. I stared into the reflective face, polished clean from the surrounding dust. The portal to Shadelorn.

I twisted around to face Darian, who stood at a respectful distance, eyes focused on Silaine and paying me no attention. How could he do this? Had he been on Silaine's side this whole time? That would explain why he rescued us from the Fae king, but not why he got us an audience with him in the first place. Just what game was Darian playing at?

As my blinding panic faded to mere seething panic, Silaine's words came into focus. She assured her slaves and followers that their hard work was about to come to fruition. The bloodkey had been found, and Shadelorn would soon be their allies against the perverse paradise ruled by a bloodless king.

"A deathless land is a dead land," she proclaimed, words ringing with passion and power. "Peace is death. Avalon is death. Are you shades, or Fae? Are you the dead, or the living?"

The Fae in the crowd shouted their wordless support, zealots of her cause.

I stretched my wrists against the cord until it cut into my flesh, but nothing broke. The sword in Silaine's hand was *my* sword, I realized. The one I'd appropriated from Soren and used to communicate with him. Now it had turned against me, the same way he had.

Silaine finished her rousing speech to thunderous approval. She turned to me, triumph gleaming in her dark eyes.

I glared back. "You can't kill me." I shouted so the crowd could hear. "You made a blood deal to spare my life."

As she passed Soren she touched his shoulder again, and he shuddered. She towered over me, nearly vibrating with power. "Oh yes," she agreed, whispering through her wicked smile. "But I'm not going to kill you."

Then she stabbed me.

My nerves sang in pain as the sword connected with flesh, piercing the crook of my right arm. I cried out and lifted my hands to my chin but blood gushed from the wound anyway, down my elbow and into a cup Silaine held ready.

I lunged at her but she was too quick for me. I ran out of slack and jerked back with a painful tug to my raw wrists. The hot center of magic glowed in me but could not burst forth. Blood soaked into my velvet dress.

Silaine approached the end of the walkway and held the golden cup aloft. It shone in the sun. My heart ached like it would break apart in my chest. Even Soren even looking at me now. He was watching her. The whole world was watching her. Silaine was a goddess of vengeance, War incarnate at the height of her ascension.

"Citizens of the true Fae realm," Silaine thundered, "I deliver your victory!"

The cup began to turn.

In that moment, it seemed as if everyone who ever worked or bled for Briar cried out through me, mourning our defeat. My snow-cursed land, my fallen family, my fragile dreams, everything I was and wanted to be—it all converged in a zenith of love and agony. The apocalypse I tried so hard to avoid was at hand. Caught in my ties, there was nothing I could do.

Nothing, except what I'd already done.

A glowing blue arrow sliced through the flesh of Silaine's hand.

Her arm flung outward. The cup tumbled through the air in a haze of red, landing at last on the black stone portal.

One drop of my blood could open the portal. An entire cup dissolved it. The black stone fizzled into nothingness.

Silaine screamed a blood-curdling cry as she broke off the tip of the arrow and pulled it from her hand. Though the arrow shone with Fae-killing runes her wounds healed at once, and she held her sword out over the pit. "Children of Earth, if you are Fae at heart, then fight! Fight!"

A cloud of arrows rose from the trees and landed among the screaming crowd, downing human and Fae alike.

Soren barreled into me, forcing me to the ground and covering me with his body, but just as quickly he was up again, on orders fleeing with Silaine into her castle.

I lay on the stone, stunned, but behind me Darian stood calmly, smiling with amusement. "Darian," I yelled. "Untie me! What's happening?"

"It seems Oberon has decided to defend his throne after all. Well done, human." Then he walked away, though I screamed at him to come back.

Tied to the walkway, I could only watch in terror as the battle began.

Warriors from Avalon emerged through the tree line, white-plated armor gleaming in the sun. Bodies lay in the mud, some still writhing, but the Fae simply stepped over them. They filled the clearing, skirting the edges of the pit. Oberon strode through their midst, whistling a tune I could clearly hear above the clamor of fleeing slaves. It was calm and entrancing, as if unconcerned by the chaos he caused.

Heart in my throat, I pried at the knots around my legs, but the cord was so thin and pulled so tight that I couldn't loosen them at all. I wrapped the cord around my boot and tried to jerk it free of the metal loop in the stone, but it wouldn't break.

Silaine's warriors had fled to the stronghold, but it was a strategic retreat. Before long they streamed back out to the battlefield, having donned their own armor. Turrets filled with archers, and from a balcony on the highest level Silaine reappeared, a smear of red against the gray and brown castle. At her side was Soren in his stark white blouse. Whatever they planned, they were silent, observing the onslaught of warriors filling the clearing while Silaine's forces huddled against her castle walls.

I flopped onto my belly and rubbed the cord on my wrist against the edge of the walkway, but it wouldn't fray. I stayed there, praying I'd be forgotten in the impending struggle and no arrow would make its way to my unprotected flesh.

Despite my fear, my stomach gave a twist of excitement. Somehow my gambit had worked. Oberon was finally here.

The merry tune he whistled turned ominous, notes growing longer and lower, until finally one solid, haunting note loomed across the field. It grew into a fever pitch, then widened to encompass the battle cry of the Fae king, axe raised as he signaled his army's attack. His soldiers rushed Silaine's.

The armies met like two rivers merging, in a whirling mix of chaos and noise. Even those separated by the pit jumped down into the dirt and began to spar, watering the earth with Fae blood. Swords clanged, arrows hissed, and soldiers cried out as they killed or died.

Silaine's army couldn't keep this up, and for a moment my vision blurred with the ecstasy of relief. But a dark cloud gathered on the horizon, and a keening moan rang over the field. The flesh on my arms rose. I knew that sound.

Galloping in like some misbegotten cavalry, three giant white beasts broke through the trees to the east, wide jaws already snapping and six legs crushing Fae beneath their feet. At their heels ran other beasts called back from the snowy wastelands. The swelling cloud rushing towards us was not a thunderhead but a legion of mavens, and they joined the battle in droves, turning the field nearly black with their numbers.

Sparks and streaks of magic leaped from the middle of the fight—it was Oberon, singeing mavens to dust, but even he could do little against their vast numbers. Oberon's forces were aided only by the cannibalistic nature of the birds, which soon fell to eating their fallen comrades and the bodies of the newly dead.

Somehow amidst this chaos no creature approached me. I huddled on the walkway, pressing myself as flat as possible but unable to look away. Every part of me ached for a weapon, but just as equally I ached to know that Rowan had escaped, that he'd managed to free what human slaves he could and lead them to safety. From this side of the castle there was no way to know.

A flurry of movement high on the balcony caught my eye. I watched in horror as Silaine held her arm above the battle, and with the shining sword cut herself so that a stream of blood fell onto the ground below.

In Soren's memories I had seen her create monsters, but always using human blood. Now I saw what it was to command creation from the blood of a Fae. Her red puddle seemed to ooze along the ground, adding blood of fallen soldiers on both sides until it was a force of its own, slithering down into the pit and sucking up the blood there, too.

Finally, it began to grow.

Surging from the red lake came an oblong shape, black and dripping. The neck and torso pushed up next, longer even than Oberon. Then came man-like arms with black claws, and finally two legs supporting a hulking back. The creature, at least fifty feet tall, lurched among the battlefield, swiping at soldiers that didn't even come up to its knees.

How could Oberon's warriors fight against such a beast when their swords were as needles to it?

The creature moaned as it clawed across the field, and somehow above the din I heard Silaine's shrieking laughter. Oberon himself hacked at the creature's legs, and vines burst from the earth to ensnare it, but it always broke free. Arrows pierced its slimy skin in droves, covering it like a pincushion.

I wondered who controlled that creature—Silaine or Soren. Winged lizards and flocks of gargrayles joined the fight, adding their shrieks to the din.

Then something plummeted from Silaine's balcony like a comet with a flickering black tail. I was already screaming when I realized it was Soren.

His body smashed to the ground and broke apart like a splintering log. My scream turned into a breathless agony. All the air seemed to have gone out of the world.

It was one thing to live in his skin and know what came after the darkness. It was entirely another to watch the boy I loved jump to his death before my eyes.

Around us the battle pulsed, half the beasts seeming to lose their focus and lash out indiscriminately before Silaine took control of them, but this was not a symphony meant for one conductor. I could feel the battle flagging, even as the body I couldn't take my eyes off seemed to be piecing itself back together.

At last his hand jerked, and he pushed himself to his feet, lurching through the fracas and stumbling in my direction.

"Soren!" I screamed. "Soren!"

I prayed my screams would drown out Silaine's, that he could focus on my voice and forget to listen to her orders. Across the field her giant monster fell to its knees.

"Rose!"

A voice behind me. I turned to find Rowan running down the walkway. He sank to my side, and I leaned against him as we crouched together.

"You stupid idiot," I shouted while my heart leaped for joy. "Don't you ever listen?"

"About as much as you do." With the Fae blade Darian had given him, Rowan sliced through my cords as if they were cobwebs.

As he pulled me to my feet I searched the place where Soren last floundered through the battle, but couldn't see him. Rowan tugged on my arm but I stood my ground, waiting for one glimpse of Soren so he would know I was free. A spear clattered against the walkway. With no other choice, we fled.

I followed Rowan into the maze of the compound. The halls were dark and empty, but elsewhere there was shouting, and the clank of steel.

"Wait," I cried, pulling him to a stop. "Where are we going?"

"The slaves," Rowan said, dragging me another step towards the exit. "I got them out of the cages before the fight. Everyone's fleeing. Gile and the men are waiting for us, we have to go!"

I stood firm as he tugged on my arm. My sleeve was wet with blood, and it streaked Rowan's hand. But I couldn't spare the energy to heal myself, not for something so trivial. Not when

I could use it to purchase something else.

"Please," Rowan said to whatever expression I wore. "Please let me save you."

But I shook my head, pulling out of his grasp. "I have to stop her, Rowan. It's what I'm here for."

"You already did your part! All that matters now is getting out alive."

I put one hand on the wall to steady myself. "No. Alair dreamed I'd stop Silaine. Your father died so I'd have this chance."

Rowan gripped my waist with both hands, his forehead bending to almost touch mine. "They'd want you to be safe, now. Rose, come with me!"

I felt breathless in a way that had nothing to do with fear. "You can't keep protecting me, Rowan. I have to do this."

His dark eyes darted across mine, reading the determination there. "I'm not trapped," he blurted. "I choose you."

"Rowan—"

He kissed me.

For a moment I was too surprised to react. If he'd asked me first I would have said no, would have explained my heart still belonged to Halen, even though he'd died long ago, and the person he'd become was likely dying now.

But I loved Rowan, too. As my friend, as my last semblance of family, as the person who had shared these past agonizing weeks with me, who fought for me and would die for me. Who believed in me. Who had hurt me, yes, and regretted it. Who held me while I cried, and held me in joy, and held me while he reached inside my soul to expose the magic there.

Pressed against him, lips and noses touching, I felt a familiar intimacy—the comforting scent of his skin, the warmth of the feeling between us. It reminded me of Halen in a way that both thrilled and ached, loss and discovery mingling together in a wave of exquisite agony.

It would have taken hours to explain everything tangled up in my heart. But as all these thoughts flickered instantly across my mind, they added up to one conclusion:

I kissed him back.

Only for a moment. And though a thousand unconsciously-planted seeds of desire scattered between us miraculously burst into bloom… the fact is we simply did not have time for this.

I broke away. "*Rowan.*"

"I know, I know, I'm sorry," he said, pulling back, a faint smile on his lips. "I just... had to do that at least once, before we die."

"We're not going to die," I muttered, turning away to suppress my own smile, the flutter in my stomach, and the heat in my cheeks. "Come on."

We ran back the way we came, taking new turns into main hallways and climbing stairs as we found them. The battle still raged outside, but it was impossible to tell who might be winning as we dashed by rare windows.

Finally, we found the spiral stairs that seemed to indicate a tower. Praying this was the right one, we climbed and climbed though my calves quickly ached and my lungs cried out for air. Silaine's shouts echoed down to us, and the strange excitement in my stomach turned to dread.

We slowed to a creep and came to a wooden door. By the mutterings and shouted curses I knew Silaine was on the other side.

Rowan nudged the Fae dagger into my hand, but I shook my head. My fingers crept towards the latch and I pressed slow and firm, praying the hinges wouldn't creak. But it wouldn't open. I pressed harder, leaning with my shoulder against the door. It was locked. We only had one option.

Rowan wrapped his arms around me. "You can do it," he whispered in my ear, breath tickling my neck. "Remember."

Yes. I remembered his hands on my back as he and Maeve broke the block on my magic. I remembered the way the flowers bloomed in the dream grove, and how it felt to conjure the arrow in Avalon under Soren's approving eyes. I remembered Rowan's arms around me, like now, as he touched the magic I couldn't find in myself, defying Silaine's curse and revealing the power within me. I remembered that magical, momentary kiss.

Open.

The door swung open. I pulled away from Rowan's arms. Silaine stood before us, leaning over the balcony. Her blood stained the gray stone. In a breath, I was there.

In the end, it didn't come down to magic at all. I pushed Silaine over the ledge.

TWENTY-NINE

Her scream filled the world.

Below us the battle seemed to pause as Silaine tumbled to the earth. Joy and horror stole the breath from my chest as I realized what I'd done. If she died now, humanity would win— but I'd never see Soren again. My hands groped into the void.

Something dark barreled through the air. A gargrayle snatched Silaine from the sky. It lurched, the velocity of her body too much for its wings. They sped towards the ground, but slower this time. When it finally released her she fell the last few feet into the mud, alive if not unharmed.

But Oberon was already there. He stepped onto her gasping chest and swung his sword, the blade stopping a hair's breadth from her neck. His growl reached us. "Call them."

Whatever answer she whispered was lost to the wind.

He pressed the sword to her neck until blood jeweled around the blade. "Call them, or die in the mud."

A moment of defiance. Then...

"Stop," Silaine commanded, voice magically magnified, ringing over the battlefield. "I yield."

The last lingering swordfights stilled. Her monstrous giant had already been toppled and hacked apart, but the beasts that were still alive quieted their roars and knelt to receive their death. Oberon's soldiers delivered the killing blows swiftly, eliminating Silaine's beastly army. As for her warriors, they threw down their weapons and were escorted at sword-point into the bloody pit.

"It's over," I breathed, leaning against the railing where Silaine had stood just a minute before.

Rowan pulled me away from the edge and we clung to each other in dawning joy. I closed my eyes, relaxing into him as he spoke my name over and over. "Rose. You did it." We'd survived. For a moment I savored my victory, and felt the pressure of the world ease off my shoulders.

Then I gasped. "Soren!"

My feet fairly flew down the spiral staircase, Rowan trailing behind. I tore through the castle and out into the battlefield, in time to hear Oberon address his army.

"The sorceress Silaine was cast out of Avalon for conspiring against the crown, and now she will be cast out of Earth for the same crime. All of you... Bear witness to her death so that you see what becomes of those who defy your rightful king."

Silaine knelt at his feet, bound in glowing cords, but it wasn't she who lost her head first. Down in the pit Oberon's warriors beheaded hers, one by one. They were killing traitors first, saving Silaine for last.

My heart lurched. It was so fast. I didn't think it would be so fast.

I cast about desperately for Soren, seeing only the hostile eyes of the Fae. Oberon himself glanced at me with silent disdain, and I feared for my safety, but they couldn't execute her. Not now. Not yet.

"Where's Soren?" I cried out, power in my voice.

"Who?" Oberon said, but someone stepped up and whispered in his ear.

Darian. Without a hair out of place, looking as if he hadn't bothered to even lift a blade during the recent skirmish.

"Oh. The *damnsoír*." Oberon waved his hand in the general direction of the forest, and my heart lurched in frustration.

I had to find him.

I told myself I hadn't hoped, but it wasn't true. Deep in my heart I'd hoped we'd have some time. Time to go back to the place where we met. To go home. To maybe glimpse Halen again in the face that had become Soren's. To speak with the shell of my beloved now that I knew him again.

Because when Silaine died, Soren would die also. And now I might not even get to say goodbye.

"Hurry," Rowan said, pushing me towards the trees. "You can make it. Go!"

I flew. Over the bodies, across the mud and into the shadow of the forest. I knew where to find him. I ran to the grove, to the place where Silaine's castle of mud and blood couldn't be seen through the trees. Where birds still sang and leaves whispered in the breeze. He stood beyond the black portal, head tilted up to look at the sky.

He turned when he heard me approach. Soren smiled.

I fell into his arms. He held me while I cried into his chest. "It's not fair," I managed to say. "I don't want you to go."

"Shh," he whispered, stroking my hair. "Don't be sad. Not after you've won."

"But I'm losing you."

"Be happy for me. This is the kindest thing you could do for me. I'm only sorry I have to leave you behind." He pulled back and wiped the dampness from my cheeks. "Don't cry, Rose. You've given me a wonderful gift. You freed me."

I tried to hold in my gasping breaths. I wanted to see him clearly, and I didn't want his last image of me to be of a blubbering mess. I nodded, and wiped my eyes.

His soft smile grew. "You have to promise, Rose. I waited a hundred years in hell to see you again. Don't put all that to waste. You have to promise you'll stay safe, and be happy."

I brushed them away, but the tears kept coming. I nodded again.

"I'm so sorry," he said. "For everything. I never wanted to hurt you."

"I know," I sighed and the pain rushed out of me. There was no avoiding this. There was only goodbye.

We sat on the grass and he lay his head on my lap, his hands wrapped in mine. He stared up at my face framed by the clear sky, and smiled.

I knew the moment Silaine died because he started to change.

In the space of ten seconds he aged a hundred years, and I watched his body travel through the lifetime it had deferred.

First, a slight widening of his shoulders, a deeper shadow on his cheeks, then a hardening of features as he settled into his adult face. Laugh lines sprouted by his eyes, and a field of gray rippled across his hair. His features grew blunt, his fingers thick, and the gray hair pulled back on his forehead as his skin grew mottled. His cheeks sank, his hands softened, and wrinkles washed up on his face like waves on a shore, mixing with the scars until I could not tell which was which.

At last, I held an old man, one who had lived far beyond what nature intended. I watched the man he would have become, the summer of his prime, and the winter of his decline.

I loved him every moment.

When it was over, I pulled my hands from his and laid him on the ground. I planted a kiss on his forehead, and stood back from the body. Eyes closed, arms spread, I reached into that whirling center inside myself and let the golden light pour forth.

Vines burst from the ground and covered Soren's body, thorns interlocking and leaves layering over each other like scales on a fish. Flowers surged into existence, heavy red blossoms turned towards Soren as if he was the sun. Roses cradled him, roses shielded him, and roses protected him.

After a time Rowan came to the clearing, hesitantly, prepared to go if I didn't welcome him. But I did. He stood beside me and looked over my monument, one hand awkwardly seeking a place to land. It eventually settled on my shoulder. I leaned closer and wrapped an arm around his waist.

"I'm so sorry," he said. "You were right about him."

"We were all just trying to do the right thing."

"The snow's started to melt, if you wanted to come see."

"Yes," I said, feeling the ghost of a smile return. "I'd like that very much."

We spent some time regrouping with our men and gathering the human survivors. The reunion with Gile was fierce and joyful. Most slaves had fled but some had stayed to see the battle finished, fearful of the snows or what would happen to runaways if Silaine won. They were filthy and wide-eyed, so broken down they barely sighed with relief when Rowan announced Silaine was dead. Led by Gile, our men managed the assembly of supplies for our return journey, stealing from Silaine's stables and storerooms.

Rowan and I made our way to the other side of the stronghold to keep an eye on the Fae. We found them prying a stone block from Silaine's castle to cover the portal to the Shadelands. The pit had become a mass grave, Silaine's body gracing the top of the pile. They buried everyone at once, sealing away both the portal and all evidence of the traitors.

I watched grimly, bearing witness to the gritty end of a century-long struggle. I noticed, though, before they covered the portal, that the world it led to was not roiling with dangerous beasts, and in fact didn't seem dangerous at all. I spied green, and a peaceful forest.

So perhaps, as Soren had told me, our legends about Shadelorn were wrong.

While his soldiers worked, I approached King Oberon, pretending to be confident even though I was quaking in my boots. "Thank you, Your Majesty," I said with forced calm, "for saving my kingdom." *Even though it was you who caused this mess in the beginning*, I didn't add. "I hope that Avalon and Valeria will continue to be allies in the future."

Oberon lifted an eyebrow. "We are not allies, little one. When greater rulers than you come to take this land, do not ask me for help. Avalon is forbidden to you."

My stomach dropped. He was a thousand times my age, as large as a giant, with more magic than I could ever hope to wield. I clenched my fists to hide my shaking hands, and drew myself up to my full height. "Then I suggest you kill your traitors next time, instead of exiling them to Earth."

"No need," he said with unnerving calm. "The infection of Silaine's heresy has been purged. Avalon is the true home of the Fae. We'll not return to this tired, little world again."

"Then I look forward to peace between us."

Oberon raised one eyebrow in amusement. "Magic is fading on earth," he said ominously. "You are boring—the gods have turned their eyes towards better places. If I wanted your world, I would take it. But what would be the point?"

Oberon returned his gaze to the labor of his soldiers, and with nothing more to say I stormed off, excitement about my freed lands shattered by his words.

I didn't know about magic, gods, and worlds, but he was right about Valeria. With the snow melting our borders would be unguarded, and the only residents of Valeria were the slaves around the corner. I called it 'my country', but there was no country anymore.

Not yet at least.

The Fae eventually left in a somber procession, carrying their faithful dead through Avalon's portal in a long line. Rowan, Gile, and I bore witness to their passing. Despite our harsh words Oberon inclined his head at me as he passed, and I took grim satisfaction from that.

Darian was the last to leave, lingering in the clearing with us and smiling like the cat that stole the cream. Rowan thanked him for his assistance these past hundred years, and Darian bowed like an actor reaping applause.

"So what was your game?" I asked, not matching his smug smile.

"Whatever do you mean, Your Highness?"

"If you're truly working for Oberon, why did you take me to Silaine?"

"He—What?" Rowan's hand twitched towards his dagger.

"Silaine didn't *capture* me. Darian hand-delivered me so she could open Shadelorn," I explained. "And I want to know why."

Darian only laughed. "Appearances, of course. How would it look if I were sent to bring you and never came back? I didn't know how long it would take the king to act."

"The king who doesn't seem to mind that you stole me and Soren out from under his literal nose. I figured he'd have left you in the pit."

Darian waved a hand airily. "Appearances. Politics, plots within plots, I don't expect you to understand all the complexities of the Fae court."

"You didn't have to help Silaine open Shadelorn," Rowan growled. "I think you were on her side, until she lost."

"Well, appearances can be deceiving, can't they? Come now, princess," he said. "Don't be angry with me. We should be friends, you and I. Here, perhaps this will make you forgive me." Darian pulled a silver chain up through his tunic until its pendant swung free—an opal sphere cradled in a wire net.

"What is it?" I asked as he set the necklace onto my outstretched palm, the stone heavy and faintly warm.

"His heart," Darian said simply.

My own skipped a beat. "What?"

"Silaine was right, the Fae have lost their souls," Darian said as I stared into the glimmering stone. "Oberon let the very blood stagnate in his veins. But battle will have woken him again. We cannot linger in Avalon with the memory of a true Hunt fresh in our minds. We'll be back. And when we should meet again, princess... I hope you will remember this moment."

With Fae quickness he turned and disappeared into the portal.

"Wait!" I shouted, but the wall had closed up again.

I leaned against its reflective surface, light glowing from where my skin touched the black stone. For a moment I considered opening the portal to chase after Darian and make him tell me how this white stone could be Soren's heart, and what it meant to hold it in my hand. But if Darian had wanted me to know, he would have stayed, and I couldn't risk Oberon's displeasure with another journey into Avalon.

If only I could close the portal forever and lock the Fae away in the world they'd made. But that's not how the portal worked. The Fae King could open it as easily as I could, and despite Oberon's disdain of Earth earlier, Darian's words rang in my ears. I would see him again, of that I had no doubt.

Rowan touched my shoulder. "Rose?"

I stood, lifting the silver chain over my neck and slipping the stone under my shirt so that Soren's heart lay next to mine. It was all that remained of him, and whatever Darian's intentions were, I was glad to have it.

Rowan's eyes searched my face. "Are you all right?"

I took a breath, and nodded. He pulled me into his chest and I rested my head on his shoulder. "You know I'll always love him."

"I know," he said. "Come on. It's time to go."

We returned to the front of the castle where the doors to the slave cages swung free, locks broken by the Fae dagger Darian gave Rowan. The slaves—no, the survivors—waited for us with tense curiosity, packs and carts packed for the journey ahead. Some had homes to return to. Some didn't. We would all travel together until we reached the main roads.

Gile observed our approach with weary pride. "There she is," he announced to the assembled crowd. "That's the girl that stopped Silaine. Princess Rose."

"Queen Rose," Rowan corrected, smiling at me. "Once Princess Talia. The rightful ruler of Valeria."

I observed the survivors, nervous for their reactions. Some were still too deep in their misery to react to anything. Many looked back with curiosity. A few smiled, perhaps only in gratitude.

I still didn't know how to be a queen, but as I thought about it, I figured I hadn't done too poorly so far. I'd rescued my kingdom, freed my people, and banished the Fae. Not bad for a peasant girl from the mountains.

Looking back at Rowan, I finally met his smile with my own. Whatever happened to Valeria in the future, Rowan would be there to help me figure it out.

So perhaps it was time.

Soren had told me one final thing, in our last few minutes together. While the surviving humans were preparing for the journey, I'd braved the maze of Silaine's strange castle. I'd found the room where Darian prepared me for Silaine's bloodletting ritual. In a chest, under the bed, waited a familiar, velvet-lined box. Confiscated when the Fae captured Rowan's team, Soren had found it, and kept it safe for me.

I put the tiara on my head. Then I mounted the white horse Gile held waiting. Silaine's stables were several orders of magnitude better cared for than the human pens. We had oxen to pull supplies, and carts to carry those too weak to walk.

"Everyone is free to go," I said from atop my new gray-legged mare. "Everyone." I looked at Gile and the remaining men of Briar in particular. "But for those that want to be part of the new Valeria, you're welcome to come with us."

"And where are you going?" A woman with hollow eyes asked.

I glanced at Rowan. "Home."

What few sentries of Briar were left sent up a cheer. Rowan

grinned from atop his black stallion, and soon we left Silaine's compound behind, traveling south through damp lands as the snow melted back into the earth.

Days later, Rowan and I separated from the group. We followed ancient deer trails over a ridge and down the hill to the village of my childhood. The huts were mere wreckage, crushed by decades of ice and snow, but everything else was as I remembered.

I showed Rowan where Alair and I used to sit on a log over the river together, where I met Halen for the first time, and my favorite hunting trails and perches. Around us wandered the ghosts of the past, always just out of sight, going about their lives with peace and happiness. At least… in my memory.

The roses that grew over the doorway of my home were dead, of course, petals bled of color, frail and delicate as ash. They reminded me of the monument Soren made in the castle of my birth, covering me in my namesakes out of love and sorrow.

Out of ashes can come new life. I resurrected the roses, until they climbed over every fallen home and bloomed towards the sun, my own monument to the family and love I had lost. A symbol of she who would carry them in memory. A promise of the family that would come after.

Rowan took my hand and smiled. We joined our people again, enjoying the beauty of the land as we traveled south. Valeria's capital awaited, the site of our new home, in our new nation. The days of lingering in the past were over.

We had a future to build.

To be continued...

ACKNOWLEDGEMENTS

When a book takes fifteen years to cross the finish line, as this one did, there end up being so many people who touch the story in various ways, and I am grateful to you all. Thank you especially to the following people:

Florence + The Machine for the gorgeous music that inspired this story.

Laura Bradford, for believing in me enough to sign me to your agency, and for taking Rose's story through several rounds of submissions. Your time, effort, and editorial advice were so deeply appreciated.

Kat Zhang, Caitlin Vanasse, and Laura Wardle for reading various versions of this story and providing feedback. Kat, thank you especially for all the brainstorming help with plots and titles!

Emmanuelle Morgan, for the validation and encouragement. You inspired me to pick up this story again, and run with it.

Cade, for your love and enthusiasm for all my ideas, including this one. Friend of my life, you know how much you mean to me.

My family, especially my sister Ciera, for supporting my writing journey. Ciera, thank you for your fierce loyalty, encouragement, and girlboss attitude. Your courage gives me courage. Mom, thank you for all the hours you spent reading to me as a child, which jumpstarted this lifelong passion.

Steve Mesker, for your friendship, excellent brainstorming skills, and artistic support.

The staff at Café 153 for all the lattes, green teas, and chicken salad sandwiches, Maryssa Gordon for editorial feedback, Muhammad Kaleem for the gorgeous cover art, Justin Miller of Five Points Recording, Kiss09 for the book trailer illustrations, and of course all my beloved "beautiful creatures."

AUTHOR'S NOTE

I wrote the first draft of this story in 2011, at the ripe age of 22, inspired by the song BLINDING, by Florence + the Machine. These lyrics in particular haunted me:

No more dreaming of the dead, as if death itself was undone
No more calling like a crow for a boy, for a body in the garden
No more dreaming like a girl, so in love, so in love
No more dreaming like a girl, so in love with the wrong world

Although the song itself specifically mentions Snow White, most of the lyrics directly reference tales of Sleeping Beauty. I was captivated by the idea of a girl in love with the 'wrong world'—the world she'd been torn from forever by a century of sleep—and dreaming of a lost love as if her longing could bring him back to life.

I listened to this song countless times on my daily commute, reliving the angst and agony over and over again. All my book ideas derive from glimpses of these extreme emotional moments, and the desire to form a plot that justifies and explains their existence. When I started writing, I didn't know or plan for the tangled motivations and explanations Rose would receive from Soren and Alair. I only knew both parties cared for her very much, and both had reasons to deceive her. It took multiple drafts and hours of brainstorming to determine what 'really' happened.

In early drafts, Rose woke up having lost all her memories.

I liked the simplicity of this, and it made sense for Silaine to have stolen Rose's memories as part of the sleeping curse—another hidden trap for Soren. Unfortunately, a main character who doesn't know anything about their world, family, or history makes a poor tour guide for the reader. Catching Rose (and the reader) up to speed took too much info-dumping, in a book already necessarily heavy on that front. I reduced the amount of memory loss and changed the responsible party in order to keep things moving.

In fact, this book commits several writing 'sins' typically advised against… It begins with a character waking up, Rose describes her features to the reader by use of a mirror, a perspective change occurs halfway through the book, and—worst of all—there's a prologue (Gasp!) However, I think all these devices make sense to use within their contexts, and I hope this is one of those situations where you learn the rules so you know when it's appropriate to break them. Also, I will never capitulate to prologue-haters. I love prologues. I wish there were more of them.

The first title used for this story was ROSES OF ASH. It wasn't until my literary agent at the time, Laura Bradford, suggested changing the title before going on submissions to editors that a real title brainstorm began, and we settled on A CURSE OF ROSE AND SNOW.

Again, this was 2011. The title craze of A Blank of Blank and Blank was not yet in full swing, and I still love that title the most. But after rounds of submissions and then rounds of edits over the next few years, we changed the title once more to THE ROSE CURSE, in an effort to rebrand and acknowledge how much the story had evolved. I was writing other books, you see, and growing as a writer with each one. Repeatedly I brought those new skills back to my 'sleeping beauty story', improving it in both increments and chunks.

I love this story. I love it more than any other book I've written thus far, and I love them all quite a lot. One of the most inspiring pieces of writing advice that ever pierced my heart as a young writer came from the exemplary Toni Morrison: If there is a book you really want to read, but it hasn't been written yet, then you must write it. As a teenager, I'd written that quote on a scrap of paper and pasted it to the wall of my room, as I did with all the quotes that struck me so.

AWAKENED is a book I really, really, really wanted to read. And I'm so glad I got to, in all its various incarnations. I truly hope you enjoy it as much as I do. As you can tell, AWAKENED is the final title I went with, but I couldn't help adding A CURSE OF ROSE AND SNOW as a subtitle, because that's still the name of the book in my heart. Even if it is terribly cliche these days.

It's been fifteen years since I started working on Rose's story. She's lived with me through so much, and if the fates are on our side she'll keep living with me through the sequel. The story isn't over, you know. There's a kingdom to build, and worlds to explore, and destinies to decide. I've written half the manuscript, but it will only be finished if enough people want to meet me at the end of that journey. If you love Rose's story, please tell your friends. Books live and breathe in the hearts of readers, and they propagate by recommendation. The power is in your hands to make Rose's story bloom.

Savannah J. Foley
Huntsville, Alabama
April, 2026

ABOUT THE AUTHOR

Savannah J. Foley is a writer and artist who grew up in Auburn, Washington but has spent most of her adult life in Huntsville, Alabama. She writes fantasy and science fiction, and illustrates the webcomic Pickles and Pitch. She is over 6'2, can wiggle her ears, and types like a maniac. Although not a witch herself, Savannah loves witchery and witchy things. She believes real-world magic is mostly quantum physics, but isn't that just as wonderful?

Learn more at www.savannahjfoley.com

Savannah has an account on your favorite social media site @savannahjfoley

www.ingramcontent.com/pod-product-compliance
Lightning Source LLC
LaVergne TN
LVHW090550110826
845146LV00001B/93

* 9 7 9 8 9 9 5 5 8 5 6 6 4 *